# DON'T YOU CRY

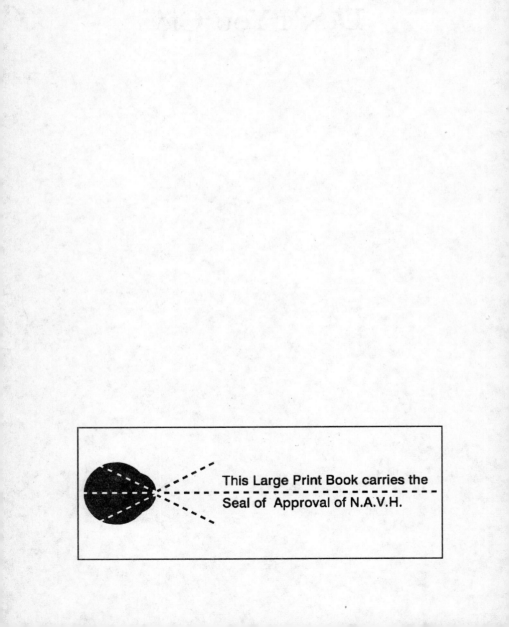

# DON'T YOU CRY

## MARY KUBICA

**THORNDIKE PRESS**
*A part of Gale, Cengage Learning*

GALE
CENGAGE Learning·

Farmington Hills, Mich • San Francisco • New York • Waterville, Maine
Meriden, Conn • Mason, Ohio • Chicago

## GALE
CENGAGE Learning®

**LIBRARY OF CONGRESS CATALOGING-IN-PUBLICATION DATA**

Names: Kubica, Mary, author.
Title: Don't you cry / Mary Kubica.
Description: Large print edition. | Waterville, Maine : Thorndike Press Large Print, 2016. | Series: Thorndike Press large print core
Identifiers: LCCN 2016015585 | ISBN 9781410489890 (hardback) | ISBN 1410489892 (hardcover)
Subjects: LCSH: Large type books. | BISAC: FICTION / Thrillers. | GSAFD: Suspense fiction.
Classification: LCC PS3611.U23 D66 2014 | DDC 813/.6—dc23
LC record available at https://lccn.loc.gov/2016015585

Published in 2016 by arrangement with Harlequin Books, S.A.

For Pete

■ ■ ■ ■

# SUNDAY

■ ■ ■ ■

# QUINN

In hindsight, I should have known right away that something wasn't quite right. The jarring noise in the middle of the night, the open window, the empty bed. Later, I blamed a whole slew of things for my nonchalance, everything from a headache to fatigue, down to arrant stupidity.

But still.

I should have known right away that something wasn't right.

It's the alarm clock that wakes me. Esther's alarm clock hollering from two doors down.

"Shut it off," I grumble, dropping the pillow to my head. I roll over onto my stomach and swim beneath a second pillow to smother the sound, throwing the covers up over my head, too.

No such luck. I still hear it.

"Dammit, Esther," I snap as I kick the covers to the end of the bed and rise. Beside

9

me there are rustles of complaint, blind eyes reaching out to reclaim the blanket, an aggravated sigh. Already the taste of last night's alcohol creeps up my insides, something called a cranberry smash, and a bourbon sour, and a Tokyo iced tea. The room whirls around me like a Hula-Hoop, and I have this sudden memory of twirling around a dirty dance floor with some guy named Aaron or Darren, or Landon or Brandon. The same guy that asked to split a cab with me on the way home, the one that's still lying on my bed when I nudge him and tell him he has to go, yanking the blanket from his hands. "My roommate," I say, poking him in the ribs, "is awake. You have to go."

"You have a roommate?" he asks, sitting up in bed, yet beset by sleep. He rubs at his eyes and it's then that I see it in the glimmer of a nearby streetlight that glares through the window and across the rumpled bed: he's twice my age. Hair that looked brown in the hazy burn of bar lights — and under the influence of a healthy dose of alcohol — is now a pewter-gray. Dimples are not dimples at all, but rather laugh lines. Wrinkles.

"Dammit, Esther," I say again under my breath, knowing that before long, old Mrs.

Budny from downstairs will be pounding the ceiling with the hard end of her sponge mop to silence the rumpus.

"You have to go," I say to him again, and he does.

I follow the trail of noise into Esther's room. The alarm clock, a droning noise like a cicada's song. I mutter under my breath as I go, one hand dragging along the wall as I make my way down the darkened halls. The sun won't rise for another hour. It's not yet 6:00 a.m. Esther's alarm screams at her like it does every Sunday morning. Time to get ready for church. Esther, with her silvery, soothing voice, has been singing in the church choir every Sunday morning at the Catholic church on Catalpa for as long as I can remember. Saint Esther, I call her.

When I enter Esther's bedroom, the first thing I notice is the cold. Drafts of frosty November air sail in from the window. A stash of paper on her desk — held secure by a heavy college textbook: *Introduction to Occupational Therapy* — blows in the breeze, making a raucous noise. Frost covers the insides of the window, condensation running in streams down the panes of glass. The window is pushed up all the way. The fiberglass screen is removed, set to the floor with cause.

I lean out the window to see if Esther is there on the fire escape, but outside the world — on our little residential block of Chicago — is quiet and dark. Parked cars line the street, caked in the last batch of fallen leaves from nearby trees. Frost covers the cars and the yellowing grass, which fades fast; soon it will die. Plumes of smoke escape from roof vents on nearby homes, drifting into the morning sky. The whole of Farragut Avenue is asleep, except for me.

The fire escape is empty; Esther is not there.

I turn away from the window and see Esther's covers lying on the floor, a bright orange duvet with an aqua throw. "Esther?" I say as I make my way across the boxy bedroom, hardly big enough for Esther's double bed. I trip over a stash of clothes tossed to the floor, my feet getting tangled in a pair of jeans. "Rise and shine," I say as I smack my hand against the alarm clock to shut it up. Instead, I wind up turning the radio on, and a cacophony of noise fills the room, morning talk against the drone of the alarm. "Dammit," I swear, and then, losing patience, "Esther!"

I see it then as my eyes adjust to the darkness of the room: Saint Esther is not in her bed.

I finally manage to shut off the alarm clock and then turn on the light, grimacing as the bright light makes my head ache, the aftereffects of an overindulgent night. I do a double take to make sure I haven't somehow or other managed to miss Esther, checking under the heap of blankets lying on the floor. Ridiculous, I know, even as I'm doing it, but I do it nonetheless. I check in her closet; I check the single bathroom, my eyes scanning past the prolific collection of overpriced cosmetics we share, tossed at random on the vanity.

But Esther is nowhere.

Smart decisions aren't really my forte. They're Esther's. And so maybe that's why I don't call the cops right away, because Esther isn't here to tell me to do it. In all honesty, though, my first thought isn't that something *happened* to Esther. It isn't my second, third or fourth thought, either, and so I let the hangover get the best of me, close the window and go back to bed.

When I wake for the second time, it's after ten. The sun is up, and all along Farragut Avenue people scuttle to and from the coffee and bagel shops for breakfast, or lunch, or whatever it is that people eat and drink at 10:00 a.m. They're blanketed in puffer jackets and wool trench coats, hands forced into pockets, hats on head. It doesn't take a brainiac to know that it's cold.

I, however, sit on the small apartment sofa — the color of rose petals — in the living room, waiting for Saint Esther to arrive with a hazelnut coffee and a bagel. Because that's what she does every Sunday after singing in the church choir. She totes home a coffee and a bagel for me and we sit at the small kitchen table and eat, talking about everything from the children who cried their way through mass, to the choir director's lost sheet music, to whatever vapid thing I'd done the night before: drinking too much, bringing home some guy I barely knew, some faceless man who Esther never sees but only hears through the paper-thin walls of our apartment.

Last night I went out, but Esther didn't go with me. She had plans to stay home and rest. She was nursing a cold, she said, but now that I think of it, I saw no visible symptoms of illness — no coughing, no sneezing, no watery eyes. She was on the sofa, buried beneath the blanket in her comfy, cotton pajamas. *Come with me,* I'd begged of her. There was a new bar open on Balmoral that we'd been dying to go to, one of those chic, low-lit lounge types that only served martinis.

*Come with me,* I begged, but she said no.

*I'd be a killjoy, Quinn,* she said instead. *Go without me. You'll have more fun.*

*Want me to stay home with you?* I asked, but it was a halfhearted suggestion. *We'll order takeout,* I said, but I didn't want to order takeout. I was in a new baby-doll dress and heels, my hair was done, my makeup was on. I'd gone so far as to shave my legs for the night; there was no way I was staying home. But at least I offered.

Esther said no, go without her and have fun.

And that's just what I did. I went out without her and I had fun. But I didn't go to that martini bar. No, I saved that for Esther and me to do together. Instead, I wound up at some shoddy karaoke bar, drinking too much and going home with a stranger.

When I came home for the night Esther was in bed, with her door closed. Or so I thought at the time.

But now I can't help but wonder as I sit on the sofa, considering this morning's turn of events: What in the world would make Esther disappear out the fire escape window?

I think and I think, but my thoughts only land on one thing: an image of Romeo and

Juliet, the famous balcony scene, whereby Juliet professes her love for Romeo from the balcony of her home (which is more or less the only thing I remember from my high school education, that and the fact that a pen barrel makes the best artillery for shooting spitballs).

Is that what sent Esther clambering out the window in the middle of the night: *a guy*?

Of course at the end of that tale, Romeo poisons himself and Juliet stabs herself with a dagger. I read the book. Better yet, I saw the movie, the 1990s adaptation with Claire Danes and Leonardo DiCaprio. I know how it ends, with Romeo drinking his poison and Juliet shooting herself in the head with his gun. I think to myself: I just hope Esther's story has a better ending than that of Romeo and Juliet.

For now there's nothing to do but wait, and so I sit on the small rose-colored sofa, staring at the empty kitchen table, waiting for Esther to arrive home, regardless of whether she spent the night in her bed or crawled out the third-floor window of our walk-up instead. That doesn't matter. I still wait in my pajamas — a waffle henley and flannel boxer shorts, a pair of woolly slipper socks prettifying my feet — for my coffee and bagel to arrive. But today they're a no-show and I blame Esther for it, for the fact that this day I'll go without breakfast and caffeine.

By the time noon rolls around, I do what any self-respecting adult might do: I order Jimmy John's. It takes a good forty-five minutes for my Turkey Tom to arrive, during which time I convince myself that my stomach has begun to digest itself. It's been a solid fourteen hours since I've had a thing to eat, and what with the surplus of alcohol, I'm quite certain I've got the whole stomach bloating thing going on like those starving kids you see on TV.

I have no energy. Death is imminent. I may die.

And then the buzzer beeps from the first floor and I rise quickly to my feet. Delivery! I greet the Jimmy John's guy at the door, handing him his tip, a few measly dollars I manage to find in an envelope Esther stuck in a kitchen drawer with the description *Rent*.

I eat my lunch hunched over an industrial iron coffee table, and then do what any self-respecting human might do when her roomie has gone AWOL. I snoop. I let myself into Esther's room without a hint of remorse, without a whisper of guilt.

Esther's room is the smaller of the two, about the same size as a large refrigerator box. Her double bed spans the room, popcorn wall to popcorn wall, leaving hardly anywhere to walk. That's what eleven hundred dollars a month will buy you in Chicago: popcorn walls and a refrigerator box.

I slip past the foot of the bed, tripping over the pile of bedding that's still left on the scratched wooden floors, and peer outside at the fire escape, a collection of ladders and platforms in steel gratings that adheres to Esther's window. We joked about it when I moved in years ago, how she got the smaller room, but by virtue of the conjoined fire escape to her window, she'd be the one to survive a blaze should the entire building one day go up in flames. I was okay with that. Still am, really, because not only do I have a bed and a desk and a dresser in my room, I have a papasan chair. And the building has never once caught on fire.

Once again, I find myself wondering what in the holy hell would make Esther climb out her fire escape in the middle of the night. What's wrong with the front door? It's not as if I'm worried because, really, I'm not. Esther's been on that fire escape before. We used to sit out there all the time, staring at the moon and the stars, sipping mixed drinks, as if it was a balcony, our feet dangling over a repugnant Chicago alleyway. It was sort of *our thing,* spreading out along the uncomfortable steel gratings of the dingy black fire escape, sharing our secrets and dreams, feeling the lattice grilles of the unforgiving metal dig into our skin until our backsides fell asleep.

But even if she was there last night, Esther certainly isn't on the fire escape now.

Where could she be?

I peer inside her closet. Her favorite boots are gone, as if she put on her shoes, opened the window and climbed outside with intent.

Yes, I tell myself. That's exactly what she did, an assumption that reassures me that Esther is just fine. *She's fine,* I tell myself.

But still. Why?

I stare out the window at the quiet afternoon. The morning's coffee blitz has given way to a caffeine downer; there's not a soul in sight. I imagine half of Chicagoland perched before the TV, watching the Bears claim another stunning defeat.

And then I turn away from the fire escape and begin my search of Esther's bedroom. What I find is an unfed fish. A heaping pile of dirty laundry spilling out of a plastic hamper in the closet. Skinny jeans. Leggings. Jeggings. Bras and granny underwear. A stack of white camisoles, folded and set beside the hamper with care. A bottle of ibuprofen. A bottle of water. Grad school textbooks piled sky-high beside her ready-to-assemble IKEA desk, in addition to the one that lies on top of it, holding random papers in place. I set my hand on a desk drawer handle, but I don't look inside. That would be rude, somehow, more rude than riffling through the items left on top of the desk: her laptop, her iPod, her headphones and more.

Thumbtacked to the wall I find a photograph of Esther and me, taken last year. It was Christmas and together we stood before our artificial Fraser fir, snapping a selfie. I smile at the memory, remembering how Esther and I trekked together through mounds of snow to collect that tree. In the picture, Esther and I are pressed together, the boughs of the evergreen prodding our heads, the tinsel getting stuck to our clothing. We're laughing, me with a complacent smirk, and Esther with her gregarious smile. The tree is Esther's, one she keeps at a storage facility down the street, a ten-by-five box where, for sixty bucks a month, she keeps old guitars, a lute and whatever else she can't fit into her pint-size bedroom. Her bike. And, of course, the tree.

We'd gone to that facility together last December, on a mission to find that Christmas tree. We trudged through embankments of newly fallen snow, our feet getting stuck in it like quicksand. It was snowing still, the kind of snowflakes that poured down from the sky like big, fat, fluffy cotton balls. The cars that lined the city streets were buried deep; they'd have to be dug out or wait for a forty-degree thaw. Half the city was shut down thanks to the blizzard, and so the streets were a rare quiet as Esther and I slogged along, singing Christmas carols at the tops of our lungs because there was hardly anyone around to hear. Only snowplows braved the city streets that day, and even they skidded along in a zigzag line. Work had been canceled, for Esther, for me.

And so we plodded to the storage facility to hunt down that small plastic tree to haul home for the holiday season, stopping in the concrete corridor to do a giddy dance for the security camera and plunging ourselves into hysterics as we did. We imagined the employee — a creepy, quiet introvert — sitting at the front desk, watching as we danced an Irish jig on screen. We laughed and laughed, and then, when we finally stopped laughing, Esther used her padlock key to let us inside and we began to search unit 203, me prattling on and on about the irony of that number, seeing as my own parents lived at 203 David Drive. *Fate,* said Esther, but I said it was more like a stupid coincidence.

Seeing as the tree was disassembled and stuffed in a box, it was hard to find. There were a lot of boxes in that storage facility. A lot of boxes. And I inadvertently stumbled upon the wrong one apparently, because when I lifted the lid of a box and exposed a mound of photographs of some happy little family sitting beside a squat home, lifting one up and asking of Esther, *Who's this?* she snatched it quickly from my hand and said point-blank, *No one.* I didn't really have a chance to see the picture, but still, it didn't look like no one to me. But I didn't push the issue. Esther didn't like to talk about her family. That I knew. While I groaned and griped about mine all the time, Esther kept her feelings on the inside.

She tossed the picture back in the box and replaced the lid.

We found that tree and lugged it home together, but not before first stopping by our favorite diner where we sat nearly alone in the vacant place, eating pancakes and sipping coffee in the middle of the day. We watched the snow fall. We laughed at people trying to drag themselves through it, or excavate their cars from pyramids of snow. Those who were fortunate enough to dig themselves out called dibs on their parking spots. They filled them with random things — a bucket, a chair — so no one else would park there. Parking spots were like gold around here, especially in winter. That day, Esther and I sat in the window of the diner and watched this, too — we watched our neighbors lug chairs from their homes to stake a claim in the scooped-out parking spots, ones which would soon fill again with snow — feeling grateful all the time for public transportation.

And then Esther and I carried that tree home where we spent the night prettifying it with lights and ornaments galore, and when we were done, Esther sat crisscross-applesauce on the rose-colored sofa and strummed her guitar while I hummed along: "Silent Night," "Jingle Bells." That was last year, the year she bought for me a pair of woolly slipper socks to keep my feet warm because in our apartment I was cold twenty-four hours a day, seven days a week. I could hardly ever get warm. It was a thoughtful gift, an attentive gift, the kind that proved she'd been listening to me as I complained time and again about my cold feet. I look down at my feet and there they are: the woolly slipper socks.

But where is Esther?

I continue my search, for what I don't know, but I find stray pens and mechanical pencils. A stuffed animal from her childhood days, ratty and worn, hides on the shelf of a piddling closet whose doors no longer run on the track. Boxes of shoes line the closet floor. I peer inside, finding every last one of the pairs to be sensible and boring: flats, loafers, sneakers.

Absolutely nothing with heels.

Absolutely nothing in a color other than black or white or brown.

And a note.

A note tucked there on top of the IKEA desk, in the stash of paper beneath the occupational therapy textbook, among a cell phone bill and a homework assignment.

A note, unsent and folded in thirds as if she was on the verge of sticking it in an envelope and placing it in the mail, but then got sidetracked.

I put the cap back on the water; I pick up the pens. How was it that I never realized Esther was such a slob? I muse over the thought: What else don't I know about my roomie?

And then I read the note because, of course, how could I *not* read the note? It's a note, which is all sorts of stalker-ish. It's typed — which is such an anal-retentive Saint Esther thing to do — and signed *All my love,* with an *E* and a *V. All my love, EV.* Esther Vaughan.

And that's when it hits me: maybe Saint Esther isn't such a saint, after all.

# ALEX

One thing should be clear: I don't believe in ghosts.

There are logical explanations for everything: something as simple as a loose lightbulb. A faulty switch. A problem with the wiring.

I stand in the kitchen, swallowing the last of a Mountain Dew, one shoe on and one shoe off, stepping into the second of the black sneakers, when I see a spasm of light from across the street. *On. Off. On. Off.* Like an involuntary muscle contraction. A charley horse. A twitch, a tic.

*On. Off.*

And then it's done and I'm not even sure if it happened anymore or if it was just my imagination playing tricks on me.

Pops is on the sofa when I go, his arms and legs spread out in all directions. There's an open bottle of Canadian whiskey on the coffee table — Gibson's Finest — the cap lost somewhere in the cushions of the sofa, or clutched in the palm of a clammy hand probably. He's snoring, his chest rattling like an eastern diamondback. His mouth is open, head slung over the arm of the sofa so that when he finally does wake up — hungover, no doubt — he's sure to have a kink in his neck. The stench of morning breath fills the room, exuding like car exhaust from the open mouth — nitrogen, carbon monoxide and sulfur oxides flowing into the air, making it black. Not really, but that's the way I picture it, anyway — black — as I hold a hand to my nose so I don't have to smell it.

Pops wears his shoes still, a pair of dark brown leather boots, the left one untied, frayed laces trailing down the side of the sofa. He wears his coat, a zippered nylon thing the color of spruce trees. The stench of old-school cologne imparts to me the details of his night, another pathetic night that would have gone scores better had he thought to remove his ring. The man has more hair than a man his age should have, cut short, and yet bushy on the tops and sides, a russet color to tag along with the ruddy skin. Other men his age are going bald, thinning hair or no hair at all. They're getting fat, too. But not Pops. He's a good-looking guy.

But still, even in sleep, I see defeat. He's a defeatist, a calamity much worse for forty-five-year-old men than love handles and receding hairlines.

He's also a drunk.

The TV is on from last night, now playing early-morning cartoons. I flip it off and head out the door, staring at the dumped home across the street where I saw the light coming just a few minutes ago. *On, off.* It's a minimal traditional home, school-bus yellow, a concrete slab in place of a porch, aluminum siding, a busted roof.

No one lives in that house. No one wants to live there any more than they want to have a root canal or an appendectomy. Many winters ago, a water pipe froze and burst — or so we heard — filling the inside with water. Some of the windows are boarded up with plywood, which some of the wannabe gangs defaced. Weeds choke the yard, asphyxiating the lawn. A rain gutter hangs loosely from the fascia, its downspout now lying defunct on the lawn. Soon it will be covered with snow.

It isn't the only house on the street that's been abandoned, but it is the one everyone always talks about. The economy and the housing market are to blame for the other rotten, forsaken homes, the blight that abraded the rest of our homes' value and made a once idyllic nabe now ugly.

But not this one. This one has its own story to tell.

I ram my hands into the pockets of a gray jacket and press on.

The lake this morning is angry. Waves pound the shores of the beach, sloshing water across the sand. Cold water. It can't be more than thirty-five degrees. Warm enough that it hasn't thought to freeze, not yet, anyway — not like last winter when the lighthouse was plastered with ice, Lake Michigan's swell frozen midair, clinging to the edges of the wooden pier. But that was last winter. Now it's fall. There's still plenty of time for the lake to freeze.

I walk a body length or two away from the lake so my shoes don't get wet. But still, they get wet. The water sprays sideways from the lake, the surf a solid four- or five-feet high. If it were summer — tourist season — the beach would be closed down, dangerous swimming conditions and rip currents to blame.

But it's not summer. For now, the tourists are gone.

The town is quiet, some of the shops closed until spring. The sky is dark. Sunrise comes late and sunset early these days. I peer upward. There are no stars; there is no moon. They're hidden beneath a mass of gray clouds.

The seagulls are loud. They circle overhead, visible only in the swiveling glow from the lighthouse's lantern room. The wind whips through the air, upsetting the lake, making it hard for the gulls to fly. Not in a straight line, anyway. They float sideways. They flap their wings tenaciously and yet hover in place, going absolutely nowhere like me.

I pull my hood up over my head to keep the sand out of my hair and eyes.

As I crisscross the park, heading away from the lake, I pass the old antique carousel. I stare into the inanimate eyes of a horse, a giraffe, a zebra. A sea serpent chariot where a half dozen years ago I had my first kiss. Leigh Forney, now a freshman at the University of Michigan, studying biophysics or molecular something-or-other, or so I heard. Leigh isn't the only one who is gone. Nick Bauer and Adam Gott are gone, too, Nick to Cal Tech and Adam to Wayne State, playing point guard for the basketball team. And then there's Percival Allard, aka Percy, off to some Ivy League school in New Hampshire.

Everyone is gone. Everyone but me.

"You're late," Priddy says, the sound of a bell overhead tattling on my overdue arrival. She stands at the register, counting dollar bills into the drawer. *Twelve, thirteen, fourteen . . .* She doesn't look up as I come in. Her hair is down, tight curls of silver rolling over the shoulders of a starched no-nonsense blouse. She's the only one in the room who's allowed to have hair that is let down. The waitresses who beetle around in their black-and-white uniforms, filling salt and pepper shakers, bowls of creamer, all have theirs tied back in ponytails or cornrows or braids. But not Mrs. Priddy.

I tried to call her *Bronwyn* once. That is, after all, her name. It says so right there on her nametag. *Bronwyn Priddy.* It didn't go so well.

"Traffic," I say, and she sniggers. On her ring finger is a wedding band, given to her by her late husband, Mr. Priddy. There's speculation that her incessant nagging was the cause of his death. Whether or not it's true, I can only assume. She has a mole on her face, right there in the sallow folds of skin between the mouth and the nose, a raised mole, dark brown and perfectly round, which always sports a single gray hair. It's the mole that makes the rest of us

31

certain Priddy is a witch. That and her maliciousness. There's rumors that she keeps her broom in a locked storage closet off the kitchen of the café. Her broom and her cauldron, and whatever other Wiccan things she needs: a bat, a cat, a crow. It's all there, tucked away behind a locked metal door, though the rest of us are sure we hear them from time to time: a cat's meow, the crow's caw. The flapping wings of the bat.

"At this time of day?" Priddy asks about the traffic. But on her face, there's a smile there somewhere, under the peach fuzz that seriously needs to be waxed. She compensates for it somehow, for the peach fuzz, by drawing eyebrows on — dark brown on hair that is meant to be gray — to take the attention off her 'stache. Priddy pauses a moment in her counting to raise her eyes up off the dollar bills, as I stand there in the entryway stripping off my sandy jacket, and she says to me, "Those dishes aren't going to wash themselves, you know, Alex. Get to work."

I think she secretly likes me.

The morning comes and goes as they always do. Every day is a rehashing of the day before. The same customers, the same conversations, the only difference is a change of clothes. It goes without saying that Mr. Parker, who walks his two dogs at daybreak — a border collie and a Bernese mountain dog — will be the first to arrive. That he'll tie the dogs up to a streetlamp outside and ramble inside, the soles of his shoes leaving leaf clippings and muddy footprints before the display case, which I'll later be called upon to wash away. That he'll order coffee, black, to go, and then let Priddy talk him into some kind of pastry, which erroneously claims to be *homemade,* which he'll say no to twice before he says okay, sniffing the air for the faint scent of yeast and butter that isn't even there.

It goes without saying that at least one waitress will spill a tray full of food. That nearly all of them will gripe about the inadequacy of the tips. That on the weekend, the morning customers will loiter around, drinking endless cups of coffee and shooting the shit until breakfast blends into lunch and they finally leave. But during the week, the only customers hanging around after 9:00 a.m. are retirees, or the school district's bus drivers who double-park their Blue Birds in the back lot and spend the morning kvetching about the disrespectful nature of those in their care, namely all children between the ages of five and eighteen.

There are no unknowns this time of year. Every day is the same, unlike in the summer months when random tourists appear. Then it's a crapshoot. We run out of bacon. Some egghead wants to know what's really in the chocolate croissants, leaving Priddy to send one of us to drag the box out of the trash in back and see. Vacationers snap photos of the café name in the front window; they take pictures with the waitresses as if this is some kind of tourist attraction, a hot-spot destination, spouting on and on about how some Michigan travel guide claims ours is the best coffee in town. They ask if they can buy the cheap mugs that bear our name in an old-style font, and Priddy will up the price from the bulk fee she pays — a dollar fifty apiece — to $9.99. A rip-off.

But none of this happens in the off-season when every single day is a rehashing of the day before, the same of which can be said for today. And tomorrow. And yesterday. At least that's the way the day sets out to be as Mr. Parker arrives with his two dogs and orders a coffee, black, to go, and Priddy asks him if he'd care for a croissant, which he says no to twice before he says okay.

But then at the end of the morning something happens, something *abnormal*, mak-

34

ing this day different than all the days before.

My Dearest,

It's one of the last memories I have of you, your arms clinging to her neckline, the gentle curve of her breast pressing into your skin through the thin cotton of a wispy white blouse. She was beautiful to say the least, and yet it was you I couldn't take my eyes off of — the shimmer of your skin and the radiance of your eyes, the gradual curve of your lips as she traced over them with the pad of a forefinger and then placed her own to yours. A kiss.

It was through the window that I saw you. I stood there, in the middle of the street, not hiding in the shadows or behind trees. Smack-dab in the middle of the street, impervious to the flow of traffic. I'm surprised she didn't see me, that she didn't hear the blare of a car horn suggestion that I move. Recommending it. But I didn't move. I couldn't be bothered. I was too busy watching the two of you gathered together in a warm embrace. Too intrigued and too angry.

Maybe you did. Maybe you did see me, but only pretended not to see or hear.

It was nighttime, just after dusk as I pressed my face now to the glass to see inside. The curtains were open, every single light in the house on as if you wanted me to see. As if you were gloating, rubbing it in, exulting in your victory. Or maybe that was something she came up with all on her own: leaving the lights on so that I could see. It was, after all, her victory. Like a spotlight illuminating dancers onstage, the way you laughed, the way she smiled, no one noticing my absence because I'd already been replaced as if somehow I'd never even been there in the first place.

Except that you weren't onstage at all, but rather in the living room of a home I was meant to share with you.

I have to know: Did you see me? Were

37

you trying to make me mad?

All my love,

EV

# ALEX

Her hair is dark brown. Sort of. A dark brown that lightens steadily so that by the time your eyes reach the end of it, it's nearly gone blond. Ombré. It's got a subtle wave to it, an understated wave, so you're not really sure if it's a wave at all or if it's just windblown, the hair that sits below the shoulders. Brown hair to accompany the brown eyes, which — like the hair — seem to change colors the longer I stare. She arrives alone, holding the door for a couple of old fogeys who follow on the heels of her overpriced Uggs. She steps back and waits while they're seated, though it was clearly she who arrived first. She stands there in the entranceway, somehow looking sure and not so sure all at the same time. Her stance is that of aplomb: upright posture, nothing fidgety or twitchy, simply waiting her turn.

But her eyes are aimless.

I've never seen her around here before,

but for years now I've been imagining she would come.

When it's her turn, she's seated at a table beside the window so she can watch the same predictable customers who come and go and come and go, though it goes without saying that they're anything but predictable to her. I watch as she slips from a black-and-white checkered pea coat. There's a marled black beanie on her head. She removes the hat and drops it on an empty brown banquette chair beside her canvas bag. Then she peels a knitted scarf from around her neck and drops that, too, on the chair. She's petite, though not like those überskinny models you see on the fashion magazines in the grocery store lines. No, not like that. She's not pin thin, but her build is slight. More short than tall, more skinny than not skinny. But still, not short and not skinny, either. Just *average* or *normal,* I guess, but she's really not any of those things, either.

Beneath the pea coat and the beanie and the scarf, there's a pair of jeans with the Uggs. And a hoodie. Blue. With pockets.

Outside, day has broken. It's another sunless day. There are leaves on the sidewalk, brittle, crumbly leaves; what remain on the trees will lose their hold by the end of the afternoon, if the westerly wind has any say in it. It whips around the corners of the red-brick buildings, sneaking under a kaleidoscope of awnings where it lies in wait for the perfect opportunity to snatch someone's hat or steal scraps of paper from their glove-laden hands.

There's no threat of rain. Not yet, anyway. But the cold and the wind will keep plenty of people inside, forestalling the promise of winter.

She orders a coffee. She sits by the window, sipping out of the discount ceramic coffee mug, staring out the window at the view: the brick buildings, the colorful awnings, the fallen leaves. You can't see Lake Michigan from here. But people like to sit at the window, anyway, and imagine. It's there somewhere, the eastern shore of Lake Michigan. Harbor Country, we're called, a string of small beachfront towns just seventy-some miles outside of Chicago, seventy-some miles that are somehow equivalent to three states and another world away. That's where most of our clientele comes from, anyway. Chicago. Sometimes Detroit or Cleveland or Indianapolis. But most often Chicago. A weekend getaway because it's not like there's anything to do here that will keep you busy for more than two days.

But that's in the summer mainly, when people actually come. Nobody comes now. Nobody but her.

Our café is far enough off the beaten path that where we sit at the far edge of town the shops and restaurants give way to homes. It's an assorted mix, really — a souvenir shop to the north, a bed-and-breakfast to the south. On the opposite side of the sett street is a psychologist's office, followed by a succession of single-family homes. Condos. A gas station. Another souvenir shop, closed until spring.

A waitress passes by, snaps her fingers before my eyes. "Table two," she says, a waitress I call Red. They're all just nicknames to me: Red, Braids, Braces. "Table two needs to be cleared."

But I don't move. I continue to stare. I give her a nickname, too, because it feels like the right thing to do. The woman staring out the window is building castles in the air. Daydreaming. It's a big deal, really, something different happening around here when nothing different ever happens. If Nick or Adam were still around, and not away at college, I'd call them up and tell them about the girl that showed up today. About her eyes, about her hair. And they'd want to know the details: whether or not she really was different than the dime-a-dozen girls we see every day, the same girls we've known since first grade. And I'd tell them that she is.

My grandfather used to call my grand-mother — also a brunette, though in my lifetime I'd never seen her as anything other than a mass of weblike gray — Cappuccetta. The nickname Cappuccetta purportedly came from the monks of Capuchin, or so my Italian grandfather claimed, something about the hoods they wore bearing resemblance to the coffee drink, a cappuccino. That's what Grandpa said, anyway, when he looked my grandmother in the eye and called her Cappuccetta.

Me, I just like the sound of it. And it seems to suit this girl well, the modicum of brunette hair, the ambiguity that surrounds her like the hood of a monk's cowl. But I'm not a coffee drinker, and so instead my eyes drop to her narrow wrist where there sits a pearl bracelet that looks much too small for even her small hand. It's pulled taut, the elastic cord showing through the creamy beads. I imagine it leaves a red imprint along the skin. The pearl beads are worn along the edges, losing their sheen. I watch as she plucks habitually at the band, pulling the elastic up off the skin, and allowing it to snap back again. It's mesmerizing, almost, that simple movement. Pluck. Pluck. Pluck. I watch for a while, unable to shift my eyes from the bracelet or her fluid hands.

And that's what cinches it. Not Cappuccetta, I decide. I'll call her Pearl instead.

Pearl.

It's then that a cluster of churchgoers appear, the same ones who arrive every week about this same time. They claim their usual table, a rectangular slab that seats all ten. They're delivered carafes of coffee — one half-caf, the other leaded — though no one asks. It's assumed. Because this is what they do every Sunday morning: cluster around the same table, talking passionately about things like *sermons* and *pastors* and *scripture.*

The waitress Braids disappears for three consecutive smoke breaks so that when she returns she reeks of a cigarette factory, her teeth a pale yellow as she dribbles another inadequate tip into the pocket of her apron and moans. A dollar fifty, all in quarters.

She excuses herself and heads to the restroom.

The café takes on a vibe of normalcy, though with Pearl in the room — the lady with the ombré hair, staring out the window at the colorful homes and the redbrick buildings across the way — things are anything but normal. She eats from the plate of food now set before her: scrambled eggs with an English muffin on the side, smothered in butter and strawberry jam. A second cup of coffee splashed with two tubs of creamer and sprinkled with a single sugar substitute, the pink stuff, which she drinks without ever bothering to stir. I find myself staring, unable to take my eyes off her hands, and she raises the mug to her lips and sips.

It's then that the sound of Priddy's thin, metallic voice summons me by name, inter-rupting my thoughts. "Alex," she says to me, and as I turn, I see her long, crooked finger draw me to her side, her fingernails painted a cantaloupe orange. Before Priddy, on the display case, is a cardboard box and a plastic cup complete with fountain drink. Inside the box are a BLT with a mountain of fries and a pickle on the side. Same as always. We don't do deliveries, but for Ingrid Daube we do. And today it's my turn to go. Usually I look forward to the trips to Ingrid's home — a break from the mundane routine of the café — but today isn't one of those days. Today I'd rather stay.

"Me?" I ask stupidly, staring at the box, and Priddy says, "Yes, you, Alex. You."

I sigh.

"Take this to Ingrid," Priddy says to me, with no *please* and no *thank-you,* but rather an edict: "Go." I loiter a fraction of a second, my eyes on the woman with the ombré hair — *Pearl* — as Red passes by and refills her coffee mug for a third time.

Pearl has been here for an hour now, maybe two, and although she finished her meal long ago, she doesn't go. The dishes have been cleared. It's been a good thirty minutes since Red placed the check on the table beside the coffee mug. The waitress has asked three times if there's anything else she needs, but the girl only shakes her head and says no. Red is getting antsy, eager to gather up another measly tip that she can complain about as soon as Pearl decides to split. And yet she doesn't split. She remains at the window, gazing out, sipping coffee with no apparent plans to go.

I tell myself I'll hurry. That I'll be back before she leaves.

Why? I don't know why. For some reason I want to be here when she goes, to watch her put the black hat back on her head, obscuring the ombré hair. To watch her wrap the scarf around her neck and gather the canvas bag in her hands. To see her slip into the checkered pea coat. To see her rise

46

up off the chair, to see which way she goes.

I tell myself I'll hurry; I'll be back before she leaves. I say it again. If I time it just right, maybe she'll be leaving just as I return — back from my delivery to Ingrid. Maybe.

I'll hold the door for her. I'll say to her, *Have a nice day.*

I'll ask her her name. *New to town?* I'll say.

Maybe. If I time it right.

Also, if I'm not being a chicken shit, which I probably will be.

I don't bother to put on my coat for a quick trip across the street. I grab the box and the drink and slip through the glass door backward, using my backside to open the door for me. The wind nearly swipes the box from my hands as I step outside, and I think it's times like these that I wish I had hair. More hair. Much more hair than the burr cut on my head, which does nothing to keep my scalp and ears warm. I could use a hat, too, and my coat. Instead, I wear my café-issued attire: the cheap, pleated pants, the white button-down shirt and a black bow tie. It's tacky, the kind of thing I'd prefer not to have to be seen in public in. But Priddy gives me no choice. The sleeves of my shirt flutter in the breeze, the wind getting trapped beneath the polyester, making it puff up like a parachute or a birthday balloon. It's cold outside, the air temperature reaching no more than forty degrees. The windchill is another story. The windchill — also known as the one thing everyone will be talking about for the next four months to come. Only November and already meteorologists are calling for a cold winter, one of the coldest on record, they say, with subzero temps, record windchills and bounteous snow.

It's winter in Michigan, for God's sake. What else is new?

Ingrid Daube lives in a Cape Cod right across the street from the café, a small Cape Cod circa 1940- or 1950-something. It's a light blue house with dark blue shutters, a roof almost as tall as it is wide. It's a good house, a charming house. Quaint and idyllic, save for the hustle and bustle of the main street, which does anything but hustle or bustle this time of year. It's quiet. From Ingrid's upstairs dormer window, she has a bird's-eye view of the café and there I see her, standing in the window like an apparition, eyes watching mine as I wait for a passing car and then scamper across the street. She waves at me through the glass. I return the wave and watch as she disappears from view.

I start climbing the steps of Ingrid's wide, white front porch, and that's when I hear the high-pitched squeal of a squeaky door hinge, followed by the slamming of a screen door from the home next door, a blue cottage converted into an office for Dr. Giles, the town shrink. It's been less than a year since he moved his practice in. As I peek over, there he stands in the doorway, saying goodbye to a patient before peering up and down the street — hands in pockets — as if waiting for someone else to appear. Does he hug her? I'm quite certain he does, an awkward one-armed hug not meant to happen in plain sight. That's what makes it weird. He checks his watch. He looks left, he looks right, up and down the street. Someone is late, and Dr. Giles doesn't want to be kept waiting. He seems miffed that he has to wait. I see it in his squinty eyes, in his vertical posture, in the way his arms are crossed.

I don't like the man one bit.

The patient who leaves thrusts a hood up over her head, a fur-lined hood on a thick black parka, though whether it's for warmth or privacy, I can't say. I don't know. I never do see her face before she scurries away, down the street the other way. I don't see her, but I hear her. Half the town hears her.

49

I hear her crying, a distraught wail that can be heard a half block away. He made her cry. Dr. Giles made the girl cry. Add that to the list of reasons I don't like the guy.

There was a whole scandal when Dr. Giles moved his office into the tiny blue cottage. A scandal because the ladies in town took to lurking around the café, to puttering up and down the street, so they could see the comings and goings of Dr. Giles's clientele: which of the town's members was seeing the headshrinker and why. Proving what people hated most about small-town living: there is no such thing as privacy.

Ours really is the paradigm of a small town. We've got one stoplight, and we've got a town drunk and everybody knows who the town drunk is: my father. Everyone gossips. There's nothing better to do than throw one another under the bus. And so we do.

Ingrid opens the door before I knock. She opens the door and I step inside, wiping my shoes on the woven floor mat. She smiles. Ingrid is about the same age my mother would be if my mother were still here. Don't get me wrong, my mother's not dead (though sometimes I wish she was dead), she's just not *here*. Ingrid has one of those short hairdos forty- or fifty-year-old women sometimes have, the color of wet sand. She has welcoming eyes. She has a nice smile, but a sad smile. There isn't a person in town who could say a bad thing about Ingrid, but rather the bad things that have happened to Ingrid. That's what they talk about. Ingrid's life is the definition of tragic. She's gotten the short end of the stick, that's for sure, and as a result she's become the town's charity case, a fifty-year-old woman too terrified to step foot out of her own home. She has panic attacks any time she does, chest pressure, trouble breathing. I've seen it with my own two eyes, though I don't know her whole story. I make it a point not to meddle in others' business, and yet I've seen Ingrid get loaded into an ambulance and whisked off to the emergency room when she thought that she was dying. Turned out everything was fine. Just fine. Just an ordinary case of agoraphobia, as if it's ordinary for a fifty-year-old woman to stay in her home because she's scared to death of the world outside. She doesn't leave her house for anything, not to get the mail or water a flower or pick a weed. Within the gypsum walls she's perfectly fine, but outside these walls is another story.

But all that said, Ingrid isn't crazy. She's about as normal as they come around here.

"Hi, Alex," she says to me, and I reply, "Hi."

Ingrid dresses like a fifty-year-old woman should: a bright orange sweatshirt kind of thing, and black knit pants. Around her neck, a locket and chain. In her earlobes, stud earrings. On her feet is a pair of flats.

Before Ingrid has a chance to close the door, I turn around for a quick peek. There in the storefront glass I see her, Pearl, obscured in part by the reflection of nearly everything on the opposite side of the street. What's inside and what's outside are complicated by glass, so it's no wonder that birds fly headlong into it sometimes, plummeting to their deaths on the porous concrete.

But still, through the marquee of trees and in the manifestation of half the world on one pane of glass, I see her.

Pearl.

Her eyes stare out the window, but not at me. I follow the path of Pearl's eyes to a sign that hangs with scroll brackets from the neighboring home: Dr. Giles, PhD. Licensed Psychologist. And there he stands, Dr. Giles, with his dark, trim-cut hair and well-groomed style, waiting impatiently for a patient to appear.

Well, I'll be. She's watching him.

Does she have an appointment with Dr. Giles? Maybe. Maybe that's it. My perception shifts, but not so much that I stop thinking about her hair or her eyes, because I don't. In fact, they're there every time I so much as blink.

Ingrid closes the door, and she asks of me, "Can you lock it?"

Ingrid's home is on the small side, but more than adequate for a single occupant as I kick the door closed, turn the dead bolt, and bring Ingrid's lunch to her kitchen table. On the marble countertop is an open cardboard box, a small reserve of novels set beside it. Something to pass time. There's a knife set there, too, a professional-grade carving knife, used to slice through the packaging tape.

The television is on, a small flat-screen TV that Ingrid doesn't watch, though I can tell she's listening to it and my guess is that the sound of actors and actresses on the TV screen tricks her into feeling like she's not alone. That someone is here even if they're only make-believe. It's a spoof she plays on herself. It must be lonely, not being able to leave your own home.

The house is otherwise quiet. Once upon a time there was the sound of boisterous children and stampeding feet, but not anymore. Now those sounds are gone.

"I was hoping you'd do me a favor, Alex," Ingrid says, drawing my eyes away from a lady on the TV screen. Her home is a crisp white: white walls, white cabinets. The floors are a contrast to the rest of the home, stained plank flooring, so dark they're almost black. Her furniture and decor are austere, shades of neutrals and gray, not much in the way of knickknacks or accessories, unlike my own home, Pops being the hoarder that he is, unable to part with anything. It's not like he collects years' worth of rubbish, piled miles high in the middle of our living room, stray cats procreating in every crevice of our home so that it burgeons with feral kittens, some living, some dead. No, not like that; not like those hoarders on TV. But he is sentimental, the type that has trouble parting with my junior-high report cards and baby teeth. I suppose this should make me feel good. Deep down I guess it does.

But it's also a painful reminder that Pops has no one else in this world but me. If I were to leave, where would he be?

"I made a shopping list," Ingrid says, and without waiting for her to voice the words — *Will you go?* — I say, "Sure thing. Tomorrow, okay?" And she says that it is.

From a window in the kitchen of Ingrid's home, I've got a decent view straight to the inside of Dr. Giles's office. Ingrid's Cape Cod sits just above his, the window at the ideal angle to see right in. It's not a great view, but still, it's a view. As Ingrid sorts through her purse for two twenty-dollar bills and hands them to me, I catch sight of something shadowy and vague, just the movement of shapes through the glass. Someone is there. I stare, but I don't stare long. I can't. I don't want Ingrid to think I'm some Peeping Tom. Instead, my eyes meet Ingrid's and I tuck the two twenty-dollar bills into a pocket and tell her that I'll go tomorrow morning. I'll go to the grocery store in the morning. I've done this routine many times before.

I take the list, say my goodbyes and go.

The minute I emerge from Ingrid's house and step down the wide porch steps and onto the sidewalk, I see it.

The café window is now untenanted.

The girl is gone.

# QUINN

I often thought that Esther was transparent, like a pane of glass. What you see is what you get. But now, sitting on the floor of her boxy bedroom, on my legs so that they've gone numb, holding the note to *My Dearest* in my hand, I think that maybe I was wrong. I've gotten it all wrong.

Maybe Esther isn't transparent, after all. Not a pane of glass but rather a toy kaleidoscope, the kind with intricate mosaics and patterns that change every time you so much as turn the edge.

It was a listing in the *Reader* that brought me to Esther.

"You can't be serious?" asked my sister, Madison, when I showed her the ad: *Female in need of roommate to share 2BDR Andersonville apartment. Great locale, close to bus and train.* "You have seen the movie *Single White Female,* haven't you?" she probed from the edge of her twin-size bed, science flash cards spread out before her, proliferating like rabbits on the bedspread.

I picked up a flash card. "You're never going to need this junk, you know?" I asked, staring at the garbled definition on the back. "Not in the real world, anyway."

And then Madison gave me that look like she always did and said, "I have a test tomorrow," as if that was something I didn't know.

"No shit, Sherlock," I said, tossing the flash card back on the heaping pile. "But after high school," I mean. "You're never going to need this crap."

I was the last person in the world who should be giving anyone advice on anything, the least of which was education. I had graduated five months ago from college, a crappy college at that, one which didn't quite make the cut of best colleges in the US of A. But the tuition was cheap, or cheaper than its counterparts. They also let me in, the same of which couldn't be said for the other colleges to which I applied thanks to a little thing known as learning disabilities. Between the ADHD and the dyslexia, I was a lost cause. Or so said the multitude of rejection letters I received from the colleges to which I applied, with the big, red Rejected stamp across the returned applications.

That's quite good for the self-esteem. Really, it is.

Or not.

I spent the first two of my eight semesters on academic probation. But when the dean threatened to dismiss me from school, I got my act together and cracked open a book. I also remembered to take my Ritalin from time to time, and admitted to the learning disability, which I wasn't too keen on having to do.

But still, somehow or other I managed to graduate from college with a 3.0. And yet no one needs academic advice from me, least of all Madison, my little sister, on schedule to graduate with high honors. And so I shut my mouth. On that subject at least.

I had, by the way, seen the movie *Single White Female.* Of course I had. But desperate times called for desperate measures, and I was desperate. I was twenty-two years old, five months post–college graduation and desperately in need of fleeing my parents' suburban home where they lived with my mastermind sister and her smelly guinea pig. Madison was still in high school, a science geek with a whole medical career ahead of her. That or an embalmer, maybe, with her whole morbid fascination of things

that were dead. She had a taxidermy squirrel she bought on the internet with her allowance, the same thing she planned to do
with the guinea pig when it finally kicked
the bucket — skin and stuff the pathetic
thing so she could set it on a shelf.

Madison was happy as a clam living at
home. She couldn't understand my need to
get out. It was more than just dullsville for
me; it was nails on a chalkboard, the way
my mother's minivan greeted me at the
suburban Barrington Metra station each day
after work, Mom behind the wheel, always
on my case to know how the day had gone.

*Did you make any friends today?* she had
asked that first day of my new career as a
project assistant at an illustrious law firm in
the Loop, as if it was the first day of kindergarten and not a job. I got the job based on
a little white lie, claiming interest in law
school when law school didn't interest me
at all.

*Did you learn anything new?* my mother
asked there, that day, in the front seat of
her car.

*Nope, Mom. Nothing.*

But I did, didn't I? I learned how much
the job sucked.

And then my mother and I drove home,
where I was forced to listen to the parental

figures go on and on about how Madison was *oh so smart,* about how Madison *aced* another exam, about how Madison had already been *accepted* to some smarty-pants college, while I'd picked one based on the simple fact that it was cheap and they'd actually accepted me as opposed to the mass of rejections I received following a poor performance on my SAT.

I had to get out. I was feeling suffocated, smothered. I couldn't breathe.

And that's when it happened. I was riding the Metra home from work when I flipped open to the classifieds and saw the ad in the *Reader.* Esther's ad, a beacon in a dark night sky. I'd looked for apartments before, but my entry-level job barely paid minimum wage, and though I tried cutting corners — *studio* apartments, *garden* apartments, apartments on the *south* side — the simple fact was that I couldn't afford an apartment in Chicago all on my own. And an apartment outside of Chicago was out of the question because then not only would I need an apartment, I'd also need a car, some mode of transportation to drive me to and from the train station rather than mother dearest.

*Female in need of roommate to share 2BDR Andersonville apartment. Great locale, close to bus and train.*

I was sold! I called immediately and we made arrangements to meet.

The day I was to meet Esther for the first time, I mentally prepared myself for a meeting with Jennifer Jason Leigh. Truth be told, Madison had psyched me out with the whole *Single White Female* bit. To make matters worse, I watched the movie before our meeting, watched as Jennifer Jason Leigh, aka Hedy, turned all psycho or whatnot, assuaged only in the fact that, as the one moving *into* Esther's apartment, I was in fact the Jennifer Jason Leigh in our situation, and she the charming Bridget Fonda.

And indeed she was charming.

Esther was running late that day, held up at work by a coworker who'd called in sick. She phoned as I was heading to the apartment, and we made plans to meet instead at a bookshop on Clark, where I soon found out she worked. Just a part-time gig while she finished up a master's degree in occupational therapy, she said. She was a singer, too, the type who performed on occasion at one of the local bars. "Just something to pay the bills," she said, though in time I would come to learn it was more than that. Esther had a secret craving to be the next Joni Mitchell.

"What's an occupational therapist?" I asked as she led me through the stacks of books to a quieter spot in back and we sat on blood-orange poufs meant for children's story time, apologizing for dragging me down to the bookshop and veering me away from our original plan. It was a Saturday; the shop was full of cosmopolites, browsing the shelves, picking their books. They looked smart, every single one of them, as did Esther, though in a cool, contemporary sort of way. She was doe-eyed and polite, but possessed traces of an inner devil, be it the sterling silver nose stud or the gradient hair. I liked that about Esther right away. Dressed in a cozy cardigan and cargo pant ensemble, Esther was cool.

"We help people learn how to care for themselves. People with disabilities, delays, injuries. The elderly. It's like rehab, self-help and psychiatry all rolled into one."

Her teeth were aligned successively inside her mouth, a brilliant white. Her eyes were heterochromatic — one brown, one blue — something I'd never before seen. She wore glasses that day, though I learned later they were only for show, a prop for her role as book salesman. She said they made her look smart. But Esther didn't need faux glasses to look smart; she already was.

The day we met, she asked me about my job and whether or not I'd be able to afford my half of the rent. That was Esther's only qualification, that I pay my own way. "I can," I promised her, showing my latest paycheck as proof. Five-fifty a month I could do. Five-fifty a month for a bedroom of my own in a walk-up apartment on Chicago's north side. She took me there, down the street from the bookshop, just as soon as she finished reading to the tiny tots who pilfered from us the blood-orange poufs. I listened to her as she read aloud, taking on the voice of a bear and a cow and a duck, her voice pacifying and sweet. She was meticulous in the details, from the way she made sure the little ones were attentive and quiet, to the way she turned the pages of the oversize book so all could see. Even I found myself perched on the floor, listening to the tale. She was enchanting.

In the walk-up apartment, Esther showed to me the space that could be my room if I so chose.

She never said what happened to the person who used to live there in the room before me, the room I would soon inhabit, though in the weeks that followed I found vestiges of his or her existence in the compact closet in the large bedroom: an indecipherable name etched into the wall with pencil, a fragment of a photograph abandoned on the vacant floor of a hollow room so that all that remained on the glossy image was a wisp of Esther's shadowy hair.

The scrap of photo I did away with after I moved in, but there was nothing I could do to fix the closet wall. I knew it was Esther's hair in the photograph because, like the heterochromatic eyes, she had hair like I'd never before seen, the way she bleached it from bottom to top to get a gradual fade, dark brown on top, blond at the bottom. The tear line on the picture was telling, too, the barbed white of the photo paper, the image gone — all but Esther.

I didn't toss the photo, but rather handed it to Esther with the words, "I think this is yours," as I unpacked my belongings and moved in. That was nearly a year ago. She'd snatched it from my hand and threw it away, an act that meant nothing to me at the time.

But now I can't help but wonder if it should have meant something. Though what, I'm not so sure.

# ALEX

I wait for hours for the girl to return — trying hard to stare through the window coverings of Dr. Giles's cottage office — but she doesn't show. I consider sneaking into that space between Ingrid and Dr. Giles's home, standing on tiptoes to try and see in. I contemplate a return visit to Ingrid's home — feigning I forgot something, that I *needed* something — to try and catch a glimpse from her kitchen window. I imagine that Pearl is in there, in Dr. Giles's cottage, doing what people do in a shrink's office: sitting on a sofa, spilling her guts to a man who gets his kicks listening to other people's problems. But then the time goes by — thirty minutes, an hour, *two* hours — until I tell myself it's been too long for her to be in there, chatting it up with Dr. Giles. No psychiatry appointment lasts two hours. Or do they? I'm not one to know.

In time, I give up. She's not in there, I tell

myself. But of course I'm not sure. I can only guess.

In the middle of the afternoon, I go home. I retrace the steps I made this morning, down the streets of town, past the small stores that are closing up shop for the night, flipping Open signs to Closed, locking the doors. I'm tired; my feet hurt. My head swims with the image of that girl at the window, here one minute, gone the next.

The streets are paved with setts, rectangular granite blocks like cobblestones. The two restaurants remain open, but the boutique stores — the cutesy one with baby stuff in the front window and the one that carries nothing other than novelty items and a poor selection of cheesy, overpriced greeting cards — will soon close. The streets are sleepy, the gray sky contemplating rain. To the side of the road, there's a big, black crow feasting on a rabbit carcass: roadkill. Everyone gets a little desperate this time of year. A squirrel scampers across a telephone wire, praying the crow doesn't see. Down the street a group of preteen boys in shorts and T-shirts walk home, as if unaffected by the cold. The sound of their laughter cuts through the autumn air. One of them puffs on the end of a smoke; he can't be older than twelve or thirteen.

I pull my hood up over my head. I tuck my hands into the pockets of my pants and walk quickly, head down, through town, past the carousel, and to the beach.

The town is lonesome and I am feeling blue.

I think of my pals Nick and Adam and Percy, off at college, having the time of their lives. Meanwhile, I'm thinking of some girl I don't even know, may never see again, likely a head case, too.

The lake pounds the shore, no different than it did this morning. It's only in daylight that I can see the choppy waves out at sea, the steady flow of whitecaps that charge the sand, livid and swift like knights on horseback — a charging cavalry. The sand is a washed-out brown. The lake has a smell to it, not an unpleasant one, but one that just smells soggy and wet and cold. The sand sticks to my black gym shoes as I make my way past the tall beach grass, the dense bursts that emerge through the sand. The grass is brown and brittle now. No longer green. Soon it will be gone, torn from its roots by the cold and the wind and the snow. My eyes rove the sand for crinoid stems — the tiny disks I find in the gravel and in the sand — just as they always do. It's a fixation for me, a weakness, a habit.

Crinoid stems, Indian beads, sea lilies. It's all the same to me, the fossils of prehistoric creatures that once inhabited Lake Michigan. I gather a crinoid stem from the sand and admire it in the palm of my hand. Much more beautiful than shale or basalt rock to me; much more meaningful than granite or slag, though, really, they're nothing much to look at. People string jewelry with these, but me, I collect them in a Ziploc bag. For now, I slide it into the pocket of my pants, holding tight, careful not to let go.

There's a couple out on the pier, a man and a woman, not far out, but far enough to get the gist of it without being knocked into the water by the wind. They hold each other by the hand — steadying one another in the stubborn gale — as they take in the sweeping lake views and the apocalyptic sky, and then they turn and go, trooping to a car parked in the adjoining lot, stomping the sand off their shoes as they do.

But I don't go. I stay, taking it all in for myself.

It's only after they've left and I've watched the black car spin out of the lot and out of town that I see her sitting all alone on the playground's belt swing, her feet dragging through the sand below. Her hands clutch the chain, though she doesn't pump her legs, allowing the wind to move the swing for her. It's a measured swing to say the least, deliberate and lazy, as one does when they're thinking about something else and not at all about the swing.

Pearl.

Her coat is on; her hat is on. Her hands are ungloved and look to me to be cold. Her scarf is wrapped around her neck, though the wind grabs it by either end and pulls, so that the scarf floats this way and that on the current of the wayward wind. It's begun to rain — just a slight drizzle — something she seems repellent to, as if she's waterproof. She doesn't seem to mind the rain, which pelts me in the eyeballs and soaks my insides. I can't stand the rain. I could scurry home; I *should* scurry home. I should run. But I don't. Instead, I move to a covered spot, a picnic area with wooden tables and, more importantly, a roof. I sit on the timber tabletop, a solid fifty feet from where Pearl sits.

She doesn't see me.

But I see her.

When I get to the end of the note, I have one, simple, undeterred thought: Who the hell is *My Dearest*? I have to ask Esther about this. I just have to. The last line screams over and over again in my ear: *Did you see me? Were you trying to make me mad?*

I want to ask Esther, *Who?*

I scurry out into the living room to see if she's come home yet, slipped in quietly while I was in her bedroom. I half expect to see her sitting on the rose-colored sofa, crisscross-applesauce as she says to those tiny tykes at the bookshop's story time. I picture myself confronting Esther about the note, thrusting the typed sheet of paper under her nose. *Who is My Dearest?* I ask. I see myself shake that note in front of her rueful face and demand to know, *Who is he?*

A line runs through my mind: *Or maybe*

*that was something she came up with all on her own: leaving the lights on so that I could see. It was, after all,* her *victory.*

In my musings I shake Esther by the shoulders and ask over and over again: *Who is she? Who is she, Esther?* as Esther's face turns contrite and she begins to cry.

But no. I wouldn't do that to Esther. I wouldn't want to see her cry.

But still, I want to know. *Who is she?*

Of course it doesn't matter, anyway, because when I come barreling out of the bedroom she's not there. Of course she's not there. It's just me and an empty room. The TV is off and so other than the hiss of the radiator the room is silent. The room itself screams of Esther, all the mismatched furniture she owned before I moved in: the rose-colored sofa, the industrial iron coffee table, a mod plaid chair in black and white, throw pillows in moss and yellow and blue. And then, of course, there was the frieze rug that we carried home together from some yard sale on Summerdale — my only contribution to the decor save from, of course, *me.* We must have walked three blocks with that rug, Esther in front, me in the rear, laughing all along the way from the sheer weight of it, from the fact that it was a bilious green. I take in the walls of the apartment themselves, a blinding white, which we're prohibited from painting by order of Mrs. Budny. Mrs. Budny, an eighty-nine-year-old Pole who lives in the unit beneath us, and also my landlord. The walls instead are covered in coat hooks and candleholders and a dry-erase board where Esther and I leave each other curt little messages, missives and other forms of communiqué.

*Pick up milk.*

*Did you eat my cheese?*

*When life gives you lemons, make lemonade.*

*Ran out. Be home soon.*

It's lonely, I realize again then. The apartment is lonely without Esther home.

I pick up my phone to call Ben, a coworker and also a friend. Ben is, more or less, the only person I talk to at work unless of course I'm being paid to talk to them. The lawyers who beckon me to fetch files and make photocopies — I only speak to them because I have to speak to them. It's required. Part of the job description essentially.

But Ben I speak to because I want to. Because I like him. Because he's nice.

He's also handsome as all get-out, a twenty-three-year-old PA like me, though one with legitimate plans of law school ahead. But he's got a girlfriend. A college coed, another law school hopeful like him. As soon as she finishes up a prelaw degree at UIC, they'll both apply for law school together in Washington, DC. So romantic. His girlfriend's name is Priya, a name that even sounds beautiful.

I've never met her in person, Priya, but I've seen the assemblage of photographs Ben stores in his smallish office cube: photos of Priya alone, photos of Ben and Priya, photos of Priya and *Ben's dog,* a one-eyed Chihuahua named Chance (and if that doesn't say something about the size of Ben's heart, I don't know what does).

I find Ben's number in my call history and click on his name, and then proceed to listen to the phone ring five shrill times before it sends me to voice mail. I listen to Ben's message, the simple and robotic and yet entirely charming sound of his voice as he says, *This is Ben. Leave a message.* I could listen to that message on repeat all night. But I don't. Instead, when the phone beeps, I take my cue and leave a vague message. "Hey," I say. "It's Quinn. I have to talk to you. Call me back, okay?" I don't say a thing about Esther. That's not the kind of message you leave on a voice mail; it's tacky. Important things aren't meant for voice mail. I've been dumped that way before, and so I should know. I'll fill Ben in when he calls back, but then I picture Ben and Priya together and wonder when he'll call back, or if any of this will matter any more when he does. Esther will surely be home soon, I think, although now I'm not so sure.

I sit on the sofa all alone and watch as the apartment is besieged by blackness. Nighttime. The only light derives from a streetlamp or two outside our apartment window — and even those are few and far between — our little residential Chicago neighborhood too far from the Loop to be illuminated by the likes of the Willis Tower or Donald Trump's posh hotel. As darkness takes over, I start to fill with a sense of unease. *Where is Esther?* Esther has done strange things before, don't get me wrong, but never before has she left me for a whole day without saying where she was going or when she'd be home. Never before has she climbed out that fire escape window and disappeared into the darkness of night. I stare at the clock on the wall and realize it's been twelve long hours since Esther's alarm clock first woke me from sleep, and still she's not here.

I start to worry. What if something has happened to Esther, something bad?

And so I contemplate a second phone call. Not to Ben this time, of course, but to the police. Should I call the police? My mind vacillates back and forth between *Call the police* and *Don't call the police* like a game of eeny, meeny, miny, moe, before landing on *Call the police.* And so I do. I dial 311, the city's nonemergency phone number, as opposed to 911. This isn't an emergency, or at least I don't think it is. I pray it's not an emergency. A woman answers the phone, and I picture her, some telephone operator, sitting at a computer desk with a headset on her head, flattening her hair.

At the operator's request, I state the nature of my nonemergency. "My room-mate," I tell her, "is missing." And then I fill her in on the details of Esther's quick departure — the window, the screen, the fire escape.

She listens attentively, but when I'm through, her words are wary. "Have you checked the local hospitals?" she asks.

"No," I admit, feeling suddenly like a fool, "I haven't."

It didn't occur to me for one split second that Esther might be hurt.

"That's a great place to start." And I

gather from her comment that calling the police isn't a great place to start. "You've checked in with your roommate's family? Other friends?" she asks, at which I shake my head in silent admission. I did not. Well, I called Ben, that's one step in the right direction, but I didn't even think of calling Esther's family, not that I know a phone number, anyway, or have the slightest clue how to find it. I don't even know her mother's or father's names, nothing other than Mr. or Mrs. Vaughan, or so I assume. And I'm guessing there are tens of thousands of people in the world with the last name Vaughan. Besides, I rationalize in my head, Esther and her family aren't close. Esther doesn't like to talk about them, but I gather that her father's out of the picture; her mother and she are estranged. How do I know this? Because while my own mother sends care packages galore and shows up without warning at our door, Esther's mom doesn't even call to say hello. I asked Esther about her family once; she said she didn't want to talk about it. I didn't ask again. One time a card arrived, but Esther let it sit on the kitchen table for four days, unopened, before throwing it in the trash.

"Any reason to believe there was foul play?" the operator asks, and I say no. "Does the missing person have a medical condition that would make the issue life-threatening?" she asks, and again I say no. Her voice is detached and unfriendly, as if she doesn't care. She probably doesn't, but you'd think an emergency or nonemergency operator would have at least a scant amount of sympathy. I almost want to make something up, to tell this woman that Esther is diabetic and that she's left all her insulin at home, or that she has asthma and is without an inhaler. Then maybe this woman would show concern. Maybe I should tell her the window screen was gashed, the glass broken in. That there was blood, a pool of it, enough for Esther to have completely bled out. Then maybe I'd be redirected to 911 and suddenly Esther's disappearance would be deemed an emergency.

Or maybe the operator is trying to clue me in to something: this isn't an emergency; Esther is fine. She says to me then, "Nearly seventy percent of missing people leave of their own free will and return within forty-eight to seventy-two hours, voluntarily. You're more than welcome to come to the station and file a missing-persons report, though there's only so much the police can do in the case of missing adults. Without evidence of foul play, we can't immediately think something criminal has happened. People are allowed to up and disappear if they want to. But if you file a report, your roommate will be placed in a missing-persons database and our investigators will look into it.

"Does your roommate drink, do drugs?" she asks then, and I quickly shake my head and say no. Well, Esther does drink, a margarita here, a daiquiri there, but she isn't an alcoholic or anything.

It's then that the operator asks about Esther's mental state — does she suffer from depression? — and I picture Esther's magnanimous smile and think to myself that she can't be. She just can't be.

"No," I say without delay, "of course not."

"Did you two get into an argument recently?" she asks, and I realize she's trying to insinuate that *I* did something to hurt Esther. Did Esther and I get into an argument? Of course not. But was Esther upset that I went out last night without her, though she'd told me to go? I don't know. I reiterate to myself that she told me to go. *I'd be a killjoy, Quinn. Go without me. You'll have more fun.* That's exactly what she said. So how could she be mad?

"We didn't get into an argument," I say, and the operator leaves me with two options: I can come in and file a missing-persons report, or I can wait it out.

I feel silly for calling the operator, and so I decide to wait it out. The last thing I need to do is stare an officer in the eye and feel like a fool in person. I have plenty of experience with this. I'll call the hospitals; I'll try and track Esther's family down. I'll wait for Ben to call, and with any luck, Esther will come home of her own free will, just like the operator said, within forty-eight to seventy-two hours. Two to three days. *Two to three days,* I think. I don't know if I can wait that long for Esther to come home.

I hang up with the operator and will Ben to call. *Please, Ben, please,* I silently beg. *Please call.* But Ben doesn't call. I search online for the numbers of the closest area hospitals, starting with Methodist, and then I call, asking the receptionists one by one if Esther is there. I state her name and then I describe her — the shaded hair, the hetero-chromatic eyes, the ungrudging smile — knowing that Esther has that kind of face that once you've seen it, you never forget. But Esther isn't at Methodist Hospital or Weiss or any of the local urgent care facilities. I lose hope with each apathetic reply. *No Esther Vaughan here.*

I'm feeling lost and alone when I hear the

sound of a telephone ringing. Not my phone, but a phone. Esther's phone, which I know from the ringtone, some 1980s Billboard hit that nobody listens to any-more.

Esther's ringtone. Esther's phone.
Esther's not here, so why is her phone?
I rise to my feet to find it.

# ALEX

I wonder if she has any idea she's being watched.

I watch the girl twitch her hands, scratch her head. I watch her cross her legs this way — and then that way — on the park swing, trying to get comfortable. Then she uncrosses her legs and kicks at the sand. She looks left, right, and then peers upward and opens her mouth to catch droplets of rainwater falling from the sky.

I have no idea how long I stare. Long enough that my hands go numb from the cold and the rain.

It's after some time that the girl rises to her feet and stands. Her feet, in the chestnut-colored Uggs, sink into the sand as she moves through it and toward the beach. Closer and closer to the water. It's hard for her to move through the sand thanks to the density of it, for one, and the wind. It pushes her modest body this way and that, her arms out at her sides like the arms of a tightrope walker. One foot in front of the other. One step at a time.

And then three feet before the tide line, she stops.

And I stare.

And this is what happens. It starts with the boots first, which she draws from her feet with great balance, one foot, and then the other. She sets them side by side in the sand. The socks are next, and I think to myself, *Is she crazy?* Thinking she will dip her feet into the frigid waters of a November Lake Michigan. It can't be more than forty degrees. Ice cold. The kind of water that gives rise to hypothermia.

The socks get tucked into the shaft of the boot so they don't blow away. I watch and wait for the girl to totter to the lake's side and walk right on in, but she doesn't. There's a moment that passes — or many moments, maybe, I don't know, I've lost all sense of time — before she reaches for the buttons of the coat and starts to unbutton from top to bottom. And then the coat comes off. Set in the sand beside the boots and the socks. It's as she starts to remove the jeans from her legs that I think, *This can't be happening.* I peer around for another onlooker, someone, anyone, to tell me this is real and not only a figment of my imagination. Is this really happening? This can't be happening. This can't be real.

I've stood now and moved closer, two, maybe three feet, hidden behind the wooden columns that frame the picnic shelter. I wrap my hands around the columns and squint my eyes so that I can see the way Pearl unbuttons and unzips the jeans, the way she sets herself down in the wet sand and drags the denim from her legs, setting that, too, by the coat and the shoes. The rain has picked up its pace now and barrels down harder, blowing sideways in the wind. It sweeps through the orifices in the enclosed shelter space and soaks me through and through. The girl stands then, hands in the pockets of her blue hoodie, with nothing else on. Just the hoodie and a pair of underpants. And the hat and scarf.

But then the hoodie goes, too.

And it's then that she enters the water. In nothing more than her undergarments, her scarf and a hat. She walks right in, insouciant to the cold like an emperor penguin, diving right into arctic waters. She doesn't stop when she gets her feet wet. Or her ankles. Or her knees. She keeps going. I think she might walk right on to Chicago if she could, hands dragging along the surface of the water as the waves run up and splash her, soaking her head to toe with the lake's callous spray.

Without realizing it, I've moved from the picnic shelter and stand, myself, in the sand. How did I get here? I don't know. All common sense tells me that I should call someone for help. The police? *Dr. Giles?* How long does she have before the cold water leads to hypothermia? Fifteen minutes? Thirty minutes? I don't know. But I can't call someone because I'm completely dumbstruck and speechless, feet frozen to the sand, unable to lug my phone from the pocket of my pants. Because I can't get my eyes off Pearl, there in the water, swimming the sidestroke, long enough to call for help. Watching the way her unhurried arms rise up out of the water one at a time, and then drop back in. The gentle, rhythmic kicking of feet in water, proffering no splash at all. The way she goes and goes without turning her head for a breath, like a fish with gills and fins.

If I had something better to do with my time, I probably wouldn't be standing here watching her swim. But I don't and so I stand here and watch her swim.

And there, as I stand, gawking, the girl rises up to her feet and begins a retreat from the water. While any normal human being would sprint shivering from the water and into something warm and dry, she doesn't. Her steps are slow, calculated. She isn't in a hurry. She takes her time, emerging from the water soaking-wet, the little she wears now completely sheer. The sand clings to her feet, her ankles, grainy sand changing colors before my eyes. Turning darker.

I would avert my eyes. I *should* avert my eyes.

But I can't.

I can't be blamed for this. What eighteen-year-old would turn his head away, refuse to look? Not me, that's for sure. Not anyone I know.

Seems to me, anyway, that she wants to be seen.

And there she stands in the wet sand, the water likely freezing to her bare skin in the cold, autumn air. She makes no attempt to dry herself off or to get dressed. Her back is to the lake now and she takes in what's on the other side: the playground and carousel, the beach grass and a line of vacuous trees.

And me.

And that's when she turns to me and waves.

And I prove to the world that I really am

a chickenshit when I turn and walk away,
pretending I don't see.

# QUINN

I rise to my feet and follow the ringing of
the phone to the kitchen, fully expecting to
see Esther's cell stashed there on the countertop beside canisters of flour, sugar and
cookies. But no such luck. I'm not one to
answer her phone or even notice its ring,
but now I'm worried. Perhaps Esther *is* in
trouble; perhaps she needs my help. Perhaps
it's Esther on the other end of the line calling me for help on her phone. She's lost,
doesn't have enough cash for a cab. Something along those lines.

But she could just call me on my phone,
then. Of course she could. That would make
more sense. But still. Maybe . . .

I flip on the stove light and continue to
search, tracking the subdued ringtone as
Hansel and Gretel tracked bread crumbs
through the deep, dark woods. It sounds far
away and hard to hear, as if there's cotton
in my ears. I open and close the stove, the

refrigerator, the cabinets, though it seems utterly absurd to do so. To look for a phone inside a refrigerator. But I do, anyway.

I continue on my search. The phone rings once, twice, three times. I'm nearly certain the call will go to voice mail and this will all be for naught, when I find it tucked away inside the pocket of a red zip-up hoodie that hangs from a hanger in our teeny-weeny coat closet.

I snatch up the phone, ousting the hoodie from its hanger as I do, watching it fall to the floor as I answer the call, the caller ID reading Unknown.

"Hello?" I ask, pressing the phone to my ear.

"Is this Esther Vaughan?" probes a voice on the other end of the line.

And then I utter the three words that in about thirteen seconds I'll regret having said. "No, it's not," I say, wishing instantly that I would have said, *This is she.* But then again, why would I when my interest has yet to be piqued? It takes much more than a blocked phone number to get my attention. I get blocked calls all the time, mainly debt collectors calling to collect unpaid bills. Old credit cards with cringe-worthy balances I haven't made payments to in years. Student loans.

"Is she there?" asks the voice. It's a gruff voice, a male voice, that isn't going to fool around with any pleasantries or wisecracks or banter.

"No," I say, and then, "Can I take a message?" I ask as my hand fumbles through the near-darkness for the dry-erase board and a marker. I drift across the room to the board that hangs aslant from a wall, fully prepared to jot down a name and phone number below the arcane message: *Ran out. Be home soon,* a phrase that suddenly takes on an abundance of meaning.

*Ran out. Be home soon.*

Esther wrote that. I know she did. It's not my handwriting; it's hers. The fusion of cursive and print, upper- and lowercase words. Both feminine and masculine all at the same time.

But when did she leave the message, I wonder, and why?

Was it last week when she ran back to the bookshop to find her forgotten faux glasses? Or just a couple days ago when she hurried to the Edgewater branch of the Chicago Public Library on Broadway to return a book before closing time, so that it wouldn't be late? Esther is a stickler for returning books on time.

Or, I wonder then while waiting for the

guy on the other end of the cell phone to decide whether or not he's going to leave a message, did she leave the annotation last night before she opened her bedroom window and climbed on out? That's it, then, I tell myself. There's no reason to be worried. Esther left me a note; she'll be home soon. It says so right there on the board.

*Ran out. Be home soon.*

And then to my dismay, the man on the other end of the line curtly replies, "It's a confidential matter." His voice is ticked off. "We had an appointment this afternoon. She didn't show."

Apparently *that* information — Esther's sloppy, negligent behavior — isn't quite as confidential as who he is or why he's calling. There are voices in the background that I try hard to decrypt: cars, the lapping sound of ocean waves, a blender. I can't be sure. It all fuses together until it is one thing and one thing alone: noise. Clamor. Racket. A whole hullabaloo.

"I can tell her you called," I suggest, exploring for a name. A reason for calling.

"I'll call back," he says instead, and the line goes dead. I stand there in the kitchen, my bare feet cold on the black-and-white checkerboard tile, watching as, in my hand, the cell phone screen fades to black. I press the home button and swipe my finger across the screen. The phone prompts me for Esther's password. *Password?* My heart starts to race. *Damn!*

I start pressing digits at random until I'm locked out of the phone altogether, the device disabled, and I'm stuck waiting an entire minute — sixty long, maddening seconds — until I can do it again. And again. And again.

I'm not the sharpest tool in the shed, nor the brightest crayon in the box. I've been told as much before. So it shouldn't surprise me in the least bit that I have no idea how to break into Esther's phone without her password or thumbprint. And yet it does.

I placate myself with the simple fact that he promised to call back. The gruff voice on the other end of the line said that he would call back.

I'll do better the next time, I tell myself. I will.

# ALEX

It's evening at my house. I'm cooking. Pops is watching TV, feet on the old coffee table, a bottle of beer in his hand. He's drunk, but he's not wasted. He still knows his left hand from his right, which is a big accomplishment some days. He was awake when I got home from work this evening. Also a big accomplishment. Seems he managed a shower, too. He'd changed out of his striped shirt and no longer reeked of the god-awful cologne or the rank morning breath as he did when I left for work that morning. Now he just reeks of booze.

On the TV is a football game. The Detroit Lions. He screams at the TV.

There are chicken nuggets in the oven and a can of green beans warming on the stove. Pops wanders through the kitchen for another beer and asks if I'd like one, too. I look him in the blasted eyes and say, "I'm eighteen," though I'm not sure that means too much to him. On the fridge door is a picture I drew about a dozen years ago of outer space: the sun, the moon, the stars, Neptune and Jupiter, in Crayola crayons. Worn along the edges, a corner missing, having fallen from its magnet about a million times. The colors are faded. Everything, these days, seems like it's starting to fade.

Sharing the same magnet is a postcard from my mother. I threw it in the trash when it arrived in the mail, but Pops found it there, mixed up with lunch meat scraps and corn kernels, and pulled it back out again. This one's from San Antonio. *The Alamo,* it says.

*You shouldn't be so hard on her,* he'd said to me when he found the postcard in the trash. And then that line was trailed by the same one it always was when Pops talked about my mom. *She did the best that she could do.*

*If you say so,* was what I'd said before leaving the room. I wonder if it's possible to hate someone and feel sorry for them at the same time? I felt sorry for her, sure. She wasn't cut out to be a mother.

But I also hate her, too.

Pops is a lousy drunk, and the more he drinks, the more he thinks about my mother. About the way she left us all those years ago, without ever saying goodbye. About the fact that he still has their wedding photo framed and hung on the bedroom wall, about the fact that he still wears his wedding band, though she's been gone a whole thirteen years. Since I was five. A little boy with Legos and Star Wars toys. That's when she left.

If it was up to me I would have chucked that ring long ago. Not that I hold a grudge or anything, because I don't. I just think I would have tossed the ring. Or pawned it like he pawned my high school class ring for booze. Instead, it becomes a hot topic of conversation in the many botched dates Pops has with the single ladies around town — a reservoir that is drying up quickly and will soon be completely sapped. Chances are he's dated them all. Except for Ingrid, maybe, the agoraphobic, for reasons I don't need to explain. Pops spends his dates at the tavern in town, getting loaded and talking about how my mother left him and me when I was five years old. It's supposed to be a sympathy trigger, but instead he ends up looking like a patsy. Pops ends up crying and scaring the ladies away one by one, like old cans lined in a row for target practice.

He has no clue why he's still alone.

It's pathetic, really. But he's still my dad

and I feel sorry for him, too.

I dish the nuggets and green beans onto a chipped dinner plate and call him to dinner, where he lumbers in — beer in hand — and takes his place at the head of the table, the only chair from which he can still see the TV. "Catch the fucking ball!" he screams, smacking the table hard with the palm of a sweaty hand, sending his fork spiraling into the air before it crashes down to the ground. As he reaches down to grab it, he smacks his head on the corner of the wood table and curses. And then he laughs as his forehead swells and turns bright red.

Just another night in our house.

Tonight we don't make small talk. Instead, I model good behavior, the way you're supposed to use a knife to spread butter, the way you're supposed to eat the beans with a fork and not your hands. I watch as Pops drags half of a dinner roll through the tub of margarine and think: no wonder this guy is still single. He had a lot more to offer my mother when he was young, employed and sober. Needless to say, he's no longer any of those things. But the reason she left had nothing to do with any of those things, anyway. The reason she left? Motherhood. Me.

I try not to let this go to my head.

"They're not French fries," I say as he plucks the fancy-cut green beans up one at a time with a hand, drawing them to his mouth and chewing with his jaws open wide. "Use your fork." He ignores me and screams at the TV, spittle flying out. Green spittle, like the beans.

He rises to his feet and hollers, "False start!" pointing a finger at the referees on TV as if they can hear. "What are you, asshole, are you blind? That was a *false start.*"

And then he sits back down.

I watch as he sits there at the table, eating his food. I note the way his hands shake. Pops has a tremor, whether or not he knows it exists. I know. His hands shake, the small, rapid movements when he's trying to use his hands for something: picking up his nuggets, snapping the top off another bottle of beer. They remind me of my grandpa's hands, though his only shook because he was old. There are times Pops's hands shake so badly I have to open up his beer for him. The incongruity of it? The more he drinks, the less his hands shake, like some sort of paradoxical reaction. The hands find placidity when he's completely tanked. Seems to me it should be the other way around, but still, the shaking hands are a good benchmark for me of how much he's had to drink.

It's never worth asking how much he's had to drink; he's either too drunk to remember, otherwise he'll lie. Tonight, not enough.

He stands up again quickly to chastise the coach who decides to run it up the middle instead of a sweep play. And then back down. And then up again when the ball gets knocked out of the running back's hands and there's an interception — this time managing to overturn his chair as he does. He watches in dismay as the Giants trot down the field with the ball. I don't even have to turn my head to see the TV. He narrates it for me before tossing the other half of his dinner roll at the screen. And then he gets up to get another beer, damning to hell every Lions player on the field.

So it's really no wonder then that when he says, "Squatters," I don't pay much attention. He's talking about the TV. It's someone's last name, or some epithet he's come up with for one of the coaches or players. *Fucking Squatters.*

"Did you hear me?" he asks, and that's when I realize he *is* talking to me. His shirt is wet; at some point or other he managed to spill his beer. There's a piece of green bean stuck to his chin. Classy.

I notice that Pops isn't looking at me, and I turn in my chair, my eyes copying his line of vision, out the front window of our home and across the street.

And there I see it again, that light: *on, off.*

Like an involuntary muscle contraction. A charley horse. A twitch, a tic.

*On, off.*

And Pops says, "Damn squatters are living over there again," about the school-bus-yellow home on the opposite side of the street from ours. The one with the story to tell, the kind of story no one ever talks about but everybody knows. It isn't the first time squatters have lived over there before. All sorts of vermin have inhabited the place at one time or another. The occasional drifter has been known to move into that house and live there for a while, scot-free. They usually leave on their own without any need to call the cops or anything, but it's unsettling nonetheless, knowing there's some bum in a vacant house right across the street from yours.

In the backyard hangs an abandoned tire swing from a fated oak tree, forgotten along with the home. Curtains hang from the window still, dated gossamer curtains, which were once white. They're yellowish now and sheared at odd angles as if someone took a pair of scissors to their ends. Instead, it's likely the mice eating their way through the lace. The concrete crumbles from around the house like cookie crumbs, breaking off in bits and littering the lawn. There are posted signs, which no one pays attention to, anyway: No Trespassing and Not Approved for Occupancy. They're black signs with a bright orange font. Hard to miss. And yet people do. They ignore the signs and go right in.

A bum is living over there or maybe . . . No. I shake my head. That's not it. I said it already. I don't believe in ghosts.

But that's just me. The rest of the people in town, they do.

Every single town in all of America has its own haunted house.

Ours just so happens to be right across the street from mine.

I never knew the family that lived inside that home. All it's ever referred to anymore is *that house.* It's been empty for years, since before I was born. I guess I never cared enough to ask who used to live there. In my mind, they're long gone, leaving behind trace memories of a once-happy family and a derelict home. The only inhabitant people speak of is the dead Genevieve, though she is only ever referred to as *her,* or sometimes the even less humane *it.* There are claims that people see her, the ghost, moving throughout the home, her soul trapped inside for all of eternity.

But I know better than to believe those things. It's just a bunch of malarkey. There's no such thing as ghosts.

"Fucking squatters," says Pops one last time as he rises from the table and stumbles to the fridge for another bottle of beer. He puts the cap on the countertop; he wanders into the family room to resume watching the football game. He leaves his dirty plate behind for me to clean, his napkin lobbed to the floor for me to retrieve.

# QUINN

I don't have to wait too long to be put to the test again.

As I stand in the kitchen, in my hand the phone rings. Esther's phone. I jump. This time it's not a blocked call, but a local 773 number. The caller has an easygoing voice, upbeat, maybe the same age as me, though it's hard to tell through the phone because of course I can't *see* the woman on the other end of the line. She asks if this is Esther, and this time I assert proudly, "It is."

It's fun, masquerading around as Esther. I hold Esther in the highest regard. If there was one person in the world I'd like to be, it's Esther. She's beautiful and intelligent and kind. She's dauntless and spunky sometimes, and a good roommate to boot.

But all those thoughts fall quickly by the wayside when the caller on the other end of the line announces, "I was inquiring about your ad in the *Reader.*"

"What ad?" I ask, forgetting for a fleeting moment that I am supposed to be Esther. She's trying to sell some things, I figure, maybe cleaning out the crap in that storage facility. Who needs an old lava lamp, anyway? They're way passé.

But when the woman on the other end of the line declares, "The ad for the roommate," my mouth drops. I'm all but stunned speechless. "Have you already found someone else?" she asks, and a tremendous amount of time passes before I find the ability to speak.

A thousand thoughts run amuck in my mind, but at the very core of them is one question that comes to me again and again: Why? *Why* did Esther place an ad in the *Reader, why* is she looking for a new roommate, *why* does she want to do away with me? I'm hurt. My feelings are hurt like I've been stabbed in the back with Romeo's dagger. I get it that I'm a slob and I pay a measly forty-five percent of the rent rather than the afore-agreed-to fifty, that I don't always have the cash to cover my share of the utilities or that I leave lights on and forget to turn off the sink water. *But still, Esther,* I snap silently in my head, wondering suddenly who is the lousier roommate: Esther or me. *How could you do this to me?*

Where did she possibly think I would go if she kicked me out? Back home to suburban America to live with my mother and father and Madison the dweeb? No way. Esther could have pointed out my deficiencies for me; we could have had a conversation about it. She could have given me some warning before deciding to kick me out. Some time to find a new apartment, a new roommate. My heart sinks. I thought Esther was my friend, but maybe I was wrong. Maybe Esther was just my roommate all along.

"It's okay if you did. I mean, it's not a big deal," says the caller, but I clear my throat and swallow the overwhelming sense of betrayal and say to her, "No. I didn't. I'm so glad you called," and it's then that I make arrangements to meet the young lady who's about to be my replacement, who's to take over my spot at the kitchen table, my place on the rose-colored sofa, the one who will soon inhabit my room, and become best friends with my best friend while I get tossed like leftover food.

I think of myself, all alone in the big city, without Esther. I can't afford the rent in a city apartment on my own if my life depends on it. Eleven hundred dollars a month this unit costs, which in Chicago is quite the steal. Esther has lived in this apartment for years, the reason it was cheaper than all its other walk-up counterparts in the neighborhood: rent control. If I walked into Mrs. Budny's office today and told her I wanted my own apartment, identical to the one I share with Esther, she'd charge me sixteen hundred bucks a month and I don't have anything in the realm of that kind of money.

I agree to meet with my replacement after work tomorrow at a small coffee shop on Clark. We say our goodbyes and I pull up the *Reader* online, and sure enough, there it is, the ad. *Female in need of roommate to share 2BDR Andersonville apartment. Great locale. Call Esther,* and there she leaves her cell phone number beside a photograph of our walk-up from the outside, the autumn leaves tumbling from the trees as if she'd taken that photo yesterday or maybe just the day before.

*Why, Esther?* I silently beg. *Why?*

■ ■ ■ ■

# MONDAY

■ ■ ■ ■

# ALEX

I rise early, well before the sun, and head out into the cold morning air for the long haul to town to retrieve Ingrid's groceries for her as promised. The air is nippy today, making it hard to breathe. It burns my lungs, freezes my hands and ears as I close and lock the door behind myself, shutting a dozing Pops inside. In my hand I carry bills to discard in the mailbox outside. I used last week's paycheck to cover them, the gas bill coming with a Final Notice that we'd soon be without heat. Its arrival a week ago yesterday prompted a scolding of Pops about how he'd better get his shit together and find a job.

I'm glad to see he took it to heart.

As I make my way to the mailbox, I eyeball that old, abandoned home across the street, searching for potential squatters or other signs of life. It's an ugly sight, it is, one of the few scars on our otherwise toler-

107

able street. There are vacant houses, properties foreclosed on, new homes stymied in the midst of construction, plywood and two-by-fours and other building supplies still taking up residence on the weedy lawns. It's a sign of the times, the housing crisis of our generation that other generations will read about in history textbooks to come. I'm kind of stoked about it in some weird way, knowing these abandoned, beaten-up, unloved homes are making history as we speak.

The people in the neighborhood are mostly blue-collar workers, many commuting from as far as Portage, Indiana, or Hobart, to earn a paycheck and pay their bills. They work mainly in the manufacturing industry, if they're not working retail for some shop in town. Money is harder to come by here than it is for others, and yet we're better off than those in the slummy apartments off Emery Road, the subsidized housing units, low-income apartments paid for in part by the US government.

But regardless of how many scourged homes there are on the block or in town, this is the house everyone always talks about: that school-bus-yellow, minimal traditional home with its aluminum siding and its busted roof, right across the street from mine.

That house wasn't always a blot on the landscape. Though I've never seen it as anything but a blight with my own two eyes, I've heard this from neighbors who stand on their front lawns from time to time, arms crossed, frowning at what it's become over the years. It wasn't always such an eyesore, they tell me. *A damn shame,* they say. There was a time when the house was actually lived in and nice. Neighbors want it demolished, but the bank that owns the property doesn't want to pay for that. That costs money. And so they leave it be. The house is a pockmark now, though it's always been this way, since I was a little thing myself. Like the rest of the world I wish someone would level it to the ground and take it out of its misery.

And then of course there are the stories of the ghost of Genevieve.

Kids (gutsy, stupid or otherwise) have been known to creep to the windows and peer in, spying her wraith through the panes of glass. But it isn't just the kids. No, adults claim they see her, too, a tiny apparition in white drifting from room to room, lost and alone, calling for her mommy.

In middle school, it's a rite of passage, being dared to spend the night inside the haunted house. I did it myself when I was twelve. Sort of. We made it a couple hours, at best. Half the battle was getting out of your own house without your mom or pop taking notice, though my pop was so ripped he didn't know whether I was here or there or anywhere. But the other guys had to lie to their folks, saying they were sleeping somewhere else, or climb out their bedroom windows long after they were supposed to be asleep.

But it was an initiation of sorts, being recruited from the nerd herd to the in-crowd, all by spending the night with a spook.

And so we did. Or tried to at least. A bunch of buddies and I packed bags full of flashlights, lockback knives, binoculars and food, and double dog dared one another to spend the night there, in that yellow house with a ghost. Why? Don't ask me why. We just did.

We had a disposable camera with us, too, to take pictures to show off the next day at school. Proof that we did it. We spent the night with a spook and we survived. Some guy tagged along with night-vision, another with a camcorder. Another with something he claimed was a thermal imager (it wasn't). We climbed in through a busted window — me scratching my shin on a shard of glass

— and set up camp in what was one day the living room of a happy family, with sleeping bags, pillows and all. We snapped photos, the guys and I — beside the cobwebbed fireplace, sitting on an old sunken-in sofa that seethed with bugs, crossing the threshold to her room. *Her* room.

Genevieve's room.

From the stories I've heard over the years, Genevieve was a naughty little girl. In the five years before her death, she was caught more than once upsetting bird nests, and pulling the legs one by one off the thorax of ensnared bugs. It's the kind of thing people remember about Genevieve, little Genevieve climbing a tree to jettison robin fledglings to the ground, whereby she scampered down the tree and stepped on them, while mama robin watched on, defenseless, unable to do a thing to save her babies. The kids in the neighborhood at the time, adults now, long gone — though their parents remain — recall the way their children didn't want to play with Genevieve. Genevieve was cruel. Genevieve was mean. She pulled their kids' hair; she called them names. She made them cry and fake stomachaches, saying they didn't want to go to school, because once there Genevieve would punch them in the gut and kick their shins. She had a temper, a nasty temper, or so I've heard, and not just the typical pouting, crying, whining behavior of a usual five-year-old child, but a five-year-old who could've used a straitjacket or, at the very least, some mood stabilizing drugs.

No wonder half the town is certain she came back as a ghost, to haunt them even in death.

The guys and I made it in that old house a few hours at best before figuring out we weren't the only ones there, and we ran. It had nothing at all to do with a ghost. It was the rats that did us in. The damn rats. Roof rats. We didn't make it past 11:00 p.m., when they came out in search of food.

Even these days, all these years later, there are allegations of strange noises at night. A child singing lullabies, a child's cry.

Me? I'm pretty sure it's just the wind.

But others aren't so sure. Some people are superstitious enough not to walk past the house, and so they cross the street to my side instead. Others hold their breath the whole darn way, like passing a cemetery and holding your breath to make sure you don't breathe in the spirit of the dead. They tuck their thumbs inside their fists, too, but I don't know why. I just know that they do.

Death superstitions are the norm around here.

If your shadow is headless, you will die.

An owl sighting during the day means death is coming.

A bird crashing into a window also means death is near.

Death comes in threes.

And corpses should always be removed from a home feet-first. Always.

I don't buy any of it. I'm far too skeptical for that.

Funny thing is, she didn't even die in that house. That's where she lived, sure, where Genevieve lived, but that's not where she died. So how could her spirit be there?

But maybe that's just me being overly pragmatic.

# Quinn

The night comes and goes but Esther doesn't come home. The next day I can hardly drag myself out the front door and on to work, for what I want to do most is sit at home and wait for Esther. Forty-eight to seventy-two hours the 311 operator assured me, and Esther has only been gone for twenty-four. Seventy percent of missing people leave of their own free will; she told me that, too. I also know that Esther is on the lookout for a new roommate — one to replace me — and so I connect the dots in my head and easily surmise that Esther's leaving has something to do with me and my laxity. I'm a lousy roommate; I get that. But still, whether or not it *is* my fault, it doesn't make me feel any better. It feels like a kick in the teeth to me, the fact that Esther wants me out.

But I can't sit home for the next two days and wait for Esther to magically appear. I have to work, and hope that if and when she does return, we can talk this out.

Monday morning I'm riding the 22 into the Loop in a short skirt for some ungodly reason. At every single bus stop — at every single intersection — the doors burst open and the nippy, November air rushes in to assault my bare legs. I have panty hose on, don't get me wrong, but sheer hosiery does nothing to fend off the merciless wind in the Windy City. There are pumps in my bag, a pair of gym shoes on my feet: my working-woman image.

If only my mother could see me now! She'd be so proud.

I have headphones on, a tablet on my lap playing music so that — more than anything else — I can drown out the litany of coughs and sneezes and breathing of those around me. So I can pretend that they're not here, though the crooning voice of Sam Smith begging me to stay isn't such a bad way to start the day.

Some dunce has left a window open a crack so that the temperature on the bus can be no more than sixty-two degrees. I pull my coat tightly around me and snap at the itinerant man sitting behind me to stop touching my hair, *please*. This isn't the first time he's been on the bus with me. He's a vagrant, the type of man who spends every last penny he owns to ride the bus. Not because he has anywhere to go, but because he doesn't. He does it to stay warm. He rides as far as the driver will let him, and then he gets off. He begs for more money, and when another two dollars comes his way, he pays his fare and rides again. I kind of feel sorry for the man. Kind of.

But if he touches me again, I'm changing seats.

The Loop comes into view, the buildings rising higher and higher into the sky as we leave Andersonville and pass through Uptown, Wrigleyville, Lake View, Lincoln Park.

And that's when it returns to me, as the 22 bus galumphs down Clark Street, gooseflesh on my skin, some creep to my rear fondling my long golden locks. I'm mad. Esther is trying to replace me.

It's like stubbing your toe or passing a kidney stone. It hurts. Better yet, it's like smashing your fingers in a car door. I want to cry out and scream. There's this hollowness in my heart, this knowledge that I can't quite wrap my head around. I hear that girl on the phone last night — Esther's phone — the credulousness in her cheerful voice as she happily declared, *I was inquiring about your ad in the* Reader. *The ad for the room-mate.*

Little does she know that in less than a year Esther might give her the boot, too.

I get off the bus and scurry to my office building, a high-rise on Wabash. It's a tall, black building with fifty indistinguishable floors of office upon office. Its once-gorgeous view is now obstructed by the latest and greatest skyscraper monstrosity: ninety-eight floors of steel framework and curtain walls that popped up in the city almost overnight, smack-dab on the opposite side of the street from my place of employment. The lawyers who I work for, the ones with their panoramic office views and offices as big as my parents' home, are peeved about it, about the fact that they no longer overlook Lake Michigan because some business tycoon and his superstructure has stolen their view.

First-world problems.

I take the elevator up to the forty-third floor, smile at the receptionist, who smiles at me. I'm pretty sure she doesn't know my name, but at least she no longer asks to see my ID. I've had this job for an entire three hundred and sixty days. That's a whole lot of Mondays. I don't like the job one bit, a project assistant job that is lower on the totem pole than the janitors even, the men and women who wipe the floor and clean urine off the toilets.

The reason I wanted this job was that it paid. Not much, but it paid. And there wasn't a whole lot I could do with a liberal arts degree from a crappy college. But this I could do.

The first thing I do when I arrive at work is try to find Ben. Ben, who never returned my call last night because he was too busy doing things with his girlfriend, Priya. But I won't let my mind go there; I can't. I don't want to think about Ben and Priya right now, Ben and Priya and my insatiable jealousy. Instead, I focus on the task at hand. I have to find Ben. I have to talk to Ben about Esther.

And so I slip into the stairwell and start to make my ascent to Ben's floor. Our firm, a national law firm with well over four hundred attorneys, occupies eleven floors of office space in the black building. Each floor is essentially the same, with the paralegals and project assistants like me shoved into small cubes in the interior of each floor, forced to dwell among the stacks and files and photocopy machines. Where we reside, there is no such thing as natural lighting, but rather fluorescent troffers, which do nothing for the tone of my skin or the shade of my hair. The lighting makes me look yellow and sickly, so one might think I'm afflicted with a serious case of jaundice, caused by some sort of liver or bile duct disease. Now that's classy.

I work on the forty-third floor. Ben, the forty-seventh. I start climbing the steps one by one, trying hard to ignore the creepiness of the office stairwell. I don't use it all that often, but there are times when a girl doesn't want to be crammed on a small elevator with three or five or even one hotshot attorney, and today is one of those days.

When I get to Ben's cube on the forty-seventh floor, it's empty. His computer is on, and beside his swivel chair is a leather bag and a pair of black running shoes. I know that he's here, somewhere — in the building — and yet he's not here in his cube. I ask around to see if anyone has seen Ben, trying to mask the angst I feel with a weedy smile. "He was here," some blonde paralegal tells me as she scampers by with a box in hand, her sling-back heels clickety-clacking down the wooden floors, "but now he's not." Obviously.

I find a piece of scrap paper and jot down a quick note in the best handwriting I can muster, though my hands shake for about a million reasons, or maybe a million and one. *We need to talk. ASAP,* I write, and leave the note on the plastic keyboard before returning to my own cube, disgruntled.

This morning I'm given the all-important task of Bates labeling documents. It sounds important, it really does. It has a name even, Bates labeling, like the fact that those little dots over a lower case *i* or *j* have a name — a *tittle* it's called, a simple fact I discovered while searching the internet and charging my time to one of the firm's more opulent clients — or when your second toe is bigger than your big toe, it's called a Morton's toe. Important things worthy of names. Like Bates labels. Matters of life or death.

But no. What I'm doing is placing hundreds of thousands of numbered stickers on a looming document production before being given the task of photocopying them three or five or ten times. There are boxes of documents, and worse yet, they're not even full of scandalous details like the divorce lawyers get, but rather *financial* documents. Because I get to work for transactional lawyers, boring men who get their kicks staring at financial documents and talking about money all the livelong day while paying me pennies above minimum wage.

As I settle into my task of Bates labeling, my movements become hurried and repetitive, my mind far removed from the stacks of financial documents that lay before me. I'm at work, but I certainly can't focus on work. All I can think about is Esther. Where is Esther? I can't focus on a single thing, not Bates labeling the piles of documents before me, nor skimming through a mountain of correspondence and pleadings, marking over and over again our client's name with a red Post-it flag, until all the words start to blur before my eyes. I replay our last conversation in my mind. Did I miss something hidden there in the tone of her voice or her weary smile? She was sick; she didn't feel well. *I'd be a killjoy, Quinn. Go without me. You'll have more fun.*

But now I have to wonder: Was this a test? Was Esther putting me to the test? Seeing what kind of roommate I really was, and whether or not I'd put her needs before my own.

If that's the case, then I guess I failed. I went out without her; I had fun. I didn't even think to stop by Esther's room when I got home to see how she was feeling and if she was okay. The thought never even crossed my mind. I didn't offer to bring her a blanket or warm up a bowl of soup. Another roommate, a better roommate, would have made soup. Another roommate would have said, "No way," to Esther's insistence that I go. "No way, Esther. I'll have more fun here with you."

But that's not what I said. I said okay, and left in a hurry out through the front door. I didn't think twice about my decision not to stay.

"Damn," I say out loud now as a sheet of paper slices the fragile skin of my index finger, and red blood swells to the surface, leaving its mark on a statement of cash flow. "Damn, damn, damn," I repeat, knowing my escalating frustration is directed far more at Esther than this insignificant amount of blood loss. My finger hurts and yet my heart hurts even more.

Esther is trying to replace me.

My mind considers for one split second a world without Esther, and it makes me feel sad.

"Bad day?" a voice asks then, and I peer up from my paper cut to see Ben in the doorway, standing arms akimbo (that, too, is a thing also discovered on a random internet search, meaning: standing with hands on hips), as he spies the driblets of blood on my hand and says to me, "Here, let me help."

Ben wears a pair of slim cotton chinos, taupe, and a piqué polo shirt the color of peacock feathers. He's impeccably dressed and looks amazing, though chances are he rode his bike to work as he so often does, a Schwinn hybrid that he locks to the galvanized steel bike rack outside the building. He's got a runner's build, lank but muscular, always adorned in tight-fitting clothes — tailored tops and skinny bottoms — so you can see each and every one of the gluteal and abdominal muscles. Or so I imagine you can see them.

It's no secret I have a crush on Ben. I'm pretty sure everyone in the world knows but him.

Ben grabs a tissue from a box and presses it firmly to my hand. His hands are warm, his movements decisive. He holds my hand in his, inches above my heart. He smiles as he tugs on my arm and raises it higher. "It's supposed to help slow the bleeding," he says, and for the first time in a while I smile, too, since we both know good and well no one ever bled out from a paper cut. The only thing it will do is leave a mess on these stupid financial documents — nothing a little Wite-Out can't fix — but I'll be just fine.

"Sorry I missed your call last night," he says to me, then, "What's up?" He carries with him my note: *We need to talk. ASAP.*

I have this urge to unload on Ben right here and right now, to tell him everything: Esther, the fire escape, the bizarre letter to *My Dearest* and more. There's so much to tell Ben, but I don't. Not yet, anyway, not here. I don't want to talk here. Gossip in this place spreads like wildfire, and the last thing I need is the nosy PA down the hall telling the rest of the firm about what a shoddy roommate I am or how Esther has renounced me.

Ben, Esther and I are like the three stooges, the three musketeers. It was me who brought us together. I knew Ben from work — we started working at the firm on the same day, and together sat through eight painful hours of filling out mounds of human resource forms, watching mindless videos, surviving orientation. I was bored beyond belief when two hours in Ben turned to me in our swivel chairs at some fancy-schmancy conference room table and parodied the HR lady for what was clearly a surfeit of Botox injections. Her face was frozen stiff; she couldn't smile.

I laughed so hard I was pretty sure coffee shot up my nose.

We've been friends ever since, sharing lunch together almost every day, an extravagance of coffee breaks, rumors about the firm's attorneys.

And then came the day when I moved in with Esther, about two weeks before Ben and my twosome became a threesome. Esther suggested we host a party to celebrate my arrival. She put up decorations; she made hors d'oeuvres galore. Of course she did; she's Esther. That's the kind of thing Esther does. She invited a whole slew of people she knew: people from the bookstore, from grad school, from the building and around the neighborhood; Cole, the physical therapist from the first floor; Noah and Patty from down the street.

I invited Ben.

Everyone else came and went, but by the end of the night it was just me and Esther and Ben, rattling on and on about nothing until morning came and Priya called him home, interrupting our fun. He went, grudgingly, and then the next weekend when Priya was too busy studying for a midterm exam to hang out with Ben, he came back.

*You like him, don't you?* Esther had asked knowingly once Ben was gone.

*It's that apparent?* I'd asked of her, and then, stating the obvious, *It's not like it matters, anyway. He has a girlfriend,* as she and I sat on the sofa side by side, staring at a blackened TV screen.

*Well,* said Esther in that unselfish way that was all Esther, *he's missing out on something really great. You do know that, don't you, Quinn?* And I said yes, though of course I didn't know. *His loss,* Esther told me, and she made me repeat it so that in time I'd start to believe.

The next weekend, Ben was back, chilling with Esther and me.

If there's anybody in the world who can help me find Esther, it's Ben.

And so there in my tiny little cube when Ben asks, "What's up?" I ask instead, clutching that tissue to my hand to clot the nearly nonexistent blood, "Want to go to lunch?" and though it's not even eleven o'clock, Ben doesn't balk.

"Let's go," he says, and I rise from my chair and together we leave.

We go to Subway, as always, and as always I have the same thing to eat: roast beef on wheat while he has the chopped chicken salad. And it's there as we slide into the booth beside the windows, watching the city life pass by on the street, that I admit to

Ben, "Esther didn't come home last night," adding on quietly and penitently, my voice just above a whisper, "Esther didn't come home Saturday night, either."

There's construction on Wabash and so things are loud: jackhammers, saws, sanders and such. I try to block out the noise, all of it, inside and out. The construction noise outside. The dozen or so patrons inside the restaurant beside us, hovering in a long, mushrooming line, impatient, hungry, talking on their phones. The so-called sandwich artist asking the same question over and over again like words on a scratched CD: *White or wheat? White or wheat?* I pretend for one nanosecond that it's only Ben and me in the room, that we aren't being inundated by the scent of veggies or cheese or fresh baked bread, that we're someplace romantic, say Trattoria No. 10 on Dearborn, or Everest, up on top of the Chicago Stock Exchange (a place I'll likely never get to go), dining on rack of lamb or loin of venison while staring out at the Loop from the fortieth floor. Waiters and waitresses who refer to us as *sir* and *ma'am,* who deliver champagne followed by a single sorbet for us to share with two spoons — cutlery that I probably couldn't even afford. Now that would be romantic. I imagine the force of Ben's knee pressing against me beneath the bistro table, an unswerving hand traveling across the starched white tablecloth to find mine as I admit to him sadly, *Esther didn't come home Saturday night, either.*

Ben lifts his fork to his mouth and then sets it back down, neglecting the salad before him. "What do you mean Esther didn't come home?" he asks. The concern manifests itself in puckers and folds along his forehead and temples. His hands reach to his pocket to find his phone where he pulls up his contacts and flips through to Esther.

"She might be mad at me," I say.

"Why would she be mad at you?" he asks, and I tell him I don't know, but the truth is that I do, and it isn't any one thing, per se, but a series of things leading to the fact that I'm a bad roommate. "I don't know," I say. "I've let her down, I guess." But Esther has let me down, too, and now I'm mad and sad all at the same time. I watch as Ben attempts to call Esther on his cell, but with a hand to his arm, I say that it's no use.

"Her phone," I tell him contritely, "is at home."

And because Ben is smart, logical, systematic (all of which I'm not, making him the

128

perfect yin to my yang), he pushes his feelings aside and focuses on the task at hand. He says, "Call the bookstore. See if she showed up for work today. What about her parents?" he asks.

"It's just her mom," I say, or at least I think it's just her mom. Esther has never made mention of a dad, a brother, a sister, a family dog, a guinea pig, though of course there was the photograph of a family — some family, *her family?* — inside that storage unit, the one Esther nearly amputated my finger over last December when I snuck a peek inside the box. *Who's this?* I'd asked, followed by Esther's pithy reply as she slammed the box lid down on top of my hands: *No one.*

"Did you try calling her mom?" he asks then, and I shake my head.

"I don't know her name. Or her number," I admit, though I tell him I called the police. One step in the right direction, I guess, but more likely one step forward, two steps back. I seem to be making no progress at all.

"Check Esther's phone," he suggests, but I shrug my shoulders and say, "Can't get in. I don't have her password."

Unless Esther's family calls us directly, that's a dead end. But Ben, not willing to concede defeat, says to me, "I'll see what I can dredge up." He gives me a wink and says, "I have connections," though I doubt he does. More likely he's handy on the internet and has a log-in for LexisNexis. That's about the only bonus of working for a law firm, access to a database that allows for a search of public records and background checks.

I'm feeling frustrated, to say the least, like I can't do anything quite right. I'm not one to cry, but for a whole two seconds I think that's exactly what I'd like to do. I'd like to smash my face into my Subway napkin and cry my eyes out. But that's when Ben reaches across the table and runs a brisk hand across mine. I try not to read more into it than there is — just a friendly gesture — but it's hard not to completely liquefy when he says to me, "I doubt Esther's mad at you. You're best buds," and I think to myself that I thought we were, I thought Esther and I were best buds. But now I'm not so sure.

"So you'll call the bookstore and I'll hunt down Esther's mom. We'll find her," he promises. "We will." And at this I realize I like the sound of his voice, the take-charge, no-nonsense way he's made this task his own, and I smile because my lone manhunt for the missing Esther Vaughan has now become a two-man job. And I'm quite pleased with my partner in crime.

# ALEX

I stand at the door to Ingrid Daube's house, noticing the way the yard snowballs with fallen leaves. I make note of this: bring a rake. Rake Ingrid's leaves. It's the least that I can do.

It's not like she can do it herself because that would involve going outdoors and that isn't about to happen. The snow will come soon. I don't want her grass to die.

I carry two paper sacks in my hands. In my pocket is her change, a dollar and seventy-three cents. I have one bag in either arm. I lift up a leg and depress the doorbell with a knee, waiting for Ingrid to answer my call.

Outside there is sun. It's not warm — far from it, in fact — but there is sun. The day is crisp. The gulls are clamorous this morning, making a rumpus. They soar overhead in their colonies, perching on the roofs on the town's buildings and awnings.

When Ingrid opens the door, there's a frowzy look to her. Hair mussed up, she's still in a nightgown and robe. Her skin lacks makeup, and there are trenches in the folds of her skin, deep marionette lines made visible without the camouflage of makeup. One thought and one thought alone comes to mind: Ingrid looks old.

She says to me, "Good morning," and I say, "Good morning" back. But today her voice is clipped, and she ushers me in quickly, pushing the door closed against the weight of the wind. She does it in a hurry, trying hard to keep the outside air out. This is Ingrid sometimes. Sometimes the fear of the outside world starts and ends at the doorsill, and so long as her feet are behind the threshold, she's A-okay. But other times she fears the air itself: germs, pollen, pollution, smoke, breath and whatever other horrors the air may hold. Today is apparently one of those days. She pulls me in by the arm — eyes doing a quick sweep of the street outside to make certain I haven't been trailed, that the wind isn't lying in wait behind me, ready and waiting to attack — and slams the door at once, latching the lock and the dead bolt, too.

And then she takes a deep breath, exhales and smiles.

133

Phew, says that smile. That was a close call.

Ingrid has good days and Ingrid has bad days, but it really isn't any of my business which is which, and so I pretend not to see or care. I don't know much about agoraphobia, but I do know that the mailman brings her mail to her door sometimes, when there's so much stuffed inside he can no longer close the door. A little neighbor boy lugs her trash bins to the curb. I, or some other twerp like me, run her errands. From what I know, it started with a panic attack at the market in town. It was a Saturday in summer a few years back, and it was crazy busy around here. The market was packed, and so that's what the rumor mill blames for Ingrid's very public panic attack. The crowds. It was also hot out, stiflingly hot, hard to breathe. The lines were seemingly endless, swarming with people she'd never seen before and didn't know. Tourists. Some bystanders saw her grope at her neck, gasp for air; others heard her scream, *Go away* and *Leave me alone,* and so they did, phoning 911 to help instead. *Don't touch me!* Ingrid purportedly screamed.

The fear of a repeat attack is what keeps Ingrid inside these days. The fear of losing control, the prospect of dying in the local market with everyone watching on, staring, pointing fingers. She's never said as much, but that's what I assume. 'Cause that's the last place in the world I would want to die, at the local market, surrounded by the smell of fish fillets and tourists.

Ingrid takes a bag from my hands and I follow her into the kitchen where, spread across the farmhouse table, is a deck of cards. She's playing solitaire. How sad. She's got a pad of paper set beside the cards, ticking off the times she wins a game. She's up three to one.

Also on the table are all of Ingrid's beading supplies. The ribbons and the wires and the cords. Beads and clasps. Empty cardboard jewelry boxes. A rainbow of tissue paper. A handwritten list of orders that need to be filled. Trapped at home and yet surprisingly resourceful, Ingrid manages to make her own beaded jewelry and run an online shop. Supplies are delivered to her, while the mail carrier collects the outgoing packages, pint-size jewelry boxes with necklaces or earrings tucked inside. Ingrid makes a living without ever having to step foot outside her home. She tried to show me how to make her jewelry once, a necklace for no one in particular, not as if I had someone to give a necklace to. But still, my bungling hands couldn't figure out how to bend the wire, how to put on the beads. Ingrid smiled at me sweetly — this was years ago — and confessed that I made a lousy apprentice. After that I stuck to running her errands and delivering her meals. But still, she made me a necklace, nothing girlish or sissified, but rather a shark's tooth necklace on an adjustable cord with just a few black and white beads. *For strength and protection,* she told me as she set it in my hands. She said it as if I was in need of these things. Supposedly that's what a shark tooth represents: strength, protection. It became my talisman, my good luck charm.

I wear it all the time, but so far it hasn't worked.

Today we shoot the shit. We talk about the Lions' loss to the Giants last night, the fact that she's going to bake cookies this afternoon. We talk about the weather, we talk about the gulls. *Never heard them so loud,* says Ingrid, and I say, *Me neither.* But of course I have. The gulls are always loud. I think if I should mention the squatters in the yellow house across the street from mine, deciding that no, that's not the kind of small talk she wants or needs to hear. I help her unpack the sacks, laying the items on the table so that she can put them away.

She hands me another twenty for my time. I try to refuse. She shoves it into my hand. I take it this time.

We go through this routine every week.

As Ingrid unpacks the sacks, she hums a song. It's not one I know, but it's a gloomy song, a morose song, one that I can't place, but it makes me feel sad. It's depressing. It makes Ingrid sad, too. Tired and sad. Her movements are plodding, her posture is slumped. "Can I help you there?" I ask, pulling the empty paper sacks from the countertop and folding them in two.

But Ingrid says, "I'm just about done," as she sets a box of microwave popcorn on the shelf and closes the pantry door.

"Did you eat lunch, Alex?" Ingrid asks, and she offers to make me a sandwich. I lie. I said I ate. I say no thanks. The last thing I want to be is an inconvenience, or my own charity case, which I already am. It's hard to say which of us has the more miserable life, Ingrid or me.

And then, for whatever reason, when the sacks are empty and I know I can say goodbye to Ingrid and go, I pick up that deck of cards and start shuffling, anyway.

"Ever play gin rummy?" I ask, and before me, Ingrid relaxes and smiles. She's played gin rummy before. I know because I've played it with her on some other day just like today.

We sit at the table and I deal.

The first game I let her win. It seems like the right thing to do.

The second game I put up more fight, but she wins that, too. Ingrid is quite the cardsharp, drawing and discarding with nimble hands. She stares at me from above the fan of cards, trying to think through what I have in my hands. A queen of clubs, a jack of diamonds. An ace.

She's also good at meddling, though she does it with such tact it's hard to get mad.

"You're working full-time for Mrs. Priddy?" she asks as I shuffle the cards for a third time, and I say, "Yes, ma'am." She runs her hands through her hair, relaxing the frowziness. She tugs at the robe, making sure it's tied tight. She slackens in her chair, and yet the signs of stress are still there, in the lines of her face, in the restive eyes. She rises and moves to the two-cup coffeemaker, asking if I'd like some. I say no, and she helps herself to a mug, adding the creamer, the sugar, and again I think of Pearl, of her body rising up out of the waters of Lake Michigan, dripping wet. Since yesterday, I haven't been able to get that image out of my mind.

"The rest of the kids have gone to college," she says, as if somehow I'm in the dark about this little fact, the fact that all the kids I grew up with are no longer here. "Not for you?" she asks as I lay the cards out on the table before us. Ten for her, ten for me.

"Couldn't afford it," is what I say, but of course that's not true. Well, it *is* true — Pops and I couldn't afford it, but we didn't need to. I was offered a full ride that I turned down. Tuition and housing included. I said thanks, but no thanks. I'm a smart kid, I know that as much as the next guy. Though not in an ostentatious, inflated kind of way, more of a sly, witty kind of way. I know big words but that doesn't mean I'm going to use them. Though some of the time I do. Sometimes they come in handy.

"How's your father?" asks Ingrid in a knowing way, and I say point-blank, "Still a drunk."

Pops hasn't been able to hold down a job for years now. Seems you can't show up at work completely pie-eyed and plastered and plan to still get paid. After the bank nearly foreclosed on the mortgage years ago, I started working part-time for Priddy because she turned a blind eye to the fact that I was only twelve years old. I washed dishes in the back room so that no one would see, and Priddy graciously paid me under the table so the IRS wouldn't find out. It was another one of those things that everyone in town knew about, but nobody mentioned.

And then I change the subject because I no longer want to talk about my dad. Or college. Or the fact that the rest of the world has moved on, while I'm stuck in a life of stagnancy.

"Supposed to be a cold winter," I say as the wind turns tight corners around the periphery of the house like a race car driver, brakes squealing, tires shrieking.

"Aren't they all?" asks Ingrid.

"Yup," I say.

"Ever hear from your mom?" she asks as if she just can't quite let it go, this conversation about my father, about my mother, and I say, "Nope." Though sometimes I do, sometimes just a random postcard from a place I'll never see: Mount Rushmore, Niagara Falls. The Alamo. Funny thing is they never say anything. She doesn't even sign her name.

"It's not easy being a mother," she says under her breath, not looking up at me as she speaks. Ingrid is a mother, though her children are long gone, her husband gone, too, thanks to a particularly virulent strain of the flu that passed through many years ago. But Ingrid is a much better mother than my mom ever was, whether or not her kids are still around. She must've been. She looks like a mother, the considerate eyes and good-natured smile. Flaccid arms that look like they give great hugs. Not that I would know.

I consider Ingrid's words: *It's not easy being a mother.* To this I don't say anything. Not at first, anyway, but then I finally offer up, "Must be," because the last thing I want to say is something that will exonerate my mother for leaving me. There's no excuse for that, for disappearing in the middle of the night, hopping the train out of town without ever saying goodbye. There's a photograph Pops keeps of her. In it, she's about twenty-one. They'd been together only a short time when the photograph was taken, my mother and my father. A month, two months. Hard to say. In the photo, she's not smiling. But that's not saying much. It's hard to remember my mother ever smiling. Her face is narrow, tapered at the bottom to a point. Her cheekbones are high, her nose slender. Her eyes solemn, verging on stern, maybe even mean. Her hair, brunette, cut above the shoulders, is fanned out around her head, a fallout of the generation. It's the

1980s, early 1990s. She wears a dress, which is strange because I don't ever remember seeing my mother in a dress. But in this photo she wears a pale gray and foggy lavender dress. The dress is ruffled and tiered and shifty, but it's also simple, as if trying to be something that it's not. Just like my mother.

"We all make mistakes," she says, and I say nothing.

And then before I know it, we're talking about the dreaded winter again. The cold, the wind, the snow.

It's after the fourth game that Ingrid tells me to go. "You don't need to stay here and keep me company," she says while gathering the playing cards in her hands. "I'm sure you have better things to do," though of this I'm not so sure. But I go, anyway.

I bet Ingrid has better things to do than hang out with me.

I say my goodbyes and I head out the front door, letting it slam closed. From the front porch I catch the sound of the dead bolt latching. I hurtle myself down the steps and into the middle of the street as a sedan sluggishly pulls into a parking spot before me and cuts the engine. A young lady climbs out, a cigarette pinched between her thin lips. I step around the sedan and that's when I see the shadow of a lone figure ambling down the road. In a black-and-white checkered coat, a black beanie set on her head. Her canvas bag crisscrosses her slight body; her hands are shoved into the pockets of her pants. The ends of her hair blow in the wind.

Pearl.

She disappears into the morning air, over a single hill on the far end of Main Street — over the hill, getting consumed by the large homes and the enormous trees that fill that part of town, swallowed up and digested, so that before I know it, as I stand, feet frozen to concrete in the middle of the street, she's no longer there.

And then I hear the squeal of a screen door and I see Dr. Giles standing outside his cottage home, watching this scene, too.

I am not alone. Dr. Giles and I, the both of us, watch as the woman goes, watch as she evanesces over the hill and into the morning's fog.

# QUINN

I call the bookshop on the ride home, apologizing effusively for the poor reception on the bus. I try hard to sound sincere. I really do. I don the kindest voice I can possibly round up, a whole mishmash of kindness, sincerity and concern like a fragrant potpourri.

The woman who answers the phone is a lady by the name of Anne, who's uptight, high-strung and rule abiding, all attributes I gleaned the one and only time we met, when I'd come to the bookshop to keep Esther company for her thirty-minute lunch break. As I walked in the shop that day and announced the reason for my visit, Anne quickly pointed out that I was early, that although it was 12:24 and the shop was destitute, hollow and wanting for life, Esther's lunch break didn't begin until twelve-thirty. And then she proceeded to watch like a hawk as Esther organized books — face out and spine out — on a wooden shelf until twelve-thirty arrived and we were given permission to leave. And in that moment I decided I didn't like Anne one bit.

So it's quite unfortunate, really, that of all the booksellers in the shop, Anne is the one to answer my call. I tell her who I am. I try to play it cool, not letting her in on my little conundrum, the fact that it's been thirty-six or more hours and I still don't know where Esther is.

From the other end of the phone, there's silence. At first I picture the old, cadaverous woman searching the bookstore for Esther, and a faint trace of hope fills me with the possibility that Esther really is there, at the bookstore, working, arranging those books face-out on the wooden shelves. At least that's what I hope is happening in the ten or twenty seconds of dead air. But then the silence goes on so long that I'm absolutely certain we've managed to disconnect somehow, our conversation broken up by the faulty connection on the bus. I pull the phone from my ear and stare at the display screen, watching the seconds of the call time rise. Fifty-three, fifty-four . . .

She's there. Somewhere.

"Hello?" I ask. "Anne?" I think I say it more than once. But it's hard to hear.

Around me there is noise, the diesel engine of the CTA bus, people talking inside, the honking of horns outside. It's rush hour and there is traffic. Surprise, surprise.

"Esther was supposed to be here at three," Anne says to me. "Do *you* know where she is?" she asks rather brusquely, as if I've pulled a fast one on her, lacking all the sincerity and effusion of my request.

I don't bother to check my own watch, knowing good and well it's after five o'clock. The evening commute is busy and loud. Bodies press into mine on the bus as I stand, holding on for dear life. It smells. The people smell of body odor and bad breath, evidence of a long day at work. An arm presses against me, leaving a trace of sweat on my skin.

This, of course, strikes me as odd, the fact that Esther didn't show up at work. Esther always goes to work, even on those days she drags herself out of bed complaining that she doesn't want to go. She still goes. She works hard; she goes out of her way to please everyone. She tries her hardest to make a good impression on her boss and her coworkers, even Anne, though I tell her that's a waste of time. She'll never please Anne. But still, it's not like Esther to not show up to work, and no matter how angry

I am with her over the roommate quandary — that betrayal still stings — I don't want Esther to get in trouble or lose her job and so I decide to cover for her.

"She's sick," I say to Anne then. It's the very best I can come up with on the spot. Esther would do this for me; I know that much is true. "Bronchitis," I say, "maybe pneumonia." And I describe in detail a croup-like cough. I tell her about the phlegm, a yellow-green, and how for over twenty-four hours now Esther has been unable to get out of bed. There is a fever. There are chills. "She was going to try and make it into work today," I say, citing Esther's conscientiousness and industrious nature; she was going to try to go to work despite the fever, despite the chills. "She must be feeling really lousy not to go."

But despite all this Anne says that she should have called in sick, sure to tack on, "She seemed fine on Saturday," as if maybe, just maybe, Esther isn't sick at all.

"It came on very quickly," I lie. "Knocked her out cold."

"Well, I'll be," is what she says, but what she means is, *You're full of shit.*

If the coffee shop has a name, I don't know what it is. To me, it's just the one on the corner of Clark and Berwyn. That's what I call it. It's a place Esther and I like to hang. To us, it doesn't even need a name. *Let's meet at the coffee shop,* we'll say, and like magic, we both appear. That's my boiled-down definition of *best friend.* You always know what the other is thinking.

Except for right now, when I have no idea what Esther is thinking.

I see her through the window of the shop before I go in, taking in her layered ginger hair, the alabaster skin. It's evening, darker outside than it is on the inside, and so I can see right in, into the industrial designed space with its bold, unfinished look, the steel tables, the salvaged and recycled things that hang from the ceiling and walls. She sits, slouched on a bar stool at one of the wooden window counters, picking at the deckled edges of the coffee cup's paper sleeve, staring out the window, waiting for me, and I think to myself: she's got it all wrong. That's not where Esther and I sit, but rather at one of the smaller, more intimate steel bistro tables near the back, beside a custom brick fireplace and the exposed brick walls. And we wait until we've both arrived and then we order together, the very same thing, some caffeinated concoction that we agree to while waiting in line for our turn. But this girl has gone up to the counter all on her own and ordered her drink without waiting to see what I'd have. She sat at the wrong table.

This girl is not a good match for Esther. Not at all. That's what I decide.

I walk in and cross the room, traversing the patchy, polished concrete floors, staring down at them, in fact. I don't look at the girl, not yet, not until I'm closer. It's hard to look into the eyes of the person who plans to take over your life — knowingly or unknowingly. It isn't her fault, I get that, and yet it doesn't make me dislike her any less. I might just hate her.

I focus on my feet instead, on the rounded toes of a pair of leather boots, as I walk.

Her light eyes move from the window to mine, and it's then that she smiles, a pleasant smile, yes, but also one with reserve. "You're Esther?" she asks, extending her tiny hand, and I say that I am. I'm Esther, though of course I'm not. I'm Quinn, but right now, that's neither here nor there. I'm Esther.

Her name, she tells me, is Megan, and then, as if she doesn't even know her own name or hasn't quite decided on who she is, she says, "Meg." Her handshake is lethargic to say the least. Prissy. I'm not even sure that we touch.

I don't bother to get a coffee, knowing this will be quick. I'm not even sure why it is that I agreed to meet, but for some reason I wanted to see her with my own two eyes. She strikes me as young and naive, the kind of girl who probably has no clue how to hail a cab. The kind of girl I used to be. I slide onto a bar stool beside her and say, "You're interested in the apartment," and she assures me she is. She's a recent grad, or will be come December, and looking for a new place to live. Right now she lives with her single mom out in Portage Park, but is looking for something closer to the Loop, more trendy, a younger crowd. She has a job all lined up for after graduation in the west loop. She needs an apartment close to transportation. She tells me dramatically with a flip of the ginger hair, "The commute from Portage Park would take *years.*"

The thing that exasperates me the most is that she sounds a lot like me, or the me I was all those months ago when I saw Esther's *other* ad in the *Reader,* her first roommate request. My lucky break, I'd thought at the time, but now I wasn't so sure. Now I feel like some kind of mass-produced commodity rather than someone unique. My heart breaks a little with each of Meg's words, when she tells me her gig is in graphic design, how — as an avid environmentalist — she plans to bike to work in the summer. How the hardest part of moving away from home will be leaving her cat behind. How she loves to cook, and is a self-professed neat freak. My heart breaks not because any of these things appeals to me but because I think Esther would like Meg. I think Esther would really, truly like Meg.

But the question is this: Would she like Meg more than me?

"You're looking for a new roommate?" asks Meg, and I nod my head, staring out the window as a sea of people walk by, commuters just stepping off the 22 bus.

"My roommate," I tell her sadly, "is about to move out." And then I tell her how she sometimes has trouble paying her fair share of the rent. How sometimes she shorts me on her half of the utilities, or eats my food without asking first. And it's true; I do each and every one of these things. But that doesn't make me a bad roommate. Or does it?

What will I do, I wonder, if Esther makes me leave?

Where is Esther, I wonder, and why won't she come home to me so we can figure this out?

Why won't she talk to me?

Meg asks questions about the apartment, logical questions about first and last month's rent payment, security deposits and whether or not there's laundry in the building. Questions I never thought to ask. But when she asks if she can see it, the apartment, I say no. Not yet, is what I say. "I'm speaking to a few other applicants first," I lie, though I wonder, over the course of the next few hours and days, how many calls Esther's phone will receive. One call, ten calls, *twenty* calls? Twenty young people wanting to chase me from my home, to take my bed, my bedroom, my best friend?

"I'll be in touch," I tell her, but then mumble under my breath so that she can't hear, as I walk quickly away, out of the coffee shop and onto the city street, *But I just don't think you'd be a right fit, Meg.*

Though of course she could've been Jane Addams or Mother Teresa or Oprah Winfrey, and I still wouldn't have thought she was good enough for Esther, whether or not Esther brought her here because she thought *I* wasn't good enough for her.

Talk about ironic.

# ALEX

I wander the streets, searching for Pearl.

It's a path that takes me through the neighborhoods of town, from the stately homes where the stinking-rich people live, to the smaller, more provincial houses like mine, something just slightly above a hovel. I walk from the shores of Lake Michigan inland, where the waterfront community becomes bucolic. I pass the schools, an elementary school, a middle school and a high school, all three lined in a row, three bland, light brick buildings that have to bus kids in from surrounding towns to fill the halls. The American flag flutters before each one, beating in the wayward wind like the webbed hands of a bat's wings. The noise is loud; not a single bat, but a colony of bats. There are kids outside, on the playground, thronged together to keep warm, gym classes in uniform running laps around the archaic high school track. A fire engine soars by, lights and sirens blasting — the town's volunteer fire department. I stand on the side of the road and watch it go, looking for signs of smoke in the distance, its four big tires kicking gravel up along the road. I hope Pops hasn't managed to start our own house on fire. Thankfully they head the other way of our home.

I continue on, past the old Protestant church, the old cemetery, the new cemetery, the café. I lumber beneath power lines, listening to the electricity's buzz; I tread past farms, past desiccated stalks of corn, stripped of produce and waiting to be cut down; past livestock farms with fat cows and thin cows and everything-in-between cows. It's Michigan, the Midwest, our town right on the rim of the Corn Belt; you don't have to walk too far in any one direction to see a farm. I walk in circles, having nothing better to do with my day. Work would be a blessing, a lucky break. But today I don't work.

In time I find my way to the old beach-front carousel, closed this time of year. I wonder if, perhaps, Pearl will be here. She's not, not that I can see. But I scale the partition, anyway, and take my place on the sea serpent chariot, some kind of mythological blue creature, part dragon, part snake. The

154

seat is hard and cold, an ornate, Victorian design, and though now it's still and quiet, I hear the tunes of Rogers and Hammerstein playing in my mind. That and a stranded aluminum can, one that gets propelled across the asphalt parking lot by the wind, making a racket. Hard to believe one can — lifted from the jam-packed garbage bin by the deranged November air — would make so much noise. And yet it does, lurching back and forth across the lot like a ship in a sea storm.

There's a girl who lives there at the periphery of my dreams: a cross between Leigh Forney, the girl who stole my twelve-year-old heart, and a whole assemblage of girls I think I've been in love with, from Hollywood starlets like Selena Gomez to the weather lady on the Kalamazoo news. She's part of the dream, too, this composite of a girl with an oval face and fair skin and close-set hazel eyes, eyes that sit right there at the bridge of the button nose. Her hair is light brown, like caramel, and smooth; in my dreams it glides on the surface of the wind, always drifting. Her smile is wide and airy. Carefree. She doesn't reside in the deepest stages of sleep, REM sleep, where most of my vivid nightmares exist, the reoccurring dreams where Pops drinks himself to death, or burns the house to smithereens with the both of us trapped inside. Rather, she lives in the place of light sleep, where the variance between *sleep* and *awake* is often blurred. She lives with me in the moments before I fall asleep for the night, and in those moments that I wake up, coming to, pulling myself from sleep, this ethereal figure who strokes my cheek or grazes my arm, or pulls me by the hand, whispering, *Let's go . . .* though always — always — as I become fully roused from sleep, does she decide to leave, dematerializing before my eyes. When fully awake it's impossible to summon her hair or her eyes or her blithe smile, though when I close my eyes I know that she'll be there, calling me, rallying me to leave. *Let's go . . .*

When I was twelve years old I kissed Leigh Forney for the very first time. The very first and the very last time, right here, on this sea serpent chariot. It was summer, night-time, and the carousel was — as it is now — quiet. The park was empty for the night. I'd carried my telescope to the park where, on the beach's edge, we sat in the sand and stared through the eyepiece, me pointing out the Double Cluster, the Orion Nebula, the Pleiades, and she pretending to care. Or maybe she really did care. I don't know.

Leigh was a childhood friend of mine, the kind I'd played kick the can with when I was five years old. She lived just down the street in a 1950s tract home like mine. I'd lugged that bulky telescope all the way from my house — arms burning by the time I arrived — with the promise I had something to show her, something cool. Something I thought she'd enjoy. Why we didn't just look through the telescope at home, I don't know. I thought this would be more special. And she did, for a minute or two, she did enjoy it, and then she said, "Bet I can beat you to the carousel," and like that, we were off and running, feet sinking in sand, through the parking lot, and over the orange partition onto the sleepy carousel. We forgot all about the telescope and the nighttime sky. We fell, laughing, onto the chariot. I'd let her win as I had so many times before when we raced from her house to mine or mine to hers.

And it was then and there that she kissed me, the stiff, wooden kiss of two twelve-year-old kids. For me, not much has changed since that day. It's hard to get good at something when you never practice. But I'm betting Leigh has learned a thing or two over the years.

After that we sat in silence, knowing we

would never go back to being friends; something had changed with that kiss. If it could even be called a kiss, the way we sat, lip to lip, for two seconds at best.

By the time we made our way back to the beach so I could retrieve my telescope, someone else was there, a handful of jocks from the middle school's basketball team, staring through the eyepiece at a couple making out farther down the beach. I peered over my shoulder at the carousel and wondered what else they'd seen. They had names for me when I tried to repossess the telescope from their hands: loser and geek. Faggot. They stood, three feet away, making me grovel for my own telescope. They told Leigh she could do better than me, and for whatever reason she believed them, because I remember that night, walking home sad and alone with my telescope in hand, while Leigh drifted away with those boys.

Even then, I knew my role in the social hierarchy.

Six years later, not much has changed.

Leigh is gone, those boys are gone. But I'm still here, sitting on the carousel all alone, chasing down some girl that's unreachable; she's far out of reach as are most of my dreams.

# QUINN

Esther is a great roommate. Most of the time. I've hardly ever seen her angry, except for the day I rearranged the foodstuff on her cabinet shelf. Then she got angry, really angry, and by that I mean she nearly flipped her lid.

I didn't *rearrange* her foodstuff, per se. I was looking for something, dill weed to make a seasoning for my microwave popcorn. A little salt, a little sugar, a little garlic, a little dill weed, and presto! It was one of my many obsessions. Esther was at school, a night class for her occupational therapy thingie, and I was at home, settling in to watch some show on the TV.

Esther and I each have kitchen cabinets that are our own. The ones with the bowls and plates we share, but the ones with the foodstuff we do not. There's mine, packed to capacity with junk food galore, and then there's Esther's, complete with one-off cooking and baking supplies: kelp noodles and basil seed, dill weed, peanut flour, garam masala, whatever the heck that is. And Frosted Flakes.

I made the popcorn. I could have settled on salt, I know, but knowing Esther had the ingredients for my special seasoning, I dug through her spices and noodles and whatnot for the dill weed.

I didn't think I'd made a mess, but Esther sure did. I was on the sofa with my delish popcorn when she returned from class, the volume on the TV quiet so as not to disturb Mrs. Budny down below, old Mrs. Budny, who I imagined often stood in the middle of her own home, her dough-like head wrapped up in a babushka, her skin an anemic white, upthrusting a mop with shaking, old-lady hands, pounding the ceiling to shut up Esther and me.

But not that day. That day the TV was so quiet that I could hardly hear. Esther came home in a fine mood, one which disappeared quickly when she reached into her cabinet for the Frosted Flakes and then said to me, "Quinn," her voice a tad bit Hannibal Lecter–like when she appeared in the living room and snapped off the TV. *Hello, Clarice.*

"Hey!" I griped. "I was watching that," I

said as she tossed the remote control to the mod plaid chair.

"Can you come here for a minute?" she asked, leaving the room without waiting for me to respond. And so I set my popcorn aside and followed her into the kitchen, where her cabinet door was ajar. It didn't look like a mess to me. I could hardly tell a thing had been moved. The dill weed was right where it needed to be, between the cumin and the fennel seed. Alphabetical order.

"Did you touch my food?" she asked with a strange tremor to her voice that I'd never heard before.

And I said, "Just a little dill weed." And, "I'm sorry, Esther," when I saw how upset she'd suddenly become. It wasn't like Esther to become upset, and so I was taken aback. "I'll buy you more," I promised as her face turned red, as red as a field of poppies, so that I thought smoke might come out of her ears like steam from a train engine. She was mad.

She marched to the open cabinet and said, "The dill weed goes here," as she lifted and lowered the dill weed container into the exact same spot I'd left it. "And the peanut flour goes here," she said, doing the very same thing with the bag of flour so that when she dropped it to the cabinet shelf, flour sprayed everywhere.

I hadn't touched the flour. I thought to tell her that — to tell Esther I never touched the flour, not once, not one single time — but I saw now that she wasn't in the mood for a rational discussion on peanut flour.

Then Esther said, "Now look what you've done. Look what you've done, Quinn. Look at the mess you made," meaning the pinpricks of flour that dotted the countertops, and she tromped out of the room, leaving me to clean a mess she made in response to my bogus mess.

You live and learn, I told myself, and the next day I bought my own damn dill weed.

I return home from the coffee shop, walking down the worn hallway to my apartment. The carpeting is frayed and tattered, a henna color to mask the mud and dirt and other gunk we carry in on the soles of our shoes. The walls are scuffed. One of the corridor lightbulbs has burned out, making the walkway dim. It's dreary. Not dirty or dangerous or any of those things that urban dwellings can sometimes be, but just dreary. Used. Overused. Like a tissue that no longer has any usable parts. The hallways need new paint, new carpeting, a little tender loving care.

Though if it wasn't for the *homeliness* of the walk-up corridor, I wouldn't quite appreciate the *hominess* of Esther's and my space. Snug and comfy, cozy and warm.

As I slide my key in the keyhole and turn the door's handle, there's a part of me expecting to see Esther on the other side of the steel pane, making dinner in her favorite button-back sweater and a pair of jeans. The smells that greet me are delectable and divine. Either the TV is on — The Food Network — or the stereo, some kind of folksy acoustic thing emanating from the three-piece, overpriced speakers with Esther singing along, her legato and range even more impressive than the voice on the stereo that's getting paid to sing.

If the radiator hasn't kicked into high gear, Esther will greet me at the door with my timeworn fleece and a pair of slippers. Because that's Esther. Saint Esther. The kind of roommate who greets me at the door, who makes me dinner, who would bring me coffee and bagels every single day of the week if I asked her to.

But Esther's not there and I'm more than a bit discouraged to say the least.

And so, without Esther, I find my fleece

myself. I find my slippers. I turn the stereo on.

I ravage the freezer for something to eat, settling on a frozen pizza jam-packed with pork fat and mechanically separated chicken beef. I'm not known for my healthy eating habits, but rather one who likes to indulge on fatty, greasy things — and ice cream. It's an act of rebellion, naturally, a way to get back at my mother for years and years worth of Shake 'n Bake chicken, Hamburger Helper casserole and the unvarying mound of mixed frozen vegetables (lukewarm): the peas, the corn, the cut green beans. She'd always make me sit at the table until I'd finished my meal. Didn't matter if I was eight or eighteen.

The first thing I did upon moving in with Esther: splurge at the grocery store on everything my mother never wanted me to eat. I asserted my independence; I took control. I claimed a kitchen cabinet and a freezer shelf as my own in Esther's and my passé kitchen, loading them with potato chips and Oreo cookies, enough frozen pizzas to feed a football team.

Until, of course, Esther helped me see the error of my ways.

Esther is a good cook, the very best, the kind who can make things like cauliflower and asparagus taste good, or even better than good. She makes them taste delicious. She searches for recipes online; she follows cooking blogs. But me? I don't cook. And Esther isn't here to do it for me. So I find a baking sheet and slather it with cooking spray.

As my pizza cooks I wander into Esther's bedroom. It's dark as I go in, and so I flip on a table lamp that sits on the edge of her desk. The room comes to life, and there it is again, that fish — the Dalmatian Molly — pleading with me for food. I see it in its beady black eyes: *Feed me.* I sprinkle in a small handful of flakes and start pulling at desk and dresser drawers at random. While yesterday's search was a simple reconnaissance mission, this one is the real deal. A strip search. A no-holds-barred search. It's more intelligence gathering than a fishing expedition (no pun intended).

And as I pull and pluck papers at random from inside the drawers, I realize the fish and I have a little something in common: Esther has abandoned the both of us. She's cast us aside and left us both for dead.

What I find is doodles. Restaurant menus. An essay on adaptive response, and another on dyspraxia. Jottings on kinesthesia with words like *hand-eye coordination* and *body awareness* inscribed on the lines of the notebook paper in Esther's script. A greeting card from her great-aunt Lucille. The lyrics for a church hymn. Post-it notes with reminders like *Pick up dry cleaning* and *Get milk.* An arbitrary phone number. A box of contacts, *colored* contacts, that makes me stop dead in my tracks.

I stop and inspect the packaging. They're blue, *brilliant blue,* as the box says. And I picture Esther's cherubic face, one brown eye and one blue, a physical mark that proved she was special. Chosen.

*Does that mean . . . ?* I wonder, and *Could it be . . . ?*

Is Esther's one blue eye an imposter?

No, I tell myself. No. It can't be.

But maybe.

But there are other things I find, too. Things that leave me equally as confused. Handouts on grieving, the grieving process, the seven stages of grief. I try to convince myself that this has something to do with her getting her occupational therapy degree — *if Esther was sad, wouldn't I have known?* — and that this isn't real life. Not Esther's life, anyway. Someone else's life. But that belief only lasts so long. From the piles of paper a card falls to my lap, a monochromatic card with a monogram on the front, a

166

name, address and phone number on the rear. It's a business card for a doctor. *Licensed Psychologist,* it reads. I pick up that card and stare at it for a good three minutes, making sure it doesn't read *podiatrist, pulmonologist, pediatrician.* Some other kind of doctor that starts with a *p.* But no. It says psychologist. Esther was sad. Esther *is* sad. She's grieving, and I didn't know a thing about it.

But why, I wonder, why is Esther sad?

And what else hasn't she been telling me?

There's more. Another document that I find in the pile of documents. A form, an official-looking form that reads State of Illinois across the top. In the circuit court of Cook County. Petition for name change.

It's complete. Signed, dated and stamped. Esther is no longer Esther, but now *Jane*? It seems preposterous, imagining Esther as something as banal as a Jane. Something so ordinary for Esther, who isn't in the least bit ordinary. If she had to change her name she should have gone for something along the lines of Portia, Cordelia, Astrid. That's far more suiting to Esther than *Jane.*

But no. Esther is now Jane. Jane Girard.

I'm hit with a sudden flash from the past: Esther and I sitting on the apartment sofa, watching TV. It was three months ago,

167

maybe four. She'd been somewhere for the day, which she was pretty tight-lipped and buttoned-up about; she wouldn't tell me where she'd gone. And since she didn't, my mind made up for lack of details, envisioning some unscrupulous man with a wife and kids meeting Esther at that shady hotel over on Ridge, the one that was still offering en suite bathrooms and color TV, as if this was the latest and greatest in hotel accommodations. It wasn't like Esther to do such a thing, but it was fun in my mind to pretend. She didn't want to talk about where she'd been, and muttered one-word responses to every darn question I asked: *Yes* and *No* and *Fine.*

She said two weird things then, two weird things that I remember. First, she said, "Have you ever tried to make something better, and ended up making everything worse?" Though when I asked her to explain, she wouldn't elaborate. I told her yes. *Story of my life,* was what I said.

And she also asked this, out of nowhere, from beside me on the sofa, sad and contemplative. "If you could change your name to anything, what would you choose?"

I chose Belle. And then I went off on a rant on how I loved the name Belle and hated the name Quinn. What kind of name is Quinn, anyway? It's a boy's name is what it is. Or maybe a last name, I don't know. Either way, it's not a name for a girl. That's what I said.

I never knew what Esther would choose — she didn't tell me — but now I did. Jane. Esther chose the name Jane.

Esther had changed her name. *Legally.* She had stood in some courtroom before a judge and asked that her name be changed, and I didn't know. How did I not know about this?

I also find a paper shredder plugged into an electrical outlet on the white wall. I yank off the top of the shredder and stare inside at the millions of ribbons of paper bits. It's filled to the brim; I don't think she could get one more sheet of paper in. How long would it take me to sort the ribbons of paper out and tape them back together again? Would it even be possible?

I return to the desk and find a bookmark, a coupon, a gift certificate and what looks like a passport photo, three passport photos tucked in a Walgreens sleeve, the fourth image missing, sheared off the page evenly with a pair of scissors. No passport, just the remaining photos, and I have to wonder who they belong to, Esther or Jane?

I also wonder where the passport is.

I search everywhere, but there's no passport here.

If Esther changed her name to Jane and got a passport for Jane, she'd need other things changed to Jane, as well, such as a driver's license and a social security card. Is Esther walking around someplace with a driver's license that bears the name Jane Girard?

But then, when I'm about to give up hope of finding anything else in the drawers, I see another note, typed and signed, *All my love,* with the same *E* and the same *V. All my love, EV.* Esther Vaughan. Folded in thirds as the first note had been, and stuffed at the bottom of the bottom desk drawer.

*My Dearest,* I read as the oven timer hollers for me, the odor of burning pizza cheese threatening to ignite the entire building on fire.

I drop the note on the desktop and run.

# ALEX

There isn't anything you can't find on the internet these days, especially for a public figure like Dr. Giles. Thanks to sites like *HealthGrades* and *ZocDoc.com* I can easily access any and all reviews on the shrink. The first thing I discover is that he really does have a first name, something other than *doctor.* Joshua is his name. Dr. Joshua Giles.

For some reason that changes everything when I picture him as a helpless babe, in a mother's arms, being given a name. *Joshua.*

He's also thirty-four years old.

Married.

A father of two.

Graduate of Chicago's Northwestern University, with above-average ratings in *wait time* and *office cleanliness, ease of scheduling appointments.* By the looks of *HealthGrades* and *ZocDoc.com,* people like him.

I spend the afternoon at the public library, reading the reviews on a computer I've reserved. Unlike the rest of the world, Pops and I don't own a computer. This computer, a dated HP desktop, sits in a small terminal in the equally as dated library. The town library, a 1920s relic, is old. Though it's expanded twice since the original seven-hundred-square-foot library was opened in 1925, it's still small. The collections are lacking and out of date, a has-been of some other generation. Books are in short supply. And then there are the videocassettes, movies still available on VHS, which far surpass the number of DVDs.

Here at the computer terminal (I'm surprised we even have computers, rather than typewriters, word processors, the Roman abacus), there are no doors or walls and so I'm constantly peering over my shoulder to ensure I'm not being watched, that some looky-loo or nosey parker isn't surveilling my internet search. Because that's the kind of thing people around here do. I make a mental note to clear the search history before I leave, too, so some librarian doesn't stop by later and see what I've been seeing, the glowing reviews for a Dr. Joshua Giles, PhD, that appear on the screen one after the next, after the next. *Kind,* say the reviews. *Good listener. Heartwarming. Grounded. Easy to talk to.*

*He is the best!!!* says one review, with an overkill of exclamation points that makes me question the reviewer's mental health and state of mind.

As for Dr. Giles's personal life, he's married to a Molly Giles and has two kids, a four-year-old son and a two-year-old daughter, according to a blip in the local paper. There's no mention of their names. There are pictures of Dr. Giles — professional photos of him in a navy sport coat with a stock gray backdrop like every other doctor in the whole entire world has — but zilch for the rest of the family. His home was purchased about a year and a half ago for 650,000 smackeroos. Everything is there: his name, date of purchase, address, what he pays in property taxes. There's no such thing as privacy anymore.

"Finding everything okay?" a passing librarian asks, and I jump quickly, minimizing the screen. The librarian is a relic from the 1920s herself, a gray-haired woman well past her prime. I tell her I am; I'm finding everything just fine. Except that I'm not, not really. I don't even know what it is that I'm looking for, but I do know that I'm not finding it here. I guess deep down I was hoping for something scandalous and bad. Patients claiming he was a creep, a freak, a pervert, something along those lines. Citations from the American Psychological Association, code of conduct violations or just plain bad reviews. He missed appointments, he made his patients wait too long, he fell asleep in his chair midsession.

But as far as I can tell, people like him. The man's history is squeaky clean.

I rise up out of my chair, the steel legs skating across the ugly maroon carpeting, getting tangled on a loose thread. I drape a coat over my hooded sweatshirt and prepare to leave. I double-check that I've closed all search engines, and then do a quick sweep of the search history to make sure there's nothing there. There isn't. It's clean as a whistle.

I'm about to leave when I hear a voice. "Alex?" asks the voice. "Alex Gallo?" and I turn to see her, Mrs. Hackett, my high school science teacher, standing before me with some paperback in her hand, a winter coat draped over an arm. She's hardly changed a bit in the six months since I've been there, and I'm struck by a sudden moment of homesickness. I miss school, my friends, roaming the halls of that aged, light brick building with its rows and rows of cherry-red lockers and vinyl floors. Mrs. Hackett still has the same dark long hair, parted at the center and pulled into a low ponytail on the side; the same dark eyes; the same thick eyebrows; the same soft smile. Where her body used to be narrow and trim, there's now a bowling ball protruding, right in her midsection, which she has her hands laced around. She wears a long, tunic-type thing that bulges at the center, hanging low to cover up the protuberance. A baby. Mrs. Hackett is going to have a baby, and soon. For some reason this makes me smile, even if she is giving me a look of arrant disappointment, her arms crossed, a pout on her pretty face.

"I told them no, surely not," she says. "I said I wouldn't believe it until I saw it with my own two eyes. But here you are," she adds, wielding her hands in my direction, and I force a smile and say, "In the flesh."

Her disappointment turns to heartache as she asks, "Why, Alex? Why? Why did you turn that scholarship down?"

I shrug my shoulders. "I'm a homebody, I guess. Couldn't be away from home."

It's true, of course, and it's not true. And everybody knows the reason why, though no one's too keen to say the words out loud.

"How is your father?" she asks.

"Just fine," I say. She sighs.

"You used to come here all the time," she says then, of the library. I did. I used to come here all the time and hole myself up in the stacks all day, with a tower of astronomy books, and read them until the librarians told me to leave. I'd been fascinated with the sky since I was a little kid, since long before I could read. Pops bought me a telescope once, back when he could actually afford a telescope. I can hardly remember life that long ago. I haven't looked through it in years, not since that night with Leigh Forney out on the beach. That's the last thing I need to see, my dreams floating off to space with clouds of interstellar dust and nebulae.

It's what I always thought I would do when I grew up, work as an astronomer or, if that fell through, an aerospace engineer. Design spaceships and airplanes. Study the universe, find life out there somewhere, confirming what I already knew was true: we are not alone. Not working for Priddy full-time, bussing tables. I never thought I'd be doing that. There's a letter at home somewhere to prove it, a full ride to the U of M, which I turned down two days after Pops drank so much he had to be hospitalized for alcohol poisoning. I'm pretty sure we're still paying for that visit, a no-interest payment plan I managed to negotiate with the hospital's billing staff.

My eyes stare off into the distance, to the spines of books lined in a row, as Mrs. Hackett says, "I haven't seen you around here in a while."

"I've been busy," I say.

"You're working?" she asks.

"I'm working," I say. And then I point at that big, round belly and ask, "Boy or girl?" Anything so that we can stop talking about me and what an utmost disappointment I am, and she confirms that that bowling ball inside her shirt is in fact a girl. Elodie, she'll be. Elodie Marie Hackett.

I say that I like it. She asks if I want to touch her belly, but I say no.

And then I go because I can't stand that look of disappointment in her eyes.

Outside I backtrack from the library through town, fully intent on heading out to the beach and finding my way home, along the same path as I always do. It's almost five o'clock; it'll be getting dark soon. Pops is likely hungry, wondering where I am and why I'm not making dinner. Tonight we're having SpaghettiOs and a can of corn. I'm a regular sous-chef. I might even heat up some kielbasa and throw that in, too.

But this is where the plan goes south.

I'm cutting down Main Street, past In-grid's house and the café, for a return to the beach. I'm thinking about Pearl, and whether or not she'll be there for another evening swim — *hoping* that she'll be there, so that this time I might actually manage a return wave and not practically shit my pants when she smiles at me — when I hear a screen door slam shut, and standing there, just outside the blue cottage door, is Dr. Joshua Giles.

Locking up for the night.

He wears a coat and gloves, a leather satchel in the clasp of a hand.

His patients have all come and gone, the day is done, and Dr. Giles is heading home. The rest of the street is quiet. Most of the shops are closed for the night, though cars pass up and down the street, going slowly, stopping to take turns at an intersection that bears no stoplight, but rather a yellow yield sign. A block away, a woman walks her dog, a small terrier-like thing that she scoops into her arms to cross the street as a conversion van drives past. The sky has begun to fill with stars, Sirius first, the brightest star in the nighttime sky. I stop on a street corner and stare. In the distance, the train pulls into town as Dr. Giles begins his trek home.

All of that makes perfect sense.

What makes no sense to me is why I follow him.

My Dearest,

I've forgotten many things. But there are many more I will always remember: your voice, your smile, your eyes. The way you smelled, what it felt like when your hands first touched mine.

I didn't ask for you. You should have just gone away like I asked you to. Like I told you to. Just go. But you didn't go, and then you were there, and there was nothing I could do.

You stayed until it was me who had to go.

I wonder, sometimes, if you even remember me.

Do you remember me?

All my love,
EV

# QUINN

There are few worthwhile lessons I actually remember my mother teaching me. *Don't pick your pimples, they'll scar.* And *Floss your teeth. You don't want to lose your teeth before you turn thirty-five.* That's what she said, citing cavities and gingivitis as the cause of tooth loss. There was also the fact of bad breath, and how bad breath scared eligible bachelors away, and I didn't want to be a spinster forever, did I? That's what Mom asked those nights she hovered in the doorway to the bathroom in our split-level suburban home, insisting that I floss my teeth. I was about twelve years old and already she was picturing me as an old spinster living alone with a thousand cats.

But there was one lesson that stood out above the rest. One good one. I was fifteen. I'd gotten into a fight with my best friend, Carrie, of eleven years over something as inane as a boy. I had my heart set on asking some football jock to the high school's turnabout dance, but she asked him before I had the chance. *You snooze, you lose,* Carrie had said to me, and it was in that moment I decided we'd no longer be friends. What I wanted to do was scream at her, berate her in public, start some hideous catfight in the crowded halls of our public high school, pulling hair and arousing our retractable feline claws so we could scratch each other's eyes out while scores of teenagers watched, picking sides and jeering us on.

But my mother wisely cautioned that this would help nothing. She was right. Carrie was bigger than me, for one. She was tall, an athlete, a basketball and volleyball player to boot. She could kick my ass if given the chance, and so I didn't dare give her the chance.

Instead, my mother suggested I write notes to my friend-turned-archenemy, Carrie. "Jot your feelings down on paper. Tell her how you're feeling," she said, with the PS: "Don't send the letters. Don't give them to her. Keep them to yourself. But once you get your feelings down on paper, you'll be able to move on. You'll be able to think through your emotions. You'll find closure."

And she was right. I wrote the letters, long

scolding notes on lined purple notebook paper with my favorite gel pen. And in those letters I read Carrie the riot act. I tore into her, I took her into the woodshed and reamed her out. I called her names. I told her I hated her. I said I wished she'd die.

But I never gave the letters to Carrie. I wrote them and threw them away. And in the end, I felt better. I found my closure. And I found new friends, too, though never any as dear as Carrie had once been.

Until the day I met Esther.

Sitting there that day on Esther's bedroom floor, eating my pizza, mozzarella cheese streaming down my chin, I'm absolutely certain of one thing: that's why Esther was writing the notes to *My Dearest.* That was her intent, to get her emotions down on paper, to feel better, to find closure with this two-timing man who has broken her heart.

The notes were never meant to be seen.

After searching a few more drawers, a shoebox or two in Esther's raggedy closet and under the bed, I give up. I'm not going to find any more answers in here, anything other than the contacts, the information on loss and grieving, the passport photo, the change-of-name form, all things which raise far more questions than they solve —

183

namely, who is Esther, *really*?

I'm feeling frustrated to say the least. Assumptions come to mind: Esther, aka Jane, has taken her passport and fled the country; or maybe Esther, aka Jane, is sitting somewhere, so afflicted by grief she can't bring herself to come home. I just don't know, but it makes me sad, thinking that Esther is sad and I didn't know. And so I find that business card and dial the number embossed on its surface, the one for the psychologist. It rings five times, but he doesn't answer, sending the call to voice mail, whereby I leave a message delineating my concerns. *My roommate Esther Vaughan is gone,* I tell him, and I explain that I found his card in her things. I ask if maybe he knows where she is. I beg, in fact, hoping, wondering, if Esther might have revealed to him some place she likes to go to hide, or whether or not she planned to leave the country without her phone. Maybe she told him the reasons she decided to place an ad for another roommate in the *Reader,* or why she wants to replace me with Meg from Portage Park. Perhaps he knows. Perhaps Esther sat there in some dimly lit room across from the man and confessed to him that I made for a lousy roommate. That I didn't pay my fair share of the rent, that I didn't cook. That I ate her dill weed. And maybe he encouraged her, as a good psychologist would do, to cut ties and to do it quickly. To kick me to the curb. To be ready to leave at a moment's notice, in case my abuse went beyond the realm of shiftless and slovenly. To not let me take advantage of her anymore.

Perhaps it's his fault I'm in this predicament.

Or maybe it's mine.

But then I'm hit with another query: Does he even know who Esther is? Perhaps to him she is Jane. And so I say this, too, on the phone. I say that my roommate also goes by the pseudonym of Jane Girard — as I take a look at the petition for Esther's name change and I'm stricken by how completely outlandish this is, admitting to some person I don't know that my roommate has a double life I know nothing about. On his answering machine, no less. I pinch myself. *Wake up!*

I don't wake up. Turns out, I'm already awake.

I press End on the phone, feeling miffed at how many questions I've formed — many — and how many answers I've found: none.

I think and I think. Where else could I possibly look for clues? I put in a call to

Ben to see if he's had any luck in tracking Esther's family down, but again he doesn't answer his phone. Damn Priya, drawing his attention away from the task at hand. I leave a message, and as I do, my eyes swerve to that photograph of Esther and me thumb-tacked to the wall — Esther and me posing before the artificial Christmas tree for a selfie. Seeing the photo, my mind starts to wonder about that storage unit where we found the tree, that winter day we dragged the tree home through the snow. What else does Esther have hidden in there besides a Christmas tree? It's not like I have the key to the storage unit, but still, I wonder if I'd be able to sweet-talk some employee into letting me inside. Doubtful. That's the kind of thing Esther could do, but not me. I'm not the type of person able to sway someone with my bright eyes and a beguiling smile, which is Esther to a T.

That night, before I go to bed, I gather the collection of clues I've found and sit before the arched windows of the living room, going through them one by one, rereading the notes to *My Dearest,* familiar-izing myself with the grieving process, run-ning my fingers over the embossed name on the psychologist's business card. It is dark outside, the lights of the city like a million sparkling golden stars. The number of neighbors who have curtains drawn is trifling; they, like me, sit in a fully illuminated room into which everyone outside can easily see. It's part and parcel of city living or so I've learned, leaving the window coverings open wide to welcome in the city's super-abundant lights but also neighbors' prying eyes. My mother, in our split-level suburban home, never would have gone for this. Curtains and blinds were closed at the first indicator of dusk, as soon as the stars and planets became visible to the naked eye and the sun began to dip. I stare out the window and admire it all: the lights of the buildings, the stars, the planets, the flashing wing lights of a passing jet plane, flying silently overhead at thirty thousand feet. From up above, I wonder what the passengers see. Do they see me?

And then my eyes return to the street, and I spy a sole figure standing in the shadows of Farragut Avenue, staring in the window, up at me. A woman, I believe, with strands of hair that flitter around her head like a dozen butterflies flapping their flimsy wings. At least that's what I think I see, though it's nighttime and I can't see so well, but still, the figure doesn't make me feel in the least bit scared or creeped out, but rather hopeful. Esther? The form stands far enough away from streetlights to be inconspicuous, to be invisible, to hide. But someone is there.

*Please let it be Esther,* I silently beg. She's home; she's come home. Or at least partway home, though she's not yet convinced to come inside. I have to convince her. I rise quickly to my feet, a fish in a fishbowl, knowing that whoever is outside can see me with clarity, and for this reason I wave. I'm not scared.

I search for signs of movement, hoping and wishing that the sole figure will wave back, just a twitch of movement from the street, but no. There's nothing. Not at first, anyway. But then there is. A wave, albeit a small wave, but still a wave. I'm just sure of it. Or at least I think I am.

Esther?

I drop the items in my hand and run quickly through the apartment door and down three misaligned flights of stairs before she has a chance to leave. If it's Esther, I have to convince her to stay. I run. *Stay,* I think to myself and, *Don't go.* I slip more than once, my shoes losing traction on the floor as I run faster than I've ever run in my whole entire life. I almost fall, catching the hand railing for support and righting myself before my rear end hits the ground. I come barreling out the main entranceway and onto the quiet street, down the steps and into the middle of the road without looking left or right for traffic.

"Esther," I call out two times, the first a forced whisper — to avoid waking neighbors — and the second, a scream. But there is no response to either. I dart across the street, to the blackened expanse where thirty seconds ago I saw the figure — or thought I saw the figure, though now I can't be sure — but there is no one there. Just parked cars, a line of flats and low-rise apartments, a vacant street. I look every which way, but there are no signs of life. Nothing. The street is barren. Whatever I saw, or whatever I thought I saw, is gone.

Esther isn't here.

I turn sadly back to my own four-flat, but I don't go straight home. Instead, I wander through the streets of Andersonville, past the places we like to hang, searching for Esther. Our favorite restaurants, our favorite coffee shop, the snazzy little gift and boutique shops that line Clark and Berwyn, cupping my hands around my eyes to peer inside and see if Esther is there, but in each and every one of these places, she's not there.

I pass a theater on Clark Street where a satirical play has been gracing the stage. Esther has been dying to see it but I've refused to go. *I like my shows with surround sound and popcorn,* I told Esther at the time, weeks ago, when she'd asked if I'd join her for the play. *Lots of popcorn,* I said, spouting on and on about how live theater was lame.

Now I wish I'd just shut up and gone.

A group of artsy urbanites comes bounding down the steps of the theater and I quickly dig up a photo of Esther on my phone and thrust it into one man's hand. "Have you seen her?" I ask with shaking hands. "Was this woman inside?"

The man shakes his head and returns my phone to me. He hasn't seen Esther and I watch sadly as he and his pretentious friends turn and walk away, happy and laughing, talking about what a great time the play was, what a riot.

I wind my way up and down the quieting city streets, watching as they slowly become uninhabited as nighttime draws near, footsteps escaping off into every darkened direction. I pass the Catholic church where Esther sings in the choir, a huge neo-Gothic structure whose doors, even at this late hour, remain unlocked. I pull on the blackened handle and let myself inside, calling out quietly and yet hopelessly for Esther. "Esther," I hiss, moving with stealth two steps in, knowing this was where she was supposed to be, this is where she was *meant* to be, when she was not sleeping in her bed.

But the church is empty and the only words that return to me are mine, my desperate plea for Esther echoing off the wood paneled walls. Esther is not here.

In time I know that I'll have to return to the vacant apartment all alone, without Esther in tow, and that when I arrive, Esther will not be there waiting for me. Not tonight, anyway, though I take comfort in the fact that maybe Esther will be home tomorrow. Tomorrow will be forty-eight hours that she's been gone, just like the 311 operator said. They usually come home in forty-eight to seventy-two hours. Tomorrow then, I tell myself. Tomorrow Esther will come home.

Maybe.

At home that night, I can't sleep. Driven by insomnia, I slip quietly into Esther's bedroom and flip on a light. For whatever reason, my feet lead me to the paper shredder on the floor. I remove the top and dump its contents to the hardwood floors and then stand back to assess the mess. Some of the ribbons are traditional white computer paper, while others are colored, green and blue. Yellow. Some are heavy, like cardstock, and others are sparse and thinning, like a receipt. But it's the ribbons of glossy photo paper that catch my eye as I run my fingers over the smooth, sheeny surface, wondering who it's a picture of, assuming it's even a picture at all. I start plucking the shreds of photo paper from the rest, making a pile on the floor.

How long would it take me to sort the ribbons of paper out and tape them back together again? Would it even be possible? I don't know, but I'm sure as heck going to try.

# ALEX

He walks with an abnormal gait. His footsteps are short, the weight of his body placed more on the heels of his feet rather than the soles or the toes. It isn't overly evident, and yet it is unmissable as I trail Dr. Giles by a good twenty paces to keep from being discovered. I probably walk with a gait abnormality, too, as I creep warily down the street, hiding behind tall, fat oak trees any time he so much as breathes. I've got my cell in the palm of a hand, texting invisible digits onto the screen so I can play possum if he turns around and sees me. Though I've got the phone on vibrate to deflect the sound of any incoming calls.

Dr. Giles didn't plan on walking home. He planned on driving in his car, a functional sedan parked in the driveway of the blue cottage where he keeps his office. Though a lot of people walk or ride bikes in these parts, even when the temperature drops to a meager forty-five degrees, that wasn't the reason Dr. Giles walked home. The reason? The puncture holes in the tire of his car, rendering the tire flat. I watched from the street as he ran his hand over the gashes, as he stared at the flattened tire in dismay. Probably a slow leak thanks to a nail or a rock. Or maybe somebody slashed his tire. Who knows?

And so he turned and walked home, leaving the car behind.

Dr. Joshua Giles is a good-looking guy. I'd be lying if I said I didn't think so. Not that I'm into that kind of thing, but he just *is*. He's a good-looking guy, and he knows it, too. That's the worst part. That's what makes me mad. He's tall, maybe six foot two or six foot three. Dark hair and eyes, the kind that women seem to like. He wears trendy, thick, black-framed glasses that hide his kindhearted eyes. I wonder if they're natural, those eyes, or if that's something they teach you in shrink school. To have kind eyes. A sympathetic smile. A rhythmic, measured nod. A solid handshake. I'm guessing it's all a ruse.

He dresses nicely. While I've got on ripped jeans and a hooded sweatshirt the color of gunmetal and torn at the hem, the drawstring missing, he's got on some kind of dressy, olive-colored pants dad-types wear. Not my dad, but other people's dads. Working dads. I have no idea what else is tucked under the black topcoat, but whatever it is, I'm guessing it's classy. And then there's the leather satchel that swings from the palm of his hand, all the way through town and into the adjoining neighborhoods where the burghers live, the rich people, in the older but renovated historic homes — Tudor cottages and American foursquare homes — that Pops and I couldn't afford. Everyone knows that's where the rich people live, tucked behind their decorative metal fences and sweeping lawns. It's a scant quarter-mile walk from Main Street in the opposite direction of my own house, overlooking Lake Michigan from a small bluff. From up on the hilltop, these homes overlook the downtown area, the fringes of town, the lake.

It's dark by the time we arrive. Cars drive past us, slowly heading home from work. Their headlights are on, navigating the way home. At some point a cell phone rings — his, not mine — and I freeze in place like a chipmunk, entirely motionless. The wind blows through me rather than around. It hurls itself right to my core, making everything down to my liver and spleen cold.

"Hello," he says, pausing on the street, answering the phone. His voice is gentle, telling the person on the other end of the line that he'll be home soon. He got held up at work; he's running late. He doesn't mention the tire of the car. He sounds strange and hollow in the vacancy of the nighttime street, his voice bouncing off concrete and trees. The call is short and sweet, laced with words like *darling* and *dear.* His wife. And then they say their goodbyes and he ends the call.

He walks quickly, the sound of his feet taking consistent steps on the pavement. I walk quickly, though my steps are silent. He steps over a pothole on the narrow street. I do, too. At one point he pauses and turns around, as if he knows he's in pursuit, and I fall quickly to the street in the prone position behind a parked car, feeling like an idiot as I do, but I do it, anyway, waiting, holding my breath, until the shrink gives up and continues on his way.

As Dr. Giles pushes through a squeaky metal fence and hikes up the long driveway, I remain on the other side of the street, squatting behind a parked car, a beat-up black Nissan that certainly doesn't belong on this street. I have no idea what I'm here to do or see, why I trailed him home. What was I hoping to gain from it? I don't know. But at least I know now where he lives, in a Cotswold cottage that should really be in some small English hamlet rather than here, in our dinky Michigan town. He lets himself in through the arched doorway, and there in the casement window she appears, the missus. She runs to him with small, precise footsteps, and he sweeps her into his arms where they kiss with that familiarity husbands and wives often share, a mastery of where hands and lips go, of whose head goes in which direction when they kiss, of how long they have before the rug rats appear. And then, like that, they do appear, two sprogs standing at his feet, arms raised, begging to be picked up. And he does; he picks them up, one at a time, the bigger one first followed by the little one. The whole scene is something I have no awareness of. No comprehension. No knowledge. It's as strange to me as a foreign language, the image of a happy, nuclear family — a mom, a dad, two kids and, no doubt, a dog. As conflicting to my family as black is to white. Polar opposites.

My childhood was something much different than this. My mother and Pops never fought; rather, it was the silence that did them in. The fact that they could go for days, occupying the same space, breathing in and out the same oxygen and carbon dioxide, without speaking, but rather moving around and around in silent isolated spheres, one for Mom, one for Pops and me.

But then again, unlike Dr. Giles and his wife, I hardly think Pops and my mother were in love. Well, one of them wasn't, anyway, while the other was head over heels.

His wife is pretty, but in this dolled-up way that doesn't really appeal to me. Even from this distance I can see that she's got on too much makeup, too much hair spray in her flaxen hair. She's just shy of me thinking she's a prima donna, but more like a lady who tries hard to look good for her husband when he comes home from work. Maybe that's not such a bad thing. She leans into him, his hands falling to her waistline, hers rising to his shoulders, so that for one split second I think that there, in the large bay windows, for all of the world to watch and see, they might just dance.

I can't hear the rug rats, but through the window I see them. I see the gigantic smiles on their faces as they giggle, watching their mother and father embrace, and for some strange reason it makes me mad. Jealousy is what it is. I'm jealous.

They have no idea I'm watching. If they did, I wonder if they'd care. Doesn't seem so to me. But still, I've seen enough. I don't need to watch this anymore.

I stand and turn to go, and as I do, I'm all but certain I hear something — a mewl, a bleat, a whine. A cry. I don't know. Some kind of noise, echoing up and down the street, through the trees.

"Hello?" I call out, but there's no response. Only the rustle of leaves in the trees. "Is someone there?" I ask, feeling again like a chicken as my heart starts to race and my head spins. It's dark out here, nearly black, the gleam of porch lights barely stretching down to the middle of the street where I stand. The wind blows again and I shiver, an earthquake of a shiver that rattles me from head to toe.

Is someone there? Is *something* there? Not that I can see. All I see are houses and trees, houses and trees. A car passes by, headlights illuminating the scene. I peer in the glow of the passing light, but still, I see nothing.

But then again I hear that noise.

"Hello?"

Nothing.

It's a squirrel, I tell myself. A chipmunk, a raccoon. A bird nesting in the trees. Garbage on the street. Litter. A hawk, an owl. The last few crickets that haven't been done in by the cold, singing their own little dirge.

But still, as rational as all that sounds in my head, I'm overcome by the strangest sensation that I'm not alone.

As I walk away, I realize this: someone is here with me, matching me stride for stride.

■ ■ ■ ■

# TUESDAY

■ ■ ■ ■

# QUINN

I wake up early the following morning and spend a few minutes putting together my puzzle pieces on the floor of Esther's room. I'm making progress, albeit not much, just the berry blue of a sky and nothing more. The rest of the image lies in an unkempt pile on the floor. I shower and dress for work. Ben calls early to see if there's been any word from Esther, and I tell him sadly no. He hasn't had any luck with his search, either.

Before leaving, I snatch some cash from Esther's and my Rent envelope in the kitchen drawer, one twenty-dollar bill and a couple of singles. It's empty now — the envelope — thanks to my Jimmy John's purchase and now this, and so I step on the foot pedal of the trash can, ready to toss it in.

And that's when I see the ATM receipts tucked away in the garbage can.

Normally they wouldn't catch my eye — I'm not one for picking through trash — but I see Esther's bank's insignia right away and know that they're not mine. They're Esther's receipts. I reach my hand inside the trash can, steering clear of a splatter of ketchup on a dirty napkin that the receipts are hidden beneath. I pull them out, three of them, three receipts dated Thursday, Friday and Saturday afternoons, each a withdrawal for five hundred dollars, cash. That's fifteen hundred bucks. One thousand five hundred dollars. A whole lotta moola, to be sure.

What in the world would Esther need fifteen hundred dollars for, taken out over the course of three days? I don't know for certain, but strawberry daiquiris in Punta Cana come to mind. Seems like a nice place for Jane Girard to take a vacation. Seems like a nice place for *me* to take a vacation, but I doubt in my life I'll ever make it to Punta Cana. Five hundred dollars is the maximum withdrawal limit for most banks, not that I'm one to know; I don't even have five hundred dollars to my name. Everything I make at work gets handed over to Esther straightaway to cover rent and utilities, leaving only some spare change for the occasional night out or a pair of new shoes.

*What is Esther doing walking around town with fifteen hundred dollars stuffed in her purse?* I wonder. But I can't think about this right now. Right now there are other things on my mind.

I'm about to head out the door when I throw it open and there, standing on the other side, is the building's maintenance man, John, who's, like, eighty years old and wears navy blue coveralls, though it's not like a person needs coveralls to change the occasional lightbulb or battle a colony of carpenter ants. His hand is raised in the air, ready to knock. Beside his feet is a toolbox, and in his hand is a whole assortment of things, tools I don't recognize, tools I do, a brand-new door handle and a dead-bolt lock, to boot.

"What's this?" I ask, staring down at the dead-bolt lock as he tears into the plastic box and removes it from its packaging.

For as much as I don't like Mrs. Budny, John I do. He's like a grandpa, like my grandpa who died when I was six years old, with his shock of white hair, wire-rimmed glasses, and his denture smile. "You asked for a new lock," John says to me, and it's snappy the way I say, "No, I didn't," though I don't mean to be snappy with John. I like John way too much to be snappy.

John's answer is immediate, as well. "Then it must have been the other one," he says, his left hand moving up and down around his face. "The one with the hair."

I know right away what he means. He's referring to Esther's hair, distinct and prominent, unmistakable, a conversation piece. The day my parents loaded up a U-Haul and helped move my twenty-nine cardboard boxes and me into the city apartment they were consternated by Esther's hair to say the least. It appalled them. In suburban America, people had blond hair or brown hair or red hair, but never some sort of odd combination of two or three. But Esther did, this piecemeal hair color that changed like paint swatches, brown to mocha to tawny to sand. My mother pulled me aside by the arm and begged, "Are you sure you want to do this? It's not too late to change your mind," while keeping one eye on Esther all the time.

I was sure. I wanted to do this.

But now, of course, I'm wondering if I should have been a little more judicious, a little less sure.

I ask John again if he's certain Esther requested to have the locks changed and he says yes, he is certain. He even shows me the paperwork to prove it, an order by Mrs.

Budny to change the locks in unit 304. The date of the request is three days ago. Three days ago Esther got on her phone and called Mrs. Budny's office to request our locks be changed.

*Why, Esther, why?*

But I don't have to think on this too long. The answer comes to me before John fires up his electric screwdriver and starts removing the old dead bolt from the steel door. I've been a bad roommate and Esther wants me gone. She wants to replace me with Megan or *Meg* from Portage Park, or someone akin to Meg. Someone who pays the rent on time, who helps finance the utilities, who doesn't leave the lights on all the time, who doesn't talk in her sleep.

Before I leave, I snatch a spare key from John's extended hand. I'm sure that wasn't in Esther's plan. And then I take a cab out to Lincoln Square and head to the police district station, a light brick building that spans an entire city block, surrounded by flags and parked police cars, the white Crown Victorias with their red lettering and a blue stripe along the side. We Serve and Protect, it says.

I don't know if I should be here, but nevertheless, I am.

I stand outside for a good ten minutes or

more, wondering if I really want to step foot inside the police station. Esther is missing, yes, maybe. But also maybe not. I could wait it out, give it a few more days to see if she comes home. The 311 operator more or less told me, anyway, that there wasn't a whole lot the police department could do, whether or not I filed a report. *People are allowed to up and disappear if they want to,* she'd said. There's nothing illegal about that. Other than putting Esther's name into some sort of database, I wasn't certain there was much they could do.

But what if filing a police report helps bring Esther home? Then it's totally worth it.

On the other hand, what if Esther doesn't want me to file a report? What if she'd rather I just leave her alone?

And so I'm really in quite the conundrum as I stand there, back pressed to the light bricks, wondering what to do: file a missing-persons report or no.

In the end I do. I file the report.

I meet with an officer and provide the basics for which he asks, including a physical description of Esther and the particulars into her quote-unquote disappearance. I'm sparse on the details, leaving out many things of which I assume Esther would rather not be made public knowledge, such as the fact that she's been meeting with a psychologist. I provide a photo, one I find on my cell, an image of Esther and me together at our neighborhood's Midsommarfest, a summer street festival, listening to live music and feasting on ears of corn, as behind us, the setting sun glinted off the buildings, turning the world to gold. We asked a passerby to take the photo, some dude who could hardly stop salivating over Esther long enough to snap the picture. She had corn in her teeth, melted butter on her chin and hands, and yet he, like I, thought she was beautiful. She *is* beautiful. Magnetic, really, the kind of individual who draws people with her idiosyncratic hair and heterochromatic eyes — whether or not they're a sham. But more than her hair and her eyes and her impossibly flawless skin is her kindness, that tendency of hers to make people feel special whether or not they're as ordinary as, well, as ordinary as me.

I pass the photo along to the officer and even he takes a second look and says, "Pretty girl," and I say that she is, and I'm half certain we both blush.

The report will be filed; someone will be in touch. Esther isn't met with the same regard as, say, a four-year-old girl who's gone missing. I'm not sure quite what I expect: a search team to line up before me with orange vests and search-and-rescue dogs; squad cars; helicopters; volunteers on horseback wandering the streets of Chicago with a rope tracker, calling out her name in tandem. I guess this is what I hoped would happen, but none of it does. Instead, he tells me I could hang up posters, ask around town, consider hiring a PI. The officer also says, with an unsmiling face, that they'll likely need to search our residence. I assure him I've looked; she's not there. He gives me a look reminiscent of my little sister's looks — as if he's Einstein and I'm a giant ignoramus — and then again says that someone will be in touch. I say okay, before heading on to work, not quite sure whether I accomplished something, or made things even worse.

# ALEX

Morning begins like every other day: waking up at the crack of dawn, chugging down a Mountain Dew, slipping past a passed-out Pops on my way to work. My mind tries to make sense of the footsteps that followed me home last night in vain. Was someone there — and if so, then who? — or was it simply my brain playing a trick on me, a figment of the imagination? I don't know. Already this morning I'm predicting how the day at the café will go, and I'm dreading every single minute of it, from Priddy harassing me for my persistent tardiness, to me, wriggling out of the sandy jacket and getting down to work, washing mounds of dishes left behind by cooks in the sink, the water so hot it scalds my hands. Red and Braids bellyaching about the meagerness of their tips. Broken dishes. Spilled food. Eight hours of feeling like a loser.

My only hope as I lumber along the restive shores of Lake Michigan on the way to greet Priddy is that Pearl will be there, sitting at the window of the café, eyes again on the office of Dr. Giles. This is the only thing that gets me through the monotonous, repetitive trek to work, through the dismal prospect of the next eight hours on my feet, scurrying around the café, gathering other people's used forks and knives in my hand. Washing their dishes. Wiping spilled food off the tables and floors. Day after day after day, knowing in the back of my mind that this will never end.

I continue on along the lake, past the stationary carousel, and head into town.

There's an Amtrak station in town, not too far from the beach. A half mile, a quarter mile, I don't know. I can't say. Just on the other side of the sand-strewn beach parking lot. It's small, a waiting area and the ticket booth, with a few bike racks that remain empty at this time in the morning. There isn't even a john. The train passes through a couple times a day heading one of two ways: Grand Rapids — eastbound — or Chicago — westbound. Today it's eastbound, the Pere Marquette to Grand Rapids, Michigan. I've never been there before.

The station is quiet when I pass by on my daily morning trek to work, only a couple riders climbing on board for the two-and-a-half-hour ride. Another stepping off, having just arrived from Chicago. They carry duffel bags and suitcases in their hands. Some have hands that are empty, just a purse strung over the shoulder or the wallet in the pocket of their jeans. It's a short commute either way, the kind you can pull off, round trip, in a day. There and back again in the very same day.

And that, it seems, is just what Pearl's done as I watch her drop down the large steps of the Superliner and set foot into town.

Again.

She's gone and come back again, and it seems that I'm the only one who knows.

Turns out, I'm none the wiser for it, though I can't help but wonder why.

I wait all morning at the café for her to show.

The day is generally quiet. The morning crowd — a word I use loosely, *crowd* — is made up of old folks mostly, those who don't have to scurry off to work or school. In time they disappear and are replaced with the school district's bus drivers who, in time, disappear, too.

And that's when Pearl appears.

It's all as it was the day she first arrived.

She stands with poise, waiting for a table, and then, when it's her turn, asks for a spot by the window, out of which she can watch and stare, taking in Dr. Giles's office across the way, the few, random pedestrians who come and go up and down the street.

I surveil her as she peels the scarf from around her neck and removes the hat, setting them both on an empty chair to her left. She shakes out of a coat and drapes it over the back of her chair, and I think to myself: *Don't stop there,* imagining the way that on the lake's shore she stripped down to her underwear. But of course she does. She asks for coffee when Red arrives, sits in her chair and crosses her legs at the ankle, the Ugg boots wet as if she'd been foot-slogging through the lake all day. There's sand on them, too, wet sand, adhered to the sheepskin like burs.

Red is a big girl, her arms squashy like bread dough, a chalky white that's been hidden from sunlight by a cheesecloth towel, the yeast inside making it rise. Her voice, her mannerism, everything about her, is raunchy and crass. And then there's the smell of her, something along the lines of feet, stinky feet, a miasma of feet. Her thighs rub against each other as she walks, overlapping.

But then there is Pearl, the antithesis of everything Red is, whether or not she's as mad as a March hare. She's older than me, but that doesn't matter these days. Five, maybe ten years older. Enough that she carries a poise and finesse about her that most eighteen-year-old girls don't have.

But not too old that it's weird for me to stare.

As Red passes by again, Pearl orders her meal. Her voice is quiet, nothing more than a whisper. Red leans in close to ask what she said. From where I stand I tune out all the other noise so I can hear Pearl's somnolent voice over the chaos of the café — the ding of a cash register, the opening and closing of a door, hushed music coming from a CD player. It's not that she's shy. No, that's not it. Instead, it's an act of diplomacy, a subtlety, tact. Not screaming over the noise, because that would be crass.

Red disappears to shout the order to one of the short-order cooks — her voice all gritty and gravelly like someone who smokes too much, which, like Braids, she does, the two of them teeter-tottering outside all day on their rotating smoke breaks — while Priddy gives me the death stare, telling me to get to work. Talk about ironic. Sexism is what it is. I'm being harassed. I should sue.

And yet, I return to wiping tables down, swiping the dirty dishes off and into a dishpan where they plink, glass on glass, silver on silver.

The November sun blazes through the window as it so often does around this same time every day, at noon, crossing over the meridian at its highest peak and right into our space. I watch as patrons' placid faces begin to glare, eyes squinting, hands on head as if in salute, blinded by the light.

If it weren't for the sun I wouldn't have approached the window in the first place. But I do, crossing the room to tug at the strings on the Venetian blinds, lowering them just enough to keep the sunlight at bay, and yet not restrict Pearl's view of the street. That's the last thing I want to do. To take away her view. I know how much she likes it, staring out the window, monitoring Dr. Giles's office from here.

It's her shampoo that I smell first — or lotion, maybe hair spray, how the heck would I know? — some sort of blend of grapefruit and mint that stings my olfactory receptors. Truth be told, it also makes me weak in the knees. I'm not one to swoon. But this time I do. My hands tremble, glassware jiggling in the dishpan so that I set it down so nothing will break. I wonder to myself if she could be the woman, the ethereal figure, living at the periphery of my dreams? The one who comes to me at night and begs of me, *Let's go . . .*

"I've seen you before," she says as I approach, her words halfhearted and meandering, her eyes never looking at me.

Is she talking to me? I look around to be sure.

I'm the only one here.

She says it again, different this time but still the same. "I saw you the other day."

"I know," I say, my voice flickering like a lightbulb that's about to conk out and die. A tiny voice inside my head reminds me that I'm a chicken. A loser. A pansy. The closest I ever get to beautiful women are the nudie girls from magazines who live in my closet so that Pops can't see. I've dated exactly three girls in my life, not a one that lasted for longer than two weeks.

"By the beach," she says.

"I know," I say. "I saw you, too."

It's the best that I can do.

From behind me, I hear a little boy's mother tell him to sit down and eat. I turn to see. As he leans across the table to touch his mother's hand, she pulls back quickly, and snaps, "Don't touch me." It's emphatic, the way she says it, a proclamation that

217

reminds me of my own mother. *Don't touch me, Alex.* But this mother's words come with a postscript. "Your hands are covered in syrup," she says, handing the boy a napkin.

My mother never told me why she didn't want me to touch her. It was simply, *Don't touch me.*

"You could have said hi," Pearl tells me then, drawing me away from the memories of my mother. Her eyes run this time from down to up, taking in my black gym shoes, my cheap pleated work pants and uniform shirt and bow tie, and I think, *What do I say to this?* All logic would have me ask why she was swimming in the bitter cold lake in the middle of November. Why she didn't have a bathing suit, a beach towel? Doesn't she know about hypothermia and freezing to death? Frostbite?

But that would be lame.

"Do you have a name?" I ask instead, trying hard to play it cool, and she says, without ever once looking at me, "I do."

And then I wait, on the edge of my proverbial seat, for her to tell me what it is. I wait so long that I start to form ideas in my head: Mallory, Jennifer, Amanda.

But then her food arrives — Red elbowing me out of the way to get through with the hot plate — and just like that she starts to eat, staring out the spotted window at pedestrians on the street, completely incognizant of the sun in her eyes or me, lingering a half step behind her, waiting for a name.

She has a name.

But she doesn't tell me what it is.

# QUINN

At work I find that I can concentrate on nothing but Esther. Little does she know it, but she occupies every spare moment of my time. My phone rings and the first thought on my mind is Esther. Is it Esther? But it's not Esther. I hear my name called over the PA system, beckoning me to reception, where I run quickly down the gleaming hardwood floors of the law firm, certain it's Esther, that she's there at the receptionist's desk, waiting for me, but instead I see a bombastic attorney sending me to deliver documents to the office of some expert witness to be analyzed. I scurry quickly off on my task, my mind still consumed with Esther, feeling hurt and worried all at the same time. It comes to me in random moments, this fact that Esther is trying to get rid of me, a betrayal that is sometimes overshadowed for this unmistakable feeling that something is wrong, that something has happened to her.

The minute I return to the law firm from my errand, I seek out Ben and come to learn that he's at a stalemate in his search, as well. Though he's made attempts to track down a Mr. or Mrs. Vaughan, his search turned up empty. Ben is seated at his own office cube when I come in from behind, startling him in his swivel chair. He rubs at his head and sighs, losing hope like me. On the computer screen before him are three tormenting words: *no records found.*

"No word from Esther?" he asks.

I shake my head and say, "No word."

I am not the only one who finds it impossible to focus on the tedium and stupidity of work. I couldn't care less right now about things such as Bates labels and document productions and what kind of deadline some deranged attorney needs me to photocopy thousands of documents by. It all seems so frivolous and petty when Esther is missing.

I'm not the only one feeling frustrated by this strange turn of events. Ben feels it, too, and there in his cheerless cube we lament on how impossible it is to focus on work when work is the farthest thing from our minds. We make a pact to leave and by two-fifteen we both phony up an illness at work:

food poisoning. We grope our midsections and claim to have eaten something rotten, putrid, rank. *The roast beef,* I say, and Ben blames his chopped chicken salad. We threaten to vomit, and it's immediate, almost, the way we're told to go home. *Just go.*

And so we do.

We share a cab, my treat because Ben is trekking out to my apartment in Andersonville to help me sort this mystery out. He offers to split the fare with me — of course he does, my very own knight in shining armor (he just doesn't know it yet) — but I say no. The cabbie hurls us through the streets of Chicago, tossing us this way and that on the torn leather seat. He leaves the Loop and hops on Lake Shore Drive, exiting at Foster. I watch Lake Michigan out the filthy car window as we pass, the water blue, as is the sky, but that doesn't mean either of them are the slightest bit warm. It's a clear day, the kind of day where they say you can see all the way to Michigan from the top of the Willis Tower. I don't know what you can see, just the other side of the lake pouring onto the shores of some negligible town, I suppose. Outside it's cold, the wind pitiless, and though I'm pretty sure it has nothing to do with our tempestuous weather, the nickname Windy City feels entirely apropos.

The cabbie reaches a good sixty miles per hour on Lake Shore Drive and though we're both scared as all get-out, in the backseat Ben and I laugh. It feels wrong to laugh. Almost. Esther could be in real danger. But there's also a bit of desperation in it, a bit of agony and misery. It isn't a lighthearted laugh.

I'm concerned about Esther, of course, and yet there's a part of me still put off by Esther's whole lavish plot to replace me. So many of the clues point to Esther: Esther wrote the creepy notes to *My Dearest;* Esther placed the ad in the *Reader;* Esther changed her own name; Esther had a passport photo taken; Esther requested the locks be changed on our apartment door. Esther, Esther, Esther.

So why should I be worried for Esther when this is all her doing?

Also, if I don't laugh, I might just go berserk.

As we emerge from the cab on my little residential block of Farragut Avenue, the wind whips through my hair, dragging it some way other than the way which my feet need to go. It's with instinct that I grab for Ben's arm and he steadies me before I release my hold and let go.

"You okay?" he asks, and I say, "Yeah. I'm okay. It's windy." But still, I feel his arm upon my skin. What is it that he sees in Priya, after all? Why not *me* instead of *her*?

But I can't think about that right now.

Ben goes first, and I follow closely behind, up the concrete steps, through the white front doors and into the vacuous entryway. There's nothing there but sixteen mailboxes and a dirty, gray doormat, smothered in grime and debris.

Welcome, says the doormat, though it's placed upside down so you see it as you leave.

I have no idea what Ben and I plan to do, or how it is that we'll attempt to find Esther. But I do know that I'm happy as pie to have someone here by my side, someone practical like Ben who can help me sort through all these inane ideas running amuck in my mind. It's also lonely and I'm desperate for someone, anyone, to keep me company, for the sound of voices other than those which live inside my head. But more than anything, I'm happy it's Ben.

I gather my mail from one of the mailboxes, and up the stairwell we go, Ben in the lead, me in the rear. I'd be lying if I said I didn't stare at his tail end.

At the door I fumble with my keys, having almost forgotten that my key — the little copper thingie I've had for nearly a year — no longer fits inside the door, and I fish around in my pockets for the new one, the one I snatched from John the maintenance man's aging hands. Once inside the apartment, I kick the door closed and drop the stash of mail on the countertop and walk away, thinking nothing of it until Ben holds up a catalog for me to see.

"I have to know," he asks, "which one of you shops here. You or Esther?" And there's a smile on his face, a teasing smile, but suddenly I feel irritated and confused. I've seen that catalog before. It's a regular in Esther's and my mailbox, the kind of thing that hits the recycle bin the moment it arrives, like the takeout menu from the deli where Esther and I both got sick. Why do we keep getting this catalog? On the front is a woman, no more than twenty years old, with some sort of occult ensemble on, a tunic dress that could be cute if it wasn't decked out in skulls and crossbones, platform heels with spikes extruding from all sides. There's a choker on her neck, black leather, pulled so taut it's a wonder she doesn't gag.

I reach out for the catalog in Ben's hand and for whatever reason flip to the reverse side to see why this catalog keeps winding up in our mailbox. Does this catalog belong to Esther? Was she a vamp in a former life? A goth? Did she dress in all black and go around clubbing under the pseudonym of Raven or Tempest or Drusilla? Did she have an odd fascination with death, a fetish for the supernatural? I don't know. I have this pesky feeling that I don't know who Esther is anymore.

But instead of seeing Esther's name there on the address label as I expect to see, it reads, *Kelsey Bellamy or current resident of 1621 W. Farragut Avenue.*

That's my apartment building, but who is Kelsey Bellamy?

I never asked Esther about her old room-mate and she never said anything. It was as if she didn't exist, though I knew she did, of course. It was the reason for the vacant space, for Esther's need to fill a room once complete with life but suddenly void of it.

I have one thought then, one memory: the name etched into the wall in my bedroom closet, the forgotten fragment of a photograph bearing traces of Esther's hair, the one I found in the closet of the vacant bedroom after I'd moved in.

I hurry quickly from the room and into my bedroom. Ben follows behind asking,

"Where are you going?" and there in the bedroom I show him. I slide open the doors of the reach-in closet and start pulling out items at random, tossing dresses on hangers to the floor, pushing aside a rolling suitcase I've never used, a graduation gift from my folks in case I ever had the urge to *get up and go*. Right now I have the urge to get up and go. But where?

"What are you looking for?" asks Ben as I point a quivering hand at six consequential letters placed on the drywall, scored into the popcorn walls with something like a carving knife. An hour ago they meant nothing to me, but now they do.

*Kelsey.*


It's all just fun and games until somebody gets hurt.

Isn't that how the saying goes?

It couldn't be more apropos.

We're sitting in my apartment, Ben on the rose-colored sofa, me on the black-and-white mod plaid chair because it seems like the right thing to do, the *unassuming* thing to do. I could have sat next to him; he'd sat first and he left me room. But that, of course, seemed foolhardy and pert. And what if after I sat, he rose and found another chair? That wouldn't be good.

No, this way I'm in the driver's seat, in the saddle, at the helm. I'm the one in control. And anyway, from the other side of the industrial iron coffee table, the view is more clear. *The better to see you with, my dear.*

His light brown hair is a sleek square cut, the kind that sends him to the barber every other week for a trim. His expression has taken on that serious air as it does when he's working, completing the all-important task of Bates labeling documents like me. But instead of Bates labels, his fingers type across the keyboard quickly, and then he stares at the screen. And then he types and he stares, and he types and he stares. His feet rise up to the coffee table, his work shoes removed. His socks are black, a crew cut, pulled halfway up to his knee. He's discarded the tie and unbuttoned a button or two of a vintage oxford shirt. He wears no undershirt beneath, the skin there tanned and smooth.

I want to touch it.

And he says in a grisly, morbid sort of way, "This is weird," and his eyes rise up to meet my eyes, which are already on his.

Outside it's nearing five o'clock. Soon our coworkers will go home, fleeing the black high-rise like rats fleeing a sinking ship.

Dusk is falling quickly out the apartment windows. The close of day. I rise from the mod plaid chair to flip on a light, an arched floor lamp that fills the space with a yellow hue.

"What's weird?" I ask, and Ben says, "Listen to this."

He clears his throat and reads. "Kelsey Bellamy, twenty-five, of Chicago, Illinois, died Tuesday, September 23, at Methodist Hospital. She was born on February 16, 1989, and moved to Chicago from her childhood home of Winchester, Massachusetts, in 2012. She worked as a substitute teacher in the Chicago Public School system for two years before her death. Kelsey is survived by her fiancé, Nicholas Keller; her parents, John and Shannon Bellamy; siblings Morgan and Emily; and countless grandparents, aunts, uncles, cousins and friends. Visitation will be from 3:00 p.m. to 8:00 p.m. Friday, September 26, at Palmer Funeral Home in Winchester, Massachusetts. In lieu of flowers, donations can be made to Food Allergy Research and Education."

He searches for a date of the obituary: last year. September of last year, mere weeks before I moved in with Esther. *Weeks!*

"Well, I'll be damned," I say, and I think

to myself, *How sad,* but also, *Holy shit.*

"Are you sure she's the one, the *right* one? *She's* the Kelsey Bellamy who used to live *here*?" And then I think, *My God!* I hope she didn't die *here,* and I have this image of a dead Kelsey Bellamy, dead on my bedroom floor. I shake the image from my mind.

"Well, I can't be sure," says Ben, "but she's the only Kelsey Bellamy in all of Chicago that I can find. The age seems right, too. Can't imagine Esther living with a sixty-year-old."

"I can't believe Esther didn't tell me this," I say, but the thing is, I can. Two or three days ago, I'd have said, *No way,* but now I can't be sure. I'm starting to discover there are many things about Esther's life that I didn't know.

Esther, Jane or whoever the heck she is.

"How'd she die?" I ask.

"Doesn't say," Ben says, "but I'm guessing . . ." And then his voice trails off, only to be interrupted with, "Look here," as he scoots over to make even more room for me on the small apartment sofa. He doesn't have to ask twice, though I'm slightly offended by the amount of space he believes is needed for my rear end. He's pointing at his tablet screen as I toss a throw pillow to the ground, and slide in beside him. And there on his tablet is an image of Kelsey Bellamy.

She's lovely. That's the first thought that runs through my mind. Though not in your typical blond hair, blue eyes kind of lovely. More like a gothic lovely with jet-black hair and smoky eyes, hence the goth catalog delivered to her this afternoon. Her skin is an ashen white. It's whiter than white as if it's been slathered with baby powder — or as if, perhaps, she's a ghost, already dead. She dresses like a goth, I guess, but with a certain femininity to it — a black Lolita skirt, a ruffled blouse, black lipstick.

I have a hard time picturing Kelsey Bellamy as a substitute teacher.

"This is weird," I say, "really weird."

"You're telling me," says Ben as he continues his search to see what else he can find. As we sit there — pressed together on the small apartment sofa so that our knees hover mere inches from each other, eyes staring at the same pinwheel on the same display screen as the tablet thinks, me inhaling his crisp, citrusy cologne — we come across Kelsey's Facebook page, whereby friends and family leave mournful, tear-jerking status updates about their beloved daughter, granddaughter, niece and friend, with claims made by some that Kelsey's roommate was the one responsible for her death. *A terrible accident,* some say, but others call it negligence. Some claim she should be convicted of manslaughter. *She* as in Esther. *The roommate,* they say. They say Esther — my Esther — did this. That she killed Kelsey.

"You don't think . . ." asks Ben, but he stops just short of finishing that thought out loud.

But yes, I do think. I think exactly what Ben is thinking though neither of us can say the words aloud.

I can't even begin to describe what goes through my mind.

And then there's my stomach, which has sunken somewhere down to my toes.

All at once, I think I may puke.

# ALEX

In the end it's curiosity that makes me decide to step foot inside that derelict house across the street from mine. It's dark out, nighttime, as I walk home from another long day of work, my feet and legs bone-tired. As I close in on the house, I see the flicker of light, same as Pops and I did the night before: *on, off.*

And that's what gets my attention.

A bird, a common grackle, sits on the contorted roof shingles, singing a rasping, croaky song, its luminous blue head glowing in the glossy moonlight. It sits there perched on the old, sunken-in roof with black bug eyes that stare down onto the street at me, its cusp-like beak pointed in my direction. I take it all in: the bird's shiny body; the lustrous blue head; its long, attenuating tail; its feet, brown and gnarled like an old lady's hands.

The moon, a perfectly round sphere,

ascends high into the nighttime sky as lazy clouds float by.

I run home first to grab some tools, and then from a distance appraise the house, trying to figure out the best way to get inside. I want to know who it is that's living in there and whether or not it really is, as Pops thinks, a squatter. I bring with me some pastry I carried home from the café. A chocolate croissant, stuffed inside a pocket. Whoever's living in there might just be hungry.

I cross the street and settle on the fragmenting sidewalk, seeing the names at my feet, names sculpted decades ago into the solidifying concrete, proof that someone once lived here. That this home wasn't always abandoned.

It's the blue hour, the time of day when the entire world takes on a navy hue, the derelict house becoming blue, too. A few of the windows have been boarded up with plywood, and so those entryways are out. I'm not about to wrangle with the plywood with my bare hands. It's pinned to the window casement with rusty old nails so that I'll probably die of tetanus if I touch the darn things. That's not really something I want to mess around with — the spasms and muscle stiffness, the risk of death —

and so instead I use the tools I brought from home, a Craftsman nail puller that belongs to Pops and a pair of industrial work gloves.

I slip my hands into the gloves and use the nail puller to pry the rusty old nails from a boarded-up, busted window — in the back of the house where I'm less likely to be seen — and remove the plywood from the yellow siding. I drop it to the ground. And then I rely on a stepstool I dragged along to climb inside, using the end of the nail puller to push out any remaining bits of broken glass so I don't get cut. It's getting dark out here — hard to see much of anything — and yet it's as I'm climbing in that the moon's glow hits the rear of the house and I realize it's all been for naught, for less than ten yards away stands another window, plywood removed, glass already smashed. Squatters.

Inside, the ceiling caves right on in, hunks of drywall falling off, leaving the framework of the home exposed. It's dark inside, but thankfully for me, I brought a flashlight, too. I feel a wall for the light switch, surprised — and yet not surprised — to find the home is without electricity, probably shut off years ago. Just means whatever illegal tenants have been camping out here also have their own flashlight, the light Pops and I spied radiating from the open window.

*On, off.* A flashlight or a lantern. Maybe a candle.

Inside I discover that when the owners left, they left quickly. They didn't take much with them when they went. But still, it's been stripped of appliances, and furniture is missing, things other people could sell and profit from. What remains are the knick-knacks and other novelty items, things with sentimental value but not monetary. A vase, a chessboard, a defunct clock whose hands will forever be stuck at 8:14. In time many of the utilities were shut off for nonpayment, the water only after the pipes froze and burst. The bank tried to sell the home at auction, but no one made a single bid. It wasn't worth the cost to level it to the ground, and so instead the home remained. The neighbors had half a mind to light the thing on fire and watch it burn; wouldn't be such a bad idea in my opinion. But no one wanted to mess with the ghost of Genevieve, a thing that doesn't even exist.

Inside there is writing on the walls. Graffiti. Some kind of creeping vine grows right through the splintered walls and into the home. The lawn is a mess, overgrown shrubbery all but taking over the home's facade. In the backyard, there are downed trees everywhere, their remaining stumps blackened with rot. Inside there are the oddly normal facets of life: a stack of melamine cereal bowls resting in the cabinet, covered with webs and rodent droppings. There are chunks of fallen drywall from where the roof sank into the room, the shingles of the roof exposed. An impromptu skylight. Insulation falls out of the walls like stuffing from a torn teddy bear.

What I expect to see as I tiptoe my way through the derelict home is a squatter, maybe even a small family of squatters, huddled together in blankets on the floor. Or maybe a bunch of teenage hoodlums, smoking pot where they don't think anyone will see, or some hobo passing through town, looking for a warmer, dryer place to get some sleep beneath a somewhat intact roof.

But maybe I'm not as smart as everyone seems to believe, because it doesn't ever cross my mind, not one time, that I might see Pearl standing there in the abandoned living room, but there she is. I spot her ombré hair, which falls in waves down her back, the redness that strikes her cheeks as if she'd been slapped. As I watch on, she presses her fingertips to those cheeks; I can tell they're cold. Even inside, in the unheated home, with broken windows that embrace the autumn night, they've gone numb. Her eyes glisten, starting to water in the cold November air. Her nose does, too, as puffs of air emerge into the room from her salmon-colored lips, whitish-gray puffs like clouds.

And now, standing in near-darkness, out the open window, the bird — the grackle — again begins to sing, a creepy little elegy, and a plump full moon shines in through the barbed broken glass, and Pearl turns to me and smiles.

"Hi there," she says. "I was wondering if you'd ever come."

"What are you doing here?" I ask, and she says, her voice calm like a millpond, "The same thing as you." Her tone is poetic, rhythmical, and as she says these words, she turns her small feet in my direction. "Just nosing around," she says as her index finger traces a line of dust on the fireplace mantel, and she stares down at the filth on her skin before wiping it on the leg of her pants.

It's dark in the room, not black, but still dark, the full moon trying hard to find its way in. It glints from behind the obese clouds, the light flickering on and off, as does the light from the flashlight in Pearl's hand as she presses the power button again and again. *On, off.*

I think of Pops, sitting all alone in the house across the street, watching the blinks of light from the window. *Damn squatters,* I hear him say. *Damn squatters are living over there again.*

But no, I think. Not squatters. Pearl.

These things are mutually exclusive; they are to me at least. This girl cannot be a squatter because, well, because she just can't. She deserves more than this, more than the dirt, the grime, the filth. She deserves better.

I come into the living room slowly, not quite sure what to say or do. This is the living room, I know, because there's a couch here still, a plaid sofa, and the remnants of what was once a fireplace, a cast-iron insert surrounded by a marble mantel that's covered in dust, Pearl's finger now traced through it like a road map.

On the floor beside her feet lies a blanket, a holey, moth-eaten blanket, and a flat cushion, one that I'm guessing she took from the sofa, a place to lay her head. The fabric matches the couch, the blue country plaid that I have trouble believing was ever in style. But it was. Once. Long ago. My heart splinters a little bit, thinking of Pearl laying her pretty head on that ratty pillow and spending her night sleeping on the dirty, rigid floor. Before me, she wraps her arms around herself and shivers. It's no more than fifty-some degrees, I'd bet. My eyes rove again to the fireplace, the hearth empty and cold.

"You're sleeping here?" I ask, though the answer is obvious, and I want to tell her about the rats, the bugs, the signs outside that say No Trespassing and Not Approved for Occupancy, but I don't. I'm guessing she already knows about these things. She doesn't answer my question, but simply stares, her bewildering eyes trying hard to read mine, as mine do her. Instead, I say, "You know they say this house is haunted," and I wonder if I should say more, about Genevieve, about the little girl that died in a bathtub, her spirit said to haunt all who enter this home. But I don't. I don't have time to say a thing before she smiles at me, a confident smile, and says decisively with a shrug of her shoulders, "I don't believe in ghosts."

I smile back at her and say, "Yeah. Me neither," as my hands inadvertently find their way to my pockets, coming across the chocolate croissant. But my smile isn't confident at all, and my words come out thick and breathy as if I've swallowed cotton and can hardly find the voice to speak. They shake, too, as do my hands. I might even wheeze. I draw the croissant from my pocket, flattened now and a tad bit pathetic, and offer it reluctantly to Pearl. She shakes her head and says to me, "No."

Before me, she stands: an ingénue. That's the way she looks to me. The girl next door or, maybe, the damsel in distress. Something along those lines, or maybe that's just who I want her to be. She looks tired, cold and maybe even a little bit scared. Up close, I see that her clothes are shabby — and not, of course, shabby chic, but the kind that looks like she's been trekking across the country for days, sleeping on some dirty, dusty floor. But still, she brings out the introvert in me, that kind of anti-social loner who doesn't know the first thing about talking to girls. It has nothing to do with her, but rather the fact that she is a girl — a *woman* — and a pretty one at that. That's what makes my hands shake, what makes my words hard to find, makes my sight line fall to the repulsive floors beneath my feet instead of into her eyes.

"What's your name?" she asks me, and, glancing at her quickly, transiently, I say that it's Alex.

But when I ask her her own name, she says sagely, "My mother told me I shouldn't talk to strangers," and it's the smile on her lips that says it all. She isn't as bashful as she'd like for me to believe. There's a bit of playfulness going on here, maybe even subterfuge, but I can't say that I mind. In fact, I kind of like it.

"You're already talking to me," I say, but still, she's not going to tell me her name. I don't pry. There could be any number of reasons why she won't. She's on the run, here to hide. She's in trouble with the police, or maybe even some guy. It's none of my business. I think of her and Dr. Giles, the way her eyes gazed through the café window at him. The way I saw her yesterday, ebbing away on the street, his eyes watching as she disappeared over the hill at the far end of town. Had she been there already, in the blue cottage, talking to him? I don't know. I'm guessing her being here has something to do with him, that maybe she's a patient, but the way she stares out the café window with fascination and curiosity, maybe even a bit of nostalgia mixed in, I think that it might be more than that. There might be something more to it, something that goes beyond the realm of a doctor-patient relationship. But that's just a hunch, some bedtime story I've made up. I don't really know.

"How long have you been staying here?" I ask, and she shrugs.

"A couple days," she says. "I guess."

There's a cheap motel in town, a bed-and-breakfast and one of those extended-stay hotels. There are summer rental homes, beach homes, a campground or two. But I'm guessing these are things she can't afford, so I don't tell her this. I'd give her money if I could, but I don't have money. Though it's hard to see in the murkiness of the room, I look, anyway, for signs of maltreatment or abuse, such as healing bruises, a fractured bone, a limp. Something to tell me she's on the run from something or somebody, but there's none.

It's as she wraps those spindly arms around her body, and shudders from the cold, that I say to her, "Too bad we can't start a fire in there," as my finger points to the dilapidated fireplace, now little more than a grubby hole in the wall.

As I step forward to the fireplace, I feel the floors beneath my feet start to give, and I move quickly, as if I hover long enough I might just disappear into quicksand, a black hole. Thankfully, I don't. As I pause for a moment to gather my bearings — seeing the way the carpeted floors just sank a good inch beneath my feet — I feel grateful that

I'm still here. Not Approved for Occupancy, the sign says, and now I know why. When I get to the fireplace, I eyeball the inside, absolutely certain the chimney itself must be filled with bird nests, squirrel nests and other soot and debris. I'm no chimney sweep, but I'd bet my life the bricks of the chimney are missing and the mortar desperately needs to be fixed. And that's all on the outside; the inside alone, the cast-iron insert, is covered with so much grime and smut it'd probably be the first thing to combust if I were to start a fire, that or the inside of the house would fill with carbon monoxide, and before either of us knew it, we'd drift off to sleep and die, joining Genevieve in the afterlife.

"You sure?" she asks me as she eyes the fireplace herself, and I consider this — fire, carbon monoxide, death — and say quite simply, "It'd be a bad idea."

But I have something else in mind.

I lower the zipper on my sweatshirt and remove it, handing it to the girl. "Here," I say, "put this on," but she doesn't take it right away. Instead, she stares at the sweatshirt in my shaking hands, and I start to feel like a fool, as if I've crossed some sort of malapropos line. I think about pulling it back, about putting it back on and pretending this never happened. I feel her eyes watching me, looking at the sweatshirt in my hand.

But then she takes the sweatshirt into her own grasp and says to me, "That's sweet of you. Really it is. But won't you be cold?" And I shrug my shoulders and mutter, "Naw," but of course it's not true. I'm already cold. But soon I'll head home for the night, into a soft bed with blankets and a house whose thermostat is set to sixty-eight degrees. Soon I won't be cold. But she will. She'll be here in this cold, dilapidated home all night.

As she slides my sweatshirt over her own hoodie, her long, rippled hair falling over the bulgy hood, her hands getting stuffed into the soft, worn cotton of the already-warmed pockets, I realize I kind of like the idea of my sweatshirt keeping her warm for the night.

I don't stay long. I don't want to overstay my welcome.

But even more importantly is the fact that I haven't done a thing yet to humiliate myself, and I'm hoping to keep it that way. But for a few minutes I do stay. I stay and watch as she sets herself down on the floor, covering her body with the moth-eaten blanket. I stay while she folds her legs up in what we used to call Indian-style and hums quietly beneath her breath. I cross my own arms across myself — warmed now by only a thin T-shirt — and think to myself that Pops and my garage would be warmer than this. So, too, would our wooden shed. But this girl doesn't know me from Adam. I find it impossible to believe she'd spend the night in my garage.

Heck, with Pops likely out cold, I could bring her right on into my room and there, in my bed, she could sleep, snug and cozy and warm — with me on the floor, of course. I let that image dwell in my brain for just a little while.

But she doesn't look that naive, and so I don't bother to ask.

She'd just say no, and then I'd feel like some degenerate for even thinking that was a good idea. She'd think I was a creep. Open mouth, insert foot.

"You from around here?" I ask, and she replies rather aloofly, "Sort of. Not really," and I smile self-consciously and ask what that means.

She shrugs. "I guess you could say that I am," and still, even with this I'm left wondering.

"Closer to Battle Creek?" I ask, knowing it's a stupid thing to ask. There could be a thousand towns and cities in all of Michigan, maybe two thousand. Why Battle Creek? But I ask it, anyway, because when I open my mouth, it's all that comes out. To my surprise she nods her head impassively and I know it was either a lucky guess on my part, or she wishes I'd just shut up.

"You like to swim?" I ask as an alternative, thinking of that day at the lake, but instead of saying yes or no, she asks of me, "Do you?" It's a technique, spinning my queries so she doesn't mistakenly share a single thing about herself. She doesn't want me to know a thing.

"I like it enough," I say, "though the water gets pretty cold this time of year."

"You think?" she asks, but still I can't tell whether or not she agrees, and I envision her back floating along the surface of a frigid Lake Michigan as raindrops plummeted from the sunless sky. I'm not sure if it's a question or a statement or something in between, but I nod, anyway, and say, "Yes, I do. It's cold."

"Are you from around here?" she asks.

"Born and bred," I say, watching as she plucks at that strained bracelet that hugs her wrist, that habitual pluck, pluck, pluck that earned her the nickname of Pearl. I have no idea how long I watch.

When she lays her head on the blue country plaid pillow, I say my goodbyes and go. But by then her eyes are already half-closed, and if she does say goodbye, I don't hear it. I go, anyway, watching for one last minute as she drifts off to sleep.

As I retrace my steps through the old home and back out the busted window onto the stepstool placed outside, knowing fully well that Pearl will take center stage in my dreams tonight — if I even manage to sleep — I realize this: out of sight, but never out of mind.

# QUINN

Ben holds my hair for me while I puke.

The good news is that I only picked at the roast beef sandwich at lunch. What comes out of me is mainly stomach acid and bile. And I made it to the toilet in time, so it's not as if there's a mess left behind to clean.

We sit together on the cramped bathroom floor, a black-and-white checkerboard tile like all the other tile in the apartment. There are dust bunnies there, that and soap residue. Which makes no sense because it's not as if we bathe on the bathroom floor. But still, it's there. I'm pretty sure there's urine on the toilet seat, too, and I silently curse Landon or Brandon, Aaron or Darren — whoever that man was I brought home Saturday night — because he's the only one who could have possibly made the mess. It's not like Esther and I pee on the seat. Little did I know that sixty-some hours after our little tryst I'd be staring his pee straight in the eye as I hovered over the porcelain throne and puked. That's quite some parting gift.

When the puking mutates into dry heaving and slowly draws to a close, Ben lays a cool washcloth on my head and brings me a 7-Up with a pink plastic straw.

"You should go," I whisper to him, knowing good and well that it's nearing six o'clock. Priya, in her own apartment miles away, will wonder where he is. They don't live together, but Ben would like to. He's said as much and I've pretended to care, knowing that if they did, they'd save rent. *Loads of rent money,* Ben says. But Priya says no. He's confessed this to me once and only once, the fact that it drives him nuts the way Priya keeps her guard up all the time, as if she's got only one foot *in* the door. Not one foot out the door — she has no plans to leave — but she's not quite ready to step completely inside. He wonders if she'll ever be. She's überindependent, which was something that intrigued him from the get-go — self-sufficient and self-reliant, the kind of girlfriend that didn't cling. Now it seems as if he'd like someone who clings, or rather, he'd like for Priya to cling. Or maybe he'd just like for Priya to need him the way that he needs her.

But still, they have dinner together many nights, and tonight it's Priya's turn to cook. He's due there at six. She's making *aloo gobi,* not that I asked, but still he told me — though that was before the notion of food sent me running to the john.

"I'm not going anywhere," he says, and he excuses himself and leaves the room. From the bathroom floor I hear his voice. He's in the hallway, just outside the door, telling Priya the reason for canceling their plans. "Hey, babe," he says, but he makes no mention of me.

Or of being at my apartment.

Or of Esther.

Or the fluky death of her former roommate.

Instead, Ben blames a document production, which needs to be overnighted via FedEx by the time the store closes at nine o'clock. It's not that far-fetched; it's happened before, dozens of project assistants running to and fro to Bates label and photocopy documents so they can reach the opposing side by some imminent deadline. "I'm so sorry," he says, "the lawyer just sprung it on us this afternoon. It's going to be a long night." And Priya being Priya — not that I would know — absolves him completely of his sin. "Thank you for understanding," Ben says, and, "You're the best," and then he ends the conversation with a *love* and a *you* and a nauseating air kiss that makes me want to hurl all over again and so I do.

He returns to the bathroom and joins me on the floor.

"Are you ready to talk about it?" he asks, his tablet — as always — within reach. "We should talk about it, don't you think?" he asks, sure to add, "When you're ready," and I tell him I'm ready. Though I'm not quite sure I am.

Ben scours the internet and comes across an article, one which states that paramedics responded to a 911 call at Esther's and my address, that they found Kelsey Bellamy unresponsive, that she was transported to Methodist Hospital, and it was there that she was pronounced dead. I picture emergency room physicians trying hard to work their magic before some EKG flatlines and a grim man states point-blank, *Time of death: 8:23,* though of course I don't know what time she died.

But then another image comes to me: handouts on grieving, the grieving process, the seven stages of grief. Was Esther grieving because Kelsey was dead?

Friends and relatives on Kelsey's Facebook page cite carelessness, negligence, complete disregard as the cause of death. But why? The messages are esoteric to say the least; they leave out some kind of information the average reader wouldn't be privy to, someone like me, just snooping around on Kelsey's Facebook page for the inside scoop.

She wasn't my roommate; she wasn't my friend. So why, then, do I see the photos of Kelsey Bellamy and feel sad? My eyes tear up and, as Ben hands me a tissue, I wipe the tears from my eyes. "Esther didn't do this," I say, though inside we're both thinking the very same thing.

She did.


Esther has a habit of making every task her own, of moving items from other people's docket to hers. It isn't a bad quality to have, an eager beaver with a behemoth heart.

A typical example: the time Nancy on the second floor decided the tenants of our walk-up apartment building needed to be more committed to recycling. Nancy was tired of seeing old beer bottles and never-read newspapers tossed out with the trash, and Mrs. Budny — old Mrs. Budny with one foot in the ground already, who didn't need to worry about preserving the world for her children or her children's children (neither of which she had) — wasn't going to do a thing about it.

But all Nancy did was post a flyer — delineating the recycling centers around town — in the hall, beside the mailboxes, which somehow or other every single tenant managed to ignore.

But Esther, on the other hand, took it a step further. She contacted recycling services to secure a deal. She purchased several containers for recycling — with her own money, I should add — and left them outside, by the rank Dumpster in the alley behind our home, and in the laundry room. She posted signs, listing what was recyclable and what was not, and what effect *not* recycling was having on our world: landfill overflow, and the need to create new landfills. She encouraged use of the three R's: reduce, reuse, recycle. She offered up an award for which resident was the best recycler (it wasn't me).

And unlike Nancy's master plan, which failed miserably, Esther's plan didn't fail. It was quite the success. Avid recyclers we turned out to be.

Esther was the one who encouraged me to eat more healthful foods; she persuaded me to pursue a career change. A simple remark — *I hate my job* — became Esther's cue to solve the problem, to make this conundrum her own, though she did it in a way that was never autocratic or oppressive or annoying. It was simply sweet. What Esther decided I needed to be was a teacher, instead of a dopey PA. I almost laughed at that thought: me, a teacher. It seemed ludicrous, and yet it was Esther who convinced me to try and get certified in early childhood education, after I slowly became smitten with the tiny tykes at her bookstore's story time. *You're good with kids,* she told me, *and besides, you don't want to stay in that crappy job forever, do you? You're better than that, Quinn.*

*I'm not smart enough to be a teacher,* I told her at the time as we hovered in the bookstore after story time, me on the floor with some curly-haired kid I didn't know, helping her find the perfect picture book on princesses. It wasn't as if I worked at the bookshop or anything — I didn't — but I'd become a frequent attendee of story time and had gotten to know some of the kids. I liked the stories, yes, more than I cared to admit, but even more I liked that sense of belonging in Esther's world. I've never had a friend quite like Esther. She's like a sister, one I like even more than my real sister.

*You're smarter than a four-year-old, aren't you?* Esther had asked, and I shrugged. God, how I hoped I was smarter than a four-year-old. *You can do this,* she said.

It wasn't a week later before I sought out information online for teacher certification programs in Chicago, and Esther signed on to helping me prepare for the Basic Skills test, one which tests my knowledge — or lack thereof — in language arts, reading and writing and math. I can only take the test five times; I've already failed it once. Esther has been helping me study; she swears we're going to pass it the next time around. We. Esther and me. She's told me at least twelve times already that this isn't something I have to do alone. We're a team, Esther and me. That's what she said to me.

Another example of Esther's take-charge persona: the time I made mention of the fact that I'd like to exercise more, to get in shape. I'm not a small person, not short or skinny or just plain petite. Esther is petite, but I am not petite. I am in no way small. But I'm not fat, either. I secretly blame my mythological Amazon ancestors for my tall figure and big bones, for the fact that I am mighty. That's the way I like to look at it: mighty. The way I figure it, too, when I do my shopping online, I got a heck of a lot more sweater or skirt for my money — a heck of a lot more fabric than their size-two-petite, say — for exactly the same price. Their loss, my gain.

But still, I'm not getting any younger, or smaller for that matter, and I made the mistake — or maybe it was a blessing — of telling Esther this, and at once, Esther concocted a fitness plan for her and me to follow. She isn't a hard-core runner, but she does run on occasion. She isn't about to sign up for the Chicago Marathon or anything like that, but she can last a good mile or two, and so that's exactly what we did. Esther got in the habit of dragooning me from bed early in the morning — well before sunrise — and we'd follow the same route, down Clark to Foster where we crossed under Lake Shore Drive and onto the Lakefront Trail, a paved path that spans eighteen miles, running north to south along the shores of Lake Michigan. We didn't make it all eighteen. Nowhere close. For all intents and purposes, I'm not even sure I ran. Running, by definition, requires two feet off the ground at a time, and I'm not entirely sure they were. If anything, we maybe trekked two miles along the path, which might have been a brisk walk, trying desperately to save face in the midst of all

257

those marathoners or wannabe Olympians soaring past us on the Lakefront Trail.

My legs burned; I had a cramp. I had many cramps. I couldn't breathe.

But Esther being Esther cheered me on. She was encouraging. *You can do it,* she said. She slowed down to keep pace with me so that I didn't feel like a chump, though I was pretty sure I still looked like a chump what with my arms flapping like a dying bird falling from the sky.

But Esther didn't give up. She dragged me out of bed day after day after day, though each day I tried hard to refuse, blaming blisters on my feet, the aches and pains near the joints and muscles and tendons. It hurt everywhere. I could hardly squat down to use the restroom or pull on a pair of socks or my shoes. But Esther didn't give up on me. *Wakey, wakey,* she sang to me each day, luring me from bed. She drew a warm bath for my aching limbs, adding Epsom salt — *the panacea for muscle pain,* as Esther claimed. She made me stretch. She helped with my socks. She tied my shoes. She yanked me out to the Lakefront Trail.

And I ran.

This is what I realize as I return to my bedroom closet, sitting there staring at that word carved into the drywall — *Kelsey* — like some sort of desperate cry for help. When Esther puts her mind to something, there isn't a thing she can't do.

But I can't help but wonder what it is this time that Esther's put her mind to.

In time Ben and I move into Esther's bedroom, where I show him my latest work-in-progress, the ribbons of photo paper spread across the floor.

"What's this?" he asks as I explain how I pulled these scraps from Esther's paper shredder.

"Maybe nothing," I say, "or maybe something." I shrug, admitting, "I don't know yet," and without being asked Ben and I drop to the floor in tandem and make haste of putting my shredded puzzle pieces together, more curious than ever to know who it's a photograph of.

We work quickly; we don't speak. We don't need to speak. Is it Esther in the image, or maybe, just maybe, it's Kelsey Bellamy. Together we start to engineer the brick of a building, a slab of concrete, and somewhere in the center an image begins to form of a woman: mere legs, thinner than a man's would be, sporting a pair of flare jeans. She has no face yet, nothing to tell us who she is, no telling accessories that stand out in the half-formed image. It's a zoomed-out photograph, not a close-up, and so the details are hard to see as Ben and I stay up well past our bedtimes toiling away on the task.

Outside there's a full moon, a golden globe that glares through the window, splashing its light on the floor. As the clouds roll by, they snatch with them the moonlight, and the room grows darker, the puzzle pieces lying before Ben and me harder to see.

But then the moon returns again, taunting and mocking us, its light bursting across the floor, and I have to wonder if a nefarious Esther is out there somewhere taunting and mocking us, too.

■ ■ ■ ■

# WEDNESDAY

■ ■ ■ ■

# ALEX

I wake up earlier than usual and bike to the only twenty-four-hour grocery store in town. There's hardly a scrap of food in Pops's and my refrigerator, and what's there is likely expired or is growing green with mold. It's a three-mile trip in either direction, and so I bike there and cart home a dozen eggs, a carton of milk, shredded cheese and fruit in a plastic sack that dangles from the bike's handlebars. There's not much fresh fruit in season this time of year, but I get a couple of apples and a bunch of red grapes. It'll have to do.

Back in Pops's and my kitchen, I start washing the fruit and scrambling the eggs. I add the milk and cheese to the eggs, the way Pops likes them, and some salt and pepper, too. The house begins to fill with a smell of homemade food, but even that doesn't wake Pops, sound asleep, the door to his bedroom pulled to. I sift through our dishes to find a plate that isn't cracked or chipped, and begin placing the prepared food here and there, a mound of eggs, a handful of grapes. When I'm through, the plate looks vacant still — empty and sad, a bit pathetic — and I know that I should have gotten more: toast, a bagel, sausage links. Something along those lines, but I didn't. Oh, well. I pour a glass of milk, and then second-guess it all and think that I should have gotten juice. Or coffee. Or cereal. On a whim I snatch a Mountain Dew from the fridge, just in case. You never know what it is that she likes to drink with her eggs.

And then I load it into my arms, head out the front door and cross the street. I also leave Pops a plate.

She's still asleep when I come in, but the sound of my footsteps draws her from sleep. That or the smell of eggs. She sits up slowly in her makeshift bed as only an old lady would do, the stretching of body parts — arms and legs and such — as if it hurts, the bones and muscles being thrust back into place, the reviving of limbs that have gone senseless and numb.

"Good morning," I say, maybe too spiritedly, and she says to me, "Good morning."

Her words are gruff, her voice still sluggish and dopey, but I smile, anyway.

I'm just glad that she's still here.

I thought about it half the night, about the fruit and the eggs and whether or not I'd find the house abandoned when I returned come morning. I considered the possibility that she'd be out, wandering the streets of town, or that maybe she'd have boarded the Pere Marquette and headed far away from here. But here she is, in the flesh, her hair a jumble of bedhead, creases on her pale skin. She wears my sweatshirt still, the hood pulled up over her head. The minute I arrive she attempts to shimmy out of it — as if that's the reason I came — but I say to her, "No. Keep it," and so she does. I've showered and dressed and have on a new sweatshirt today, same beat-up cotton, another shade of gray.

"I brought you breakfast," I say as I set the tray of food on the floor beside her makeshift bed. I half expect varmints to appear from every corner of the room at the prospect of food, but they don't. The house is quiet and still.

She reaches for the fork and loads the eggs onto its tines, blowing before she sets the scrambled eggs inside her mouth. I hear her stomach growl. I can tell from the look on her face that she likes it; either that or she's so absolutely famished she'd eat anything and claim it was good.

"I like it," she says. But then another look settles on her pretty face, a look of wonder or gratitude, or maybe even trust, as she says these words to me. "People don't usually do nice things for me." I am silent, not quite sure what to say to that, and she adds, "You didn't have to do this, you know."

I tell her that I know. But inside my heart fills with warmth, though the dilapidated house remains cold.

"There's more," I say, excusing myself while she eats. I tell her to keep eating. "Don't wait for me," I say. "I'll be right back."

And then I go, out the same window in the back of the home. In the backyard, in the dense underbrush that was once a nice garden, no doubt, I take in the overgrown shrubbery that needs to be hacked. It sidles its way up the home, into every crevice it can find, under the aluminum siding so that the siding slips right off the house. The stumps of deadened trees remain in the lawn, succumbing one by one to fungus and bacteria.

But the thing that really gets my attention is the tire swing, an old rubber sphere, now deflated, that hangs from an old oak tree by a rope. I wander to that swing and give it a gentle push and then stand and watch as it dithers back and forth through the gray November air. I hear phony children squeal in delight. *Wheee!* They beg: *Again, again!* Once they were here, but now they're gone.

And then I scamper off to Pops's and my garage to get what it is that I need. The street is dead quiet; it's too early for anyone else to be up.

I didn't sleep much last night. In fact, I hardly slept at all. I was up half the night thinking of Pearl sleeping on the hard floor, freezing cold. And that's when I remembered the kerosene heater in our garage and a five-gallon, half-empty container of kerosene, one that Pops used to keep handy for when power outages rattled our town, something that only ever happened in the wake of winter blizzards. We needed something to keep us warm when the heavy snow all but buried us alive, and this was it. Pops bought it years ago — ten, maybe fifteen — and many times, it's come in handy. Years ago he wouldn't let me touch the darn thing — too dangerous, he'd say. These days I won't let him near it.

I wrangle the awkward, heavy heater back to the house and inside, and there she sits, Pearl, with the plate of food on her lap.

She's about finished it all, and I can see already that she looks full, maybe even satisfied. She eyes the heater in my hand and asks, "What's that?" and I tell her what it is as I fill it up with the kerosene and turn up the wick, igniting the heater. Just like that, the flame grows orange and the room starts to warm, bringing a sunniness to Pearl's face I hadn't seen before. She smiles.

I adjust the wick to the right height and say to her, though I don't think it needs to be said, "These things can be dangerous. We need to keep an eye on it, make sure it's off before we go," but then I shrug, not wanting to make her feel like a ninny, and say, "but I'm sure you knew that already."

But it's second nature, I guess, an effect of reminding Pops all the time to turn off the oven, to close the front door, to flush the john.

Instead of saying anything about the heater, she says to me, "I like your necklace," and it's automatic, the way my hands go to the beaded shark's tooth necklace that Ingrid made for me all those years ago.

"Thanks," I say, taking in the shade of her eyes, a light brown like amber.

"Is it from a girl?" she asks point-blank, and I'm all but certain my face burns as red as the flames in the heater.

I shake my head, setting myself down on the floor. "Just a friend," I say, but I feel the inclination to tell her more, to tell her about Leigh Forney, and how, for me, there really aren't any *girls. For strength and protection,* Ingrid had told me when she gave me the necklace years ago, after I started working for Priddy to support Pops. She did it because she felt bad for me, like half the town felt bad for me at the time. My mother had abandoned me, and my father was a drunk. Such is life.

I run my hands along the tip of the shark's tooth and, staring into Pearl's eyes, I think maybe it's working, after all.

But I don't tell her any of this. Instead, I leave it at that — *just a friend* — and allow the room to grow quiet and still.

There are things I want to ask her: her name and what she's doing here — in our town, in this house — for starters. But I can't. I open my mouth to speak, but all that transpires is air.

She asks questions of me instead.

"You live across the street," she says, and it's then that I know she's been watching me, seeing Pops and me at the kitchen table, maybe, irradiated by the bright lights of our home. Maybe she knows more about me than I think.

I say, "I do."

"With your family?" she asks, and I say, *Yes,* and then, *No,* setting finally instead on, "With my father." He's family, don't get me wrong. There's just more to it than that.

"No brothers or sisters?" she asks, and I say no.

"Where's your mother?" she asks. And though so many phony, *easy* answers spring to mind — she's dead, or she's in a persistent vegetative state in a hospital following some traumatic brain injury, or she's in jail on countless drug citations and a murder charge — none of these responses prevail. Instead, I tell her the truth.

"She left," I say as I reach for a forgotten grape at the edge of Pearl's plate and pop it in my mouth so I don't have to say anything more.

There aren't many memories I have of my mom, but there are a few. They're not good. I'm standing beside her bed, having had a bad dream. Crying. And not just a whiny kind of cry, but a really scared cry because there are monsters under my bed and I need her to get them for me. She pretends to sleep before she sits up in bed and tells me to go back to my room. *It's the middle of the night, Alex.* Even for a five-year-old, I know there's no compassion in that voice of hers,

270

no affection. She's stone cold. I tell her I'm scared, but she yanks the blanket up over her head and pretends she can't hear me. Pops, working a nightshift, isn't home. I poke a finger into the blanket and beg for her to come. She pushes me away with her hands. She doesn't come, and in time I give up. But I won't step foot in my bedroom. I won't sleep in there with the monsters. Instead, I sleep on the hallway floor. In the morning, still bushed, her eyes only half-open, she steps on me. When I cry out she yells at me again. This is my fault.

Motherhood scared the bejesus out of her. She never wanted to be a mother. Any form of affection terrified her, as well. My mother's smiles were rare and her hugs were always succinct, plaited with tension and angst. As if it hurt to hug. As if it was painful. That's one of the few things I remember from my early years, the way she wiggled out of my clasp when I wrapped my clumsy little boy arms around her knees or her waist — as high as I could reach — as I tailed her, toddling, arms extended, wanting more, *just one more hug,* until she got mad.

*Go away, Alex. Leave me alone. Don't touch me.*

That's another thing I remember. My mother's small feet, barefoot, trotting down the tatty carpeting of our home, shooing me away like a fly. *Alex!* she would snap, voice on the cusp of losing it, but trying hard to maintain control. *I told you to go away. Don't touch me.*

"Where'd she go?" Pearl asks, and I say simply, "Away," because in all honesty, I don't know where it is that my mother went to and I try not to think about it, about the possibility that she could have another family — another husband, another child — somewhere out there in the world.

"That sucks," she says point-blank as she pushes the plate of food away. "People can be so selfish sometimes, don't you think?"

I tell her that I do.

And then for whatever reason, I gather the courage to ask, "What are you doing here?" And she smiles that crafty smile again and says to me, "I could tell you, Alex. But then I'd have to kill you," and we laugh, and though it's a curbed laugh, an inhibited laugh, I realize how good it feels. It's been a long time since I've laughed. Too long. The noise sounds hollow here in the abandoned home, bouncing off the rickety walls and back to our ears where I have to remind myself that the laughter is a good thing. It means that we are happy.

I've forgotten what it feels like to be happy.

I also notice that she has a beautiful smile. Simple, with small, precise white teeth that are all but hidden behind the lips. It's unpresuming and sweet. I get the feeling that she hasn't smiled in a while, too, that she hasn't laughed. Not a real, genuine, bona fide laugh, anyway.

"The truth?" she asks then, pausing in her laughter as she reaches a fearless hand across the two-foot span and runs her fingertips along my shark's tooth. I feel my body stiffen, the blood in my veins coagulate and solidify. I can hardly breathe.

"Just passing through," she says, though from the look in her eye I'm guessing there's more to it than that, and once again my thoughts retreat to one man and one man alone: Dr. Joshua Giles. As a surge of jealousy swells up inside me, I unearth one more reason not to like the guy.

She's here for him when I wish more than anything that she could be here for me.

I wonder what that means — *just passing through* — and consider what it would be like to be a drifter, to move from town to town all alone, just passing through. I wonder if somewhere, out there, she has family, friends, a boyfriend, someone who is missing her, someone who is looking for her. Someone who is thinking of her the way I now think of her.

"How long will you stay," I ask, "before you have to leave?"

She shrugs and says to me, "I'm in no hurry," and I wonder what that means: a day, a week, a year? I want to ask her. I want to know definitively which day I'll show up at this forsaken home and she won't be here. Tomorrow? Friday? Next week? Will she say goodbye before she leaves? Will she ask for me to go, to tag along with her on her trip? Doubtful, but still, I can dream.

I don't ask her any of these things. Instead, I fidget with the heater to avoid her inveigling eyes.

Today I don't stay too long; I can't stay too long. I peer down at a cheap watch on my left wrist and check the time. Before long, I'm due at work, another day of bussing tables for Priddy's minimum wage.

"You'll remember to turn the heater off before you leave?" I remind her as her hand slides from my necklace, and she says she will. I nod my head and I say that I have to go, peering back over my shoulder for one last look before I'm gone.

# QUINN

There's a dish Esther serves. It's a vegetarian recipe, a stir-fry with beans and broccoli and baby corn. And tofu. It should be disgusting but it's not. It's absolutely delicious. It also has a sauce complete with soy sauce and rice vinegar.

And a quarter cup of peanut flour.

Which doesn't matter in the least bit to me, but it does matter to Kelsey Bellamy.

She was four years old when she was first diagnosed with a peanut allergy. That's what her fiancé, Nicholas Keller, tells me as I sit across from him at his own kitchen table in a recently renovated flat in Hyde Park. It's a small glass-top table that generally just sits one.

Him.

His eyes are disconsolate, brown eyes that dampen when I mention her name. *Kelsey.*

"She'd eaten peanuts before with no adverse effect," he tells me, "but over time, things change. Especially when it comes to allergies. She was four years old, and her mother served her a peanut butter and jelly sandwich for the first time, and right away — or so the story goes — Kelsey could hardly breathe. Her throat swelled up, she broke out in hives. Anaphylaxis. From that day on, she carried with her an EpiPen. Benadryl. She was always ready.

"She was always so careful about eating peanuts. We hardly ever ate out — too risky. She read the label on everything. Absolutely everything," he says. "She wouldn't eat products that were manufactured on shared lines for fear of cross-contamination. No processed cereal, no granola bars, no crackers."

"So what happened?" I ask, and he shakes his head and says it was an accident, a horrible accident.

Nicholas Keller wasn't hard to find. There were only twenty of them in the entire United States, and only two in Illinois. He was the first I called. Lucky guess. The commute from Andersonville to Hyde Park took a good eighty minutes: one "L" ride, two buses and a half-mile walk on foot.

I waited until evening when I knew he would be home from work. According to LinkedIn, Nicholas Keller is a financial adviser, a fact he later confirms in the foyer of his home, small talk before I dive into the reason for my visit. He seems to be a pretty straitlaced guy, not quite what I would have imagined for Kelsey Bellamy. And yet, as the saying goes, *opposites attract.*

"I went to grammar school with Kelsey," I lie, "in Winchester."

"You're from Winchester?" he asks.

I say that I am. Winchester, Massachusetts. I add in, "Go Red Sox," because I don't know a thing about Boston other than they have a decent baseball team. And they drink tea, supposedly.

"You don't have that whole Boston accent like Kelsey did," he says, and I tell him how I'm an army brat, how our stay in Massachusetts only lasted a short time.

"Fort Devens?" he asks, and I nod my head and say, "Yeah," even though I'm not quite sure what I'm saying yes to. I tell him I went to fourth grade with Kelsey. "Fourth or . . ." I pause, feign thinking, "Fifth, maybe? I can't remember for sure."

My eyes take in the flat, a home that is all man. A bachelor pad. He tells me that they planned to move in here together after the wedding, he and Kelsey. They had purchased the unit, but were living apart in their separate sides of the city while it underwent renovation — she sharing an apartment with a roommate in Andersonville, he in a midrise in Bridgeport. The building was quite downtrodden the first time they laid eyes on it, a warehouse converted to loft apartments. But still, it had all the elements they were looking for in a new home: the expansive rooms, exposed pipes and ductwork, brick walls, wood cladding. And Kelsey had a vision, though she died before having a chance to see it through. Instead, what remained was a poorly furnished space with dirty dishes in the sink and laundry on the floor. And an inconsolable fiancé.

They were to be married within a year from her death. She'd purchased a dress already, and he showed it to me, a simple taffeta thing that hung in a spare closet all alone, light blue because, as Nicholas said, "She was too much of a nonconformist for white," saying these words not in any sort of carping way, but in a romantic way, as if Kelsey's nonconformity was one of the reasons he loved her. Talk about sad. They had booked a hall for the three-hundred-plus guests they hoped would attend. They were still undecided on where to go for their honeymoon, a toss-up between Romania and Botswana. "Kelsey had no need to lie on a beach in a bikini," Nicholas says. "That wasn't her thing," he tells me, and I say that I know.

I don't know. But I've seen the gothic photo, the head-to-toe black, the albino skin, and so I can assume.

"It's been a long time, I know," I tell him, "but I just heard about Kelsey. I'm so sorry. We've been out of touch for years. I knew I probably shouldn't, but I had to stop by and express my condolences," I say, and then he leads me to his glass-top kitchen table and tells me about her peanut allergy.

"How'd you find me?" he asks. It isn't censorious in the least bit. He's curious.

"A friend of a friend," I say, knowing how vapid it sounds.

"Was it John? Johnny Acker," he asks, and I say that it was. This couldn't be easier.

"I thought so," he says. "He's the only one I remember from Kelsey's grammar school days. Hard to imagine they still kept in touch after all those years."

"You're telling me."

There are photos of Kelsey in the flat. The same jet-black hair and smoky eyes, the same ashen skin, but in these photos, the gothic look has been toned down a bit. There's an edge to her still; that goes without saying. A whole lot of morbid black in her attire. And yet, no skulls and cross-bones, no fashion corsets or creepy black Victorian boots. Nothing steampunk. Nothing emo. Just dark. In the photos, Kelsey and Nicholas stand side by side beside the Statue of Liberty, the Grand Canyon, on top of Pikes Peak. They look like opposites: he prim and proper, she anything but.

They also look to be in love.

"I got a call from her roommate," he goes on to explain as tears fill his eyes. I almost ask, *Esther?* but stop myself in time. " 'Something is wrong,' she said to me on the phone. 'She's not breathing. Kelsey's not breathing.' I knew right away what had happened. I said, 'Find her EpiPen. She needs her EpiPen,' but all she said was, 'It's too late. It's too late, Nick,' over and over again. Kelsey was already dead."

And now it's me who begins to cry. I'm not usually all weepy like this. I don't get choked up. But I'm so overcome with emotion — anger, fear, sadness — that this time I do. I want to sit Esther down before me and demand of her: *What have you done? How could you do this to Kelsey?*

"I'm sorry," Nicholas says with a pat to my hand. He rises from the table and finds me a tissue. "This is hard on you, too. I forget sometimes that I'm not the only one she left behind."

"She'd eaten peanuts," I infer when I finally gather myself well enough to speak, and Nicholas says, "Yes," and then, "No," settling finally on, "Peanut flour."

He tells me about the recipe. The soy sauce. The rice vinegar. The peanut flour. A meal I've eaten so many times before. And I have this memory of Esther, coming home from night school, feeling all worn out. Tired. Her voice all Hannibal Lecter — like, saying, *The dill weed goes here. And the peanut flour goes here,* while banging those two items inside the kitchen cabinet, the buff-color flour dusting the countertops. She'd been upset that I had borrowed her dill weed. That's what I thought at the time. There was no doubt about it in my mind, but now I'm not so sure. Perhaps it hadn't been about the dill weed, after all.

"It was just a mistake, then. A horrible accident," I say, and he says yes, with a hint of doubt in his tone, that it was. A mistake. A horrible accident.

But was it?

"They'd been drinking," he says. "Margaritas. They'd both had too much. Kelsey's roommate, she said she always swapped the peanut flour with all-purpose flour for

281

Kelsey. Always. But not that night. That night she forgot," and again he says, "They'd been drinking."

He says the word *mistake,* but still, I get the sense that even he doesn't believe it. Her EpiPen, he says, was always in her purse. Always. Except that that night it wasn't. That night, the EpiPen was nowhere to be found.

Esther had added peanut flour to the recipe and for that reason Kelsey Bellamy was dead. There was no antidote to be found; the EpiPen had simply disappeared. "One mistake is one thing, but two mistakes . . ." His voice trails off. I know what he is thinking. He's thinking Esther killed his fiancée, which is the same thing I'm thinking, too.

"Kelsey never went anywhere without her EpiPen," he says.

"You never found it?" I ask.

"No," he says.

He leaves me with this: "Her name," he says, had they had the chance to get married, "would have been Kelsey Keller," and he smiles sadly — evocatively — and says how she always thought that was hysterically funny. Kelsey Keller.

I smile. "That sounds just like Kelsey," I

say, citing her swell sense of humor, as if I actually know.

# ALEX

I spend the day at work, watching through the windows as Dr. Giles's clients come and go. Each time the door squeals open, there he appears in the cottage door frame, happy as a lark, a droll little smile on that face of his as he shakes their hand or pats their back, and welcomes them inside.

And then he closes the door and pulls the blinds, and I'm left wondering what they're up to on the inside.

I make note of the fact that it's women mostly and the occasional teenage or pre-teen girl who come to see Dr. Giles. Some I recognize; others I don't. Some live in town, but others come from far away, parallel parking their cars on the street before looking both ways and dashing across to the office of Dr. Giles, PhD, Licensed Psychologist, like a member of high society slipping through the doors of the town's adult store, hoping no one sees.

Today, Pearl comes to the café, but only for a short time. She appears and almost as quickly disappears, but in the few, fleeting minutes that she's there, she takes her place at the window and, out into the street, she stares. She orders coffee this time, only coffee, and sips introspectively while staring through the glass at the world on the other side. I watch her from a distance. I stare at the back of her head. I count the measured sips of coffee, the way she returns the mug to the countertop with care, setting it down so it doesn't spill or clang. I take in the color of her skin, the prominent metacarpal bones that push through the thin skin as she lifts the coffee mug to her lips and sips. She doesn't stay long. I watch from a distance, finding it impossible to divert my eyes. I don't want to ruin the moment.

In time, Priddy tells me to get to work. I pass by, moving a foul dishrag in haphazard circles upon the dirty tables, moving closer and closer to where Pearl sits. Red brings her the check, and there, from two tables away, I watch as Pearl roots fruitlessly around in the canvas bag for money to pay the check. When her hand comes up empty, I dip into my wallet and produce a five-dollar bill.

"It's on me," I say before she has a chance

285

to say that she can't cover the fare, laying the money on the countertop and stepping back.

"Oh, no," she says, "I couldn't," but still, her hand leaves the bag without a single bill. It makes me feel warm all over, knowing I've helped her in some small, insignificant way. Her face reddens, and she's ashamed to admit she has no money to her name, nothing save for three quarters she finally digs up at the bottom of that bag. Three measly quarters, seventy-five cents.

I shrug my shoulders. "It's nothing," I say.

But it's not nothing. I've done something good.

"You're a good friend," she says to me then, her hand grazing the margins of mine. And then, when I say nothing — because I'm too staggered to speak, because I'm stricken with a sudden onset of aphasia and I've lost the ability to speak — she goes on. "We're friends, right?" she asks of me then, and this time, it's me who blushes. "You and I. We're friends."

I'm not sure if this last part is a question or not. Is she asking me, or telling me? Is she telling me that we're friends?

I nod my head. I say that we are. Or maybe I don't say it; maybe I only think it. I don't know. Either way, we're friends. I feel the need to write it down, to take a picture, to seal the deal with blood — something to prove that this is real. Pearl and I are friends.

And then Priddy ruins it all by calling my name, pointing to a round table that needs to be cleaned. I look away for ten seconds at best, and when I turn back, Pearl is gone, just like that, my five-dollar bill left behind beside the check. On the countertop I find an empty pink packet of Sweet'n Low, assuring me that she was really here. Pearl. She isn't a dream as all common sense would have me believe. She's real.

*We're friends, right? You and I. We're friends.*

And then later in the day, when Priddy finally gives me the A-okay to go home, I don't go home. I stick around outside the café, killing time on a plastic-coated steel bench — hands and ears turning red from the cold, my nose beginning to drip, waiting and hoping for Pearl to return, hoping she'll pass by en route to an appointment with Dr. Giles, or maybe stop by the café again to see me.

But she doesn't stop by the café. She doesn't go to see Dr. Giles.

I'm not ready to go home. And so instead I hover on the bench and watch as the mail-

287

man meanders down the road in his un-washed truck, collecting and delivering the mail. He's in no hurry. It's late for the mailman to be out, nearly dusk. But this is the time of year that everyone moves more slowly. There's no rush to get things done. People walk slower, they eat slower, they talk slower. Life becomes just one big waste of time until spring arrives and then suddenly everyone is in a rush.

I watch as a stray calico cat prances down the sidewalk, past an overflowing garbage bin about to spill over with trash. A store-owner plucks dead mums from a ceramic pot outdoors and fills it instead with ever-green picks and plastic holly berries for the holiday season to come. Ms. Hayes, who owns the novelty and greeting card shop, is getting ready for Christmas already when Thanksgiving hasn't yet come.

As the sky starts to darken and night slowly creeps in, I give up. Pearl isn't coming, not tonight, anyway. But still, I'm not ready to go home. I don't want to go home.

And so I rise from the bench instead and plod across the street, gathering Ingrid's mail from the copper mailbox and into my hands. I knock on the door of the Cape Cod home. "Ingrid," I call, my voice elevated so that she can hear me through the thick wooden pane. I rap my hand on the door again, for a second and then third time in a row, and call out again, "Ingrid, it's me. Alex Gallo."

Inside, through the door, I hear the TV, volume turned loudly so that she can hardly hear a thing. I press the doorbell and listen as the chimes announce my arrival, the fact that I've been standing on her front stoop now for a whole four minutes, freezing my hindquarters off. I bobble up and down in place, trying to keep warm. It's not working. I'm cold. I peer down at the stack of mail in my hand while I wait: the *Clipper Magazine,* bills, a monthly home decor mag, some misaddressed envelope from the Department of State, not meant for Ingrid but rather a lady named Nancy. Nancy Riese. I groan; the mailman is getting lax these days. Just last week, Pops and I got the Ibsens' mail, and the week before that, the Sorensons'.

When Ingrid finally does open the door, peering first through the side glass to make sure it's me, she's pleased by the sight of the mail in my hands. "You dear," she says to me, seizing the stack of papers from my hands. She stands before me in a striped azure blue apron, holding a pair of kitchen shears. She's been making dinner. I smell something warm and delicious and home-made coming from inside the home, where the TV blares, loud and livid, the voice of Emeril Lagasse, that distinct New Orleans timbre and the well-known catchphrases (*Bam!*) telling us how to cook.

But then, Ingrid says, "Come in, come in, come in," pulling me with a spare hand by the white shirtsleeve and into the foyer of her home where she makes haste of closing and locking the door, peering out the window, again, to make sure I'm not in pursuit, that the wind hasn't followed me inside.

I follow Ingrid's trail into the kitchen. There she stands before the stove, stirring whatever mélange she's cooking up tonight. I smell garlic and onion and oregano.

And then I make the mistake of telling her that it smells delicious, and she says to me, "Stay," and it isn't so much a question or an invitation even, but rather an edict: *You will stay.*

"Oh, I can't," I sputter quickly. I want to eat whatever it is Ingrid is whipping up — something that doesn't come from a box or a can — and yet I can't. I shouldn't. "My father. He's at home." And I leave it at that, too ashamed to say the rest, that he is likely shit-faced or passed out on the sofa from drinking all day, that he probably hasn't eaten a thing since I left for work this morning. That I have to hurry home before he decides to make himself dinner, warming up an oven he'll forget to use. It's not the first time it's happened.

"There's plenty here for your father, too," Ingrid tells me as she reaches into her white kitchen cabinets and begins withdrawing dishes in sets of two. "We'll save him some. I'll send you home with a Tupperware that he can warm," and it's then that Ingrid assures me I *can* stay. I should stay. And before I know what's happening, she's ladling a serving of some kind of pasta — complete with tomato sauce and mushrooms and angel hair — into a bowl for me; she's pouring me a glass of milk, too. Just like a mother should do. Not my mother, but *a* mother. I don't ever remember my mother cooking for me. But she must have, right? She must have.

There was a time after my mother left that I clung to mothers — other people's mothers — unremittingly. Years later, I'm sure that Freud would have had a thing or two to say about it, but at the time I didn't know any better and I didn't care.

When I was just six years old, I left home alone and wandered down to a playground a few blocks away. Pops was home, but Pops was drunk. He had no idea I'd gone. There at the playground I tagged along with a little boy about my own age, one whose mother sat on a nearby park bench and watched us play, but when the time came for the little boy to go, I tried to go home with him. When he ran after his mother and grabbed her extended hand, I ran, too, and grabbed the other hand. She didn't push me away; she didn't say, *Don't touch me.*

It was then that the woman realized for the first time that I was all alone. *Where do you live?* she'd asked, and I asked instead if I could go home with them. She told me no, but her eyes were kind and attentive, and yet hoping like some little lost puppy that I'd just go home.

It wasn't the only time something like this happened.

"Eat," Ingrid says to me, staring down at the table of food set before us, and, "Please. There's too much for me. I can't let it go to waste. You will stay, won't you, Alex?" she asks with a bit of humble supplication as I stand before the kitchen table, eyes on the food she's set out before me, quite certain I drool like a hungry dog. Looking into her eyes, I'm reminded again how sad they are. Ingrid has sad eyes, lonely eyes. She blames the wasted food for the reason I should stay, and yet the real reason is this: she's alone. She has no one to talk to, no one other than the celebs on TV to share this meal with her, and a one-way conversation with the television set is more than just sad and lonely; it's pathetic.

And so I sit and I eat. I eat the pasta first, followed by peach cobbler with vanilla ice cream on the side. I'm cajoled into a game of gin rummy. It's so hard to say no to Ingrid, and as time goes on, I find that I don't want to. I don't want to go. Before I know it, Ingrid and I are watching the TV from where we sit — at the kitchen table, with our dinner dishes cast aside to the edge — old *Jeopardy!* reruns, and we're calling out the answers in tandem. *Who is Burt Reynolds?* she exclaims, and me to the next question: *What is Provence?* And then she reaches for a deck of cards and starts to deal. Ten for me, ten for her.

This is what it feels like to be part of a family.

Most of my evenings I spend alone. Well, not really alone but rather with Pops, which is essentially the equivalent to being alone. We sit in the same room sometimes, but we never talk, and sometimes we don't even sit in the same room. Friends are gone; girlfriends are nil. I, like Ingrid, spend my evenings in the company of the TV when I'm not following the town shrink home from work or sneaking my way into an abandoned home.

I offer to stay and help with the dishes after *Jeopardy!* and gin rummy are through. Ingrid tries hard to refuse. "You're my guest," she says, but I insist, standing before the stainless-steel sink, watching as it fills with opalescent dish soap bubbles, which I pop one by one with an index finger. And then I submerge the dishes and start to wash. In the drying rack, the dishes quickly accumulate and clatter, a tower of saturated dishes amassing quickly so that when I set another on top, they slip, threatening to fall.

"Where are the dish towels," I ask Ingrid, rummaging through the kitchen drawers to find something to dry the dishes with.

But Ingrid says no. "Let them be," she says, telling me they'll air-dry overnight. "You work too hard," she says, adding then, "You're a good boy, Alex. You do know that, don't you?" I see it then, the gradient of the skin around her eyes, the thinning, puckering skin. The dullness of her irises, the redness of the sclera. Conjunctivitis, I think. Pinkeye. Allergies.

Or maybe just someone who is sad.

I nod my head and say yes, I know that, though sometimes I'm not so sure if it's true. Good or not good, I still feel like a deadbeat. It's that thought that haunts me in the middle of the night: the fact that this is the be-all and end-all of life for me. This is it, life as I know it. That there will never be anything other than *this.* This town, this existence, Priddy's café. A lifetime of cleaning up someone else's dirty dishes. I hear the girl from my dreams calling to me, *Let's go . . .*

Will I ever get the chance to go?

"Your mother," she says, allowing her voice to drift off before finding the guts to finish the thought, to say what she's thinking out loud. "She should have known better than to leave." And then she pats me on the arm as I turn to go, carrying with me a container of leftover pasta.

As I walk, off in the distance a coyote howls as the train rattles through town, a freight train this time, too late for the commuter train to be coming through. But it did pass through, hours ago, that commuter train. I wonder if Pearl climbed on board or whether she is still here, patrolling the streets of town.

It's well after nine o'clock and the town is

in a deep sleep, hibernating as we do until spring.

When I get home Pops is sound asleep on the sofa, facedown. Beside his overturned beer is another Final Notice, moist with the fermenting scent of alcohol. It clings to the table, threatening to tear as I lift it up and curse out loud. "Damn it, Pops." The electricity this time. Soon we will be without lights. My eyes skim past the TV, past the lamp, past an ugly, old flush-mount light on the living room ceiling, and to the open refrigerator door — all on, all being used. He's managed to leave them all on, amassing more charges on the bill. I'm going to have to work overtime to pay the bill, more time busting my ass for Priddy while Pops sits at home getting trashed. And the money he gets for the beer. Now there's the real kicker. Pops doesn't have his own money for beer. He smashed my piggy bank once upon a time, long ago, when I was just a boy. He's been known to find and forge my paychecks from Priddy, and has asked at the bank for them to be cashed. Then he started sneaking into my bedroom and stealing my things — old baseball trophies, my high school class ring — stuff he could sell at the thrift store in town. Now I keep him on a small allowance so that he'll leave my things be. But still, he doesn't leave them be. Just last week I discovered my telescope missing, another treasure sold for booze.

But these are just things to me. Material things. What matters most to me isn't worth more than a few bucks, but I keep it tucked away under my bed to be sure Pops never finds it. My collection of crinoid stems. Indian beads gathered from the seashore. Tiny fossilized creatures collected in a Ziploc bag. Pops can have the telescope if he needs it that badly, but the crinoid stems are mine.

As expected, a single stove burner has been left on, the house filling quickly with a kerosene-like smell. A grilled cheese — completely blackened — lies forgotten on the stove, burning on a frying pan while Pops sleeps and snores, runnels of drool trickling down his chin and onto a slothful hand. The butter has been left out of the refrigerator, on the countertop beside the pack of American cheese. Both look a little bit gamy to me; I toss them in the trash. The fridge door is wide open, the food inside drifting to lukewarm. There's a spilled beer on the floor, the brew seeping into the tiles of our kitchen floor, warping them before my eyes.

I try to shake him awake and get him to clean his own goddamn mess. He doesn't budge. I press my ear to his chest to be sure; he's still breathing. He better be.

This way I can kill him when he finally does wake up.

He could have burned the whole house down.

I open the windows to air out the stench and put myself to work cleaning up the mess — Pops's mess — again, my anger mitigated only by the fact that my stomach is full.

Tonight I've been fed and cared for by a mother, any mother, whether or not that mother is mine.

# QUINN

It's dark by the time I leave the apartment of Nicholas Keller. It's darker than dark. It's pitch-black, a starless November night, the sky an inky black.

I hop on the 55 bus in Hyde Park, a good six or seven miles south of the Loop. My home, at least nine miles north of the Loop, feels far away. In another world entirely, on another planet, in another galaxy, and though I want to be there, I wonder if my home will ever again feel like home.

The commute to my apartment is inauspicious even before it begins, over an hour long, retracing the steps I made on the way to the Hyde Park flat less than an hour ago as the sun was just starting its drop in the cold night sky. Two buses, an "L" ride and a half-mile walk on foot.

But that was before. Before I had confirmation from Nicholas Keller that Esther killed his fiancée, a woman now buried beneath a bronze grave marker in an idyllic cemetery in the suburbs of Boston.

What I don't get is what all these weird occurrences have in common: Esther's disappearance, the hunt for a new room-mate, the petition to change her name, the death of Kelsey Bellamy.

There's one thought I can't get out of my mind. Is Esther on the hunt for a new room-mate because she also wants me dead?

Is Esther trying to kill me?

A shiver runs down my spine, and I imag-ine spiders scaling my vertebrae like a flight of stairs, thousands of spiders climbing the skin, their long segmented legs stealing their way across, claws digging in. Spinning webs beneath my shirt.

Is Esther a murderer?

Suddenly I'm scared.

And still, none of this explains the identity of *My Dearest.* Who is *My Dearest*? *Who, who, who?* I demand to know, needing the answers now.

I think desperately of the men Esther has brought home over the months we've been together. There weren't many; that much is for sure. There was the one who liked to cook, some hottie with high cheekbones, a strong jawline and large sweet-talking eyes. There was a secret admirer who sent her flowers, a dozen red roses without a card.

Were either of these men *My Dearest*? I don't know.

And what do any of these things have to do with *me*?

One thing I know for sure: something sketchy is going on. Tornado sirens start screaming silently in my ear. Air-raid sirens warn me of an impending nuclear attack. Everywhere I look, I see a giant red flag. *Danger, Will Robinson!*

I'm scared.

The evening commute has come and gone. The bus isn't as crowded as it often is, which is both a blessing and a curse. I would welcome the noise, for a change — bodies pressing into mine, reeking of their noxious breath and body odors. I'd embrace it for one reason and one reason alone: the fact that there is safety in numbers.

But not tonight. Tonight I am alone.

I slide into a ragged seat all by my lonesome and look out the window into the shadowy night. I pull my coat around me to help keep me warm. No dice. Thanks to the LED lights on the bus, it's hard to see much of anything. The lights of the city burn ablaze in the distance, our Great Lake nothing more than a blackened abyss. A bottomless pit. I wonder what lies on the other side of that big, black lake. Wisconsin. Michigan.

Beyond that, there is nothing. Just darkness.

But it doesn't stop me from imagining the things I can't see.

I see Esther here and there, standing on the side of Lake Shore Drive, concealed behind a leafless tree. I'm overcome with this sudden, uncanny belief that she's out there and that Esther, my dear friend Esther, is after me. I'm sure I catch sight of her in the driver's seat of another car on LSD, a red, two-door coupe, a woman who stares in through the bus window at me, her eyes menacing and hostile and mean. I spy Esther's coat at a bus stop we soar past en route to the Red Line station: her black-and-white checkered pea coat, her black beanie set atop a head. I twist in my seat, desperate for a glimpse of the woman who wears these things, but when I turn around, she's gone. In her place, where I imagined her to be, is coily black hair on the head of a teenage girl. A zebra-striped sweatshirt. Jeans.

My eyes scan the riders on the bus one by one by one — not Esther, not Esther, not Esther. I mentally check them off in my mind. I inspect them all as they drop in their fare and climb on board. I do this at each bus stop — eyes scanning the hair, the eyes, for traces of Esther, reminding myself to look closely; she could be in disguise. Some middle-aged woman glares back at me and says, "What are you looking at, girl?" and I avert my eyes as she walks by in a huff and takes a seat behind me.

When I don't see Esther, I tell myself that maybe she's hired someone to do away with me. It's silly, and yet it's not so silly when I put two and two together in my mind. Esther killed Kelsey and then she found me. Kelsey with her food allergies was an easy target. Esther could kill her with her eyes closed and both hands tied behind her back. Step one: do away with EpiPen. Step two: peanut flour. Easy peasy, lemon squeezy.

But not me. I have no allergies.

And now Esther is on the hunt for a new roommate, Megan from Portage Park. Her time with me is coming to an end. That's what I tell myself, anyway, as I sit on the bus, all but paralyzed now in fear. Esther is trying to kill me.

My rationalization leads to this: Esther has hired a hit man to kill me. She can't kill me herself, so instead she's hired someone else to do the job. Why else would she have all those withdrawal receipts from the ATM that I found in the kitchen trash can? Three receipts over three consecutive days, five hundred bucks each, totaling fifteen hundred dollars.

Is my life worth fifteen hundred dollars?

It is to me.

What does a hit man look like? I wonder as I make my way off the bus and into the Red Line subway station. There, it's poorly lit and dingy, my view of passersby bleary and vague. Everyone is in a hurry. They whiz by me with places to go, people to see. I stand, in a daze, trying hard to find my fare card, but instead appraise those around me, my feet frozen to the filthy concrete. Someone bumps into me, and barks, "You're holding up traffic," but still I can't move. What does a hit man look like? I wonder again, growing more and more scared. Is he big, gruff, his voice guttural and rasping? WWF wrestlers come to mind. But so, too, do skinny men with facial piercings and a million tattoos. Drug-addicted, emaciated men. And then there are the balding, fat men with glasses. They, too, come to mind. Is a hit man any or all of them, some combination of these traits? Is he always a *he,* or can he sometimes be a *she*? Is there some sort of rule for how a hit man should look or behave, or is it better that they be unassuming like the nerdy, awkward man, dull as dishwater, standing ho-hum, reading a newspaper in the center of the platform as I pay my fare and make my way down the steps. Is it possible Esther hired this man to take my life?

His eyes rise up off the newspaper as I appear and he smiles. *I've been waiting,* say the eyes. I look closely for a weapon in his pocket or hand, for something that will kill, and then it comes to me: the "L" train will kill.

That's the one thought that crosses my mind as I step foot on the platform, eyes spinning like a chameleon with three-hundred-and-sixty-degree vision, making sure no one is hot on my trail. My heart beats quickly. I drop my fare card once, twice, three times before I manage to get it into the pocket of my purse.

There is the occasional mishap on the train, someone or other falls onto the electrified line or gets struck and killed by an incoming train. It's happened before. I've seen it on the news. It's not that common but it happens. Men or women electrocuted on the third rail; men or women run over by the train. More often than not, suicide. The CTA lines get shut down to investigate, and for the rest of the world it's nothing more than an inconvenience. Just downright annoying and rude that some fool decides to off himself smack-dab in the middle of rush hour, on the city's main mode of public transportation.

But that's not what I'm thinking about right now. No, right now I'm thinking about what it would feel like to tumble the distance, to be fried with a thousand volts of electricity, to be flattened by one of the largest rapid-transit systems in the world. To be dead. That's what I'm thinking about as I keep my distance from the man with the newspaper, the man with the tattoos, the man with the glasses and balding head and the fiftyish woman — yes, woman — with silver in her hair. One can never be too careful of anything.

What it would feel like to be dead.

That's what I wonder.

The Red Line pulls into the station and I climb on board. I stand, ready to make a run for it if need be.

I could have taken a cab. Why didn't I just take a cab? I wonder, but the truth is, safety in numbers. There is safety in numbers.

That's something my mother would say.

Maybe she's not so daft, after all.

She also told me to carry mace. A million times. I told her she was being ridiculous. A worrywart, I called her when she was terrified for me to leave the security blanket of our safe suburban life. She feared all the hooligans the city had to offer, the gangs, the high rates of crime. "Relax, Mom," I told her. "You're worrying for nothing."

But now I'm not so sure.

I want mace.

More importantly, I want my mother.

Again I go through the evidence one by one in my mind: the fact that Esther's gone missing, the notes to *My Dearest,* the obscure phone call on Esther's phone about the missed appointment Sunday afternoon, the petition to change her name, the withdrawal receipts, the quest for a new roommate, someone to replace me after I'm gone. *Gone?* Gone where? The death of Kelsey Bellamy, which, in my mind, trumps all the other evidence, though I'm left wondering if any or all of these are genuine clues, or if they're simply red herrings, misleading ploys meant to throw me off course. I don't know.

When the train pulls into the station, there's still one more bus ride ahead. I make haste down the street and to the bus station. I thank God Almighty that the bus pulls in just as I arrive, and that I don't have to wait outside in the cold, dark night. I scramble in, up the steps, and claim a seat right behind the driver. The driver will protect me, I stupidly tell myself.

He takes off before I'm fully in my seat. I almost fall from the motion. Once seated, I dig through my purse to find my keys, and anything else that might be of use to protect me: a nail file, lip balm, hand sanitizer. I'm thinking ahead of next steps. When the bus pulls to my stop, I'll hurry home. Up the three floors of the walk-up and into apartment 304. I'll lock the door, but since Esther has keys, that will be futile. It will be of no use.

Then I'll fortify the door with chairs, I decide, all the chairs I can find. The mod plaid chair, the kitchen table chairs, Esther's desk chair. I'll bolster it with the apartment sofa, too, the coffee table, a desk. Whatever I can find.

But then I remember that Esther doesn't have a key to our apartment. Not anymore. Maintenance man John changed the locks. At this I breathe a small sigh of relief, knowing I'll still bolster the door with the chairs and table, anyway. Just in case.

I won't eat anything for fear it's been poisoned with ricin or cyanide. I decide this, too.

And then there's the fire escape, should Esther opt to return the way she left, up the fire escape and through her bedroom window, back into our home. The window is closed and locked, but that doesn't mean she can't slice through the screen and break the glass with a fist.

Or maybe she'll just set the whole damn building on fire. That's what I'm envisioning, our four-flat engulfed in orange flames.

And then I feel it: the gentle stroking of my long blond hair.

And there, on the bus, I scream.

# ALEX

That night, I lie down in bed, and just as I start to drift to sleep, I awaken. That jolt of electricity that comes before sleep, the body ready to retire for the night, the mind not. Or is it the other way around? A hypnagogic jerk, a night start. That's what wakes me, or so I think.

It's quiet and then suddenly I hear the chink of glass on glass. That's what it sounds like to me. It takes a minute to get my bearings, and when I do, I figure out that the noise is coming from the window. I rise from bed and approach the glass just in time to see a small rock get catapulted into it, its trajectory taking it from the ground to the glass. It swats the window and tumbles down, rolling along the shingles of the porch roof.

I open the blinds and peer to the wilted lawn down below and there she stands. Pearl.

She's cloaked in her black-and-white checkered coat, the black beanie set on her head. It's murky outside tonight, making it hard to see clearly. But I see her; she's there, standing in the quiet night like a figure in a blurry photograph. Hazy and imperfect, but still perfect in so many ways. She waves as I open the blinds and gaze outside feeling more than a little bit flummoxed. Why is she here? I don't know why, but I thank the heavens that she is.

All my life I dreamed some girl would come to me in the middle of the night, and now here she is.

I raise my hand and wave back, a shiftless sort of wave, though inside I feel anything but; inside I forget the fact entirely that I was just on the cusp of sleep, brooding over Pops and an unpaid electric bill, the fact that he'd stolen my telescope. Feeling sorry for myself. Sulking. Wanting and hoping for something other than this life.

I hold up an index finger and mouth the words, *One second,* though I doubt she can see. I snatch a sweatshirt from the handle of my closet door and dash outside before she can change her mind and go.

"What are you doing here?" I ask, my voice little more than a whisper as I meet her on the lawn. The grass is wet, covered in dew. It seeps through my gym shoes, moistening my feet, making them cold. Her hair is wet and I want more than anything to reach out and touch it, to graze the ombré hair with my fingertips and see if the texture changes along with the tinge: gritty to coarse to syrupy and silky, like velvet. That's the way it looks to me, like velvet. It's been raining, I think, and that's why her hair is wet. But I never heard any rain. There's dew on the lawn but the concrete of the sidewalks and street is dry. Maybe she was swimming again, treading water in Lake Michigan. Maybe that's it. That's probably it, I decide. She was swimming.

But I don't ask.

"I was bored," she admits. That's why she's here, then. I don't know what to say to this, or what to think. How bored did she have to be to come see me?

But I try not to let my self-doubt get the best of me. She's here and that's all that matters to me. She's here.

She turns and starts to walk, and like some little lost puppy, I follow. The air outside is brisk tonight, the town eerily quiet. Little more than the sound of our own footfalls fills the night, the involuntary kicking of gravel beneath our feet, the rhythmic squeak of a single shoe. There are no cars, no trains, no gulls or owls. The whole world is asleep save for us — Pearl and me.

We walk. I don't know where it is that we're going, and I don't think she knows, either. As far as I can tell, we're not going anywhere. We don't say much. Sometimes that's best, so that I don't say anything stupid and mess the whole thing up. But every now and then we say something unavailing and dumb like, *That's an ugly house,* or *Looks like the streetlight is out again.* Just shooting the shit. That kind of thing.

But then, after we've gone halfway around the block for the second time, she says, "My folks gave me up." The words come out of nowhere, though I bet they've been dwelling there in the back of her mind for a long time now, trying to work their way out, like lab rats trying to work their way through a maze. "When I was a girl," she adds, and I put her words together in my head, her confession: *My folks gave me up when I was a girl.*

Admissions like this seem a lot easier in the dark, when you don't have to see the pitying look on someone else's face, a look that somehow makes you feel worse when it's supposed to make you feel better.

"What do you mean gave you up?" I ask. "Like for adoption?"

"Yeah," she says.

"Sorry," I say because I can't think of anything better to say. Doesn't seem like it's my right to try and gouge out more information, anyway. So I settle instead on a listless, *Sorry,* hoping that she knows I really mean it. She's not a kid. She's old enough that you'd think she might be over it by now, and yet I guess you don't ever really get over these things. It's not like I've moved past my mother's leaving me. That's the kind of pain that's more of an aching throb than a sudden sting. It goes on forever.

She shrugs her shoulders and says to me, "It's okay. I'm over it," but somehow I don't think that she is. My best guess is that she's twenty-five, maybe twenty-eight years old, and she's still mad about the fact that her parents gave her up for adoption. That's the thing about stuff like that. It festers. It's human nature to hold a grudge. It's hard looking forward when you have trouble figuring out what you've left behind, or rather, what's left you behind. My own mother's been gone for thirteen years now, and not a day goes by that I don't have bad feelings about it. Truth be told, I'm still mad. And I think about her all the time. I'd tell Pearl about how she needs to forget the past and move forward with the future, but that's what we call the pot calling the kettle black. I'm no hypocrite. Sometimes things like that are easier said than done.

"How come?" I ask her then. "How come your folks gave you up?"

I can't see it, but I imagine that she shrugs.

"Why does anyone give up their kids?" she wants to know. It's a rhetorical question; she's not really looking for an answer. But inside I start to come up with all sorts of replies, such as financial trouble, divorce, a young, unmarried mother, a lack of support, just some lady who didn't have a clue how to be a mom. I'm pretty sure she doesn't want to hear any of these things. She harbors a resentment in her voice; I can hear it, clear as day. If anything, she wants me to tell her that folks give their kids up because they're lousy people and terrible parents. Because they're just mean. But I don't have a chance to say this.

"Bad girl," she spits then, the intensity of her words making me jump. They're potent and angry, and then there, in the night air, to no one in particular, she points a rigid finger accusatorily, and says again, "Bad girl. You've been a bad girl."

It's bizarre, that's for sure, Pearl's declaration or memory or whatever it is that just happened. It's not like I don't already know she's a tad bit loony, and this gives me further reason to question her sanity, and yet for whatever reason I don't. Maybe it's nice to be in the company of someone who pays no regard to the norms of society, who doesn't care what other people think. And yet those words, that pronouncement — *Bad girl* — on an otherwise quiet night stays in my mind. *You've been a bad girl.* It's a slogan that sticks with her like mine does me: *Go away, Alex. Leave me alone. Don't touch me.*

The night grows silent. I listen to the rhythm of our footfalls, my feet keeping pace with hers. We walk slowly, aimlessly, not even in a straight line. *Ambling* would be a better word. We amble down the street at night, under a canopy of stars and trees. Somewhere off in the distance, a pack of coyotes passes through a forest or field, spouting their high-frequency howls as the pack reunites for a kill. We listen, imagining a pack of coyotes stalking and surrounding a prairie dog, a cat, a squirrel.

"That's what they always told me at least. *You've been a bad girl,*" she says again, but this time her words are quieter, told with reserve. I want to ask her if it was true, if she was a bad girl. I think that maybe it was true, but also, maybe not. Maybe it was taken out of context or blown out of proportion, something along those lines. Really, all kids are bad, anyway, aren't they? Self-absorbed and all that. It's in their nature. I'm guessing I probably was and that's why my mother decided to leave. But suddenly, knowing her folks gave her up makes my mother look not quite so bad for leaving me. At least I still had Pops. She didn't take me away from Pops.

"Did you just find out?" I ask. "About being given up?" But she says no; she's known for a while. "Someone told you?" I want to know, but she says, "I figured it out on my own."

She started having dreams, she tells me, about another mother, another father. About fingers getting pointed at her, angry, denunciatory fingers, and those same five words repeated over and over again like a broken record: *You've been a bad girl.* It was years ago, many years. She was still at home living with her folks. She told her adoptive parents about the dreams, though she didn't really need to. They'd already heard her, calling out in her sleep. They knew about the nightmares, or what she thought were nightmares at the time. Turned out they were flashbacks. She was remembering. And little by little she put the pieces together and figured it out. There was the fact, too, that she didn't look a thing like her family, all tall and thickset with strawberry blond hair and light green eyes. They looked nothing like her. She was upset, overcome by a sense of abandonment and sadness, whether or not she had a family who loved her. She felt hurt, rejected by the parents who gave her up. But it was more than that, too; she'd been lied to and made to look like a fool.

Her adoptive family was contrite. "They were good people," she tells me then as we walk down the splintered street. "They *are* good people." We're closer now, moving in parallel lines. We don't touch, not intentionally, no, but every now and then the swing of her arm grazes the swing of mine. "They wanted to make it better," she tells me of her adoptive parents. She doesn't tell me their names or anything about them, but she admits that they stuffed her full of love and affection; they sent her for therapy. And at the mention of therapy, a signal goes off in my brain.

Dr. Giles.

"They did the best they could with what they were given, you know? I was a screwed-up kid. Still am, I guess. I made her cry a lot, my mother. I made him mad. But they were good people. They didn't yell, they didn't hit me when I was being bad. And it's not like they were just going to drive on into the next town and leave me with some new family I didn't know. Who does that kind of thing?" she asks with a sardonic laugh. I don't say a thing. She isn't looking for me to say anything. "They were stuck with me, you know? They'd adopted me. They signed the papers and all, though still, I put them through hell. I know I did. Couldn't help it, that's just me. It's who I am. But still," she says, "when I turned eighteen, I took my cue and decided to leave. They didn't need me sticking around anymore, poaching on their family. It was their family, anyway, not mine.

"I tried to find my family," she confesses. "My real family, anyway. And I did," she says, her voice gloomy and withdrawn. There's a long hiatus in her admission. I think that's all she's going to say. *I tried to find my family and I did.* I want to know more; I want to pry. I want to ask what happened. But I don't. I leave it at that, knowing that when she's ready she'll tell me more.

Instead, I unclasp the shark's tooth necklace from around my neck and hand it to

319

her. For strength and protection. Right now, she needs it more than me.

"I can't," she says, but she does it, anyway, taking the cord from my shaking hands as we continue on into the darkness of night, walking until I think I can walk no more, but even then, I don't want to go home.

"I tried to find my family," she says again after some time, after a long time, so long that I'd decided she was never going to tell me, "and I did. I tracked them down." I can hear her breathing in the sleepy night, her breath weighted down like mud. It doesn't come easy. An upshot of the walking — or maybe the stress. Maybe the grief.

"But they still didn't want me," she adds. "After all those years, they still didn't want me," and my heart snaps for her, knowing what it did to me after my mother rejected me. I listen as she tells me how she found her family, but as soon as she did, they tried to elude her, to refuse her phone calls, to pay her to go away. And suddenly my mother's one single rejection doesn't seem so bad. If I saw my mother again and she refused me for a second time, I don't know what I'd do. I think I'd likely lose it.

# QUINN

"Pipe down, lady," says the bus driver, a big man with an even bigger voice. He hardly turns in his chair, just enough to see that I'm not being raped at gunpoint. But he doesn't slow down the bus. He doesn't step on the brakes or reach for his walkie-talkie doodad to call for help. "Everything okay?" he asks, his voice as apathetic as if he'd asked if I wanted fries with my meal.

Behind me sits the bum who likes to touch my hair. And it's instantaneous almost, the sense of relief. Not a killer, I tell myself. Just a creep.

But the relief is short-lived.

When he smiles, I see half of his teeth are missing. The rest are yellow and misshapen. He'll lose those, too. I just know it. I'm not sure I've ever looked him in the eye before, other than a sideways glance and a simple request: *Stop touching my hair, please.*

He'd be creepy even on a good day, but

this isn't a good day. He'd be creepy if the sun was out and it was the middle of day, but this is not the middle of day, and outside the world is quiet and dark. Here and now he's downright scary.

He has a lot of hair, on his head, on his face. It's frizzed and crimped and standing on end. I can hardly see his cratered skin for all the hair. He wears a hat on top of his head, a navy-colored driving cap that doesn't do a thing to keep his ears warm. He carries with him a backpacking pack with the harness and hip belt, and a trek-king pole. There isn't much to his coat, a soft-shell hoodie the color of mushrooms. But the size of him — big — might be enough to keep him warm. On his feet are mismatched gym shoes. A handout from some aid organization — Goodwill or the Salvation Army, I'm guessing, or a lucky Dumpster dive. His hands are unwashed. He smells. He wears a lanyard around his neck with a nametag that says *Sam.* I'd bet my life he's not Sam. He found the nametag or, better yet, he stole it.

I look behind him and realize that, save for a couple of scenester teens in the back of the bus, we're the only people here. They pay us no mind. They wear sunglasses at night. They send text messages to each other. They wear headphones and use words like *tight* and *dope* and *tool,* none of which have the same meaning as was intended by Merriam and Webster. One of the boys rises to his feet and says, "I've gotta bounce."

Another says, "Bless up, my friend."

They can't save me. No way.

The rest of the bus is filled with row upon row of empty pews. No one to help.

And then the creep says, "I like your hair," as he reaches out again to touch it, and I jerk back with haste, dropping my purse so that half of its contents fall to the floor: my wallet, my makeup case, my phone. I reach my hand beneath the grimy bus seat as far as it will go to make sure I haven't managed to miss something, but my hand comes up empty. Well, empty save for the spit off someone else's chewed-up gum.

"It's pretty," the creep says, and I say to the driver, "Let me off. I need to get off the bus. I need to get off this bus *right now,*" while sweeping my belongings up off the dirty bus floor and into my bag.

And what does the bus driver say to me? "Next stop's a half block away," is what he says. "Unless it's an emergency, you'll just have to wait."

And then he yells at the homeless man to leave me alone and for the next twenty seconds he does.

He stops touching my hair. He leans back in his seat and stops talking to me.

I grab my belongings and stand. I pull the cord for the next bus stop, grateful that it's my own. When the bus comes to a halt, I don't walk. I run.

My feet pound the pavement. I'm not entirely alone on the street tonight, but I *feel* entirely alone. Knowing every soul I pass is a potential threat, there's no telling who's good and who's bad.

Who I can trust.

Who I can't trust.

I bypass people, those coming and going through store and restaurant doors; women walking dogs and men with other men, talking and laughing. I watch them all. I watch them all and wonder. Are you the one? Are you? Are you?

The question runs over and over again in my head: Has Esther hired someone to kill me?

I double- and triple-check for cars before crossing an intersection; I sidestep street gutters and storm drains in case they've been intentionally removed so that I will plummet to my death. Can one die in a storm drain? I don't know. There's no telling what kind of accident might befall me. I avoid walking too close to buildings with window air-condition units in case they might become loose and tumble down onto my head. Traumatic brain injury. That can certainly lead to death. Brain hemorrhaging. Intracranial pressure.

As I leave the more bustling streets of Clark and Foster, and head onto sleepy little streets like Farragut, I'm entirely overcome with the creeps. The willies. The heebie-jeebies.

It's entirely possible I wet my pants.

I want to go home. I want to *be* home. And not in the walk-up apartment I share with Esther. I want to be in my mother and father's home with my parents and my sister, Madison. I want to click my feet together and say it three times: *There's no place like home.*

But I don't go home.

The wind whips through the trees, tousling my hair, blowing it before my eyes so that I can't see. It wraps around my eyes like a blindfold, inhibiting my vision. But just as I'm about to panic, the wind leaves the hair, slinking down my coat, copping a feel of the bare skin. I shudder, wanting to scream at the wind.

There's the sound of traffic in the distance. A man in a three-piece suit stops and attempts to ask me for directions. "Can you tell me how to get to Catalpa?" he asks, but I tell him to go away, too. "I don't know," I say. Three or four times I say it, in rapid progression. *I don't know, I don't know, I don't know* — the words all blended together into an amalgam. The man gives me a dirty look and disappears into thin air.

And that's when I hear my name, hissed on the breath of the wind. *Quinn . . . Quinn . . .* says the wind, or at least that's what I hear.

And then a laugh, a gut-wrenching laugh.

From the shadows of the trees, he appears. *Him.*

The yellow, misshapen teeth, the shaggy hair. He stands close, reaching his dirty hand out to me, trying to touch my hair. I draw back quickly, tripping over the sidewalk and falling to the ground.

"What do you want with me?" I cry from the cold concrete.

He doesn't answer, but instead reaches out that dirty hand and tries to help me to my feet. I resist. I don't want to touch the hand; I don't want to touch him. I push myself up off the ground, cutting a palm on the rugged surface as I do. In the darkness, it starts to bleed. I rub at the injured hand, begging again, "Just leave me alone."

I turn to run, but suddenly his hand is on my arm, holding tight. Curtailing the blood supply. "Let go of me!" I scream, but he doesn't. Of course he doesn't. I'm a wiggly worm on the end of a fishing hook, kicking and screaming for dear life.

And then there, in his hand, he brandishes something, a weapon, the light from a streetlamp a solid twenty feet away casting a faint glow on the shiny matter — steel, maybe, or maybe metal. Is it a gun, a knife? I don't know. I tug at my arm. I try hard to pull away. I begin to cry.

"Don't hurt me," I beg. "Please, don't hurt me." His hand is hurting my arm, making it ache, the ligaments and muscles stretching in ways they aren't meant to go.

But all he does is laugh.

There are three million people in all of Chicagoland and not a single one of them with me on this street tonight. I should scream. That's what I should do. *Help me! Help me!* But my voice is nothing more than a whisper. I open my mouth to scream but nothing comes out.

"Hurt you?" he says. "I ain't trying to hurt you."

I say it again. "Let me go, let me go, let me go."

"You left this on the bus, lady," he tells

me. "That's all. You left this on the bus."

And then I see the item in his hand. It makes a ting, a slight noise hardly audible over the sound of my cry. Not a gun, not a knife. But a phone. Esther's phone. Which must have fallen out when I dropped my bag under a seat where I couldn't reach. As I snatch the phone from his hand, he lets go of my arm and I draw back quickly, tripping again over my own two feet. But this time, I don't fall.

An incoming text message has just arrived.

I don't need a password to read this one. There it is, right on the display screen.

Payback's a bitch, it says.

# ALEX

We're sitting on the dusty, dirty floor of the old tract home. Homes likes these, there's nothing unique about them. About a hundred of these very same homes popped up almost overnight, fifty or sixty years ago, so that this one is the same as the next, as the next, as the next. They're all the same, every single one of them, except that one may be brown and one may be blue. But they're all ugly and stodgy and just plain blah. Just like my very own home across the street from here. It's ugly, too.

It's dark outside, still night. We walked until we could walk no more, and then, instead of going back home and to bed, I came here. To this home. To Pearl's home.

"Tell me about this ghost," Pearl says. She sits on the floor before me, her legs pulled up into her. How I came to be here, I don't know. I just did. She folds her hands into her lap. The scintilla of light that sneaks in through the edges of the boarded-up window reflects off the pointed, triangular tooth — my necklace, my shark's tooth necklace, which lies over the neckline of her own T-shirt. It's dark in here. Between the boarded-up windows and the lack of lights, I can no longer tell day from night. I've lost all sense of time. Pearl sits just two feet away, staring at me, until I can hardly dredge up my own name or the reason why I'm here.

"What ghost?" I ask, though of course I know what she means. She looks a bit tuckered out. Tired. I imagine it's not easy sleeping on a hard floor, spending your days roaming some small town's streets. *Just passing through,* she'd said, and I wonder how long until she leaves. Not that I want her to leave, because I don't, but I wonder when the day will come that I'll show up at this godforsaken home and she won't be here.

"You told me this house was haunted," she says. She won't believe any of the stories I'm about to tell; I don't even believe them. But it's conversation. Small talk. And anyway, what's more important than the ghost — or this stupid idea of a ghost that half the town has conjured up — is the little girl she used to be. The rest of it is just for fun. People like to make themselves feel scared. They like to tell the tales to scare other people, too. But it's all just make-believe.

Genevieve has been dead for years now, since before I was even born. What I know is hearsay. As the story goes, she drowned in some hotel bathtub while her mother was in the neighboring room, attending to a baby, incognizant of the way five-year-old Genevieve slipped beneath the water and drowned. There was no scream like people do when they're hurt or in danger, but rather a silent death, the sagging underwater and drifting off to sleep. She never cried out; she never gasped for air. That's how the story goes.

In time, the accounts of Genevieve's death became romanticized to say the least: a little girl immersed in a cornucopia of bubble bath and soapsuds so that all that remained above water were a few random strands of brunette hair. They were in a lavish hotel room, on vacation. The description of the death scene was redolent: the puce-colored bubbles with their raspberry sorbet scent, the girl's creamy skin, reddened by the warmth of the water, though none of the people telling the tale were there to see what it is that they describe: the few random bubbles, silvery bubbles floating in the air, sticking to the bathtub tiles. Genevieve had drowned, forgotten in the bathtub thanks to a little moppet in the adjoining room, her sister, only a year or two old at the time, who had fallen from the bed and cried, taking her mother's attention away from the girl in the bathtub.

It was too expensive to ship the body across state lines, or so they say, those neighbors who are old enough to remember the day the family car pulled into the driveway of the yellow home, the three-foot corpse tucked away in the trunk to skirt whatever legalese was required of moving a body from here to there. Neighbors say they'll never forget the way they hovered in the cracked, concrete driveway, waiting to help lift the rudimentary wooden casket from the trunk and into a hole they'd dug up at the cemetery in town. The news of Genevieve's death had already arrived, leading the way into town well before her corpse.

People were shattered. Little girls weren't supposed to die.

All that was left behind was Genevieve's ghost, said to haunt people even in sleep, their dreams filled with bath water spilling over the sides of a tub, a little girl like a seraph: dead. Her skin, ashen and white, wings sprouting from her body. Her hair jet-black and wet.

I don't believe any of those things.

"Genevieve," I say to Pearl. "That's her name, the girl's name who died. The ghost's name supposedly."

"It's pretty," she tells me. "It's a pretty name."

"It is."

"And she died?"

"She did."

"Here?" asks Pearl, doing a sweep of the room with her slim arm, but I shake my head no. I follow the path of her arm, anyway, to the shadows that linger in each and every corner of the room, the spider-webs that hang from the ceiling like lace. I have half a mind to excuse myself and come back with a mop and a vacuum, to clean this place up. I think that I would do that for Pearl. I would make this place somewhat more livable and nice. I couldn't fix every-thing, no, of course not. But I could sweep the floors and dust the webs. That kind of thing. She shouldn't have to stay here in this hellhole.

The cold room has drifted to hot, thanks to the heater. Hot enough that Pearl has removed her coat and my sweatshirt and sits beside them on the floor in a thin cotton shirt and her jeans. Her arms move with the grace of a ballerina, moving through their positions in the air. I want to ask her if she ever danced, if she ever took ballet classes, what the nature is of her relationship with Dr. Giles. But I don't. Of course I don't. None of these things are my business. Everyone has their own secrets. She doesn't ask me mine, so I won't ask her hers. Though I'd tell her, of course; I'd tell her anything and everything she wanted to know.

*We're friends, right? You and I. We're friends.*

"No," I say then, focusing on the conversation at hand. "Not here. Genevieve didn't die here." And then I go on to tell her about the family vacation, about the lavish hotel. The cornucopia of bubble bath and soapsuds and all that stuff. I watch as her face saddens with my narrative of little Genevieve's death.

"She didn't know how to swim?" she asks me, and I shrug my shoulders and say, "Apparently not." Because of course if she did know how to swim she would have held her breath under water, and not inhaled deeply and let the water fill her lungs. There was speculation that Genevieve tried to stand up in the bathtub and hit her head on the ceramic tile, causing her to become unconscious before she drowned. That's just one hypothesis. No one was there to say for sure. No one saw her die. There's also the assumption that she was playing a game, trying to see how many seconds she could hold herself under water, but the water won out in the end. Oxygen deprivation, they think, summoning a breathing reflex, the body's natural need to breathe even when submerged in soapy water, filling the stomach first, and then the lungs, with fluid. Hundreds of thousands of people die each year from drowning. Of these, a huge percent are five years old or less, like Genevieve was. People can drown in anything from bathtubs, to toilets, to puddles. I think of Pops drinking himself nearly to death; he's liable, one day, to die in his own bottle of beer.

"I wonder what happens when you drown," Pearl says. "I wonder if it hurts." She looks at me then, her sad eyes wanting to know.

"I don't know," I say, "but I bet it does. I bet it's scary, not being able to breathe."

These aren't the words she wants to hear; I know that. She wants me to tell her that Genevieve merely closed her eyes and drifted off to sleep. That Genevieve didn't know any better, that one minute she was blowing bubbles in a bathtub and the next she was dead. In the afterlife. Heaven. At the pearly gates, and all that. She never knew she was dying. That's what Pearl wants to hear. But for some reason or other, I tell her the truth. Maybe because I think she's been lied to enough and she deserves the truth.

"Really scary," she agrees. "Did you ever see her after, you know . . . *after*?"

"You mean, like her body? After she died?" I ask, and she says yes. That's exactly what she means. "No," I tell her. "I wasn't even born when Genevieve died. All I've heard are the stories."

"Oh," she says, and she seems a bit let down, like she wants to hear more. Like she wishes I had seen Genevieve's corpse. But I don't have any more to tell. "I bet her family was sad," she says, and I nod my head and say, "Yeah. Really sad." But this I don't know, either. I don't know anything about Genevieve's family. They were long gone before I was born.

And then I get to wondering. "When you die, do you think you'll come back as a ghost?" I ask. It's tangential, sort of, and entirely hypothetical. Theoretical and speculative and completely make-believe. Of course, *I* don't believe in ghosts, but I ask, anyway, for the sake of conversation.

"No," she tells me decisively. "No way. There's no such thing as ghosts. Besides, if there were, I hardly think anyone would be scared of me," and she holds her flashlight up under her chin and dons a morbid expression on her face, ghostlike sounds emerging from her chest. *Ohhhh . . . Ohhhh . . .*

I laugh.

She's not scary at all. She's the flip side of scary. Her tone of voice and her warm smile and her kindly eyes, they're soothing. I find that I'm not so nervous anymore. Well, sort of. I'm still scared to death I'll say something stupid to screw the whole thing up. But I'm not so scared of her. There's something about her that puts me at ease.

"What about you?" she asks, meaning whether or not I'd come back and stalk loved ones from the beyond.

I tell her yeah, I would. Well, not loved ones exactly. But other people I would. "I'd screw with all those guys who used to pick on me in school. The girls who ignored me. My boss, Mrs. Priddy, for all the times she was mean. That kind of thing," I say, and for just a minute I savor the thought of an apparition of me tormenting Priddy from the great beyond. I smile. I kind of like that idea.

"Do you ever think about it?" she asks.

"About what?" I ask.

"About death," she says to me. "About dying."

I shake my head. "No," I say. "Not really. I try not to think about that kind of thing. You?"

"Yeah," she admits to me. "I think about it all the time."

"Why?" I ask her, and I feel her body shift closer to mine. Is it real, or is it only my imagination? I don't know, but it seems suddenly that she's within arm's reach, that if I wanted to, I could reach out and touch her hand. I don't. But I imagine that I do, running the pad of a thumb along her soft, smooth skin. "It's not like there's anything you can do to stop it. We're all going to die one day, you know."

"Yeah, I know," she says. "I get it. It's just that, what if that day is soon?"

"It's not soon," I assure her, but of course I don't know one way or the other if it's soon. For all I know, a hunk of drywall could come crashing from the ceiling right this very instant and smother us both. "You just have to try not thinking about it so much. Live for the moment, or whatever they say. Enjoy life and all that stuff."

"Enjoy life," she repeats. "Live for the moment and enjoy life." And then she turns to me, and in the murky room, I'm half certain I spy a smile radiating on her face. "You're smart, you know?" she asks, and I nod my head and tell her that I know. I *am* smart.

But as it turns out, being smart doesn't always get you where you need to go. Sometimes you need guts, too. And so I take a deep breath and reach out and touch her hand. I do it before every single neuron in my brain can scream at me, *No!* Before my overly logical and judicious side can come up with ninety-nine ways why this could go bad: she'll laugh at me, she'll pull her hand away, she'll slap me, she'll leave. Instead, the pad of my cold thumb strokes the satiny surface of her skin, and when she doesn't pull back, I smile. Secretly, quietly, on the sly, I smile. A vapid, wimpy sort of smile that I'd never want her to see, but one that seeps into every orifice of my being.

I'm happy, happy in a way that I'd never known I could be.

She doesn't say a thing; she doesn't laugh; she doesn't leave. Instead, we stay like that on the floor of the old darkened home, holding hands in silence, thinking about something other than ghosts and death and dying. At least I'm thinking about something other than ghosts and death and dying, though of course I don't know what she's thinking about until she tells me.

"I want to see her," she says then, and I ask, "See who?"

"Genevieve," she says.

"You mean the ghost? Genevieve the ghost?" I ask, feeling utterly absurd as I say it. Needless to say, it's a strange request. She wants me to summon the ghost of Genevieve. I've played Ouija once, a long, long time ago, but I'm absolutely certain that game is gone. We could hold a séance, I guess. Light candles, sit around holding hands and all that crap. Try and channel Genevieve's spirit. Sounds like a bunch of BS to me, but I'm guessing there isn't any request Pearl could make which I wouldn't oblige.

But still, I'm more than a little bit relieved when she says no.

"No," she says. "I want to see her grave. Where she's buried," Pearl adds.

"It's the middle of the night," I say, not to mention that the idea is a bit bizarre. Why in the world does she want to see Genevieve's grave? Why now?

"You're not afraid, are you?" she asks me, smiling as she slips her hand out of mine and rises to her feet. She stands before me with her hands on her hips, waiting for me to reply. It's a dare.

I shake my head. I'm not afraid. I rise up to my feet, too, dusting off the seat of my pants with my hands. What kind of ninny would I be if I passed up a midnight rendezvous in a cemetery with a woman? "Live for the moment," she reminds me then as we scale the window one at a time and return outside. "Enjoy life."

"Enjoy life," I parrot as we walk down the street. The night has grown cooler in the short time we were inside; the wind has picked up speed. It's cold, but somehow, with Pearl walking beside me, closer than she was before, I feel warm. I reach out again and hold her hand. I don't think twice this time; I just do. She doesn't pull away, and so we walk like that, hand in hand, down the middle of the street and to the cemetery in town. She's got to be ten years older than me, but not for a second does it feel weird. It feels right. We don't talk, we don't shoot the shit. We don't say anything. I lead, planning to show Pearl where the cemetery is, though every now and again I get the sense that Pearl is the one drawing me there. She wants to see where Genevieve is buried.

The cemetery is old. One of two in town, and this is the older of the two. It existed before the public cemetery was built over a decade ago. The only reason I know Genevieve is buried here is because this is where the boys and I used to play ghosts in the graveyard when we were little kids. Of course, it's not really a game that has to be played in a graveyard, but somehow it made it all the more fun. This old cemetery belongs to a church, a small old-world building that sits off to the side. We cross the lawn and take aim on Genevieve's slumping tomb. There's no more space here to bury the dead and those who are here, entombed six feet below, beneath brittle, moss-covered headstones, are often forgotten, their offspring buried on the other side of town where visitors tend to go. I haven't been here in years. Not since I was a boy, maybe eight years old, and I would walk past all the headstones, wishing my mother was buried beneath one. Oh, how I wanted her to be dead. Because that would have been better. Dead would have been a better excuse than just plain gone. I'd take death over abandonment any old day of the week.

But this is where Genevieve is buried, with a small grave marker, the kind small enough for a dead pet. It's a beveled marker, gray with black details, sunken into the browning, moribund lawn.

On the grave is an offering of flowers, black-eyed Susans pulled from someone else's lawn, nothing more than withered-up seed heads lying on the ground. Bird food masquerading as flowers. But who would leave flowers here, beside this grave? Far as I know, no one comes to visit any of these graves, other than on the annual Halloween cemetery walk, meant to be spooky and not commemorative in any sort of way. Strange, if you ask me.

Pearl drops to her knees in the sodden lawn and picks at the black-eyed Susan stems. She runs her fingers over the chiseled letters, slowly, thoughtfully, as if memorizing their details, the slope of the *G,* the curlicue *e,* the hurtling *V.* I stand a foot or two back, watching, seeing a sadness in her eyes and thinking to myself that it *is* sad. Knowing that a little girl has died. It's sad whether or not either of us ever knew Genevieve. I've heard the stories; nearly everyone has heard the stories. But I'll never know Genevieve. Pearl will never know Genevieve. But still, it's depressing, thinking that she's down there, just a rotting corpse, lying beneath this spot where we now stand. It's depressing and weird.

But then things get even more weird.

Pearl, kneeling down on the wet lawn, now lies down. She folds over sideways, in the fetal position, and lies on Genevieve's grave. As if holding the little, dead girl. As if embracing her. As if comforting her in some, odd way.

She says to me, "Alex. Come here, too," and I do, but I can't bring myself to lie down in a cemetery. Instead, I sit. Or rather, I squat. I squat down on the lawn so that my calves begin to burn and I listen as Pearl begins to recite a prayer for the dead Genevieve.

"Now I lay me down to sleep," she says, and I credit empathy and compassion for the tears that drip from Pearl's eyes, but maybe there's more to it than that.

Maybe she's just plain crazy, though it doesn't make me like her any less.

In some weird way, it might just make me like her more.

# QUINN

"Slow down," Ben says to me as I sit on a tweed Breuer kitchen chair and he presses a bandage to my hand. "Tell me what happened." His face is close, a measly six inches away, so that I can smell the soy sauce on his breath when he speaks.

There are dried tears clinging to my cheeks. My hand is covered in blood.

On the kitchen chair, I tremble. In fear and because I'm cold. It's cold in the room. There's a blanket spread across my lap, a chunky blue throw. I have no clue how it got there. Somehow or other, I'm missing a shoe. My shirt is torn at the sleeve, right where that homeless man wrenched on my arm, pulling the muscles and ligaments this way and then that, the skin fiery red. Ben opens the freezer door and reaches inside for ice, filling a plastic bag with it. He lays that on my forearm and I blanch. It's cold.

There are three chairs blockading the

345

front door at my request. Ben never once said it was silly or stupid or asked why. He just did it, sliding the mod plaid chair across the room, scurrying into Esther's bedroom to retrieve the IKEA desk chair.

He didn't ask why. He just did it.

Esther's cell sits on the table beside me, the message still there when we press the Home button to revive the phone.

Payback's a bitch, it says, the text coming from some unknown number.

"She's watching me," I say to him as he pours me a glass of red wine and sits at the table opposite me on his own chair. His eyes are warm, a nice contrast to my cold.

"Drink this," Ben says. "It'll help calm your nerves." He slides the cup across the table to me. It isn't in a fancy wine glass. Rather, a red plastic cup. A smart decision on Ben's part, considering my current state. My hands shake as they lift the cup. Under the table, Ben's hand covers my knee. His touch is warm and reassuring. Soothing.

I say it again. "She's watching me."

Esther is watching me.

Ben and Priya were feasting on dim sum at some dive in Chinatown when I called, hysterical and crying. "What do you mean you can't find the file?" he said on the phone to me. "I left it on your desk this afternoon." Then he said to Priya, there in the populous restaurant on Cermak so that I could hear his crafty words over the noise, "I'm so sorry, babe. There's been a mix-up at work. A missing file. I have to go."

And then he left Priya in Chinatown, and brought me takeout: crispy sesame chicken and an egg roll to boot. And a bottle of red wine. He arrived in the doorway, his face overcome with signs of worry: the trenches of his forehead, the concerned eyes. He wore a smile, but it was utterly bogus, meant to bolster my mood.

"I got here as fast as I could," he said, his voice bleeding with sympathy. He'd changed from his office attire into something far less formal than what I was used to seeing him in at work — jeans and a heather-gray hooded sweatshirt. But his hair was perfect and he oozed the crisp, cool cologne that made me dizzy and numb. Euphoric.

"I hope Priya wasn't mad," I said when he arrived, but he shrugged it off and said it didn't matter, anyway. Truth be told, I didn't really care whether or not Priya was mad; I was just so happy he'd come. So relieved. They were just finishing up their meal, and then Priya planned to bolt, anyhow, thanks to a heavy dose of home-work. That's what Ben tells me. He offered to help — or keep her company at least — but she'd said no. "She had too much to do," said Ben, and I made believe I saw in his eyes a certain satisfaction that *I* needed him, that unlike Priya, I couldn't do this alone. I needed his help *and* his company.

And so he washed and bandaged my hand. He moved the chairs. He got ice for my arm. He poured me wine.

My knight in shining armor.

And I told him what happened: about my visit with Nicholas Keller, the commute home, the creepy homeless man touching my hair, the text message on the cell phone.

"Why didn't you tell me you were going to see Nicholas Keller?" he asks, sitting before me, a look of concern and kindness in his eyes. He runs a hand along my arm before finding its way back into his lap.

"I didn't want to bother you," I admit, and it's true. Ben has been so good to spend so much time and energy helping me figure out where Esther has gone and what she's up to. She's his friend, yes, but it seems somehow like this is more my problem than his. But going to see Nicholas was also an impulsive decision on my part. I hardly knew where I was going until I walked out my front door and hopped on the Red Line, getting ferried underground. It wasn't so much of a well-hatched plan as it was a spontaneous one, one that suddenly feels stupid. I should have asked Ben to tag along. I should have sat beside him at Nicholas Keller's kitchen table and the both of us should have heard with our own two ears how Esther killed his fiancée.

Ben leans in even closer, his hand now kneading the denim of my jeans so that my barely beating heart almost completely stops working. "I would have gone with you. It wouldn't have been a bother. That's what friends do," he says, and I nod my head sluggishly, thinking of course this is what friends do. They don't stalk each other down and make attempts on their life.

And then I repeat for a third time or maybe a fourth, "She's watching me," and he says, "Maybe," and then in that take-charge no-nonsense way that I like, "We need to call the police." He releases his hold on my kneecap and sits back in his chair. But suddenly he feels far away, too far, the six- or eight-inch distance now transforming into eighteen, the slope of his body concave versus convex. I find myself leaning in, hoping to bridge that gap. *Come back, Ben.*

"I've already done that," I say. "I went to the station. I filed a missing-persons report," and I fill him in on my exchange with the officer at the front desk who asked for Esther's name, her photograph. He said they'd be in touch, but still, no one has been in touch.

"Maybe it's time to report a crime," he says instead, though both of us know we have nothing more than an unsubstantiated hunch to report. Just a premonition. A bad feeling.

The death of Kelsey Bellamy was ruled an accident. Since then, there's no evidence of a crime because no crime has been committed. Not yet, anyway.

For now, it's just an irrational fear that Esther is out to get me. Esther, my good friend, my dear roommate. I tell myself, *Esther would never hurt me,* but even I am not so sure.

The budding lawyer in Ben knows this better than me; he knows we don't have anything effectual for the police. Paperwork on loss and grieving, and a petition for a change of name, cash withdrawal receipts. That's irrelevant. It's not illegal to change your name, or to feel sad. To take money out of your own bank account. To ask to have the locks changed on your apartment door. Esther has done nothing wrong. Or has she?

"Besides," I say then, thinking as I stare into his hazel eyes, hoping that there I might find the answers to all my many questions, "what if we're wrong about all this? What if this is all some stupid mistake and we call the police and turn her in? What will it do to Esther if we're wrong? She'll go to prison," I tell him, my voice convulsing now as I imagine Esther spending the rest of her days behind bars when maybe, just maybe, she didn't do anything wrong. "Esther is too kind for jail," I tell Ben, "too nice," but then I imagine the Esther that purposefully added peanut flour to Kelsey's meal to end her life, and not the Esther who sings hymns in the church choir. Esther can't possibly be both of these things.

But did Esther do something wrong? I don't know for certain. I ask the question out loud for Ben. "Did she kill her? Did Esther kill Kelsey Bellamy?"

Ben shrugs. "I don't know for sure, but it looks to me like she did," he says, confirming the same suspicion that now takes over my mind. Esther killed Kelsey and now she's trying to kill me, too.

"But what if we're wrong and we call the police with this false claim that Esther is a murderer?" I ask Ben. "We'll ruin her life."

Ben mulls this over.

351

"I went to high school with a guy," he says after some time. "Brian Abbing. Rumor had it he broke into some pricey bridal shop one night, and made off with a few thousand bucks from the register. The back window was smashed. The place was tossed, shattered mannequins and torn dresses everywhere. There was no proof that Brian did anything, but still, people pointed fingers."

"Why?" I ask.

"Someone saw him hanging out down the street. And he was just sort of *that kid,* the kind of kid who people like to pick on. He never dated, he talked with a lisp, he had no friends other than Randy Fukui, who was just as much of a hermit as Brian. They did everything wrong — they had the wrong clothes, wrong music, wrong hair. They talked about video games all day, and made friends with the old shop teacher, some Vietnam vet who talked about flamethrowers and rocket launchers all the damn time."

"People made fun of them because they didn't like their clothes?" I ask. I'm listening but I'm only sort of listening.

"It was high school," Ben says, and I think, *Enough said.* I hated high school. Everyone hates high school except for those in the catty and shallow cliques — the lacrosse players and the girls of the pom-

pom squad — who roam the halls, making others feel unworthy. I couldn't wait to get out of high school when I was there.

"What happened," I ask, "to Brian?" My heart suddenly goes out to Brian. I was teased for many things as a teenager, mainly my utter stupidity. It's not a good thing being stupid when you're also a blonde. I was called many things: banana head, buttercup, Tinker Bell. The blond jokes were endless.

"Police never could figure out who did it, not soon enough, anyway. There was no evidence, no fingerprints, and so it remained an open case. But the kids put him on trial, anyway. They pointed fingers, they called him names. Even Randy stopped talking to him. He couldn't walk to math class without half the school calling him a crook or a klepto. By the time the police nabbed the real culprit, some six months later, Brian had already climbed to the top of some cell phone tower and jumped."

"He killed himself?"

"He killed himself."

"Wow," I say. It seems kind of extreme for me, but I guess that's the kind of thing you never get over, the name-calling and finger-pointing. Sometimes when I close my eyes at night I can still hear my entire econ class laughing because every time the teacher called on me, it was as if I'd gone mute. *Earth to Quinn . . .*

"Same thing could happen to Esther," Ben says. "It doesn't matter if she was exonerated from charges, if charges were even made. People would always look at her and think, *Murderer,* whether or not she is," and I nod my head listlessly, knowing that's exactly what I'm thinking, too.

Esther is a murderer.

"Once a murderer, always a murderer," I say then as I sip from my plastic wine cup with shuddering hands, spilling tiny red droplets along the tabletop. Red like blood. "Esther would be hurt if it turned out we were wrong."

I'm not sure it's the best time to be worried about Esther's feelings, but I can't help myself. I am. Though of course if we're right, then I might be the one who ends up hurt, though in an entirely different way than Esther. But still, I imagine Esther all alone at the top of a cell phone tower just like Brian Abbing, about to free-fall to the ground below, and I know we can't call the police. Not yet, anyway. Not before we know more.

"There's no reliable evidence, nothing tangible, no witnesses or hearsay," Ben says, reaching for a napkin and wiping my mess away. If only everything were so simple. He agrees with me now and takes back his advice of going to the police, and the decision — whether good or bad — is made not to call.

Instead, we sit at the kitchen table in nervous silence. Ben unearths the crispy sesame chicken from a paper bag and hands me a fork. He refills my wine and pours himself a cup and then scoots his chair closer to mine, and under the small kitchen table, we touch.

The first glass of wine is, in a word, ghastly. We sit taking small, pensive sips from our plastic cups of merlot. We ignore the way my hands convulse as I raise the cup up to my lips and sip. What I want to do is scream. I want to scream loud enough that all the neighbors can hear, that Mrs. Budny can hear, but especially so that Esther can hear. *Why?* I want to scream. *Why are you doing this to me?*

By the second cup of wine, we leave the kitchen table and move into the living room where we sit side by side on the small sofa. A joke is made and we both force a stilted laugh, thinking in the backs of our minds we shouldn't be laughing at a time like this. But the laughing is contagious, one laugh which leads to two and then three. The mood in the room becomes lighter and the world takes on an air that is no longer all Debbie Downer. It feels good.

By the time a third cup is poured I can hardly remember why my shirtsleeves are torn and on the palm of my hand is a giant gauze bandage and strips of medical tape. By the fourth I'm quite certain our legs became tangled on the small sofa like a Jenga game — his on top of mine, on top of his, legs which we keep pulling out and re-arranging on top of one another, trying to get comfortable. It isn't in the least bit libidinous, but rather cuddlesome and af-fectionate, something that takes my mind off this week's strange turn of events that's transported me from a normal existence to one which has gone completely haywire and berserk. We talk about things other than Es-ther. We talk about Anita, our boss at work, the one paid to deal with the miscreant project assistants like Ben and me. We debate things like the death penalty and as-sisted suicide, whether or not orange candies really are the worst. They are (Ben disagrees, though of course he's wrong). At some point Ben asks about my love life, or com-plete lack thereof (my words, not his), and I grimace and bring up Priya instead, fueled by alcohol to ask the question that's been living at the back of my mind for months.

"What do you see in her?" I say audaciously, though it isn't meant to be trivializing or mean, but comes out that way, anyway, and I thank the wine for that as I thank the wine for many things: for the fact that Ben is here, snuggled beside me; for the fact that I have no misgivings about the way my hand reaches out to grab his, not worrying once that he won't reciprocate the gesture; for the fact that for the first time in days, I tingle with happiness instead of fear.

"Everything," Ben says, and I feel my heart sink — my hand starts a slow withdrawal from his — only to rise to the surface again as he sighs and says then, "Nothing," and I'm not sure which to believe: everything, nothing or something in between.

"I've been with her half my life," he confesses to me, staring at me with those eyes of his, his voice drowsy from the wine, his face close enough to mine to feel his breath when he speaks. "I don't know what it's like to not be with Priya," and I think that I get it. I *think* that I do, this sense of familiarity and comfort that slips into a relationship over time, completely trampling all excitement and passion. I don't get it personally, because of course my longest relationship lasted a mere seventy-two hours, but I get it. I see the way my own parents no longer kiss; they don't hold hands. I watch the way my father sleeps on the guest bed lest my mother's chronic insomnia keep them both up all night. Ben and Priya aren't even married and already there's no excitement, no passion. At least that's what I'd like to believe, but who am I to say what goes on in their private life.

But I don't want to think about that right now; I don't want to think about Priya. Instead, I press myself closer to Ben so that we sit side by side, our legs running in parallel lines, plunked on the coffee table, my ankle crossed with his.

As if this is normal. As if this is something we do.

I have no idea how he comes to spend the night, but I'm so glad he does.

■ ■ ■ ■

# THURSDAY

■ ■ ■ ■

# ALEX

"Hello?" I call out softly as I come into the quiet house through the back window, doing a sweep of the room with my flashlight. It's early morning, the sun just beginning to ascend into the November sky. The house is still relatively dark, not yet revived by the luminescence of the morning light. The home is quiet. Pearl might just be asleep, which wouldn't be such a bad thing. I wouldn't mind sitting here for a while, watching as she sleeps.

I've been thinking about her all night, since I walked her home from the cemetery and in the middle of the street in the middle of the night we said good-night.

In fact, I find that I can't get her out of my mind.

I tread quietly through the first floor, a mug of instant coffee in my hand. I don't drink coffee, but it was the only thing we had on hand at home. I don't want to wake

361

her — not yet, anyway, not before I catch a vision of her asleep, just a whisper of the ombré hair spilling across the country plaid pillow, the moth-eaten blanket pulled up to her chin, her skin rosy red, her eyes still crusty with sleep. The house is warm, thanks to the heater, the faint smell of kerosene still filling the air. That and something chemical and unpleasant, like mothballs and mold.

But when I come into the living room, the ad hoc bed is empty. She's not there. The heater is on, and so I know that she's here somewhere. She knows better than to leave the heater unheeded. I told her as much before. And yet she's *not* here, on the floor, sound asleep as I expected her to be, in my sweatshirt, with my necklace wrapped around her neck. I lay my hand on the bedding and feel that it's grown cold. And I think that she's left, that she's left me, and I feel sad and more than a little bit let down. She's gone.

But then I hear something coming from up the stairs, a sound. A voice, singing. A soprano voice crooning a song. I stop for a moment to listen, willing my heartbeats to stop so that I can hear. It's little more than a murmur that echoes throughout the hollow home, bouncing off the pared walls and the frail steps that are covered in unraveled carpeting. I hold my breath. I try to hear past the ringing in my ears.

It's her. It's Pearl, and she's singing.

I leave the coffee behind and head up the stairs, one step at a time, summoned by the melody.

On the second floor, I scan the bedrooms one by one, pitying the family who once lived here, the forgotten dolls and animals, a child's drawing that still hangs from the putrefying pink walls. It's sad. Pathetic, really, and what makes it even worse is that whoever swiped the refrigerator, the air conditioner, the copper pipes, didn't want a thing to do with the bears or dolls.

Upstairs, it's cold, the outside air bursting into the bedroom without restraint. The broken windows are open wide, and the range of the heater doesn't reach this far.

I follow the sound of Pearl's voice, and before I'm fully aware of what's happening, I'm in a bedroom, her bedroom, *Genevieve's* bedroom. I know it's Genevieve's bedroom because a wooden *G* hangs crookedly from a nail on the wall. I take in an old, cracked dresser, a shattered mirror, walls that are a cloudy pink. I step over the shards of glass on the floor, certain some vandal did that — that they broke the mirror — consigning him or herself to seven years' bad luck. There are things left behind that no one wants: a doll on the floor, an eerie, eldritch doll that stares up at me with acrylic eyes; furniture, splintered beds and the cracked dresser, left behind for the rats and mice to share.

And then there is Pearl.

She stands on the far side of the room with her back turned to me. She doesn't know that I'm here. She stares down at a doll in her arms, a soft cloth doll with filaments of blue yarn for hair. Blue, yes, blue. Don't ask me why it's blue. That's not the weird thing.

The weird thing is the look in Pearl's eye, which I glean in the reflection of the broken mirror on the floor — a patchwork of endearment and sadness — as she cradles that doll in her arms, and runs a gentle hand over the fibrils of hair. The way she lifts the doll up to her lips and places a kiss on its raggedy old forehead. The doll is dressed in a knitted green dress with matching green shoes, a pink cardigan that stretches to her fingerless hands. She's made of cloth, her smile a simple strip of red yarn. Her eyes are made of beads, but the whole of her is in tatters, badly worn, and abandoned for many long years, along with the home. Just like Pearl.

It's then, as I stare like a deaf dumb mute, that Pearl presses the doll against her chest, supporting and protecting her like a mother does her child. She closes her eyes and begins to sway at the hips, resuming the melody that first summoned me up the broken stairs and into the bedroom. And that's when I realize this isn't just any kind of song, but rather a lullaby.

I gather bits and pieces of the lullaby's refrain: *Hush-a-bye, don't you cry,* as she sings for the doll that lies listlessly in her arms. She cradles the baby with fondness and devotion, but also something akin to ownership, claim and proprietary rights.

It's weird.

I'm speechless. I can't say anything, and for a good thirty or forty-five seconds, I can't move. I can't do anything but stare as Pearl holds that doll and pitches herself back and forth, back and forth, slowly in the room. She sings, her voice perfectly pitched. It's seductive, really; it could lull me to sleep. *Go to sleep, my little baby.*

But there's something not right about this. I feel that in every single one of my bones. My body screams at me to leave. *Leave!* But I don't leave. Not at first, anyway. I can't, for I'm completely captivated and enchanted by the measured sway of her hips and the tiny, precise toe taps, the squeak of the floorboards that accompanies her every move like a three-piece band. There's a part of me that wants to say something, to reach out and touch her, to swap places with the doll so that she'll dance with me instead. And I close my eyes for one moment and one moment alone and allow myself to evoke the soft touch of Pearl's hands around my neck, to feel her warm breath in my ear, even if it is only pretend. I want to tell her to stop. To put the doll down. To come back downstairs with me so we can both pretend this never happened, that I didn't see this. I want to sit on the moth-eaten blanket and talk about ghosts and death and dying. I want to go back in time, if only ten minutes at best. I want to go back to ten minutes ago when I climbed merrily though the broken window with a cup of cheap coffee in my hands, thinking that maybe — just maybe — today we would kiss.

But there's also a part of me that wants to run.

# QUINN

In the morning, we dance the two-step in my tiny apartment kitchen, going this way and that, for coffee and mugs. We step on each other's toes. We both giggle and blush and say, *Excuse me,* at the very same time, and again we laugh. I pour his coffee; he retrieves the sugar from the canister on the counter. It's as if we've done this a thousand times before.

*Poor Priya,* is what I should be thinking, but instead: *Yay me!*

We didn't sleep together. Not in the way that is often intended by those two words. But we did *sleep together.* And by that I mean two bodies sound asleep in nearly the same space, me on my bed, he on my bed, head to toe, toe to head. There may or may not have been a kiss. But that's hard to remember, thanks to the wine.

And now, in daylight, standing in the kitchen, I ask, "Do you want cereal for

367

breakfast?" opening the refrigerator and then a cabinet door. There's not much to be seen: Esther's Frosted Flakes, some instant oatmeal, a gallon of milk that may or may not have expired.

"No," Ben says. "I'm not a breakfast person," and so he sticks with the coffee as I pour myself a bowl of Esther's Frosted Flakes and eat them dry just to be on the safe side. Certainly Esther wouldn't poison her own Frosted Flakes.

Or would she?

I take a bite and spit it out posthaste, deciding maybe I'm not such a breakfast person after all, either.

"I should go," Ben says then, speaking in one-word sentences. "Shower," he says, and, "Work."

And that's where things get awkward.

Most men who spend the night with me end up disappearing before the rise of day, usually at my request. I know how the story goes. They say they'll call, but they never call. I sit around waiting for the phone to ring, feeling sorry for myself when it doesn't, and then angry with myself for getting my hopes up. For even thinking that they'll call. I should know better.

These days I'm the first to say goodbye, and so at daybreak, before the sun has a chance to accentuate his latest mistake, I tell my dates to leave. It's far easier to be the one in the managerial position telling some man to go, rather than the one who gets left behind.

*My roommate,* I hear myself say, *is awake. You have to go.*

But with Ben it's different. With Ben, I don't want him to leave. I don't want to say goodbye. I want to thank Ben for coming to my rescue, for keeping me safe, for bandaging my injured hand. For getting me through what would have otherwise been a terrifying night. For the food and the wine and the company, and maybe, just maybe, for the kiss. If there was a kiss. I'd like to pretend that there was, just to get that awkward first kiss out of the way. The next one, I tell myself, will be far less thorny and fraught instead with romance and passion. That's what I tell myself, anyway, as I watch Ben slip into a coat and then into his shoes.

But instead all I manage is a stiff, unconvincing, "You're the best," and he says, "You're not so bad yourself," and then he goes and I'm left overanalyzing those five elementary words of his — *You're not so bad yourself* — until it's enough to make my head explode.

I run to the window to see him leave,

drooling out the window like a dog watching its owner go. Once he's gone, around the corner and out of sight, I peer at the clock on the microwave: 7:58. I peer down at my attire: pajamas. I have seventeen minutes to get showered and dressed for work. Shit.

I grab the dirty dishes and toss them in the sink; the last thing I want is the apartment looking like a sty if Esther decides to come home. I don't need to give her any more fuel for the fire, another reason to want to do away with me. I open a window a crack, hoping to air out the stench of last night's crispy sesame chicken, now hardening on a plate on the coffee table. I grab that dish, too, chuck the chicken in the trash and set the plate by the sink. It's just as I'm about to head into the shower that I hear the sound of my phone, set on the countertop beside the now-empty bottle of red wine, ringing. I grab for it and pick it up, not bothering to look at the numbers on the display screen.

"Hello?" I ask, pressing the phone to my ear. I will it to be Esther. *Please let it be Esther.*

But it's not Esther.

On the other end of the line, a flinty voice asks, "Is this Quinn Collins?" and I say that it is while listening to the sound of neighbors in the hall scurrying off to work, the slamming of an apartment door, the jingling of keys.

"This is Quinn Collins," I say, my mind predicting I'm about to be suckered into buying a new cell phone plan or donating to breast cancer research.

"Ms. Collins, this is Detective Robert Davies, following up on a missing-persons report you filed," the flinty voice says, lacking all the charisma I'd expect of a salesman. He isn't friendly; rather, he's curt and intimidating, and my first instinct is that I've somehow done something wrong, that I've overlooked some missing-persons protocol I should have known about. I'm in trouble. I've screwed up, again. I've heard this tone before from my father, from a teacher, from an employer before he fired me for some wrongdoing, or for just being plain lazy. Seems I'm always letting someone down.

"Yes," I say meekly as I press my back to the popcorn wall, the phone to my ear, and admit sheepishly, "I filed a missing-persons report." Though I can't see it, I'm certain my skin turns red.

I hear the sound of paper on the other end of the line, and imagine this man, this

Detective Robert Davies, thumbing through the report, staring at the image of Esther and me I imparted to the Chicago PD: she and I at Midsommarfest, feasting on greasy ears of corn. I uproot memories of the setting sun, the sound of some ABBA tribute band onstage, Esther laughing as she smiled for the camera with a piece of hairy husk strewn between her teeth.

*Where are you, Esther?* I silently plead.

"You're the roommate of Esther Vaughan?" he asks, and when I say that I am, he says he has some questions for me, questions he'd like to discuss in person. At this my stomach drops. Why? Why does he want to talk to me? In person, no less. Can't he ask his questions over the phone?

"Am I in trouble?" I ask spinelessly, and he lets loose a railroading laugh, the kind that isn't meant to express humor but rather be intimidating. And it works; I'm intimidated.

I glance at the clock. I now have about fourteen minutes until I need to leave for work. I don't have time to stop by the police station on the way to work, and I'm not even sure I want to speak to this detective all on my own. I need Ben.

"I can stop by the station this afternoon," I say, though of course that's the last thing in the world I want to do. "After work."

But the detective says to me, "No, Ms. Collins, it can't wait until the afternoon. I'll come to you," he decides, and already he's asking where I work — though I'm banking on the fact this is something he knows — but one thing I refuse is to let a detective show up at the office, asking questions, in a place where gossip and hearsay spread like wildfire. *Police were here,* people will say, *asking questions.* Details will be invented: handcuffs, Miranda rights, a million-dollar bail. Before the end of the day, the rumor mill will have decided that I killed my roommate and Kelsey Bellamy, too.

I shake my head. I tell him no. "I can meet you in an hour," I say to him instead, and we make arrangements to meet at Millennium Park.

"Make it two," he says then, seemingly the kind of man who always needs to get in the last word. We'll meet at Millennium Park in two hours. Detective Davies and me. Sounds quite quaint, and also a little painful and terrifying, like dental work. I sigh, pressing the end button on the phone and then I make two subsequent calls: one to work, calling in sick — a second bout of the stomach bug, I tell my boss, Anita, who is clearly not pleased — and a second call to Ben, which goes unanswered to my chagrin.

But here's the really weird thing, though of course everything about this day, this week, is weird. When I talk to Detective Robert Davies, I'm absolutely certain we've spoken before. His voice is as familiar to me as some decades-old song whose lyrics you never forget.

I'm not in a rush anymore. Now I have time to kill, two hours until I meet the detective. I drift into Esther's room and drop to the floor, assessing the photograph I'm creating, all those minced-up bits of photo paper coming together one by one: the sleeve of a plum sweater, the black of a shoe. Threads of blond hair that look uncannily like mine, the blond blown-out look bobbing on the surface of that chunky sweater with its bateau neckline. My fingers start to shake as I grab for more shreds and lay them in place, the task becoming quicker now that it's nearly through. There aren't so many pieces remaining anymore in my pile on the floor, and I've become quite the maven, knowing innately the blue of the sky versus the blue of a short-sleeve shirt of a man hovering in the background beneath a store awning, which is, of course, also blue. I gather the bits one by one and pop them into place, watching the image take shape: a city street scene. I'm not one for wearing purple, but the sweater is a favorite of mine, the boatneck that slips from the shoulder exposing the flesh of a collarbone: the closest to sexy I ever get. It's a dark purple, nothing too feminine or dainty like lavender or violet, but rather plum. A robust plum. I'm standing midstride in the image, walking down the urban street. I'm not smiling; I'm not even staring at the camera. In fact, I don't even know that the camera is there, and — as I'm flanked by dozens of other pedestrians also as incognizant of the camera as I — I imagine Esther hidden on the other side of the busy city street, snapping the photo with a long lens.

But why?

It's as I lay the last few shreds with shaking hands that the answer comes to me. As I piece together the last ribbons of skin I begin to understand, the skin no longer a summer tan but losing color quickly and drifting to a winter white as it does now. My face takes shape: the flat forehead, the thin eyebrows, the big eyes. I piece together the nose, the lips, moving downward, and as I reach the exposed neck above the collar of that plum sweater I see that someone's

taken a red roller ball pen to the flesh and
slashed clear through the neckline.

# ALEX

I run silently from the house but I don't go home. Instead, I hide in the overgrown bushes outside. I haven't quite figured out what to do and so I loiter and think, think and loiter. But I don't have to do either too long. Before I know it, there's a noise from the window of the old home. The sound of footsteps in the lawn. The crunch of brittle, autumn leaves beneath her feet. And then Pearl appears and makes the decision for me.

She is wrapped up in her coat and hat and in her hands is a shovel. *A shovel?* I think, taking a second look at the item in her hands. Yes, a shovel.

She starts to walk. She doesn't see me as I follow her by twenty paces or more, as we drift down the street and into town, heading in the direction of the old cemetery, again. I am on tiptoes, trying hard to silence my footsteps. Pearl, herself, walks as if on air.

I watch breathlessly as Pearl lets herself in through the strident iron gate, walking across a carpet of fallen leaves. I follow. It's still early morning, the sun having yet to subdue the heavy fog that impregnates the land, turning the air to clouds. We walk through clouds all along the way, Pearl in the front, me in the rear, watching as the world materializes before us in ten-foot increments so that we're utterly clueless as to what exists beyond those visible ten feet. I am, at least. I have no idea what's there or what's not there as if I'm Christopher Columbus half certain that in those ten feet I might fall off the face of the flat earth and die. Black turns to gray — the bark of the trees, the iron of the gate getting washed away by the fog. Everything is pale and bleached. Tree branches and age-old gravestones become intangible, evanescing at their edges. Before my eyes, they disappear, too, lost in the brume. Streetlamps are on, their light fading fast in ten-foot intervals as do the trees and the fence and the gravestones I falter past one by one by one, tripping over rocks and roots all along the way to Genevieve's resting spot, her grave.

Pearl has no idea that I'm here.

As I hover in the distance, completely blanketed by the thick fog and the branches of dense shrubbery, I see her take a gardening spade to the earth and start to dig.

# Quinn

Outside the day is cold. It's sunny, but that doesn't mean much. The sun reflects off the glass of the buildings, subduing me. Slowing me down. It's in my eyes so that I can't see, and I need to see as I scurry through the masses of people, looking forward, looking backward, hurrying on my way to Millennium Park. I turn around quickly, making sure I'm not being trailed.

The temperatures stick around in the mid-forties as, up and down Michigan Avenue, workers hang holiday lights on the buildings and trees. It's too early for this, only November, and yet within days Mickey and Minnie will arrive to lead the parade, the Magnificent Mile Lights Festival, which Esther and I went to together last year.

But this year we won't be going.

I consider the red line singed across my neck in the shredded photograph and think, *This year I might be dead.*

The streets are busy. Sandwiched somewhere in between the morning rush and the noon hour, the streets are still congested with people, hordes of them standing at various intersections, waiting for their turn to cross. Cabs soar by, much too quickly for the allotted speed of thirty. I stand at the intersection, waiting for the light to turn green. I watch as a cabbie slams on the brakes, startling a woman in the center of the street. She drops her yoga mat and flips him off, but he breezes past her, anyway, uncaring.

And then I scurry on to Millennium Park.

Millennium Park is a ginormous park right in the heart of the Loop, complete with a garden and band shell, an ice rink, a fountain with reflecting pool and, of course, the legendary Bean. It has a name, one I can't think of right now as I hurry right past it, but for most of us Chicagoans it's aptly known as the Bean. It looks like a bean. *If it talks like a bean and walks like a bean, then it is probably a bean.*

Tons of people gather at Millennium Park each day, locals and tourists alike. It's a hotspot. Kids kick around in the reflecting pool, being spat at by the faces of Crown Fountain. They lie on their backsides beneath the Bean to see their warped reflections in the steel plates like a fun-house mirror. They dine in outdoor cafés; they listen to live music on the lawn of the pavilion, catching some rays under the warm, summer sun. They follow paths and bridges through the gardens and eat ice cream beneath the tall trees.

But not today.

Today it's too cold.

I didn't think of this when considering a nice, public place to meet the detective.

I'm early. While I wait for the detective to show, I try to hide among the stripped November trees, but they're transparent, see-through. They offer no disguise. Tourists with a camera pass by and ask that I take their picture. I back away. I say that I'm in a hurry. I can't be slowed down.

I make the decision to steal away into a local coffee shop to kill some time. I order a latte and take a seat in back. There is a newspaper on the table that someone must have left behind, and I hold it to my face so I won't be seen. I think about the photograph scattered in a million pieces on Esther's bedroom floor. It's a threat, a blatant threat. She wants to take my life. Esther took that photograph and then marked it up with a red pen, a thin line across my neck — a telling sign she wants me dead.

I sip my latte, my hands shaking so badly it's no wonder it spills. I avoid eye contact. I check my phone three times: Where is Ben?

When the time comes, I hasten out to meet the detective right where we said we'd meet: on the west side of Crown Fountain. There are wooden benches there that frame the periphery of the fountains and pool. When I arrive, the detective is already there. I know it's him because, well, because he looks like a cop: big and stocky and grim. My guess is that he'd be a drag at holiday dinner parties but that's neither here nor there. He doesn't wear a coat, as if completely unaffected by the autumn air that all but immobilizes me. His shirt is a button-down and he's wearing black jeans. *Do people still wear black jeans?* I wonder as I stride around the reflecting pool and take aim on Detective Robert Davies. Apparently they do.

I'm nervous. Petrified, in fact. I can't help but wonder what he wants with me. Is this standard protocol in the case of a missing person? I don't know. I'm wishing that Ben would have returned my call, that he were here beside me right now, a half step ahead as we reach out our hands and make introductions with the grisly detective.

But he's not. Ben isn't here and so I have

to make do. While a knight in shining armor is great, this time I might have to save my own day.

I sit beside the detective on the cold, wooden bench. I tell him my name and he tells me his, though of course I already know. The space is not entirely vacant; there are other people here. It is, after all, Chicago. But the people are few, and they're all caught up in their own thing, taking photos of the big buildings, feeding the pigeons French fries, arguing with children. No one looks at the detective and me.

Detective Robert Davies is losing his hair. Male pattern baldness, I believe they call it. He's got a receding hairline. But his hair is brown — no gray anywhere — so I bet he's happy about that. Must be hard to get old.

He takes out a tiny notebook. "How long has Esther been missing?" he asks, and I tell him, "Since Sunday." But then I amend, feeling somehow more guilty for this admission, for the fact that it's now been five days since I've seen Esther with my own two eyes, "maybe Saturday night," and at that my gaze falls to my hands, to a blue chalcedony ring on my right hand, an oval stone on a sterling silver band. I can't bring myself to look the detective in the eye.

Her words return to me, Esther's words:

*I'd be a killjoy, Quinn. Go without me. You'll have more fun.* The martini bar on Balmoral, its grand opening. That's what I remember. I also remember Esther sitting alone on the apartment sofa, wrapped up in pajamas and a comfy plissé blanket in a seafoam green. The last time I laid eyes on my friend.

"We've spoken before," he tells me knowingly when I hesitate for a split second, not quite sure I want to admit to Esther's disappearance out the fire escape. His eyes are sharp, like an eagle or a hawk. There are lines on his forehead, a prominent schnoz. I'd bet my life he doesn't smile, not once, not ever. "You and I," he says again, "we've spoken before," and I say I know. Of course I know; it was just this morning, and I remind him of our phone call a sole two hours ago as I stood in my apartment making arrangements for this little tête-à-tête in the park. I'm pretty sure a small huff emerges from me, or at the very least an eye roll — certainly he can't be *that* incompetent that he doesn't remember our conversation this morning — and at that — *great Scott!* — he smiles.

I pray this isn't a harbinger of what's to come.

"We've spoken before today, Quinn," he

tells me derisively, and it's then that I remember the first thought I had when I pressed End on my cell phone following our call: I've heard that voice before.

But when?

I try to connect the dots, to place his voice somewhere else, to match this voice to another voice, and it's then that it comes to me, these words: *It's a confidential matter. We had an appointment this afternoon. She didn't show.*

The man on Esther's phone Sunday afternoon when I found it forgotten in the pocket of that red hoodie. Detective Robert Davies was the man on the other end of the line, the one who refused to leave a message. *I'll call back,* he'd said. But he didn't call back. Not then, anyway. Not until today, on account of my missing-persons report. But he didn't call Esther; this time he called me.

"You called Esther the other day," I say. "You were supposed to meet. You had an appointment."

The detective nods his head. "She didn't show," he says, and I solemnly admit, "By then she was already gone.

"Why were you planning to meet?" I ask, but I'm guessing he won't tell me this on account of its confidentiality. *It's a confiden-*

*tial matter.* But to my surprise he does, but only after I tell him what I know. I lay it all on the line this time; I tell him everything. The disappearance out the fire escape, the strange notes, the death of Kelsey Bellamy. And then I show Esther's phone to the detective, the threatening message still here on the display screen: Payback's a bitch. He seems rapt by this, for a fleeting bit. He holds it up close to his eyes so he can see the words more clearly. Seems he's losing his vision, too. Presbyopia, it's called — I've seen the commercials for progressive lenses — and again I'm stricken by the fact that aging must stink, not that I would know.

"Esther sent that to me," I say.

He looks at me questionably. "What would make you say that? Why do you think Esther sent this text to her own phone?"

This is something I never paused to consider. Why would Esther send this text to her own phone? Why not mine?

"I'm not sure," I say. "Maybe she knows I have her phone. Or," I begin, but then stop quickly and shrug it off. I don't know why Esther would have sent that text to her own phone. "She killed her last roommate," I reveal quietly instead, the words themselves a betrayal to Esther. I whisper the words so that Esther can't hear. "Kelsey Bellamy," I

387

say, and then, "She's trying to kill me, too."
I tell him about the shredded photograph,
the candid shot of me walking down the
street in my plum sweater, the mark of a
red pen slicing my throat in two. A threat.

"Esther isn't trying to kill you," is what he
says to me. He says it like he's sure, like in
his mind there's no doubt about it. Like he
*knows*.

"What do you mean?" I ask, and, "How
do you know?"

And then he goes on to explain.

Detective Davies tells me that he first met
Esther a year or so ago when he was investi-
gating the death of Kelsey Bellamy. It was
more or less an open-and-shut case, he says.
The girl had food allergies, which I know.
She ate something she was allergic to; she
couldn't get to her medicine in time. Hundreds of people die from anaphylaxis each
year. It's not that common, and yet it happens. That's what the detective tells me.
Negligence might have played a part in
Kelsey's death, yes, and at the time Esther
took a great deal of blame. "People pointed
fingers," he says. "People always want to
point fingers. They need someone to blame."
But once Kelsey's death was ruled an accident, life went on for Esther and for
Detective Davies. There was no doubt in his

mind that Esther hadn't purposefully tried to tamper with Kelsey's meal. "I've seen a lot of liars before," he tells me, "but Esther wasn't one of them. She passed a lie detector test with flying colors. She cooperated with the investigation. She was an exemplary witness, and clearly contrite. She felt terrible about what had happened to Kelsey. She owned up to it right away — the mix-up with the flour — and was never defensive. I can't say as much about most witnesses, and certainly not the guilty ones."

He pauses for a breath and then continues. "Esther called me Saturday night, out of the blue. We hadn't spoken in months, nearly a year. But she had something to show me," he says, adding on, "She seemed spooked," and there's such conviction in his voice I find myself holding my breath, forgetting to breathe. Esther was spooked. But why? The very thought of this makes me want to cry. Esther was sad, Esther was scared, and neither time did I know.

Why didn't I know?

What kind of friend am I?

"She didn't say much on the phone. She wanted to tell me in person. She'd received something, a note. I can only assume it had to do with Ms. Bellamy," he says.

My heartbeat accelerates and, tucked up

into the sleeves of the aqua sweater, my hands begin to sweat.

"When did she call you?" I ask.

"Saturday night, nine o'clock or so," he says. Nine o'clock. Shortly after I left for that stupid karaoke bar, leaving Esther behind in her pajamas and a blanket. Did Esther purposefully wait until I'd left to call the detective? Was she even sick?

Esther had received a note, I wonder. But no. I consider the notes to *My Dearest*. Esther *wrote* those notes. He must be mistaken. The signature line most clearly reads: *All my love, EV.* Esther Vaughan. She's signed her name to the letters. They're hers. Aren't they?

Is it possible that Esther is somehow *My Dearest*?

I'm a tad bit skeptical to say the least.

"I have the notes," I tell Detective Davies then, reaching into my purse and thrusting the two typewritten notes into his hand. "I brought them with me."

I've been carrying them around with me in my purse because I couldn't think of another safe place to leave them. But I've read them, of course, many times, and neither says a thing about Kelsey Bellamy. As Detective Davies's eyes scan the notes, he, too, seems unimpressed, though he asks if he can keep them, anyway. I nod my head and watch as he slips the notes carefully into some sort of evidence pouch where later I imagine they'll be dusted for fingerprints and some sort of forensic analyst will try and find the make and model of the typewriter on which the notes were typed.

The notes are completely madcap, don't get me wrong. They are. But inside, there's no grand confession, no mention of Kelsey Bellamy. Somehow he's got it all wrong. He must have misunderstood what Esther said or maybe she was lying or in the very least stretching the truth. Maybe Esther was trying to mislead the detective. But why?

"There was nothing else?" the detective asks, and I say no. "There must be more," he says, but I assure him there's not. The look that crosses his face makes me believe I've failed again. In some way, I've let him down.

Or maybe I've just let Esther down. Right now, it's hard to say for sure.

"But what about the photograph," I ask, "of me? The one Esther put in the paper shredder, my face with a slit across the throat. That was clearly a threat. She wants me dead."

"Or . . ." suggests Detective Davies as I feel the bile rise up inside of me like an active volcano, threatening to erupt. "Maybe whoever sent Esther the letter took the photo of you, too. Maybe that's who wants you dead."

# ALEX

The ground looks hard. Not frozen solid, but hard. The top layer, the sod, seems the hardest to get through as she begins digging into the cold morning earth with her gardening spade, pressing on the steel with the sole of a suede boot. The sod binds together, a million sheaths of grass, clinging together, refusing to let her through. It's hard work, but Pearl forces her way in, gouging out the land bit by bit. I watch in awe as she thrusts the cold, hard earth up in the blade of the shovel, tossing it into a pile behind her slender frame. As she does, she begins to sweat, a cold sweat that congeals on her skin and makes her shiver, and as I watch from a distance, she removes her coat first, followed by the hat, tossing them both onto the dew-covered lawn, and I'm reminded of the day at the lake, Pearl undressing bit by bit and then walking into the frigid water.

As the steel blade hits topsoil, the work

gets easier; the earth puts up less of a fight and the pile of dirt begins to rise. She digs and digs, and, watching her, I lose all track of time. I'm hypnotized by her movements, but also more than a little terrified. Who is this woman and what is she doing? Why is she digging up the remains of the dead Genevieve? It feels suddenly moronic that I followed her here. Suddenly stupid. Anyone with half a mind would have immediately called the police or run in the other direction, not trailed her. But now here I am, hiding in the bushes of an all-but-abandoned cemetery while some wackadoodle unearths a corpse from the ground. I squat down to the hard, cold earth, making certain that as the fog rises I won't be seen. I don't want to even think what she'd do to me if she knew that I was here. For now, the bushes will keep my secret for me.

As I watch from a distance, I dredge up what knowledge I have of the little girl who's buried in that grave. I don't know much; she was gone before I was born. But what I've heard about Genevieve is that after her death the town's members lifted the rudimentary wooden casket from the trunk of her family's car and dropped it into this very trench in the cemetery, hastily, without the praxis of a visitation or a funeral or a procession. Instead, the body was ushered rather quickly from the car and to this ditch and nobody ever bothered to ask why. People were glad she was gone. Though she might have only been five years old, she was a delinquent, the kind of child that wreaked havoc on their own children and homes, tormenting kids, vandalizing property, chasing neighborhood dogs. That's what I've been told. It wasn't as though anybody wanted to see a little girl die, but still, they were glad she was gone. "Her mother had her hands full," neighbors have said over the years, staring at that forsaken house, mumbling under their breaths something to the effect of, *What a damn shame.*

As far as I know, no one comes to visit Genevieve's grave. I can only assume her family split as soon as they abandoned that old home and buried their child in the ground.

In time Pearl's shovel begins to fill with silt and sand, followed by clay, terra-cotta-colored clay soil, and then, later — in the moments before the steel blade hits hollow wood — bits of broken-up rock fragments, gray like stone. It comes up in chunks, rocks that appear hard to carry. They must be heavy and as I watch on she takes her time, losing speed.

But then I hear the sound of metal on wood, and know that she's arrived at her destination, the reason for which she'd come here.

The cemetery is quiet, short of silent save for the sound of Pearl gasping for air. She fights for oxygen in the still November air. I'm guessing her throat is as dry as the bedrock. Even I am thirsty and I'm not doing the work. She sweats in exertion, while the numb air freezes my lungs, making them ache and burn. It's cold, winter coming quickly. Too quickly. The grass around us is a faded green, a sage green, quickly losing color, becoming dormant for the winter season ahead. It's brittle to the touch and no longer burgeons out of the ground. Soon it will be covered with snow. The fog begins to rise, and as it does, the world materializes before me: granite and marble headstones, grotesque, ill-proportioned trees, and the church: a small, one-room rectangular Protestant church, white, with a stacked limestone base and clapboard sides. The windows are plain, no frills, as is the entire building, an 1800s structure that's been outdone by the more modern, hip churches popping up around town. I'm not even sure if anyone uses this place anymore or if it's just for show, a dead thing, a cadaver, hollowed out like all these bodies buried beneath the ground.

And then all of a sudden Pearl tosses the garden spade aside and stops digging. She's reached a box, a wooden box that itself is mostly decomposed. She can't lift the box — it's wedged too tightly into the earth, in the final stages of decay. It crumbles to bits in her hand, and so instead she pushes what's left of the lid aside and peers inside.

From this angle I can't see inside Genevieve's grave, but I watch for Pearl's reaction. What I see is a look of smug satisfaction as if she was hoping to prove something to the world, and that's exactly what she did. She puts her hands on her hips; she smiles.

She leaves the garden spade where it is, the mound of dirt piled sky-high, the gravesite exposed so that all of the world can see.

And then she wipes her sweaty brow with the back of a sleeve, picks up her coat and her hat to leave.

But she doesn't leave. Not yet, anyway. Before she goes, her eyes rove the cemetery, from the old church, to century-old headstones, to me. For a second, I'm half certain her eyes linger on my hiding place, there behind the evergreen trees and leafless bushes where I squirrel myself away and try desperately to hide. She shakes her head. She sneaks a sardonic smile. She sighs.

But if she sees me, she doesn't say a thing. And then she turns and goes.

I don't move right away. Instead, I wait. I wait for a long time, until the squeak of the cemetery's iron gate tells me that she's gone for good. And then I wait some more, just to be sure. And only then do I rise to my shaky feet to see what she's discovered inside that grave.

Nothing. Absolutely nothing. That's what Pearl discovered.

The wooden box decomposing in the hard earth is completely empty.

# Quinn

Before I climb into Detective Davies's car, I insist on seeing a driver's license plus one more photo ID. Vehicle registration and proof of insurance. You never can be too careful about these things. I've seen enough legal thrillers and murder mysteries to know the cop isn't always the good guy. But in this case, I think he is. And this is why: he's not that nice. He's not that friendly.

"Good enough?" Detective Robert Davies asks when he hands me the State Farm card, and I say, "Yeah. Good enough," as I open the door and slide into an unmarked Crown Victoria that's parked in the public lot off Columbus. The car reeks of the fast-food bag that lies open on the passenger seat. He scoops it up before my rear end has a chance to squash it flat, and tosses it into a nearby garbage can. It's much warmer in the car without the cold and the wind, but the dreariness of the enclosed parking garage is still unsettling.

Detective Davies pulls out of the narrow parking spot too quickly and down the garage ramp so that my insides continue to turn. There's a blare of his horn — warning others that he's coming through at breakneck speed — as he guns the engine out onto Columbus and drives me home.

As he drives, the bile again rises up inside my chest until I feel that I could vomit. My head swims with dread. My hands shake, a tremor that makes the rest of me exhausted and dizzy. My heart, itself, has grown wings and can fly, and there it sits in my chest, flapping its birdlike wings, threatening to soar out of my body.

I think of Esther, sad and scared, and me not knowing. Was she really sad and scared, or were these things simply a charade? Who is Esther, really? Is she even Esther or is she Jane? The questions all but take over my mind until I can no longer see straight and I can scarcely think.

Detective Davies drops me off at the front door of my apartment building. Before I can turn around to say goodbye to the detective or thank him for the ride, he speeds away quickly, with Esther's cell phone and the letters to *My Dearest* now in his possession. He plans to see what his tech guys can extract from inside that phone — Esther's call activity and voice mails, her videos and photos.

In my hand, I carry his business card, and in my head, a directive: call if anything happens, if I find anything, if I hear from Esther, if Esther reappears. Just call.

As I step from the car, I peer to the window of our unit, of Esther's and my unit, and half expect to see her, standing there, staring down at me. But of course Esther isn't there. The cloudy window is bare, just the window coverings and the reflection of the other side of Farragut Avenue staring back at me.

But then I see a woman standing beside the locked door, pressing a button repeatedly on the intercom panel with a hand. She waits with a toe tap for a reply that doesn't come. She stands before the door, clutching what I know to be Esther's powder blue, quilted satchel in her leather-gloved hands. She's a small woman; she can't be taller than four foot ten with bulky hair that must weigh as much as the rest of her. I'd bet my life she weighs eighty-nine pounds. Everything she wears is tight: tight pants, tight coat, tight boots.

"Can I help you?" I ask precipitately, my eyes glued to that purse. I have a sudden, overwhelming desire to reach out and clutch that purse in my hands, to hold it. *That's Esther's,* I want to bark out loud, and I stare at my hands, which, before me, continue to shake. I'm worried. Worried for Esther. The detective's story leaves me feeling panicked and utterly confused — even more so than I already was — this strange twist of events that takes me from mad to scared to worried. Instead of thinking that someone is after me — that *Esther* is after me — I'm worried for Esther.

But still, there are so many questions running in my mind: What about Kelsey Bellamy, and why did Esther change her name to Jane Girard, and seek out a roommate to replace me? Why did she take fifteen hundred dollars out of the ATM? This makes no sense to me, none at all.

"Are you Jane . . ." the woman at the intercom panel begins, followed by a pause while she peers at some card in her hand and finishes with, "Girard?" *Are you Jane Girard?*

Who is Esther Vaughan anymore? I wonder. Do I even know Esther?

I shake my head quickly. I say no, that I'm not, but I'm Jane's roommate. Quinn. I say it, anyway, even though I'm guessing she doesn't care about my name. She's come for Jane.

"Oh, good," she says, a great wave of relief washing over the inflated facial features — the big eyes, the big smile, the big hair. "I found this," she says as she thrusts the powder blue satchel into my hands, "in a trash can of all places," and I take it, grateful to have something, some part of Esther, to hold. I press it close to me; I breathe in the scent of Esther that's begun to wear away and be surpassed by a grungy city smell, mixed with this lady's forceful perfume, the heavy scent of jasmine and rose.

"You found her purse in a garbage can?" I repeat, just to be sure, and she nods and tells me how she was about to toss in her coffee cup when she saw it lying there on top of a jillion fast-food bags, the blue of the satchel catching her eye.

"It's a pretty purse," she says. "Much too pretty to just throw in the trash. I figured it was an oversight," and then she says how she didn't want my roommate to worry. "I know I'd be worried if I couldn't find my purse."

"That's really kind of you," I say, and it is. Of course it is, if she doesn't have some ulterior motive. Right now I'm not sure of anything, other than the fact that I'm tired and twitchy all at the same time. My head hurts; my hands shake. If any more questions fill my mind, it might just explode.

What was Esther's purse doing in a garbage can?

"What garbage can?" I ask, and she points in the direction of Clark Street and says aimlessly, "Over there."

"You just found it today? Right now? Just a few minutes ago?"

But she shakes her head no. "It was a day or two ago," and then she sighs and says, "It's been a long week. A really long week," as if that should explain to me why it's taken her a day or two to return Esther's purse. "I live nearby," she says. "It's on the way." She tells me that *Jane* really should be more careful with her purse, "Carrying that much cash around," and I know two things then: number one, this lady riffled through Esther's purse, and secondly, when I look inside, I'm going to find fifteen hundred dollars in there.

Esther took the money out of the ATM, but she never used it. She didn't hire some hit man to off me. She isn't vacationing in Punta Cana, sipping a strawberry daiquiri.

Where is Esther?

"How do you know where we live?" I ask suddenly as we stand there on the front stoop, being enveloped by the cold autumn air.

"It's on her driver's license," she tells me. "I wasn't snooping," she swears before I have a chance to ask, taking on a tone that is rueful and defensive all at the same time. She *was* snooping. "I was just trying to return the purse. You'll give it to her? To Jane?" this lady asks, and I say, "Oh, yes. Of course," and then I say my goodbyes, let myself into the building and gently close the door.

Esther's and my apartment is empty when I step inside, but it smells like Esther: the scent of her cooking, the fragrance of her peony body mist. I'm struck with a wave of nostalgia.

I meander to her doorway and, as I cross the threshold into Esther's refrigerator-box room, I see the Dalmatian Molly floating dead at the bottom of the fish tank. I drift to the side of the tank, flipping off the tank light so that I can't see the poor dead fish on the hot-pink rocks, the swoosh of the filter making it look like she's breathing when I'm certain she's not. Her body lies flaccid, turning white — a sign of rot — and as I tap on the side of the glass, she doesn't move. She's dead. Esther's fish is dead. How long has she been dead?

I mouth the words, *Sorry, Fishy.* I'm not sure what I did, but I'm sure I did something wrong.

I kindle a third search of the apartment, retracing every step I've already made twice. I'm growing desperate. I *am* desperate. There must be something more here, something I've overlooked. I look through Esther's desk and dresser drawers again; I peer inside her closet. I grope at items at random and throw them to the floor, not worrying whether or not I make a mess. I crinkle her papers; I tug the drawers right off the IKEA desk, and search for a false bottom drawer. I breathe heavily, working hard.

There's nothing there.

I make a mess of Esther's room; I knock her pencil cup to the ground, angry and rash. I flip through the stack of textbooks and then toss them aside one by one, where they fall to the hardwood floors, making a clamorous noise. Down below, Mrs. Budny is likely two seconds away from reaching for her sponge mop, but I don't care.

My cell phone rings — Ben, I'm sure, finally returning my call — but I can't be slowed down. I need to find Esther. When I get to the bottom of the textbook pile, I rise to my feet and cross the room, stepping with dirty shoes on Esther's aqua throw and orange duvet, leaving dusty footprints on the fabric, though as I do, I'm reminded of Esther's words: *The dill weed goes here. And the peanut flour goes here.*

She wouldn't like this one bit.

"There's nothing here," I say to myself out loud, hands held up in defeat.

I attack the living room and the kitchen with a vengeance, canvassing every drawer, every piece of mismatched furniture, behind picture frames, under the rug. I slip a hand behind the sofa cushions and search there, too; I knock on the drywall and listen for somewhere hollow, a secret hiding spot. I check inside the air return for a stash of goodies, but still, there's nothing there. Just dust and dirt and dead air.

And then I have an idea, some place I haven't yet searched. I climb on top of the kitchen cabinets and search that half-inch gap between the cabinets for a hideaway, a last-ditch attempt at finding some clue, any kind of clue. Anything. I trek dirty footprints across the Formica countertop but I don't care.

But still, there's nothing there.

It's from up on top of the countertop that I see it, my face red and sweaty from romping around the apartment on another fruitless mission, my heart beating quickly, my breathing heavy and uncontrolled. I'm rolling my sweater sleeves to my elbows when I catch sight of the light blue item on the floor, sitting there behind the door, right where I left it.

Esther's purse.

I leap from the countertop — my knees unleashing a groan — and run to the purse. How is it possible that I didn't think to look inside her purse? Turning it upside down, I toss its contents out on the floor, shaking the purse to make sure I get everything out. I set it aside, but not before zipping and unzipping the pockets, feeling the lining for a secret compartment. But the only thing that's left behind is a stick of gum.

This is what I find spilled across the wooden floors of our apartment: a sewing kit, a headband, a little mirror, three tampons, some Altoids, Esther's light blue quilted wallet — to match the light blue quilted purse — tissues, a book and some keys. A key for the main walk-up door, a key for our apartment door, a padlock key for her storage unit.

And one more typed sheet of notebook paper, folded into thirds.

Addressed to *My Dearest,* and signed, *All my love, EV.*

# ALEX

I'm the first one at the library when it opens for the day. I'm waiting outside at the top of a small stairway, beside the white exterior columns, when the librarian unlocks the door. She takes her time inserting the key in the lock, and then checks her watch to be certain it's nine o'clock. Nine o'clock and not a moment before. And then she opens the door as I breeze past inhaling her potent hair spray, and she says to me, "First one here," as if that wasn't already obvious, the fact that I was the first one here, the *only* one here. I mutter a quick, *Yup,* and then hurry on, to one of the computer terminals, which I haven't bothered to reserve in advance. That thought never even crossed my mind. Though I'm the only one here, the librarian tracks me down, anyway, scanning my library card because, as she says, *Rules are rules.* And I've already broken one of the twenty-seven rules about using the library's computer terminals. I watch as she gives me a disapproving look and then withdraws slowly from view. The only people at the library this morning are the other librarians, two older women who file carts worth of returned books. They disappear into the stacks making the books all alphabetical and orderly so that later people can come and muss it all up. It must drive them insane.

I don't have a lot of information on which to go, but I do know that the cemetery plot where Genevieve was supposed to be buried . . . it's empty. I try hard to exhume from memory the stories of little five-year-old Genevieve before she drowned in that bathtub. I wasn't born yet; I wasn't even a blip on the radar. To me she was always a ghost. She was never a child, but rather the purported specter in the window of the home across the street, a wraith in white wafting from room to room, calling for her mother. But to others she was a child once.

I look online and this is what I come to learn. For thirty-four smackers, I can request birth and death certificates from the State of Michigan's vital records office, but I have to mail in a request, pay twelve bucks more to have it expedited and then wait. I don't have time to wait. I need the answers now. By the looks of it, the vital records office may or may not even send me the information I need; seems much of it — birth records, in particular — is confidential. I don't really need Genevieve's birth certificate, anyway, but her death certificate would come in handy, something to help me understand why that casket is empty.

I try another angle. I research the old house, hoping to find some sort of chain of title so I can track down the family that once lived there. Unfortunate thing is, that house has been abandoned so long it predates the world of Zillow and Trulia. The bankruptcies and foreclosures I pull up online all happened over the past couple of years, a dumpy duplex on the west side of town, a slummy home on the east and a couple dozen more listings in between. A sign of the times, I guess. It's sad, all those people tossed out of their homes because they can't pay the bills. Pretty soon, Pops and I will be there, too, standing on some busy four-way intersection, bearing cardboard signs that read Homeless and Please Help, feeling grateful for a buck or two.

I do a quick scan for Genevieve's obituary online, hoping to find a name there for next of kin. But this is what I find: nada, nothing. I type in her name followed by the word *obituary,* and then check twice to be sure I've spelled the words correctly. I add in the name of our tiny little town to narrow the search field, but it comes up empty. Well, not empty, per se, but it pulls up a whole bunch of trash I don't want or need: a middle-aged lady from Hamilton, Ohio; a Dominican nun from Nashville, Tennessee, dead at the age of eighty-two. Not my Genevieve. Far as I can tell, there isn't an obituary for the little girl anywhere. Maybe it's just that it's been twenty-some years since she died, or maybe it's something else.

A librarian passes by and I inquire about microfilm, hoping I might find a two-decade-old obituary from the local paper stored there. She stands before me with a pair of bifocals dangling from a golden chain, her hair a latticework of white. She might just be the oldest person I've ever seen, and while I follow her through the library and to the microfilm reader squirreled away on the other side — passing two younger librarians who are no doubt faster and more technologically adept than she and thinking this is all a colossal waste of time — it turns out she's exactly the person I need.

Before we ever even make it to the microfilm machine, she asks of me, "Doing research?" and I say, "I guess you could call it that."

"What kind of information are you looking for?" she asks in a helpful sort of way, not nosy, and though I hesitate, I tell her. "I'm trying to get some information on that old abandoned home out on Laurel Avenue."

She stops. "What kind of information are you looking for?" she asks. I have her attention, and whether or not I want it, I don't know. But I don't have the first clue how to use a microfilm machine, and so it seems I'm going to need her help with this.

"Just trying to figure out who used to live there," I say casually, like this is no big deal at all. But her answer is completely unexpected. Her voice and her demeanor change, and she looks at me like I'm either a complete idiot or I've been living under a giant sedimentary rock.

"You don't need a microfilm machine for that," she says, leaning in close, the smell of her Aqua Net hair spray making me want to retch. "I can tell you who used to live in that house," she says, her face just inches away so I can see the eroding teeth, the transparency of her corrugated skin, and though I'm expecting the obvious, for her to say something cryptic and obscure about the ghost of Genevieve, what she says turns my world on end and makes me question everything I once thought I knew was true.

My Dearest,

You took my family away from me, and now you need to know how it feels to lose something you love. It was your fault I had to go. I want to be sure you know. They told me I was a bad girl, and that was why I couldn't stay. But we both know that's not true.

It wasn't that girl's fault. You should know that. It was yours. I wish I could say that I care that she's gone, but I don't. It had to be done. It was simple, it really was, a sleight of hand: swapping the flour while you were at work. You really must get better locks on your doors, my dear. You don't want strangers skulking around your home when you're not there.

It was priceless, too, watching from my vantage point as you scooped that flour into a bowl, and then fed it to your poor, unsuspecting friend. The grasping at her neck, the vomiting, the scene spiraling so quickly out of control. Better than I could have ever imagined. Priceless, it was. Just priceless. I had to wait days for you to serve that fallacious flour, but it was well worth the wait. Well worth the wait as I watched the scene play out before me, like a performance I had scripted myself. Absolutely perfect.

Unfortunate, really unfortunate, too, that I'd done away with the girl's EpiPen. That would have come in handy, wouldn't it have? It's mine now.

It's your fault I came back, you know. You're the one who found me. You could have just let me be. Were it not for you, I never would have discovered that I was already dead.

If only you could see me now, sweet Esther. If only you could see what I've become.

I've been watching you for a while now, long enough to know your habits, your customs, your routine. I've been trailing you to work, to school. On your errands. Did you see me? Did you know that I was there?

I shop where you shop and I dress how

you dress. The same shoes, the same coat, the same hair. It wasn't hard to do. Once you were the only Esther Vaughan, but now I am Esther, too.

You thought that you could change your name, that you could simply disappear. That you could pay me to go. How naive.

You were always her favorite, but if I'm you, then maybe she'll love me, too.

All my love,
EV

# ALEX

All the way there, I run, my feet hammering against concrete, though I'm completely anesthetized. I can't feel a thing.

I pound on the door when I arrive — once, twice, three times — watching as the metal portal shifts in its casing from the momentum of my blow. And then again and again.

She opens the door with a quizzical look on her face, and stands before me, her hair pulled back from her eyes, her gentle hands folded over her abdomen.

"Alex," she says in a way that is both a question and a statement as I let myself inside and push the door to. "You look like you've seen a ghost. Everything all right?"

I can't reply. There are no words. I fight to catch my breath as Ingrid slips down the foyer and into the kitchen. I listen to the sound of her footsteps as she goes, unable to speak because I can't summon the breath to speak. I double over, dropping my sweaty hands to my knees, and then, when that doesn't do it, I squat down to the floor. "Let me get you some water," Ingrid says from a distance, and before I can say a thing, I hear the sound of a kitchen faucet spilling water into the sink; the jarring noise of ice cubes plummeting from an ice-maker and into a glass; the seagulls outside, cawing in the distance over the sound of a truck that passes by on the abandoned street, the bobbing of tires as they yoyo over the quarried stone. *Breathe,* I tell myself. *Just breathe.*

"I didn't know you were coming by today," Ingrid calls from the kitchen. "You should have told me. I would have baked something. Banana bread, or . . ." And her voice carries on, but I can't hear a thing because I'm stuck on the librarian's revealing words — newsy and gossipy. *Ingrid Daube used to live there,* she had said to me as I stood there, mouth agape, in the old library. *That was her house. She was a Vaughan until her husband passed, you know, and then she returned to her maiden name of Daube. It's Dutch, I think, Daube. Of course, no one really makes mention of the fact that that was Ingrid's home. Such a tragedy what happened there. You do know about her little girl, Genevieve?* The librarian had continued to jabber, but by then I'd already begun to run, realizing that for all those times Pearl sat at the café window, staring out across the street, it was never Dr. Giles's home she had her eye on.

"I'm not hungry," is all I manage to say. I force myself upright and begin to plod into the kitchen, one foot in front of the other, one hand dragging along the wall for balance. The room spins in circles around me. There's the strongest urge to drop my head between my legs and force the blood back up into my brain. I'm light-headed, dizzy, hardly able to breathe.

But Ingrid doesn't seem to notice.

I've taken less than four steps when the sink faucet turns off and the home becomes still, and that's when I hear the humming of a song, a morose song, a gloomy song, one I've heard Ingrid hum before.

A day or two ago I would have said I didn't know the song, but now I know: I'd recognize that lullaby anywhere.

"Hush-a-bye, don't you cry," I say, my feet standing on the line between kitchen and foyer, eyeing Ingrid as she stands before me with my glass of water in her hands. I say the words, but I don't sing them, my voice trembling, though I try to mask the rippled effect with a plumb posture, like a scared cat arching my back so that I'll look big.

"You know that song?" Ingrid asks of me with a pleased smile, and when I nod my head in a nebbish, submissive sort of way — exhausted, scared and confused all at the same time — she confesses, "I used to sing that to my girls when they were young," and without missing a beat, she trills aloud, "Go to sleep, my little baby," and all I can see is Pearl clutching that old cloth doll to her chest, the gentle hip sway as she oscillated back and forth on the dilapidated floorboards of the old home. Ingrid's old home.

Before her eyes can reveal too much, Ingrid turns her back to me and continues the low drone of a somber little lullaby she used to sing while she rocked her baby girls to sleep in her arms. At the kitchen sink she goes through the motions of washing dishes as I stand slackly by, fighting still to catch my breath, completely unsure what to say or do. Do I say anything? Do I *do* anything? Do I tell Ingrid about the young woman squatting in her old, dilapidated home, the one who dug an empty casket out of Genevieve's grave and sings the same lullaby that Ingrid now sings?

Or do I turn and slip away, pretending not to see what's there before my eyes, the way the dots connect, the way the pieces correlate?

*My folks gave me up,* Pearl had said as we walked lazily around the street, but now I'm not so sure.

It's midday now, the sun at its highest point in the sky, the time of day it lets itself in uninvited through windows. A cold flurry of air sweeps around the side of Ingrid's house as Ingrid and I stand in the kitchen. Over the stream of water running from the kitchen sink I hear the front door squeak open against the weight of the wind, causing the walls of the home to whine.

"The door, Alex," says Ingrid with a jolt. The terror takes over her eyes. "You closed the front door. You locked it." But whether I did or didn't, I don't know.

As a scalloped dinner plate slips from Ingrid's wet hands and shatters into a million pieces on the kitchen floor, she screams. "Esther," she says, staring over my shoulder as a low moan escapes from her throat and she beats a hasty retreat from the room, across the shards of glass. The water continues to pour from the faucet, rallying together a thousand polished bubbles in the sink, which threaten to overflow. Bubbles like a bubble bath. "Oh, no," Ingrid moans, a hand groping for her throat. "No, no, no."

I turn and there behind me stands Pearl.

"Alex. It's so nice of you to come," she says, but never once does she look at me, for her eyes are lost on Ingrid.

"You look just like her," bleats Ingrid, her voice far away as if she's underwater, as if she's drowning in the kitchen sink. "You look just like her. I almost thought you were . . ." As she steps forward and past me, she reaches out a gutless hand to stroke the rippled locks of ombré hair.

Pearl smiles the most pleased smile, like a child who's just made a brand-new friend. She runs a hand along the length of the bleached-out hair and offers an ostentatious curtsy so that the hemline of her checkered coat falls down to her knees. "I thought you'd like it," she says, beaming. "She always was your favorite, after all. I thought you might like me more if I reminded you of her."

And then she reaches for a knife.

# QUINN

When I get to the end of the note, I let out an unsuppressed cry. I can't help it. It just comes. A hand goes to my mouth with instinct.

In my hands, the note shakes like a leaf in the wind. I can't stop my hand from shaking. I try to process what I've just read, to *reread* the note, but the words blur before me until I can no longer tell my *a*'s from my *o*'s or pronounce the words. The letters and words meld together before my eyes, becoming one. They flit and dart on the typed page, sneering at me: *You can't catch me.*

But there are two takeaways that I do gather from the letter: whoever this EV is, she killed Kelsey Bellamy, and quite possibly she's done something to hurt Esther. She's pretending to be Esther, running around town, looking and acting like Esther. Who is she? The letter makes mention of family: *You took my family away from me*, it says, and yet it doesn't seem like something Esther would do. Esther never talked about her family to me; if it weren't logistically impossible, I'd say she didn't have one, that she was raised by dwarves in a woodsy cottage with a thatched roof. Esther shied away when I asked questions; she snapped the lid back on the box of photographs I'd stumbled upon at the storage facility, family photographs, and when I asked who those people were in the pictures, she said to me, *No one*.

But it was clear that they were not no one. And now I feel desperate for another look at those images, longing to see a visual of Esther's family, wondering whether or not the person who penned this note is in those photographs. I need to see. I run through the memories I've stored away in my mind, but they're nowhere. I can't dredge up the pictures, not that Esther gave me much of a chance to see, anyway, that winter day we stood in the storage unit, looking for the Christmas tree. It was cold that day and outside the snow came down in gobs. We stood in the cold storage facility and, though heated, the concrete walls and floors didn't do a thing to keep us warm. *I think it's over here,* said Esther, meaning the

Christmas tree, but instead I lifted the lid off a shoebox of photographs. I was snooping, yes, and yet it didn't feel like snooping with Esther in the very same room. I didn't think she'd mind.

But she did mind.

And now, my heart beats fast as the room fades in and out before me, the rose sofa drifting away before drawing near. The windows are suddenly so close I can touch them, and then, just like that, they're gone. My hearing is fading in and out, too, as if I'm trapped beneath water or have a bad case of swimmer's ear. I can't hear.

*I never would have discovered that I was already dead.*

The line runs over and over again in my mind. What does it mean?

I peer down at the items spread across the floor before me, and there I see Esther's keys, the three of them, three nickel-plated brass keys on a beaded ring: a key for the main walk-up door, a key for our apartment door, a padlock key for her storage unit.

*A padlock key for her storage unit.*

I push myself up off the floor and, bringing Esther's purse along with me, start to run, thinking of one thing and one thing alone: those pictures. I have to see those pictures.

■ ■ ■ ■

I scurry down the streets of Chicago, past shops and restaurants, a covered bus stop, a tiny space that feigns to fight off the Chicago wind but doesn't. Rather the wind whiffles the pages of a *Chicago Tribune* left behind there on the bus stop bench as I run past, all the way to the storage facility on Clark Street. The storage facility itself creeps me out — lots of doors, empty spaces, a scarcity of people. Hardly any people at all, save for a poorly paid introvert sitting behind the front desk who creeps me out, too. But I can't let this get the best of me; I can't let this slow me down.

Once there I use a keycard I find inside Esther's wallet to unlock the facility doors and get inside. There's one man on duty, a man who hovers behind a pane of glass typing words into a computer screen. He doesn't raise his eyes to greet mine.

It's one almond-colored roll-up door after another, all the way down a long, uninhabited corridor. The floor is some kind of polished concrete that does nothing to mask the sound of my heavy footsteps as I race down the hall, hardly able to tell one door from the next, though I've been here before.

I rack my mind to remember which unit belongs to Esther. I insert the padlock key into three successive small disk locks but it doesn't open a single one. I remind myself: I've been here before. Think, Quinn, think. Remember. Is it *this* almond door, or *that*? There must be a hundred of them, a hundred almond doors all with identical locks. A thousand of them! They all look the same to me. I transport myself in time; I try to remember the one time Esther and I were here. I retrace our steps, and follow the clues: the collection of smaller closet-size units, followed by larger ones with their garage door entrances; the security camera on the wall for which Esther and I danced. I smile at the memory — Esther and I doing an Irish jig for the man at the front desk, laughing, having a ball.

And then it comes to me: unit 203, the same address as my childhood home, the one where my mother and father still live. *Fate,* I remember was what Esther had called it, but I told her it was more like a stupid coincidence. I see the numbers in my mind's eye, as I stood there last December, three feet back, watching Esther unroll the door.

I find unit 203.

I insert the key into the lock, when all of a

sudden it opens. *Presto!* I'm in.

I roll up the heavy door and, taking one look inside, I scream. And not just any kind of scream. A desperate, falsetto scream that grabs the attention of the store clerk who comes stampeding through the locked metal door and into the storage unit fast, but not fast enough to catch me before I lose all cognizance of the world around me, plunging to the concrete floor with a whump.

My keys and phone scatter in all directions. The muscles of my bladder contract as urine creeps down the inside of my legs, soaking my tights. My ankle twists from the sheer weight of the rest of me bearing down on the joints and bones, and it's then that I cry out in pain. My head hits the ground, bouncing up and down on the concrete like a playground ball. To that, I don't have time to react before I'm lying prostrate on the ground, just inches from Esther, close enough to touch.

She wears her pajamas still, the comfy, cotton pajamas she wore the last time we spoke, when she sat under the warmth of a sea-foam green blanket in our living room and said to me, *I'd be a killjoy, Quinn. Go without me. You'll have more fun.* That was what she'd said, and so I'd gone. I'd gone without her and I'd had fun. But now I wonder what would have happened if I had stayed. If only I would have stayed. Would I have been able to protect Esther from this fate?

My eyes take in the boxes, torn open, their possessions scattered at random all around her body. Photo albums. Journals. Esther's baby books, the ones her mother meticulously put together when she was just a girl, photos of an infant Esther, a toddler Esther, a young Esther. The photos are now all yanked from their plastic sleeves and torn to itty-bitty shreds. Who would do such a thing?

And then there is Esther, of course, lying there before me, her body recumbent, her eyes closed tight.

Just beyond the reach of her chalky-white hand lies a single photograph of two young girls, one big and one small, and these words in black Sharpie scrawled along the upper edge of the picture: *Genevieve and Esther.*

# ALEX

The blood coagulates inside my veins, no longer delivering oxygen to my body. My legs go numb, beginning to tingle. My knees buckle, threatening to give.

"You don't look so good, Alex," she says, holding the knife in her hands, a shiny knife, over a foot of sturdy steel with an ultrasharp edge. A chef's blade plucked from Ingrid's kitchen set. She leads Ingrid and me to the living room and forces us to sit down. My footsteps are loud as I cross the room, the booming sound of gunfire at a firing range, exploding at one hundred and fifty decibels or more. A cork blasting from the neck of a bottle of champagne. A sonic boom. Thunder. The heavy pelting of rain on a car's steel hood, hollow and persistent and loud.

"You don't want to do this," I say to her as she stands in the hub of the room with the knife in her hands. There's a surety about her — she *does* want to do this —

431

and yet it's accompanied by a frenzy, a delirium. She's manic. Genevieve is manic. Her toes tap. Her leg has a tremor to it. Her eyes skitter in their sockets; her hands, the very hands which wield a weapon, shake. She holds that knife not like one about to slice into a cut of meat or a birthday cake, but rather at the ready to penetrate skin, human skin. Her grip is tight, skin taut, veins and arteries leaping out of the flesh.

"You were there, weren't you?" says Ingrid. "I saw you at the market. I know it was you."

"Of course you did. I wanted you to see," says Genevieve.

"All those years. How did you remember?"

"How could I forget? You're my mother," Genevieve says. "A girl doesn't ever forget her mother," and I see a resignation in Ingrid's eyes that says sooner or later she knew it would come to this. Her secret couldn't be a secret forever.

The market. The place where Ingrid had her panic attack. The last public place she stood before locking herself in her home. When Ingrid had her panic attack, gawkers claimed she spat off these words: *Go away* and *Leave me alone,* and *Don't touch me!* They said that Ingrid screamed.

"I followed you inside," Genevieve says,

her jaded voice, barely audible, drifting through the air.

"You looked different then," says Ingrid. "You looked like . . ."

"I looked like me," Genevieve says, "but now I look like her. You like me more like this, don't you? You always loved her more. But I don't want to talk about Esther. Not now. Not yet."

And then she goes on to talk about that day, the day she tracked Ingrid to the market in town. She watched Ingrid walk up and down the aisles with a shopping basket in hand, she says, up and down, up and down. She followed her for a long, long time. She describes the way Ingrid dropped her basket when she spotted her, Genevieve, from across the store: the dropping of the basket, the clutching at her heart, the grating scream.

"How did you know it was me?" Genevieve asks, and Ingrid says solemnly, "A mother doesn't ever forget her child."

Genevieve's feet tread back and forth across the room. Her steps are measured steps, while on the sofa, Ingrid and I sit. She is fairly composed; I am anything but. Ingrid is scared, yes, though it's a relenting fear, a telltale sign of defeat. She gives up. She sits gingerly, posture straight, her hands folded in her lap. Her hair is tame. Her eyes remain on Genevieve the entire time, never straying, hardly blinking. She doesn't cry. She doesn't ask to be let go, while I, on the other hand, want to do all of these things, but I don't. I can't. I can't speak.

I see then the similar shape to their eyes, their noses, the lack of a smile. It's there in the minute details: the thin lips with their sharp angles, the upturned noses. The angular diamond structure of their faces, the broad cheekbones, the pointy chins. The color of their eyes.

"You have to understand," Ingrid says, her voice shaking like a wooden maraca. "I did the very best I could. I tried everything. Everything," she repeats. Genevieve's feet continue to tread along the floor. I could run and tackle her or subdue her in some other way, but there's no telling where the knife would land. My lungs, my kidneys, my abdomen.

"Things were different back then," Ingrid says. "These days every child is diagnosed with some disorder. Autism, Asperger's, ADHD. But it wasn't the case back then. Back then these kids were just bad kids. You, Genevieve, you were a bad girl. These days I would've brought you to a psychologist and they'd slap a diagnosis on you and make you take some pills. But that wasn't the case back then, over twenty years ago.

"There was so much talk, Genevieve. About the things you did, the things you didn't do. The things you did to the children at school. People were talking. *At only five years old,* they'd say, imagining what you'd do as you grew older and more callous and calculated. People were afraid to imagine. I was afraid to imagine.

"And you know what they did when you misbehaved? The teachers, the neighbors. They looked down on me," Ingrid explains as a tear wiggles loose from her eye and runs the length of her cheek. It hovers there at her trembling chin, hanging on for dear life. I watch on, still trying to process the repentance in Ingrid's words, the fact that she's not in the least bit surprised a living, breathing Genevieve is standing before her in this room. She knew all along that she was alive, that the body she purportedly toted back from a hotel was not that of her dead daughter. She let the townsfolk bury an empty box, let them believe Genevieve was dead. She let them feel sorry for her.

Meanwhile, she gave Genevieve up just like that.

What kind of mother does that to her child?

*It's not easy,* she told me, *being a mother.*

"You were hard enough to handle," she says, "but that was before I had Esther. We both know how you felt about Esther, Genevieve. The things I saw you do to that girl . . . She was only a baby. How could you do those things to Esther?" she begs, and with that her voice trails off to nothingness. Just vapor. Air. She doesn't speak and for a moment the room grows quiet and still.

In time Ingrid goes on, her words clipped like the clickety-clack of typewriter keys, banging out the story for me. Genevieve was more than a headache for Ingrid. More than a pest. She had a mean streak in her, a crazy side, a fit of rage. That's what Ingrid says.

"You remember the things you did to Esther?" Ingrid asks. "Of course you do. You must." And then she reminds her, in case somehow she's forgotten. She reminds her of the time Genevieve attempted to suffocate baby Esther while she slept soundly in her cradle. Were it not for Lady Luck steering Ingrid to Esther's crib just in time, the baby would have succumbed to the weight of the pillow, the diminishing air. That's what Ingrid says, her words now plaited with anger. She tried hard to make excuses for it at the time, to tell herself that Genevieve didn't know what she was doing as she laid that pillow on the baby's dormant face and pressed, but somewhere inside she knew that Genevieve knew what she was doing. Even at the young age of four or five, Genevieve knew that this one small act could make that baby go away. And that was exactly what she wanted; she wanted the baby to go away.

Silence befalls the room. Everything is quiet. Everything except for the sound of Ingrid's subtle cry. That and a clock on the wall, the sound of the rapid *tick, tick, tick* — to accompany my own brisk heartbeats — as that secondhand moves its way around the face of the clock. And then, like that, a tiny door opens and a bird emerges. A cuckoo clock, warbling out twelve o'clock. It's noon. And the room is no longer quiet. *Chirrup. Chirrup.* Twelve times. Across the street, the café is imaginably busy, people coming and going, completely unaware of what is happening here. My only hope is with Priddy. That Priddy is packing lunch for Ingrid as we speak: a BLT with a mountain of fries and a pickle on the side.

"I knew that I couldn't keep you. It was dangerous for Esther, dangerous for me. I did the very best I could. I found a reputable adoption agency and they found you a good home. Your adoptive family, Genevieve, they were good people. They could take care of you better than I ever could."

"Or maybe you just didn't bother to try," Genevieve snaps.

"I tried," whispers Ingrid under her breath. "Oh, how I tried.

"How did you find us?" asks Ingrid then, reaching shaking fingers out to touch the pearl bracelet on Genevieve's thin wrist. *Pearl.* The bracelet is pulled taut, the elastic showing through the beads, cutting into her skin. "You have that still?" she inquires, telling or maybe reminding Genevieve, "I made that for you. When you were just a girl. You still have it," she says, and this time it isn't a question. Ingrid made that pearl bracelet for Genevieve when she was a girl.

Genevieve ignores this. She yanks her hand away from Ingrid's gentle touch. "What you mean to ask is how did *Esther* find *me*? Yeah, that's right. It was Esther who found me. She found me online. She reached out, but then just like that, she wanted me gone. She tried to pay me to go away. Can you believe that? But you see, I didn't want to go away. I wanted to be with my family. With you and with Esther. And when Esther refused, I thought maybe I could just be with you. If I looked like Esther, if I acted like Esther, then maybe you'd

438

love me, too. Especially if Esther was no longer around."

"What did you do to Esther?" asks Ingrid in distress, and Genevieve shrugs her shoulders and says, "You'll see," and then she urges Ingrid to go on, to finish her narrative about how she ended up bringing a phony casket home from that hotel, claiming the little girl was dead in a tragic bathtub incident.

"This doesn't change the fact that your potential adopters, Genevieve, *your* new parents were exemplary. I saw the paperwork. I was there behind the scenes the first time you met. He a doctor and she a schoolteacher. They would take care of you. I thought this was for the best. I thought they would take better care of you than I ever could."

"You told me you had an errand to run. You left me with some man I didn't know. *Be a good little girl,* you said. And then you were gone."

"I was there, Genevieve. Watching through the window. I saw them come, and shortly after, I saw you go. Your new mother held you by the hand. She held your hand as you left. And I . . ." she stammers, trying again, "I . . ." Her voice trails off before she completes the thought, sagging against the weight of the sofa cushions, her rigid body becoming sloppy. "I've never felt so relieved. You were gone," she says, and, "It was through."

"It was never through," says Genevieve as she rises from the sofa and again begins to pace. "You left me. You gave me up. You picked Esther over me — that's exactly what you did. All you cared about was Esther. Esther, Esther, Esther. But never me."

"I didn't think that you'd remember," Ingrid confides. "You were too young to remember what I'd done. I thought that you'd be happy."

"I was never happy," says Genevieve.

I consider my options, wondering whether or not I could bring Genevieve down. I'm thinking of the blood vessels that knife would sever on its way in through the elastic skin, blood seeping from the vascular system and into other parts of my body. I'm thinking I would be lucky if she hit the aorta, or the hepatic artery, maybe, something that would cause death quickly, immediately, rather than the slow trickle of blood from the liver, the kidneys, the lungs.

I'm also thinking about my new friend, Pearl. About the part of me that still wants to touch her hair, that wants to hold her hand. But I can't do this. Of course I can't do this, but deep inside it's exactly what I want to do. Touch her hair, hold her hand, disappear out the front door with Genevieve, holding hands and ambling down the middle of the street.

Ingrid inhales deeply, trying to flatten her breath. It comes to her in fits and starts, and at times it seems it simply won't come. There are moments when a look of terror crosses over Ingrid's face. She can't find air, she can no longer breathe, but then it arrives and placates her for a little while; she can breathe, she tells herself as she lays a shaky hand upon her chest and reminds herself to breathe.

Ingrid winces as Genevieve sits down beside her and lays the cold, hard steel against her neck, as she then hikes the cuff of a shirt up to reveal a row of blue-gray veins there on Ingrid's fair skin, at the ready to be sundered. Death by exsanguination. That's what it's called. By definition, the draining of blood. Genevieve leans in close to Ingrid and hisses into her ear, "Hold still. You don't want my hand to slip." And then she says, "Please don't tell me you're going to refuse me, too, just like Esther did."

I can't stand by and watch this happen. Ingrid is a good person, I remind myself, though right now I'm having a hard time believing it.

Though I'm scared half to death, I try my hardest to remain cool, calm and collected. In control. "You haven't hurt anyone yet," I rationalize for Genevieve, though whether or not this is true, I really can't say. On the outside I may look relatively relaxed, or as relaxed as is to be expected, but inside I'm guessing I'll never be the same again. Something has changed. And it doesn't have to do with just Genevieve, either, the woman who I thought for a whole forty-eight hours was the woman of my dreams. It has to do with Ingrid, too. I've changed.

"Ingrid is fine," I tell her. "You and I are fine," as I point a finger at myself first, and then at her. Inside, though, I don't really know if I'm fine. "You can still change your mind. I'm not even sure you'd get in trouble, not with what she's done to you, what your mother's done to you," I say. "Besides," I tack on as I aim a finger at the razor-sharp item that glints in her hand, "that isn't even a weapon. It's a knife. Just a knife. For cooking. You see what I mean?"

I sit there on the sofa beside Ingrid. "The police are on the way," I lie. "I figured it all out before I arrived. I called the police."

In the distance is the sound of sirens, though they're not coming here. I didn't call the police. I could have called the police on my way from the library, but I didn't. Instead, I came straight here. "The best thing you can do right now is surrender," I say, hoping a subtle psychological tactic might work. "Or run," I add. "You could run. If you go now, they'll never catch you. I have money," I say as I reach into a pocket and extend my hand. In it lies two twenties. That's all. But I'm guessing it's more than she has. Enough for a train ticket out of town. I peer out the window, and as I do, I see billows of thick, black smoke fill the air on the other side of town. A fire. Something is on fire.

But Genevieve only laughs, this hideous, unspeakable laugh that will forever haunt my dreams. Her muddy-brown eyes rove between Ingrid and me as she says, "Or I could kill you both right now." Her words are fast. "I just need to be quick about it. Do it before the police arrive. Then I'll take your money and run," she adds, nodding at the cash in my hand.

I nod. My knees have begun to shake and I find that it's hard to stand. But I can't think about that right now. Right now I need to focus on the task at hand. "Or you could do that, too," I concede. But I don't mean it. Of course I don't mean it. It's a strategy, a scheme. I'm building rapport with Genevieve, trying to earn her trust. My words, my tone of voice, are slow and calm, hoping that Genevieve's will follow suit. That Genevieve's words — or more importantly her actions and behavior — will be slow and calm like mine. "You have every right to be angry, Genevieve."

"That's right," Genevieve says as she draws closer to Ingrid, knife in hand. She stares her mother in the eye and says, "I'm angry." And it's the look of resignation in Ingrid's eye that terrifies me the most, the fact that she could right now give up. Let Genevieve take her life. Ingrid looks to be tired, droopy, spent. Her body sags, her posture slumped, the wooden smile that usually commandeers her face now gone. She doesn't even have the energy or desire to sustain a fake smile. She runs a hand through her hair making it stand erect, and in the course of ten or twenty or thirty minutes begins to age, decades at a time. Ingrid turns sixty, then seventy, and then eighty before my very eyes. She takes on the appearance of a decrepit old lady.

"Doesn't matter, anyway," says Genevieve. "Those sirens aren't coming here," as her eyes follow mine out the window to a mantle of smoke. The fire. There are flames now, what I imagine to be orange and red serpents that reach into the sky a mile or a half mile from here. But from where I stand, all I see is smoke. "Seems someone left the heater on in that old, abandoned home."

And then she laughs.

She burned the dang thing down once and for all.

Ingrid then asks, "Where's Esther?" her words coming out in a desperate whisper, and Genevieve laughs again, and says, "Esther is dead." Esther. Is. Dead.

"No," says Ingrid. "You wouldn't. You didn't."

"Oh," says Genevieve, smiling a cruel smile, "but I did."

And that's when the situation begins to quickly dissolve, any hope of being salvaged lost. Ingrid begins to whimper, crying out over and over again, "My baby! My baby!" while Genevieve screams at her wildly that she was once Ingrid's baby. She was Ingrid's baby, too. But then Ingrid abandoned her, and it's as this betrayal is rehashed a second, third and fourth time that Genevieve loses her rationality and becomes more angry, more mad. I try hard to get her attention, to refocus on other things instead. The money in my hand, the fact that Genevieve has yet to harm either one of us, the fact that she could still run. It's Hostage Negotiation 101: let Genevieve speak her peace, but also keep her calm. Don't let her spew. Spewing can only lead to a loss of control, an impetus or a catalyst, the inciting factor that makes her lodge that knife into Ingrid or my midsection in a moment of passion and recklessness.

But Ingrid isn't using good hostage negotiation tactics. She's drawing from despair, from this sudden knowledge that Esther is dead. Ingrid screams aloud, "You killed my baby," a poor choice of words that makes Genevieve reel.

I try desperately to abort a bad situation. "Tell me what I can do for you, Genevieve. Is there something you need? Something that will help you escape?" I ask, my voice louder than the other two, but still, losing composure as before me the scene falls to pieces. I tell Genevieve that I have a friend who is a pilot, a man who owns a small private jet, and how he might be able to help her flee. There's a small, regional airport in Benton Harbor, just two or three miles from here. I'll put in a call. I'll ask my friend to meet us there.

Genevieve looks at me then and spits out, "You're lying, Alex. You're lying. You don't have any friends," and my breath catches, thinking a knife wound would have felt better than that.

*You were my friend,* I want to tell her. *I thought you were my friend.* But those words won't help. I need to stay rational, and forget that in the mix of all of this, I, too, have been hurt. This isn't about me. This is about Ingrid, Genevieve and Esther. It's their story, not mine.

"Genevieve," I say instead, trying to catch her attention like a game of Capture the Flag. For one split second out of the corner of my eye, I think I see a shape in the window, a pair of eyes looking in at me. Chalky-white skin, hair dyed a faux red, a menthol cigarette perched between a pair of thin, chapped lips, clouds of smoke seeping into the autumn air. Red.

But then it's gone.

"Genevieve," I say again, steering my words around Ingrid's desperate keening, which is doing much more harm than good. "Genevieve. Listen to me, Genevieve. I'll help you get out of here," I tell her. "Where do you want to go? I'll take you anyplace you want to go. I can get you there." I say it once and then I say it again, quieter this time. "I can get you there."

But nobody is listening anymore to what I have to say. We've all turned our attention

447

to Genevieve. Genevieve, who regales us with the tale of the night she scaled an apartment building on Chicago's north side and forced her way in through a bedroom window. The window was closed, but she got herself in, anyway, with the help of a slotted screwdriver and some elbow grease. She climbed through the window frame and into the bedroom and there, sound asleep in her bed, was her baby sister, Esther. It wasn't the first time she'd seen her, of course. They'd met before, an attempt at reunification that failed miserably when Genevieve threatened to expose Ingrid. From that moment on, Esther didn't want a thing to do with her. She wanted Genevieve to go away. But Genevieve didn't want to go away. She wanted them to be a family.

"Esther," Genevieve spews. "Esther," she says again with an abhorrence on her tongue. "Esther refused. She wouldn't do it, she said she *couldn't* do it, to you," she says, staring into Ingrid's desperate eyes. "You'd get in trouble, she said, if people found out I wasn't ever dead. *What would people think if they knew?* Esther asked me. Do you think I care what anybody thinks?" she asks.

"And so," she says, hands up in the air as if admitting to something careless, negligent, a simple mistake, an easy oops — having forgotten a carton of milk at the grocery store or leaving a candle unattended for too long, "I killed her." She draws that knife across her very own neck — close, but not close enough to lacerate the skin or leave a mark even. "Like this. This is what I did."

And then for five long seconds the room goes quiet and still.

Five, four, three, two, one.

*Bang.*

Ingrid moves first, charging from the sofa like a linebacker and into Genevieve, though neither of them falls to the ground. Neither one falls, nor does the knife slip from Genevieve's grip. I watch and wait and hope that it will happen, that it will happen *soon,* but it doesn't. They grapple for the knife, two women locked in a gauche embrace, fighting for the weapon. And when it doesn't happen, when the knife doesn't fall, I know I need to move quickly, I need to act quickly, I need to do something. *Save Ingrid!* a voice screams in my ear. *Save Ingrid!* I'm keenly aware that Ingrid is on the verge of losing this fight. I can't sit idly by and watch Ingrid die. Ingrid is a good person; she is. They struggle for a single second before I join the scuffle, three bodies united with a knife wedged somewhere in between.

It's inevitable that someone will get hurt.

It's bound to happen.

It's then, as the knife slips through my skin with the ease of a foot sliding into a pair of socks or a shoe, that I hear it: the sublime sound of police sirens hollering through the streets of town, coming to save me.

It's as the blood begins to seep from the aperture of my skin that I feel it: a searing pain that immobilizes me. I can't move, though all around me the others have begun to drift away, watching on with round, agog eyes, mouths parted, fingers pointing. Before my eyes, Ingrid and Genevieve, the both of them, begin to blur. The knife remains inside me, protruding from my abdomen, and at seeing the knife, I slowly smile. After the commotion is through, I'm the one who's managed to walk away with the knife.

I'm the victor, for once in my life. I won.

The room around me begins to wax and wane like the lake at high tide. And this is what I see: the lake, Lake Michigan, my anchor. The cornerstone of my existence, my mainstay.

They say that your entire life drifts before your eyes in those last few minutes before you die.

This is what I see.

The room around me turns blue and begins to ripple from the walls, across the wooden floors, a breaker coming at me, my feet sinking into sand. I sink into the water then, the blue water of the lake threatening to drown me, or to carry me home perhaps. Home. The lake, Lake Michigan, my home.

Before I know what's happening I'm three years old again, toddling along the beach for the very first time, gathering beach rocks in a plastic pail. Geodes and lightning stones and quartz. Rocks, all rocks, making my pail grow heavy with time. My mother is there, loitering where the water meets sand, sitting on the beach, her feet lost in the lake's surge. The sand sticks to her feet, her legs, her hands. She wears cutoff denim shorts and a frumpy T-shirt, one that once belonged to Pops. The shorts she made herself, sheared a pair of jeans off between the waist and the knee so that the edges turn to rags. They fray at the hem, white threads falling from the denim shorts, trailing the length of her gaunt legs.

What she loves is the beach glass, and so when I find it, I collect it in my uninhibited hand and run to her, tiny fragments of beach glass in my sandy palm, pale blue and a washed-out green. My mother smiles at me, this timorous sort of smile that says smiling doesn't come with ease. But still, she smiles, a forced smile that tells me she's trying. She runs a hesitant hand along mine as she takes the pail from my hand. She invites me to sit down beside her, and together we piece through the rocks, sorting by shape, and then by color. My mother has a rock for me, as well, a tiny tan saucer that she sets in the palm of my grimy hand, telling me to *Hold tight; don't lose it.* An Indian bead, she tells me. Crinoid stems. I'm far too young for words like this, and yet they're ones that wind their way to my heart like a tree's sinuous roots, anchoring me to the ground, feeding my soul.

I hold tight; I don't lose it.

And then, like that, I am eight years old. Eight years old and sad and alone and awkward, a boy too tall for his lanky frame. Sitting by myself on the beach, kicking bare feet at the sand, my eyes obliviously searching the sand for crinoid stems. I watch the way the granules of sand rise up in the air and then fall, dispersing through the air like dandelion seeds. Again and again and again. Rise up and fall, rise up and fall. I dig myself a hole in the ground with an old toy shovel some other kid left behind. I think I might just want to bury myself inside. Bury myself inside and never come out. All I want is my mother, but my mother isn't here. I stare at that place where the water meets sand, where the waves come crashing onto the shore. I do it to be sure, but sure enough, she isn't there. She's nowhere.

But there are other mothers who are here, other mothers that I take in one at a time, wishing each and every one of them were mine.

And then it's nighttime, and the world around me is nearly black. I'm twelve years old, staring through a telescope lens with Leigh Forney at my side. She doesn't touch me, and yet somehow, in some way, I can feel her skin, barely, just barely, the nebulous sensation of skin on skin. I've never felt this way before. This is different; this is new. And it's not bad at all. I like the way I feel as I stand there on the lake's shore, looking at the sky, listening to the waves, reminding myself to breathe. It's a night committed to memory, the particulars stored someplace safe to draw on in times of need. Leigh's romper, a purple gray thing with shorts and a T-shirt conjoined at the center with a drawstring waist. Her feet, barefoot. A pair of sandals dangling over a single finger so that it stretches too far one way. On her hair: a headband. In her eyes: excitement and fear, like mine. The night is dark, save

453

for the stars. The moon is foggy and vague. And Leigh says to me in a voice that is both playful and pure, "Bet I can beat you to the carousel," and like that, we're off and running, feet sinking in sand, through the parking lot, over the orange partition and onto the sleepy carousel where it's there, as I climb on a sea serpent chariot and the dormant carousel begins to spin, that the world around me ebbs from view.

The room turns darker, the ceiling illuminated like a nighttime sky, my mother's craven smile flecked across the drywall like a constellation. I'm five years old and all around me the world is black. It's nighttime still and I'm asleep in my big-boy bed, senseless to the touch of a hesitant hand that strokes my hair in the darkness, heedless of my mother's hurting words breathed into my ear before she goes. *You deserve so much more than me.*

But I hear them now, words that ease their way into my anamnesis as the line between this life and the next softens and blurs.

And I fall.

# Quinn

We stand on the street corner. There are men and women in uniform scuttling all around us: policemen, paramedics, detectives. They move quickly, trotting between gathering spots and meeting points: their cars, the inside of the single-story stucco building, a makeshift command post where Detective Robert Davies stands, telling the others what to do. The storage facility is cordoned off with yellow caution tape. Police Line Do Not Cross, it says. And yet I stand there beneath a thick, scratchy wool blanket and watch a dozen or more men and women in uniform cross behind that line. I watch them go in, and then later, I watch as they emerge, toting a form on a stretcher, strapped to the gurney with elastic bands and covered in a blanket.

Esther.

Dusk is falling quickly. The cars on the streets mushroom in number, from the usual daytime congestion to the bumper-to-bumper, bottleneck traffic of rush hour in Chicago, further aggravated by brouhaha on the side of the street: the policemen, the paramedics, the detectives, which passing cars pause to see, further holding up traffic. The cursory cars stare at me, standing there beneath the scratchy wool blanket, holding an ice pack to my head. They stare at Esther being removed from the storage facility. They stare at a news crew complete with microphones and cameras, men and women made to remain behind a police line where they can't reach the detectives, the storage facility employee — who garners his own scratchy, wool blanket — or me.

Car horns blare.

In Chicago, in November, dusk falls before five o'clock. The sun sets in the west, out in suburbia, somewhere above my mother and father's split-level home, taking with it the sun, leaving behind scant traces of light and a cobalt sky. Beside me, Ben stands, his arm on my shoulder, though I can hardly feel its weight. I don't know how he got here; I can't remember calling. But maybe I did.

I can do little but stare at Esther on the gurney as she tries to push herself up to a sitting position with little to no strength.

The paramedic places a firm but gentle hand on her shoulder and commands her not to move. "Stay still," he says, and, "Relax."

Easier said than done.

Esther has been held captive in this storage facility for five long days. For five days she has been denied food, and only teased with water the one time her captor passed through.

"She was there. Genevieve," Esther tells me, and I'm not sure if she was really there or if it was only a dream, an illusion, a trick played on Esther by her own mind. "She gave me water. Lukewarm water, for torture, a tease, a way to prolong what should have been a certain death." Esther laid there on the concrete floors for days, cold, alone and terrified. That's what she said to me as I laid there, too, on the floor with her, waiting for paramedics to arrive, wrapping my body around hers to try and keep her warm. She had no idea what day it was, or what time. She was covered in her own bodily waste, and in her mouth was a gag so that she couldn't cry out or scream. There was little the storage facility worker could do, though he called 911 and cranked the heat, trying to get the temperature in the building to rise so that she'd stop palpitating.

But it didn't rise. Not fast enough, anyway. We wrapped Esther in our own sweaters and coats, anything we could find to bring her warmth. The man offered trifling bits of water, pressing a bottle to her lips, though he cautioned that too much would make her sick. I didn't know one way or the other, though if it were up to me I would have let her drink the whole darn thing.

And then the paramedics arrived, and the police, and the facility employee and I were sent outside.

There on the street curb Ben wraps his arm around me again and draws me near. I'm shaking, from cold, from fear. Ben tells me this as I lean into him, and beg the wind to quit. "You're shaking," he says. My hair whips around my head, the plunging temperatures chilling me to the bone. Tonight we're expected to get snow, the first few flurries of the season. Nothing that will stick, but still snow. I'm thinking of the radiator in Esther's and my little apartment, of whether or not it will be enough to warm the rooms. I'm thinking about the apartment itself, with all of Esther's and my belongings tucked inside. I fold my head onto bent knees and begin to cry. A quiet cry. A tear or two that dribble, unchecked, from my eyes. I don't think Ben sees.

I won't go home tonight; tonight I will stay with Esther.

"She's asking for you," a voice says, and as I turn, there is the detective, Robert Davies.

"For me?" I ask, somehow surprised, and my gaze follows his to where Esther and her gurney are parked inside the ambulance with a single door open wide. An EMT attends to her, administering fluids. Soon she will be ushered to the hospital for a further examination and there she will spend the night.

I cross the police staging area and draw near the ambulance door. "How is she doing?" I ask the paramedic who presses a stethoscope to Esther's heart for a listen and tells me that she'll be fine. I can't yet look into Esther's eyes. There are no wounds that I can see, no gashes or blood, and yet I imagine that everything is broken on the inside.

"I haven't been a very good roommate," I confess, peering sideways at her, and Esther's jaded face turns confused. In that moment she looks so puny to me, undernourished and scared. Delicate in a way I never knew she could be. Her eyes look tired, her hair — oleaginous and filthy — lying too long over her bony shoulders. It needs to be trimmed. I reach out a hand and stroke that hair, finding it impossible to believe that just twenty-four hours ago I was sure she was stalking me, that she was trying to take my life.

But now I see: not my Esther. No. Esther would never do anything to hurt me.

Only now do I know it's true.

"What do you mean?" she asks, her voice nearly a whisper. She's all but lost her voice. She holds a hand to her throat; it hurts. "You're a good roommate, Quinn, you are. You found me," she breathes, "you saved me," and at that word *saved* she begins to cough.

"We don't have to talk right now," I say to her. "You should rest," but as I turn to go, she reaches for my hand.

"Don't go," she says, and I take a deep breath and admit to the things I've done, how I riffled through her bedroom once, twice, three times, how I found things I know she never wanted me to see. I don't have to tell her what I found; she knows. She nods knowingly and I voice a name: *Jane Girard.* Esther's new name. I also confess that she got a phone call from a woman named Meg, a woman replying to her ad in the *Reader,* a woman who wanted to be her roommate instead of me. I try not to be sensitive; Esther has been through enough. And yet it hurts when I tell her this, when I admit to knowing she wanted to replace me with another roommate.

"Oh, Quinn," she says, and with whatever strength she has, she squeezes my hand. "The roommate was for you," she says, five words that leave me utterly confused. "I was the one who was going to leave."

And then she explains.

When Esther was a little girl, only a year or so old, her sister drowned. She died. Esther didn't know a thing about her sister, though there were photos that she'd seen, and also a story that was imparted to her over the years: they were in a hotel room, Esther, her mother and sister, Genevieve, and when Genevieve was left alone in the bathroom for a minute or two, she sunk under the bathwater and died. The reason she was left alone in the room? Esther. That's the story she was told, though her mother always finished with this addendum: *It's not your fault, Esther. You were only a baby. You couldn't have known.*

And yet Esther grew up believing it was her fault. She also grew up feeling like a piece of her was missing. Because of her, her sister was dead. The grief was hard to handle; she sought help, a psychologist in the city, the one whose business card I found: Thomas Nutting. He helped, but only ever a little bit, never enough. And the grief, it came and it went time and again, weighing Esther down. She couldn't breathe. Until the day her mother admitted to her that Genevieve was never really dead. "She'd lied to me," Esther says. "She lied to everyone. I could never forgive her for what she'd done."

And Esther, who does everything one hundred and ten percent, decided to find Genevieve, and she did. She tells me she found her, about a year and a half ago. She located her on an adoption site online, and the two of them made plans to meet. What Esther imagined was a happy family reunion. She was filled with glee.

Instead, the reunion was suffused with blackmail and threats. Genevieve planned to expose their mother for what she'd done: the adoption, the cover-up, the abandonment. She started stalking her, calling her phone over and over and over again, though twice Esther had her number changed. Genevieve kept finding her. She showed up at her apartment door; she sent her letters. But Esther wouldn't let it happen; she couldn't be a part of exposing their mother no matter how upset she was. Genevieve said she wanted to be a happy little family, but Esther knew that could never be. And so Esther planned to disappear. She changed her name; she got a passport. She wanted to leave and begin somewhere new, a fresh start without her mother and Genevieve.

"I couldn't just abandon you like that," she says to me. "I didn't want to leave you alone. The roommate," she explains, "was for you."

Esther was interviewing roommates to find the perfect one for me.

She wanted to make sure I was okay before she could leave. Now that sounds like something Esther would do.

"But then Genevieve began sending letters." They were harmless at first, she says, but always odd. Most of them she threw away, not really thinking Genevieve had it in her to make good on the threats. Genevieve was screwed up, that much she knew, but she was sure she was simply an annoyance. Harmless. Until the letter came where she admitted to having killed Kelsey.

"Kelsey," Esther says, and with this begins to cry. It was her fault, she believed, that Kelsey was dead. Dead by association. Kelsey hadn't done a single thing wrong. "That's when I knew I had to go to the police. This was out of my control. It had gone too far." And she admits to me that maybe her mother wasn't wrong, after all. Maybe she was right to get rid of Genevieve.

Saturday night, the night the last note arrived, she contacted Mrs. Budny to have the locks on our apartment door changed so that Genevieve couldn't let herself inside and do something to harm me, too. Esther was trying to protect me. She called Detective Davies and told him they needed to meet; she had something to show him. The note.

And it's in that moment that everything makes perfect sense.

That night after Esther locked the doors and climbed into bed, Genevieve rang the buzzer over and over and over again, and when Esther refused to answer, she appeared at her bedroom window and towed her away. "Either you come," she told Esther as she dragged her down the fire escape, or she would hurt me, too. She had a photograph to prove it: me walking down a city street in my purple sweater, one Genevieve slipped into the paper shredder before they left. She'd been following me. Esther was trying to protect me.

Esther had no idea where they were headed, but she knew this: Genevieve was

464

trying to pass herself off as Esther. "She was trying to be me," she says, "in the hopes that our mother would love her more. *You were always her favorite,* she said, but how would I know? I was only a baby when she went away," she cries.

For five long days and five nights Esther laid on that concrete floor, breathing through her nose because the gag in her mouth made it impossible for air to pass through. *There can't be two of us, now can there?* Genevieve said before locking Esther in the storage facility. *That would just be weird.* And so Genevieve did away with Esther so that she could be Esther. *EV.* Esther Vaughan.

It's then that Detective Robert Davies reappears with Esther's cell phone in his hand. Esther's cell phone, which he confiscated earlier for his techies to review. "It's for you," he says to Esther with a rigid, weary sort of smile, and asks if she feels up to taking the call. Esther nods her head weakly and, peering toward me, asks if I'll hold the phone for her. "I'm tired," she confesses, a disclosure which is plain to see. "I'm just so tired."

"Of course," I say, leaning in close, pressing the phone to Esther's ear, close enough that I can hear every word that is exchanged over the call. It's her mother, Esther's mother, the one from which she's been estranged all these years.

From Esther comes a great big sigh of relief at the sound of her mother's voice, and then she begins to weep. "I thought I had lost you," she says, and Esther's mother, also crying, says the same. "I thought I had lost you, too." Apologies are offered; promises are made. A clean sweep. A fresh start.

I don't eavesdrop, not per se, and yet standing within hearing range, I gather this. After Genevieve locked Esther inside the storage facility, she sought their mother out. Esther's mother and Genevieve's mother. She threatened her; she told her Esther was dead. A boy from the neighborhood saved her, giving his own life for hers. "Alex Gallo," she says. "Do you remember him?" Esther shakes her head; she doesn't remember him. "He's a hero —" I hear Esther's mother's voice through the phone, along with these conclusive words "— he saved me. If it wasn't for him, I'd be dead."

And then there's an interlude — a brief interlude which is full of sobbing and grief — before she decisively says, "Genevieve will never bother us again," for as it turns out, Genevieve will spend the rest of her life behind bars for a murder charge.

"We need to get her to the hospital," the EMT says, and I nod my head okay. I pull the phone from Esther's ear and tell the woman on the other end of the line that Esther will call her back just as soon as she can. I promise Esther that I will be there; I'm following right behind. She doesn't have to do this alone. I'm here.

I return to Ben just as his cell phone begins to ring. It's Priya. He draws the phone from his pocket and excuses himself to drift away to a quiet space where they can speak. Ben will soon leave, and when the police say that I can go, I'll go, too. To the hospital to be with Esther.

I watch as Ben and Priya talk, feeling more alone than I've felt before, though I'm surrounded by all these people.

When Ben returns, I say to him, "You don't need to stay with me," and, while pointing at the phone in his hand, I say, "I'm sure Priya is expecting you." His nod is slothful and listless.

Priya is indeed expecting him.

"Yeah," he says, and again, a mundane, "Yeah. I should go," he decides.

Priya has made dinner, he tells me. She's waiting. But I don't want him to leave. I want him to stay. *Stay,* I silently beg.

But Ben doesn't stay.

467

He embraces me in a final hug, wrapping those snug arms around me in a way that swallows me whole, that warms me from the outside in. And then he stands just inches away and says to me, "Goodbye," while I stare into his magnificent eyes, the five-o'clock shadow that now decorates his chin, the arresting smile.

But I wonder: Is it more of a *Goodbye, my love,* or a *See ya later, pal*?

Only time will tell, I suppose, as I say goodbye and watch as he goes, turning on his heels and drifting off toward the intersecting street.

But then just like that, he turns and comes back again and there — on the corner of the city street, surrounded by men and women in uniform, the gridlock of afternoon traffic, newscasters with cameras filming for the evening news — we kiss for the very first time.

Or maybe it's the second.

# ACKNOWLEDGMENTS

Thank you to the brilliant editorial team of Erika Imranyi and Natalie Hallak, whose diligence and sage advice helped make this novel shine, and to my agent, Rachael Dillon Fried, whose tireless emotional support and encouragement kept me going.

Thank you to the dedicated Harlequin Books and HarperCollins teams for helping bring my novel out into the world, with special thanks to Emer Flounders for the incredible publicity, and to the wonderful people of Sanford Greenburger Associates.

Many thanks to the entire Kubica, Kyrychenko, Shemanek and Kahlenberg families, and to dear friends for all the support and constant reassurance: for helping care for my family when I couldn't be there; for being the happy, smiling faces at my signing events; for driving hundreds of miles to hear me say the same thing again and again; for delivering bottles of wine when I needed them most; and for putting up with my forgetfulness and constant shortage of time. I can't thank you enough for your love, your support and your patience.

And finally, to my husband, Pete, and my children, my very own Quinn and Alex, who inspire me every day. I couldn't have done it without you.

# ABOUT THE AUTHOR

**Mary Kubica** is the *New York Times* and *USA Today* bestselling author of *The Good Girl* and *Pretty Baby*. She holds a Bachelor of Arts degree from Miami University in Oxford, Ohio, in History and American Literature. She lives outside of Chicago with her husband and two children and enjoys photography, gardening and caring for the animals at a local shelter.

Monica Furlong

# Zen Effects

The Life of Alan Watts

Houghton Mifflin Company
BOSTON 1986

Library of Congress Cataloging-in-Publication Data

Furlong, Monica.
  Zen effects.

  Bibliography: p.                    **721647**
  Includes index.
    1. Watts, Alan, 1915–1973.   2. Philosophers —
United States — Biography.   3. Philosophers — England —
Biography.   I. Title.
B945.W324F87   1986       191        86–15364
ISBN 0–395–35344–0

Printed in the United States of America

Q 10 9 8 7 6 5 4 3 2 1

The author is grateful for permission to quote from the
following sources: *"This Is It" and Other Essays on Zen
and Spiritual Experience*, by Alan W. Watts. Copyright
© 1958, 1960 by Alan W. Watts. Reprinted by permission
of Pantheon Books, a division of Random House, Inc.
*Behold the Spirit*, by Alan Watts. Copyright 1947, © 1971
by Random House, Inc. Reprinted by permission of
Pantheon Books, a division of Random House, Inc. *In My
Own Way*, by Alan Watts. Copyright © 1972 by Alan
Watts. Reprinted by permission of Pantheon Books, a
division of Random House, Inc.

*In advanced particle physics some remarkable phenomena occur when two particles bearing opposite charges are forced to collide. Some of these events can be explained by standard theory, but others — zen effects — cannot be explained in terms of any known processes.*

# Acknowledgments

My principle thanks go to Joan Watts Tabernik of Bolinas, California, Alan Watts's daughter and executor, who encouraged me to write the book and was full of useful information. I was also most grateful to Ann Andrews who talked with me at great length about her father and the family history, and showed me much personal kindness. Mrs. Mary Jane Watts was very generous with her time.

Other members of the Watts family who helped with time, memories, photographs, tapes, and diaries were Mark Watts, Joy Buchan, Leslie and Peggy Watts, Sybil Jordeson, and Jean Mc-Dermid. Mrs. Dorothy Watts wrote to me at length about Alan Watts.

Watts had many close and loving friends; those I talked with about him were Elsa Gidlow, Roger Somers, Gary Snyder, Gordon Onslow-Ford, Toni Lilly, June Singer, Robert Shapiro, Ruth Costello, Sandy Jacobs, Virginia Denison, and Watts's niece by marriage, Kathleen.

Others who gave information were Bishop John Robinson,

Theodore Roszak, R. D. Laing, members of the San Francisco Zen Center, Episcopal clergy who remembered Watts from his Christian days, and Joanne Kyger. Dom Aelred Graham corresponded with me about the trip he and Watts made to Japan, Felix Greene about broadcasting with Watts, and Patrick Leigh Fermor about being at King's School, Canterbury.

King's School, Canterbury, provided archive material, suggested contacts, and described to me what the school must have been like in Watts's day.

John Snelling of the Buddhist Society of Great Britain gave me good advice, and the Society produced some interesting photographs.

For much of the research on the book I was away from home, and on my various visits to the West Coast of the United States I much appreciated the hospitality of Ann Andrews, Andrew Weaver, Daniel McLoughlin, and Ruth Costello. Frank and Mary Lee McClain of Winnetka, Illinois, gave me a temporary home while I researched Watts's years in Evanston and suggested a number of local sources of help. As on so many visits to the United States, the principal sources of help, encouragement, and hospitality were Fred and Susan Shriver of Chelsea Square, New York.

# Contents

# Introduction

When I began to write about Alan Watts I paid visits to the *Vallejo*, to Druid Heights, and to the lonely stupa on the hillside behind Green Gulch Farm. In that last place, wanting to pay tribute to a fellow Englishman so far from home, I picked a few of the California poppies that grew in the grass and laid them in front of the little grave.

Watts puzzled me, then and later. The combination of spiritual insight and naughtiness, of wisdom and childishness, of joyous high spirits and loneliness, seemed incongruous. Wasn't "knowledge" in the Buddhist sense of overcoming *avidya*, or ignorance, supposed gradually to lead you into some sort of release from craving, and yet there was Watts drinking and fornicating all over California? On the other hand Jesus had said that those who lived in "the Way" would have life and have it more abundantly than others, and everything I knew about Watts gave me to think that he had abundant life of a kind that made most of the good people seem moribund. He brought others to it, as well. Many more puzzled or troubled than he were introduced by Watts to a new way of seeing themselves and the world, and sometimes to a much more rigorous regime of spiritual exercises than he would have dreamed of undertaking himself, by way of *zazen* (Zen meditation) and Buddhism in its various manifestations.

Another thing that puzzled me about Watts was that he seemed terribly familiar to me. Among clergy in the Christian churches and gurus I had met in other forms of religion, some of them, often less remarkable than Watts, had almost all his characteristics. Though so splendidly and individually himself, Watts was at the same time a type, a type that nobody talked about much in the churches or in other religious communities because representatives of the type were something of an embarrassment, they were very often the subject of scandal. Certain sorts of disgrace tended to follow them, yet of the ones I had known well, there often seemed to be a special sort of *grace* as well, as if they were people who helped to break up rigid social patterns, forcing us to ask questions about them. We seemed to need them.

I had read of shamans who performed a function of this kind, but it was not until I met Gary Snyder and he told me about Coyote, the "trickster" hero of the Shoshone and the Californian Indians, that I could take the idea a bit further. Coyote, a favorite hero in Shoshone stories, was a bit of a rogue, but he knew something important, something other people needed. He was the one who brought fire to the earth by stealing it — it was owned and treasured by a group of flies. In the process of bringing it to his tribe he caught his tail alight and nearly burned himself to death; this was one of a long list of catastrophes that made up his life. He was also the one who brought death to mankind, accidentally. In the process he inadvertently made life worth living, but when his own child died and he really began to understand what death meant, he tried to reverse the process. Too late.

Coyote is a great folk hero, but is contradictory in nature, because his approach to issues of good and evil is an ambiguous one. When he performed "good" actions, they had a way of turning out wrong. When he was "bad," and he was often bad, goodness seemed in some mysterious way to emerge. He resisted the categories beloved of moral majorities; what had appeared comfortingly simple until he came along was thrown into comical confusion. "I think the most interesting psychological thing about the trickster," says Snyder, "was that there wasn't a clear dualism of good and evil established there, that he clearly manifested benevolence, compassion, help to human beings, sometimes, and had a certain dignity; and on other occasions he was the silliest utmost fool."

Maybe it is in this contradictory way that Watts is best seen.

In a poem called "Through the Smoke Hole," Snyder tells the Indian story of "the world above this one." This world is a wigwam with a hole in the roof through which the smoke of the fire goes. There is a ladder that goes out through the roof, and through this hole the great heroes climb on their shining way to the world above. It is our good fortune, however, that a few make the journey in reverse, tumbling, backside first, through the hole, to rejoin us in this world and give us hints of what they know. Such a one was Coyote. And so, possibly, was Alan Watts.

Zen Effects

# One

# The Paradise Garden

## 1915-1920

ALAN WATTS was born at twenty minutes past six in the morning on January 6, 1915, at Chislehurst in Kent, England, the child of Emily Mary (née Buchan) and Laurence Wilson Watts. Emily was thirty-nine years old and had begun to despair that she would have a child.

Emily came from a big family of five boys and two girls. She was the fifth child, followed by her favorite brother William (Willy) and another girl, Gertrude. Her father, William, was a patriarchal figure who ran a haberdashery and umbrella business in London. Sternly Evangelical, he prayed with his staff each morning before the shop opened, and was so unwilling to dismiss employees when times were bad that his business itself finally foundered. Alan, who could not remember him, pictured him as a sort of wrathful Jehovah who filled his mother with guilt and Protestant inhibition without giving her any real feeling for the spirit of religion.

An equally important figure to the Buchan children was their father's sister, Eleanor, an elegant, wealthy lady who lived at

Bakewell in Derbyshire and who worked in subtle ways to undermine William's austere regime. "I *hope* Eleanor is saved," her brother used to observe doubtfully. Eleanor took a particular interest in the girls, having them to stay and generally encouraging them. As a result of her enthusiasm and her financial help, both Emily and her sister Gertrude were able to carve out careers for themselves. While Gertrude trained as a nurse at the London Hospital, Emily trained as a teacher. She taught physical education and domestic economy at a school for missionaries' daughters, Walthamstow Hall, at Sevenoaks in Kent, but her real talent was for needlework. She was remarkably gifted at embroidery — there are examples of her work still to be found with a fine sense of color and design — and she became a teacher and designer for the Royal School of Needlework, where some of her designs are still used.

Emily was not a pretty girl, she had a brusque way of telling people exactly what she was thinking — a relative remembers that if she didn't like your hat she would tell you so straightaway — and she had a keen intelligence that she never bothered to hide. None of this made her particularly marriageable by the standards of the period, but in 1911 she met Alan's father, Laurence Wilson Watts, and they fell in love.

Laurence was four years younger than Emily. He was the second of five boys and was educated at the Stationers' School (a school originally for poor boys, financed by the Stationers' Guild. In Laurence's day quite well-to-do families sent their sons there). Since his father had a good job with a big silversmithing firm, Laurence grew up in comfortable circumstances at Stroud Green in North London. Perhaps a less dominant personality than Emily, he was a gentle, tolerant, humorous man, well liked by those who knew him. He is remembered in the Watts and

Buchan families as "a ladies' man like all the Watts men." At
the time he met Emily, he was working for the Michelin Tyre
Company at a job that took him on regular trips to Europe.

Perhaps Laurence liked taking care of Emily, or perhaps she
brought to the relationship some sort of forcefulness that he
lacked. Whatever the cause, they remained a most loving and
devoted couple for the rest of their lives. Their marriage in September 1912 started off on a good note when they found a very
pretty cottage in which to set up house at Chislehurst in Kent.
Still a rather attractive suburb of London, Chislehurst had acres
of unspoiled commonland, a village of old world shops, a fine old
church (Saint Nicholas's), and a village pond. Three Holbrook
Cottages, as their house was then called, was tiny, with the charming air of a doll's house, and it was surrounded by a large
and beautiful garden. Emily and Laurence could not have been
more pleased with it. They planted a mountain ash or rowan
tree in the front garden and called their new home Rowan
Cottage.

From the time of their wedding they seemed to be happy, as
Emily's letters to her brother Willy in the United States make
clear. "Laurie is so good to me. He always comes down and lights
the fire for me in the morning, then brings up a tray with tea and
we have it in bed. It is nice and warm by the time I go down to
make porridge. He thoroughly enjoys our real Scotch brand of
porridge. Laurie is quite a Buchanish man and does all sorts of
things to help me."[1]

Their financial prospects seemed quite rosy to them as well.
Laurie was earning £250 a year, plus some money his firm kept
back to invest for him. In another two years he would get £300 a
year, with an eventual prospect of £400 or £500.

Despite the happiness the new marriage brought, child-bearing did not come easily for Emily. She had conceived immediately after marriage and on June 19, 1913, Emily gave birth to a baby boy, Brian, who lived for only two weeks. She herself was very ill and took a long time to recover; she worried desperately about Laurie and about who would care for him during her stay in the hospital. This tragic sequence, though common enough in those days, must have made Emily wonder whether she would be able to bear a child, since she was now nearly thirty-eight. By Christmas she was thinking of consulting a specialist, presumably about her gynecological difficulties.

In 1914 Emily had a miscarriage, but finally in January 1915 Alan was born. Emily's sister Gertrude was present to assist at the birth and to look after Emily. (Gertrude was to be an important member of the family for much of Alan's childhood — "a pretty, vivacious tomboy,"[2] as he remembered her.) Though delighted to have a baby at last, Emily did not find motherhood easy. A relative of Emily's remembers seeing her once with a neighbor's baby and noticed that she seemed to have no idea of how to hold it or what to do with it. She found it charming, but seemed to have no natural feeling for babies, and its mother was glad to take it back.

Natural mother or not, Emily longed for a daughter, and in 1919 she gave birth to another child, a boy, who lived only a few days. The Buchan women tended, tragically, to lose their babies after birth; not until the next generation was this known to be due to the rhesus (Rh) factor. Many of the Buchan women had Rh negative blood, which meant that a baby born to them with Rh positive blood was endangered and needed an immediate blood transfusion. Alan's blood group may have been Rh negative, which would have enabled him to survive.

Emily was not, in any case, burdened with the physical care

of Alan, for she hired a trained child nurse to look after him. One of Alan's Watts cousins, Leslie, once shared his nursery for a few days, and Leslie's mother told him later how shocked she was when she realized the nannie's severity, particularly with Alan: "Wouldn't let a child have a biscuit, or a cuddly toy in bed. Wouldn't let Alan have his toys much at all."

Emily herself was a loving woman, but she had an austere puritanical streak and believed in "firmness"; Alan was not to be indulged.

Nonetheless, Alan had some good memories of his early childhood, especially of the cottage and surrounding garden where he was free to play. He remembered the hedge of sweetbriar in the front garden and "an arbor of jasmine and a magnificent tree of green cooking-apples upon which we used to hang coconuts, sliced open for the delectation of wrens and blue tits." He loved the hours spent in the garden, getting lost in a forest of tomatoes, raspberries, and beans on sticks stretching far above his head, seeing himself surrounded by "glowing, luscious jewels, embodiments of emerald or amber or carnelian light, usually best eaten raw and straight off the plant when you are alone." There was a blissful time when part of the garden was allowed to go fallow "with grasses, sorrel and flowering weeds so well above my head that I could get lost in this sunny herbaceous forest with butterflies floating above."[3] For the rest of his life Alan remembered the taste of the peas, potatoes, scarlet runner beans and pippin apples that came out of that garden.

Beside the garden was a piece of land that the Wattses owned and behind that the playing fields of a girls' school, Farrington's. Beyond that was an immense estate of fields and forests. On the boundary between the school and the Wattses' land was an enormous sycamore tree, ninety feet high, which was important to

Alan in later memory, as he describes. There "the sun rose, and
. . . in the late afternoon my mother and I watched glistening
pigeons against black storm clouds. That was the axle-tree of the
world, Yggdrasil, blessing and sheltering the successive orchards,
vegetable gardens and (once) a rabbit farm which my father
cultivated in times of economic distress."[4]

From all accounts, Alan was a precocious little boy. When he
was three Emily described him in a letter to her brother Willy
and his wife as "a gay little chap and an adorer of trains. Never
still and always talking. He has a splendid imagination and is not
short of words — and makes up a good many for himself — very
expressive they are too. He can say the whole of the Lord's Prayer
by himself. You would both be rather pleased with the bairn."[5]

Alan was aware from an early age of the love his parents had
for each other — he remembered their holding hands under the
dining room table — and of the total acceptance and love he
received from his father. He had an early memory of playing
with a piece of dry excrement as he lay in his crib. "What have
you got there?" his father asked him, with the perfect courtesy of a
Victorian gentleman. Alan handed it to him, he examined it carefully, and politely handed it back.

Laurence, in fact, never seemed to get over a kind of reverent
wonder at this tiny child in their midst, and his proud astonish-
ment at his son's achievements must have done wonders for
Alan's self-confidence. Writing, in old age, a preface for his son's
autobiography, Laurence tried to say a bit about what his experience as a father had been:

> What may appear to be . . . odd . . . is that a person of Alan's
> breadth of outlook and depth of thought should have sprung from
> the parentage of a father who inherited much of the Victorian out-
> look and tradition and a mother whose family were Fundamentalists

to whom the Bible was the Truth, the whole Truth, and nothing but the Truth. . . . As a child a gift of narrative showed in him before he could read or write, and an early need was to keep him supplied with material for illustrating the tales he invented. . . . Plenty of white kitchen paper, pencils, and coloured chalks had always to be on hand.[6]

Alan's drawings, writings, and sayings were cherished to a degree unusual in a period less interested in "expression" in children than our own. As soon as he could talk he composed an interminable serial (complete with illustrations) that he dictated to Gertrude about an imaginary country called Bath Bian Street.

The Wattses were extraordinarily lucky in that the First World War seemed to affect them very little. Laurence was saved from conscription by a carbuncle on his neck, though he used to drill with a Territorial unit on Chislehurst Common. (The unit marched to the sound of drums and bugles produced by a group that Alan called "Daddy's band.") Night air raids usually resulted in the unexpected pleasure of cocoa in the dining room for Alan. And once when a bomb did fall in the middle of the village green no one was hurt.

Even without the intermittent excitement of the war, the social and domestic life of Chislehurst was interesting to a little boy. The milkman arrived amid clanging cans with his horse and cart. Next door lived Miss Augusta Pearce, "Miss Gussy," Alan called her. On Sundays church bells rang across the Common, and Alan would go to Christchurch with his mother, or, if Emily was ill, to the Anglo-Catholic delights of Saint Nicholas's with Miss Gussy. On Sundays, too, uncles and cousins sometimes came to visit — to be born into the Watts/Buchan families was to be part of an immense, devoted clan that frequently met and consumed enormous meals together.

Shopping expeditions to the village brought their own joy with visits to the sweet shop run by a Miss Rabbit, the bakery run by Miss Battle, the stationery shop and the grocer's smelling of "fresh coffee, smoked meats and Stilton cheese." There was a chemist's shop called Prebble and Bone, which displayed enormous glass jars of colored water in the window, and a dress and drapery shop run by the Misses Scriven, which gave Alan terrible nightmares. The sisters "displayed their dresses upon 'dummies,' headless, armless and legless mock-ups of female torsos, having lathe-turned erections of dark wood in place of heads. . . . In the midst of an otherwise interesting dream there would suddenly appear a calico-covered dummy, formidably breasted (without cleft) and sinisterly headless. This thing would mutter at me and suggest ineffable terrors. . . ."[7]

As with any small child, however, the life that mattered most was at home, with father and mother, and with the routines of everyday life. Looking back on his childhood from his fifties, Alan divided the house in two: upstairs and downstairs. Upstairs seemed filled with nameless longings, fears, desires, dreams, and nightmares, as well as with boredom, pain, shame, and humiliation. Downstairs was interesting, fun, sociable, the heart of culinary and aesthetic joy. Upstairs was his bedroom, which, as a small child, he shared with his nannie, and which looked across vegetable smallholdings and trees to the spire of Saint Nicholas's Church. He was sent there continually, it seemed to him, for interminable siestas, for bedtimes while the sky was still light, and for punishment. He disliked the bedroom so much that for the rest of his life he never slept in a bedroom if he could help it, preferring some kind of bed that unfolded or unrolled in the sitting room.

Worse than the bedroom was the unheated bathroom, which he associated with all the humiliations of constipation. Emily and her nannie attended to Alan's bowels with Protestant thoroughness.

"They seemed to want, above all things, to know 'Have you *been?*' They invaded the bathroom with an almost religious enthusiasm to discover whether you had made it. They insisted that you 'go' every morning immediately after breakfast, whether or not you felt so inclined."[8] Failure to "go" resulted in a dose of Californian Syrup of Figs, followed by senna pods, cascara sagrada, and in the last resort, castor oil.

Apart from the miseries of constipation, the bathroom was the place where Alan got spanked by his mother "seated on the crapulatory throne," was told Bible stories by his nannie, and was taught prayers by his mother. The first prayer he was taught was "Gentle Jesus, Shepherd, Hear Me":

> Gentle Jesus, Shepherd, hear me:
> Bless thy little lamb tonight.
> Through the darkness be thou near me;
> Keep me safe till morning light.
>
> Let my sins be all forgiven;
> Bless the friends I love so well.
> Take me when I die, to heaven,
> Happy there with thee to dwell.

Doubtless intended to comfort little children at nighttime, this prayer had the effect on Alan of making him feel frightened of the darkness and worried that death was an imminent possibility. He had heard of people "who died in their sleep," and thought that this misfortune might happen to him. (Revealingly he mispronounced the fifth line as "Let my sins be awful given.") Later for Watts the Christian religion would seem to be as bleak as this bathroom, a desert without beauty, where an impossible cleanliness seemed to be the sine qua non of godliness, where it was always Judgment Day, and where there seemed no appropriate attitude but that of shame.

Fortunately there was also the "downstairs" life of the Watts household, a life as rich and interesting as the upstairs life was drab and depressing. Emily taught the little boy to feed the birds and to imitate birdcalls (years later in California he was to teach mockingbirds to sing like nightingales), and as soon as he was old enough, his father took him on bug- and moth-hunting expeditions. They would catch the moths by putting a treacly preparation on the trunks of trees. It is typical of Alan that, forty years later, he remembered exactly what the chemical mixture was that attracted the moths. All his life he was fascinated by technical information.

The beautiful garden was the center of his childish world, but one other place had an importance for him that he was too young to understand. In the dining room there was a huge monstrosity called "the Housetop," a combined chest of drawers, roll-top desk, and hanging cupboard. In the cupboard Emily kept plum puddings wrapped in cheesecloth, fruitcake, brandy, preserved fruits, and the family silver and glass. In the desk were small pigeonholes and drawers filled with delightful things: checkbooks whose ink gave off a wonderful smell, pens, pencils, rulers, ivory gadgets, and playing cards.

> In the center of this bank of drawers and pigeonholes was a small cupboard flanked by Corinthian columns with gilded capitals. It contained mostly photographs, postcards and old letters, but there was a secret way of pulling out the whole unit to get access to two hidden compartments behind the columns. . . . From as far back as I can remember I always had the fantasy that, somewhere, the Housetop contained some mystery, some hidden treasure, some magical entity, that would be a key to the secret of life.[9]

While the Housetop was mysterious for the young boy, his mother's drawing room was positively magical. The drawing room, used only on special occasions, contained Emily's collection of

Oriental treasures. There was a round brass coffee table from India, a Korean celadon vase, two Chinese vases, and some Japanese embroidered cushions. It was not so very unusual for houses to contain a little chinoiserie or japonerie, the odd vase or hanging, or the Indian curios brought back from the far reaches of the British Empire, but Emily's deep feeling for Oriental art, her taste, her profound sense of color, and her knowledge of embroidery transformed what might have been just a room full of knickknacks into a place of wonder and beauty. Alan knew that these ornaments were his mother's choice. He recognized, later, that through her he was heir to a kingdom that might not otherwise have been his. "She turned me on, bless her, to color, to flowers, to intricate and fascinating designs, to the works of Oriental art."[10]

Yet despite all this he sensed that something was wrong in his feelings for his mother as far back as he could remember. He valued her skills, her care of him, her conviction that God was planning great things for him when he became a man. He knew her for a good woman, honest, truthful, generous, and he knew his own childish dependence on her. Yet he had a worrying sense of disappointment in her. She did not seem to him as pretty as other women, perhaps because she was older than the run of mothers, and he couldn't stand the way she looked when she woke up in the morning.

Sometimes it seemed to him that his lack of positive feeling for his mother came from the sense that she disliked her own body, and he wondered if that was because she was so frequently sick after her marriage. "When she spoke of people being very *ill* she would swallow the word as if it were a nasty lump of fat, and take on a most serious frown."[11] In fact, for the rest of Alan's childhood, and indeed the rest of her life, Emily's health was frail. She

suffered recurrent hemorrhages from her lungs as a result of an
attack of pleurisy from which she never seemed to make a complete recovery. Alan's cousins remember that the family often went
home early from family gatherings because "Emily doesn't feel
well."

Somehow underlying Emily's lack of prettiness, her illnesses,
and her dislike of her own body, Alan could sense the influence of
the fiercely fundamentalist Protestantism her father had passed on
to her. It was not so much that Emily herself had taken on rigid
beliefs — she might have been much more cheerful about it if she
had — as that she had been force-fed with them and had lived
with an uneasy and half-digested religion ever since. Intellectually
she was a tolerant and widely read woman; she and Laurence enjoyed exploring all sorts of religious ideas. It was the unexamined
and partly unconscious aspects of fundamentalism — in particular
in connection with the body — that Alan felt he detected in her.

Watts was reserved about his feelings for his mother when he
came to write his autobiography, perhaps mainly out of consideration for his father who was still alive and who took a keen interest
in the book. But to friends in private Watts spoke of the difficulty
he had in loving her. This puzzled many of Watts's family and
friends who found her gentle, lovable, and caring. Although Watts
would not have disputed her having those qualities, he felt he
lacked from his mother cuddling and sensual appreciation. What
he got instead was a dour religion that she didn't fully believe in
herself, which got mixed up with condemnation of his nascent
sexuality and with the rigor of Californian Syrup of Figs. Any infant in a Christian fundamentalist world was necessarily unsatis-
factory, unacceptable, guilty, and ashamed, an example of the
fallen and unredeemed human state. For Watts sexuality became
something surreptitious, associated with beating or other sado-

masochistic fantasies, or with dirty jokes. It seems significant that after writing about his mother and her religion in his autobiography Watts at once moved on to a limerick mocking the Trinity, and the Holy Ghost in particular.[12] For most of his life Watts was to enjoy a reputation for his impressive repertoire of funny and risqué limericks, often connected with religion.

Watts's relationship with his father was less intense, but warm and happy, giving him a level of self-confidence that Emily could never give. Laurence always seemed to have time to spend with his little boy. He read aloud to him, Kipling being a favorite, sang hymns and Edwardian ballads to him, and taught him to shoot with a rifle and a bow. In many ways Alan's childhood was amazingly secure, with the middle-aged couple pouring love and attention on one little boy.

# Two

# The Education of a Brahmin

## 1920-1932

ALAN'S PRECOCITY AND CLEVERNESS made him an object of attention and amusement in the limited circle of grown-ups he knew. He was, as people used to say then, "a proper caution." Once when he was ill in bed the doctor came and proposed to give him an injection.

"Only," said the dignified small child, "if you will give me two shillings first." He got his fee.

In photographs he looks a rather owlish little boy, bespectacled, scrubbed, combed, and very neatly and smartly dressed. He knew he was something extraordinary — Emily had made that very clear to him, as well as to all her relatives. Leslie Watts, Alan's cousin, remembers how it was simply taken for granted by everybody that Alan was "very clever."

Despite this early promise, Watts found school to be a letdown. He went, enthusiastically enough, to the Saint Nicholas kindergarten, just across the green from Rowan Cottage, a school for children up to the age of about eight. As an only child, he was interested in the other children, but for the most part, he was bored in the school. Emily had already taught him to read, he found multiplication tables uninteresting, and he didn't like the sort of "prissy paintings" they did, being used to bolder artistic sorties at home. So he spent a lot of time just gazing out of the window at the village green.

On one particularly awful day his teacher, Miss Nicholas, chose him as the blind man in blindman's buff. He was fond of Miss Nicholas, mainly because she was so pretty, but groping round the room, unable to see, chasing giggling knots of boys and girls, made him feel as if he had been singled out for humiliation. Furious at this indignity he went home and drew a picture of Buckingham Palace, which he took back to school next morning. King George V was lying dead with an arrow in his heart, and knights in armor with flaming eyes were saying, "How dared you do that to Alan?"

Miss Nicholas cannot often have been taken to task so severely by the children she taught, and she did not take kindly to it now. Showing the offending picture to the whole school, she gave Alan a lecture on his failings. School, he decided, was a waste of time.

Outside of school he spent much of his time in the "Paradise Garden" of Rowan Cottage, and there conducted elaborate funeral ceremonies for dead birds, bats, and rabbits. He still believed in fairies and magic. On the whole he preferred the company of girls, and in his autobiography he describes how, with "two adorably feminine tomboys," Margaret and Christine, he explored a local stream from end to end. He found them rather intimidating.

While Watts was carrying out his funeral ceremonies, Emily was beginning to make plans for him. In the England of those days, if you hoped to end in a distinguished profession, you needed to have a strictly prescribed, and very expensive, education — the education of a Brahmin, as Watts later called it. You abandoned the company of your little friends at the local kindergarten, junior, and secondary school, and you underwent the rigors of the private preparatory school, usually at age eight, followed by the public school at age eleven. Both were usually boarding schools, both gave you a good grounding in Greek and Latin, both were usually noted for their spartan standards.

Emily and Laurence did not have much money, but they lived very modestly and were prepared to save every penny they had to give Alan a Brahmin's education. Alan was clever; Emily believed this as an article of faith, even though his performance at kindergarten had revealed little sign of it. Still, she knew that the way to shine in the world was to pass through the series of ordeals and initiations provided by private education.

So, Emily enrolled Alan, aged seven and a half, at Saint Hugh's, in Bickley, a nearby town. It was rather early to go to a prep school, but Emily felt that Alan's "real education" could not begin soon enough, and although the school was close enough for him to attend as a day boy, Emily, no doubt suppressing some of her own longings for her child's company, decided that Alan would go as a weekly boarder. She felt strongly that an only child should not be "indulged."

The boys had to wear a uniform to which Alan took an instant dislike, finding it uncomfortable and rigid: "Tight, dark grey pants, a black waistcoat or vest with lapels and cloth-covered buttons, and a black monkey-jacket known as a bumfreezer, obviously designed for the purpose of making the bottoms of small boys more readily presentable for flogging."[1] There was also a large, white starched collar worn outside the jacket, and a straw boater, beribboned with school colors, in this case salmon pink with a white fleur-de-lis at the front.

Emily and Alan traveled on the bus to Saint Hugh's, Bickley.

Though proud of the importance of going to a new school, Alan nevertheless broke down in panic.

"Please, please, let me stay at home," he begged, adding pathetically that he was "too young" to go away. Emily was adamant. She said it would be good for him to have to hold his own in the hurly-burly of boarding school.

Alan found himself placed in a six-bed dormitory. After he had said goodbye to his mother, he went down to supper and found the food so unpalatable that he ate nothing except white bread. Going hungry to his dormitory he had a harsh introduction to Saint Hugh's. There was bullying of new boys — beating and other initiation rites. There was a new vocabulary of lavatory and sexual words. The puritan world of Rowan Cottage, in which he was the center of his parents' existence, and where every precocious word he uttered was received with admiration, was a poor preparation for this sudden descent into hell. Fear, loneliness, homesickness swallowed him up. How shocked Emily would have been if she could have read his summing up, written in middle age. "My first lesson [at Saint Hugh's] given at night in a . . . dormitory by the other occupants, was in the vocabulary of scatology and sexual anatomy, with a brief introduction to buttock fetishism."[2]

The next morning the seven-year-olds assembled in the classroom of Miss Elsie Good, "a precise and serious lady with a sharply pointed nose, who instructed us in English, French, Latin, Arithmetic, History, Geography and Holy Scripture. I suppose all this was, as my mother called it, 'good grounding,' but the whole process was carried out under such duress that only exceptionally gifted Englishmen survived it and retained any lifelong fascination with arts and letters."[3]

History was taught with a notable slant towards the splendors of the British Empire, and French by a system so idiosyncratic that

Alan would find himself translating: "Do you have some pretty jewels? No, but I have given some water to the owls."[4] Algebra remained an ominous mystery to him, and his attempts to question its dark edicts resulted in his being struck with the blackboard pointer. Music was the most depressing lesson of all. He was a naturally musical child with, at least later in life, a fine singing voice, but the severity of the teacher and the boredom of the Czerny studies and "children's pieces" he was obliged to play on the piano set up a mental block that lasted for years.

Life in the classroom was lived under a peculiar form of tension. In order to avoid being ritually whipped on a Saturday morning, the boys had to get fourteen "good" marks during the week, marks arbitrarily given by any teacher who happened to be pleased with a boy. This nerve-racking system did not serve Alan well, and he was beaten a lot. To go home briefly to Rowan Cottage after these dreadful weeks to parents who, though loving, would not really have understood his suffering even if he had known how to tell them about it, convinced as they were that it was "good for him," in fact only heightened the contrast between home and school. Sunday was passed in a gloom of apprehension about the coming week. Yet he felt he was expected to be grateful for his interminable ordeal. "My parents knocked themselves out financially to send me to this amazing institution."[5]

At least home gave him the opportunity to eat a decent meal. Though there were a few things at Saint Hugh's he could eat and enjoy — the fried sausages, and suet pudding with Lyle's Golden Syrup on top of it — Alan found most of the food disgusting. A worried school informed his parents at one point that he was eating nothing but bread.

School shattered, or at least badly damaged, the strong sense of self-esteem he had shown at Saint Nicholas's. The feeling that he was a prince among his peers vanished. "I have been told, in later years, that I look like a mixture of King George VI and Rex Harrison, but *then* the boys told me I was a cross-eyed and buck-toothed weakling."[6]

Apart from all the other hardships of school he missed the company of girls, hitherto his closest friends. No longer could he dream of marrying a schoolmate. Such love as existed at Saint Hugh's was between older and younger boys, pretty younger boys seeking the protection of strong older boys as part of the daily battle for survival. Alan was not regarded as "pretty."

Inevitably he learned in time, however, how to make the kind of compromises necessary to survival in such a place. He learned to swim and eventually got into the school rugger team, though he could never reconcile himself to cricket, having an ocular defect that prevented him from seeing the ball quickly. He enjoyed milk chocolate bars, smutty schoolboy jokes, and the quirks of the more eccentric teachers. Like all preparatory and public schools of the period, Saint Hugh's put most of its energy into teaching boys the classics.

As the years passed, the terrors of school grew somewhat less, though Alan never quite recovered from his initial shock. This plunge into a world of sadism and sexual innuendo left the puritan child in him with the lingering impression of shameful excitement and prurient curiosity. Whenever he writes of this grim rite of passage, it is with a dryness that seems understandably defensive. The brutality of upper-class British schools, he says, is already so notorious and has been so extensively described that he sees little point in going into details. "I was sent off to boarding school for instruction in laughing and grief, in militarism and regimented music, in bibliolatry and bad ritual, in cricket, soccer and rugby, in preliminary accounting, banking and surveying (known as arithmetic, algebra and geometry) and in subtle, but not really overt, homosexuality."[7]

Saint Hugh's was, like all such schools, devoutly Anglican, and while Alan was at the school, Emily did some of her exquisite needlework on the altar cloths. This brought Alan into contact with Charles Johnson, a brother of the headmaster and a gifted architect and designer, who carved the new reredos and generally supervised the work. Johnson, who was known to the boys, was regarded by them as wildly eccentric; some said he was mad, others that he was under the influence of drugs. One of the stories was that he needed a male nurse constantly in attendance, disguised as a butler-cum-chauffeur. Alan was surprised to find that he liked him very much. Johnson, who had lived for years in Mexico, built himself a Spanish-Mexican house in the grounds in splendid contrast to the school's drab architecture, and this became one of Alan's refuges from school. Johnson himself became the first of a long line of older mentors, male and female, who instructed Alan in the arts of living. Like all such people, he struck Alan as "urbane" and "utterly removed from the crickety-militaristic atmosphere of his brothers' school."[8] (The school had two headmasters, the Rev. Frederick Johnson and Alfred Johnson.) Watching him at work designing or carving, Alan thought that Charles Johnson gave him more education in five minutes than his brothers would give him in five years, mainly through his pleasure and meticulous care in his craft.

Despite his resentment of school, Alan also admired Alfred Johnson. Alfred had a real feeling for literature and even more feeling for music. He had a passion for Wagner, and taught the boys to sing parts of *Die Meistersinger*, one of Schubert's masses, and Brahms's *Requiem*. Unfortunately, Alfred's enormous pleasure in music did little to redeem the harm that the Saint Hugh's music lessons had done.

But more important than either Charles or Alfred to Alan's development was their sister Elvira and her husband, Francis Croshaw (also widely believed around the school to be a lunatic). Alan had found a friend at school, Ivan Croshaw, and Ivan took him home to a household which for some years was to be a delight to him and a powerful influence on his interests and taste. Elvira was, in Alan's view, "handsome, witty, and sophisticated," in contrast to his own mother, and she "spoke exquisite French," was "Continental and Parisian" in style, and was also very funny. Her son always referred to her as POM (short for Poor Old Mother), and in Watts's words, "she controlled us simply by casting an influence. I never saw her punish her son, nor lose her temper. . . . I cannot remember any adult with whom I felt so completely at ease, and she, if anyone, is responsible for my adoption of what is sometimes called an un-English style of life. For me she became the archetypal representative of relaxed, urbane society, seasoned with wit and fantasy."[9]

Francis Croshaw, who was too wealthy to work, was also a glamorous figure. He smoked black Burmese cigars, "the kind that are open at both ends, nubbly in texture, and burn with a blue flame and hiss," and he shared these with the eleven-year-old boys. Croshaw was given to taking off in his car for a day and not reappearing for a week, having suddenly taken it into his head to have a look at Wales; he walked about in a Moorish dressing gown carrying a dog whip (though he had no dog), and he read French paperbacks by the score. Alan was slowly finding the sort of friends he would relish for the rest of his life.

He particularly enjoyed their cosmopolitan qualities, their lack of insular "Britishness." Even his reading at this age revealed his dislike of narrow, jingoistic attitudes and "clean-limbed" heroes. At the age of eleven his passion, instead, was Dr. Fu Manchu. He fancied himself as "a Chinese villain, keeping servants with knives hidden in their sleeves, who appeared and disappeared without a sound."[10] He wanted a house with secret passages, with screens, with lacquer bottles of exotic poisons, with porcelain and jade and incense and sonorous gongs. He began filling his bedroom at home with cheap Chinese and Japanese ornaments, until Emily, who had already given him a copy of the New Testament in Chinese, took the hint and decorated his room with some fine Oriental hangings, including a Japanese *kakemono* of two herons watching a flight of tumbling sparrows. The beauty, the simplicity, but above all, the "alienness" of Oriental culture appealed to a child already feeling alien within the culture in which he was brought up. An affinity for all things Japanese was already growing in him; it was a secret link between him and his mother, a doorway to the sensuality he felt she had mislaid.

He missed the presence of girls in the male world of school, but consoled himself as best he could with his female cousins. His favorite was Joy, the daughter of his mother's brother Harry, about his own age, and "ruddy and joyous." Joy was shy in adult company, while Alan was talkative and mischievous, but Alan would talk to her and tease her until she came out of her shell, doing drawings to make her laugh. He corresponded regularly with her, as he did with other girl cousins, very often decorating his letters with rabbits (modeled rather obviously on Peter Rabbit). Even as a child, he had a "way with women."

In the Watts/Buchan clan, family was of immense importance, and there are many photographs of the various relatives gathered in the garden of Rowan Cottage, or out in the countryside on weekend or holiday walks. On Sunday nights the family often gathered at Uncle Harry and Aunt Et's house in Bromley (a local town) for a tremendous high tea, which Alan, in his less sophisticated moods, thoroughly enjoyed. The evening ended less enjoyably for Alan with hymns round the piano. He was later to feel that he had been fed relentlessly with hymns for the whole of his childhood and youth, and moralistic and maudlin as many of them seemed, they somehow never ceased to haunt him with their dignity and beauty. But the Sunday evenings were as much a statement of family solidarity as religious feeling, and gradually Alan could feel himself pulling away from the dowdy, if worthy, Protestant milieu, turning towards a world more glamorous and more cosmopolitan.

He was beginning to travel a little outside the environs of Chislehurst, and in later years the sight of Chislehurst station still recalled the thrill of going away, alone or on family expeditions. "Much as I loved my home, that station — with the knock-knock sound of tickets being issued, the tring of the bell announcing an approaching train, and the murmuring rails as a train came in from the distance — was a center of liberation."[11]

Meanwhile at home, Alan and his friend Ronnie Macfarlane roamed the countryside around Chislehurst on bicycles, carrying an air rifle. Ronnie and he despised, on the one hand, contemporaries who played cricket and talked in the affected accents of the upper classes. On the other hand they did not want to be identified with lower-class boys who dropped their aitches, talked in a "common" accent, and revealed signs of poverty and meager education. So they set themselves up as a pair of independent adventurers — the Japanese word *ronin* summed it up — needing nobody, but alive to the excitements and wonder of the world around them.

But times were growing hard for Emily and Laurence. Laurence, like so many in the Great Depression, had lost his job. The Wattses had lived simply, apart from the cost of Alan's education, pleased with all that they had, thrifty and saving. They had a little money saved, which they tried to eke out with Emily's embroidery and a rabbit farm that Laurence set up beside the house, but there was much family discussion about how they could be helped. Should they emigrate to America and join Emily's brother Willy? They wrote to ask Willy's advice. How could they keep Alan at boarding school? Saint Hugh's, pleased perhaps to help a boy of considerable intellectual ability, agreed to reduce the fees.

One burden was taken from their shoulders when, in 1928, Watts won a scholarship to King's School, Canterbury. King's School is probably the oldest school in England, with a long list of famous former pupils, including the poet Marlowe. Standing beside Canterbury Cathedral, the school is integrated into the life of the cathedral, and therefore into one of the most ancient sites of Christianity in England, the place where Saint Augustine of Canterbury initiated the conversion of a whole people, the seat of Edward the Confessor, the heart of Anglicanism.

It was a setting to which no boy with any feeling for history or visual beauty could remain indifferent. The poet and writer Patrick Leigh Fermor, a friend and contemporary of Watts's at the school, remembered the deep awe he felt at his surroundings when he first went to King's.

> I couldn't get over the fact that the school had been founded at the very beginning of Anglo-Saxon Christianity, before the sixth century was out, that is: fragments of Thor and Woden had hardly stopped smouldering in the Kentish woods: the oldest parts of the buildings were modern by these standards, dating only from a few decades after the Normans landed. There was a wonderfully cobwebbed feeling about this dizzy and intoxicating antiquity — an ambience both haughty and obscure which turned famous seats of learning, founded eight hundred or a thousand years later, into gaudy mushrooms and seemed to invest these hoarier precincts, together with the wide green expanses beyond them, the huge elms, the Dark Entry, and the ruined arches and cloisters — and while I

was about it, the booming and jackdaw-crowded pinnacles of the great Angevin cathedral itself, and the ghost of St. Thomas à Becket and the Black Prince's bones — with an aura of nearly pre-historic myth.[12]

Watts too was affected by these ancient surroundings. He de-scribed the Canterbury of his boyhood as

> a garden enclosed — walled and gated on all sides. . . . Almost every building was of pale grey stone, and the architecture Roman-esque and every variety of Gothic. The whole atmosphere was strangely light and airy, full of the sound of bells and the cries of jackdaws floating around the great Bell Harry Tower of the Cathe-dral, and when March came in like a lion the air swept through the buildings, slamming doors and rattling shutters, and seeming to cleanse the place of human meanness.[13]

The great cathedral seemed to him romantic and heraldic, reminis-cent of the tales of King Arthur and the Holy Grail. He was moved by this central shrine of English religion, the "corona" of Canter-bury.

> All around this corona are tall narrow windows of stained glass, predominantly blue — as good as anything at Chartres — which, with their colours reflecting on the pale grey stone, give the whole place a sense of light and lofty airiness, jewelled transparency and peace.[14]

The school was, in many ways, in a good phase. It had an original and enlightened headmaster in the person of Norman Birley, and it attracted a number of lively and able teachers as staff. It gave, as most public schools did, an excellent education in the classics. However, it also showed an interest in the arts and gave boys active encouragement to pursue them, which was an unusual practice for public schools at the time.

Sports, to Watts's dismay, inevitably figured largely in the curriculum as well, but even there those who were bored could escape:
"In summer, having chosen rowing instead of cricket, [I] lay
peacefully beside the Stour, well upstream of the ryhthmic creak-
ing and exhortation, reading Gibbon and gossiping with kindred
lotus-eaters under the willow-branches."[15] In many ways it was a
very civilized and cultured way of life.

Watts was in Grange House, with a housemaster, Alec Macdonald, whom he liked and admired. Macdonald had been a pilot
in the Air Force in the First World War, but, perhaps because of
this, he was "a man of peace" as well as a man of culture. He was
a good linguist, with a deep knowledge of European classics, and
a music lover who played classical records to the boys. He had also
invented a new method of musical notation — just the sort of
thing to fascinate Watts — and in general was much the sort of
person Watts hoped to become.

There were difficulties and tensions at King's School for Watts,
though perhaps fewer than at Saint Hugh's. Many years later
Watts was to tell his second wife Dorothy that he had minded
being "a scholarship boy," that this had given him feelings of inferiority. Since his father was by now unemployed, and since even
when he had been employed he had worked in "trade" instead of
being a "gentleman," it is possible that Watts was mocked or
despised for these reasons. "Trade," in that prewar England, was
still "not quite nice." Watts suffered, however, from a sort of
unwilling snobbery on his own part, a fascination with the ease
and style that went with wealth, and it must have been painful to
return to a home where every penny was counted, where his admired father was out of work, and where his mother did what she
could to make money by embroidery.

He had learned a lot at Saint Hugh's about survival, and he

reflected that, whereas he had been frequently beaten there, at King's he managed "by sheer guile and skulduggery to avoid it altogether — only to learn the curious fact that the man who uses brains against brawn is, by the brawny, considered a sneak, a cheater, and a coward — almost a criminal."[16]

At one point early on he attempted to run away from King's School. He had written a Latin exercise in Gothic script with a decorated initial capital, and his teacher decided that this attempt to "be different" was a wicked prank. His running away, though, was half-hearted, mainly because he could not see an alternative to the school. Clever non-Brahmins went to the local "county school" where, public school boys believed, everyone said "ain't" instead of "isn't," and he could not contemplate such a fate. But if he dreaded the county school, he felt that he did not really "fit in" at King's School. Instead, he acquired an armor of bravado, superiority, and clever criticism that he was rarely to shed during the rest of his life.

During Watts's first year at Canterbury, Archbishop Cosmo Gordon Lang was enthroned at Canterbury. The magnificent cathedral was packed to the doors with robed bishops and clergy, with government ministers, with royalty — the whole panoply of church and state. The archbishop's procession wound through the nave and up the long flight of steps to the high altar with Watts, wearing knee breeches, silk stockings, and buckled shoes, carrying the long red train. Already a performer and a lover of ritual, he thoroughly enjoyed it, and Emily and Laurence were overwhelmed with pride.

At thirteen he was more at home in the elegant clothes of ritual than in the drabber garments required for everyday life. The uniform for boys below the rank of sixth form was, as Watts says, designed for "dowdy dandies," an affair of a speckled straw boater, with a blue and white ribbon, a starched wing collar with a black tie, and a black jacket with Oxford gray trousers.

The food, as at Saint Hugh's, outraged Watts's growing interest in gastronomy: "a diet of boiled beef, boiled cabbage, boiled onions, boiled carrots, boiled potatoes, and slabs of near-stale bread."[17] The serious eating in such an establishment was all extra-curricular. One of the pleasures of life was to nip down to the Tuck shop run by a Mrs. Benn beneath the arches of the medieval hall and to feast on barley sugar, butterscotch, toffee, marshmallow, a chocolate bar, or an ice cream soda. Before being long at the school boys acquired their own Primus (methylated spirit) stoves, and learned to cook sausages, eggs, and bacon for themselves. Sometimes Watts brewed a sort of curry made from two onions, six frankfurters, a handful of raisins, salt and pepper, curry powder, and cooking oil. As in all such schools there was a tea shop within bounds where coffee and scones and cake were on hand, and as soon as boys began to look even remotely grown-up they would cycle out into the country to drink the excellent Kentish ale at local pubs.

In his second year at King's, Watts was prepared for confirma-tion — it was the routine initiation into Christian practice for boys of his background, one of the common rites of puberty. The teach-ing that accompanied the rite included dark warnings against masturbation, homosexuality and playing around with girls. Among the dangers they were given to understand attended mas-turbation was syphilis. Alan dimly wondered, as no doubt they all did, just what they were supposed to do with their nascent sexual feelings. The answer seemed to be: "When aroused, go and dangle your balls in cold water" — of which there was plenty.

Like another schoolboy at an English public school during the same period — Thomas Merton — Watts was depressed by the absence of girls in school life, and by the homosexual preoccupation that this lacuna seemed to impose. Officially dedicated to discouraging homosexuality, the school tried to control it by forbidding friendships with younger boys.

Patrick Leigh Fermor, more daring than most, remembers kissing a very nice fair girl, a maid at the school called Betty. He approached her first in the corridor. "She looked very surprised, then went into fits of laughter and dashed off. It happened two or three times — 'Now don't be a Silly Billy' and 'You'll get me shot!' she would say."[18] There would have been a frightful row if they had been caught by the authorities.

Later in his school career, Leigh Fermor had a more serious heterosexual encounter. He was "very smitten," as he puts it, with Nelly, a knockout beauty who was the daughter of the local greengrocer. The two of them used to sit and hold hands in the back of her father's shop. Eventually the affair was discovered and Leigh Fermor was expelled from the school. He had liked the place but had had a stormy career there largely because of an enthusiasm, adventurousness, and wild originality that the school regarded as outrageous. "Frequent and severe beatings" made not the slightest difference to his conduct, as he continued to live out his own courageous brand of romanticism. Watts, in later life, described his own response to the unbalanced life of school.

I would not go so far as to say, with Kenneth Rexroth, that English public schools are positively seminaries for sodomy, buggery, pederasty, and sadomasochism. But monastically separated from girls as we were, a good deal of this kind of thing went on, and my first serious love affair was with a younger boy. We did nothing about it physically except hold hands, and as soon as I could escape from school I sought the company of girls, but found it strangely difficult to consummate any relationship until the age of twenty-two. . . . I was afraid of rejection.[19]

Confirmation, when it came, was supposed to be one of the high spots of school life. At least half expecting to be filled with the Holy Spirit, Watts renewed his baptism promises and then went forward to kneel before the bishop. With the bishop's hands on his head, he listened to the confirmation prayer: "Defend, O Lord, this thy child with thy heavenly grace, that he may continue thine for ever; and daily increase in thy Holy Spirit, more and more, until he come unto thy everlasting kingdom." When the service was over and he left the cathedral, he could detect no difference inside him, no white-hot religious fervor or tendency to speak with tongues. Of course, the laying on of hands did mean that he could now receive the wine and the bread at Holy Communion. This too turned out to be a disappointment, lacking in any of the feeling of conviviality and joy that he instinctively felt ought to accompany it. "No sense of being turned-on, but only an intense and solitary seriousness. Everyone in his own private box with God, apologising for having masturbated, fornicated or adulterated."[20] He felt that there must be some other way of approaching the deep mysteries of existence, but no other way, at least at Canterbury, seemed to be on offer.

Religion apart, life at school was getting quite interesting. He was making very rapid progress through the academic curriculum. He was very gifted at Greek and Latin verse, and in history his teacher had already marked him down as a candidate for an Oxford scholarship. He had a passionate pleasure in learning that surprised his more philistine schoolmates — he was continually looking things up in encyclopedias and checking on the origin of words in dictionaries, an astonishing enthusiasm in a world that cared more for sport than for learning.

With Leigh Fermor he led a rich imaginative life, discussing all kinds of ideas and interests on long bicycle rides. Leigh Fermor remembered how much he loved to laugh and what a strange effect the very slight cast in Watts's eye gave — "an amusing obliquity to his glance — and you sometimes didn't know which eye was looking at you."[21]

Watts was also beginning to discover the joys of public speaking, partly under the rather questionable influence of a Welsh teacher, Mr. William Moses Williams. Mr. Williams would arrive late at the school debating society, knowing nothing of the subject for the evening, nor on which side he was down to speak. Immediately he would pitch in to the side that took his fancy, speaking with irresistible eloquence, without notes or even very much knowledge. Watts said that he learned from Williams "that you can pitch a good argument for any cause whatsoever." In later life Watts himself was a master of effortless eloquence.

At the age of fourteen, casting round in his mind for a subject for the junior debating society more original than the usual ones about war, coeducation, and corporal punishment, he remembered his own deep pleasure in Japan. He took as his title "The Romance of Japanese Culture." Mugging up his material for the occasion, he spoke of Zen Buddhism and Shintoism, of the martial arts, of calligraphy, and of painting. Japan was not a subject that British schoolboys knew much about at the period — the Japanese would probably have come, like most foreigners, under the general condemnation of being "wogs" — but Watts talked so well that their curiosity was aroused and they asked many questions. It was perhaps the first time that he had thought seriously about Zen Buddhism and its rituals.

Much of his life at the time was taken up with another set of rituals — those of High Anglicanism. The Dean of Canterbury, the famous "Red" Dean, Dr. Hewlett Johnson, had a passionate enthusiasm for Anglo-Catholic practices, a meticulous sense of the way elaborate ceremonies should be carried out and processions conducted. Watts, with his natural gifts as a performer, was a favorite server and a keen apprentice at the altar. "I have even," he reminisced, "served as master of ceremonies at a pontifical Solemn High Mass, celebrated from the throne. . . . [Hewlett Johnson] reformed the style of services in the Cathedral and, among other things, taught us how to process in the right way — not marching and swaying in close order, but gently strolling, about two yards from each other."[22] It was a much more congenial form of Christianity than Uncle Harry's hymn singing and his mother's uncompromising Protestantism. Anglo-Catholics, he found out (with the possible exception of the Red Dean who slept on a camp bed in the open air and ate a strange diet), tended to like the good things in life. One such local high churchman, Canon Trelawney Ashton-Gwatkin, was the rector of Bishopsbourne, a country parish. Watts would bicycle out there on a Sunday, enjoy a delicious meal, followed by a Balkan Sobranie cigarette, and would admire the fine collection of books belonging to the wealthy canon and his wife. It was a world away from the boiled cabbage of school.

Francis Croshaw and the witty Elvira (POM) remained Watts's favorite grown-ups, and these two broadened his horizons immeasurably by taking him abroad to Saint-Malo in 1928. At fourteen he was enchanted by the delicious, unfamiliar food and wine, much of it eaten out of doors. Forty years later he still remembered the taste of the pâté de foie gras, the œufs en gêlée with truffles, and the intoxicating local cider. He was taken to Mont-Saint-Michel, to the races, to a bullfight down in the Basque country, and to a casino at Biarritz. The pleasure of all these sophisticated adventures, and the excellent food consumed so assiduously along the

way, were like a revelation, a revelation that made what he called
the "boiled beef" culture of England seem particularly crass. Not
surprisingly, "from then on, the curriculum, the sports, and the
ideals of King's School, Canterbury seemed, with some few excep-
tions, to be futile, infantile and irrelevant."[23] Feeling himself now
to be a man of the world, Watts became rather more self-
consciously arrogant, endlessly "one up" on his hapless fellows
with their passion for cricket and football, a self-styled "European"
in the heart of British culture.

The Croshaws' style, and Watts's growing interest in becoming
a man of the world, contrasted rather poignantly with life at home,
where Laurence's unemployment had brought matters to a crisis.
In 1928 Emily had started an embroidery business in Widmore
Road, Bromley. Her brother Harry owned two houses there, which
he used for furthering foreign missions, and he allowed her to
have a workroom in one of them. She took embroidery commis-
sions, gave lessons in embroidery, and made small items such as
tea and egg cozies, which were displayed for sale in a showcase
outside the house. The embroidery business grew, and Laurence
helped with the commercial and accounting side of it, but they
still could not make ends meet. Laurence even wrote to ask Willy
in Minneapolis about the prospects of work there, but more seriously considered borrowing money to buy one of the houses from
Harry, letting rooms in it to pay for the mortgage and other expenses, and letting Rowan Cottage. In the end Harry rented the
property in Bromley to them, and they let their beloved Rowan
Cottage and its cherished garden on a seven-year lease. It was a
painful move, one to which Watts does not refer in his autobiography. It meant that they saw more of the Bromley relatives.
Uncle Harry held a religious occasion every Sunday afternoon
known as PSA, a Pleasant Sunday Afternoon, designed to offer a

little uplift in place of more worldly occupations. He persuaded Watts to conduct one of these, which he did with enthusiasm, getting Joy to illustrate some of his points on the piano. It was perhaps the first religious occasion he ever conducted. Ultimately Uncle Harry would be poles apart from Watts in matters of religion, but he nevertheless managed to convert Watts to a lifelong passion for one thing: tobacco. Cigars, pipes, cigarettes often smoked through an elegant holder — Watts was rarely without one or another for the rest of his life.

As painful as the financial bite of the Depression was Emily's failing health. While trying to start a business, she was contending with repeated hemorrhages from the lung. "The doctor assures us that there is nothing in the way of disease there and that all that was needed to effect a cure was rest so that she has spent the best part of the last fortnight in bed," Laurence wrote. "Alan is very well and happy at his school in Canterbury. I went down to see him on Friday last. While waiting for him I spent a very pleasant hour wandering round the precincts of the Cathedral, in which the School is situated. Afterwards we had a good walk together. He is growing up very fast and is a very companionable sort of boy. Both the Headmaster and his Housemaster think well of him."[24]

Watts's talent for Latin and Greek and his intense enjoyment of academic work took him into the sixth form, the top class of the school, at the age of fifteen. Now he wore a dark blue band round his boater and carried a silver-topped walking cane. He became a prefect and a monitor.

His passion for Chinese and Japanese art, always encouraged by his mother's taste, was leading him deeper into questioning his own Christian inheritance. Canon Ashton-Gwatkin's son Frank, who had worked at the British Embassy in Japan, gave Watts some hanging scrolls and a Japanese dictionary. Francis Croshaw, who had Buddhist inclinations himself, lent him books from his library, including one by a writer unknown to him, Christmas Humphreys.

One day, wandering in Camden Town during the holidays, Watts bought a fine brass Buddha and a book by Lafcadio Hearn entitled *Glimpses of Unfamiliar Japan*. He bought the book because he was under the impression that it had a lot about ghosts in it, but what ultimately delighted him was the author's description of his own house and garden at Matsue, so much so that many years later Watts went there on a pilgrimage. The poetic discourse on frogs, insects, and plants fired the boy. He felt "a certain clarity, transparency, and spaciousness in Chinese and Japanese art. It seemed to float."[25]

By reading another book by Lafcadio Hearn, *Gleanings in Buddha-Fields,* he learned about the concept of nirvana. For some time he had felt a profound distaste for public school religion and even for the adventurous liturgical life of Canterbury Cathedral; above all, perhaps, he longed to reject the repressive fundamentalism of his mother's family. Christianity, he considered, was all about accusation — God the Father was, in effect, always "telling you off" for your wickedness. The essay on nirvana gave him a "convincingly different view of the universe" — it seemed to see ultimate reality quite differently. "The ground of it all was, instead, something variously known as the Universal Mind, the Tao, the Brahman, Sinnyo, alaya-vijnane, or Buddha-nature, wherewith one's own self and being is ultimately identical for always and always."[26]

Having seen this, Watts acted. Not without a certain pleasure at the one-upmanship involved, he made it publicly known both at school and to his astonished relatives that he had become a Buddhist. There were not many Buddhists in the Britain of the 1930s, least of all among public schoolboys. (Patrick Leigh

Fermor responded to Watts's startling declaration with gratifying awe: "Do you really mean that you have renounced belief in the Father, Son and Holy Ghost?") Watts wrote off confidently to the Buddhist Lodge in London, addressing his requests for information to Christmas Humphreys, the judge, who was the best-known English Buddhist of his generation. Noting both the address and the intelligence of his correspondent, Humphreys believed for some time that he was writing to a master at the school.

Watts's Buddhist conversion was less admired by the Watts and Buchan families, and bent on persuading them all, Watts wrote a small pamphlet that he circulated to them and to his school friends. Laurence, then and later, was driven to defend his son by saying that God was a mountain to whom many different people looked up from many different angles, and Alan was entitled to his angle. Aunt Gertrude, on the other hand, wrote back suggesting that Buddhism was a selfish belief, and that its attitude to suffering would not help those who suffered as much as a belief in a loving Jesus Christ. She also suggested that Buddhism ignored women.

In a correspondence with Gertrude that allowed him to expand upon the beliefs he had set out in the pamphlet, Watts took up the cudgels, first defending Zen intellectually: "Now I have just set forward a nice little theory which is intended to be understood by the *intellectual* faculty. The Zen master aims at giving you a much wider vision of the same Truth through the *intuitional* faculty, so that you have it not as a *conclusion*, but as a *conviction*." Against a charge Gertrude had made about meditation, Watts replied, "Of course constant meditation — the constant adoption of an impersonal attitude to Life — is a remarkably difficult thing to keep up — I do not pretend to be able to do it for more than five minutes at a time."[27]

Watts refuted Gertrude's claim that suffering is a "test." "I find it impossible to believe in a personal, loving God when the world is so full of suffering and ignorance. If you say that suffering is a test for us, I must ask, why have a test?" Man, says Watts, has made God in his own image:

> I'm afraid it is hard to put faith in a man-made God. Then put faith in what? In the immaculate Law of which all things are transient manifestations. How is this done? By looking at life from a universal instead of a personal standpoint; by seeing all things as the functioning of Reality; by annihilating the distinction between "I" and "not I," between "self" and "not self," between subject and object, and by seeing all things in terms of Reality — as being just so.[28]

None of this is likely to have appealed very much to a Christian of Aunt Gertrude's Evangelical stamp. The personal relationship with Jesus, the awareness of personal sinfulness redeemed by the suffering of the Savior, the need for effort at overcoming personal failings, the acceptance of suffering as God's will, the belief in a transcendent God owing nothing to anthropomorphic projections, were all very different from Watts's puzzling talk of "I" and "not I." And besides, Buddhism felt strange and uncongenial — the sort of thing foreigners would like, as did Alan in his state of adolescent rebellion, but scarcely the sort of thing that would do in Chislehurst.

At school, a less pained and a more intellectual approach was brought to Watts's new beliefs. Watts had a new housemaster, R. S. Stanier, whom he admired so much that he copied his handwriting for a while — a useful ploy in forging permissions for boys to stay in Canterbury out of school hours. Stanier took a strongly Calvinist line against Watts, but knew his own theology so thoroughly and argued so well that they both enjoyed their verbal battles. Watts claimed that "inadvertently" Stanier taught him "all the fallacies of Western logic."

Norman Birley, a liberal and intelligent headmaster, well-accustomed to the ephemeral phenomenon of adolescent fervor, seemed not at all put out by the boy's change of faith, to Watts's secret annoyance. In the spirit of one who believed in encouraging all things educational, he sent Watts off to represent the school at a weekend conference on religion. William Temple, then archbishop of York, presided, and in spite of his own contempt for Christianity, Watts was won over by the archbishop's good mind, his humor, and his geniality. Temple had presence, a quality helped by his enormous belly and a laugh so loud that it made the room shake. Smoking a pipe with the boys late at night he told them two stories that a Zen master might have told. One had to do with the musician Walford Davies. Teaching a hymn to a choir, Davies was heard to say that they must on no account *try* to sing it, but should simply think of the tune and let it sing itself. (Both Watts and Christmas Humphreys later used this story in books to illustrate the Zen approach.) The other story was about Temple's own difficulties in composing Latin poetry as a boy: "I was working by candlelight and whenever I got stuck and couldn't find the right phrase, I would pull off a stick of wax from the side of the candle and push it back, gently, into the flame. And then the phrase would simply come to me."[29]

Back at school Watts continued to develop his religious and other interests with passionate enthusiasm. He was studying Vivekananda's *Raja Yoga*, a book that recommended abstaining from meat, alcohol, and sex, and suggested yogic exercises; despite ridicule he managed to perform yoga at night in his dormitory cubicle. Later, to his pleasure, he got the flu and was transferred to the school sanatorium. Alone in his bedroom he was free to practice all the spiritual exercises he pleased; it also gave him more freedom to read — his appetite for books just then was voracious. He enjoyed a mixed diet of religion, politics, and psychology in such authors as D. T. Suzuki, Keyserling, Nietzsche, Lao-tzu,

Feuchtwanger, Bergson, Madame Blavatsky, Anatole France, Havelock Ellis, Bernard Shaw, Robert Graves, and Carl Jung; and in such works as the Upanishads, the Bhagavad-Gita, and the Diamond Sutra.

His change of religion had not noticeably diminished his arrogance. He challenged the headmaster to abolish flogging on the grounds of "its sexual complications." Norman Birley seems to have received the admonition with his usual good-natured interest in Watts's precocity, without feeling a compelling need to act on his advice. Another of Watts's targets was the Officers' Training Corps, common in those days in most public schools. While most students accepted such a militaristic body unquestioningly, Watts expressed open contempt for the violence it represented.

To become opinionated, even eccentrically so, was not frowned upon for boys in the senior part of the school. In fact, such schools encouraged that kind of confidence, self-assurance, and independence of mind. So there was some grudging admiration for Watts's determined support of unpopular causes and unusual beliefs. No doubt he delighted to shock — as much as his contemporaries were delighted to *be* shocked — when he defended conscientious objection or attacked capital punishment. At school debating societies he talked about Chinese and Japanese art — material entirely new to the British school curriculum — and gave lectures on Omar Khayyám and the Japanese poet Basho.

Teachers do not always appreciate the sort of outstanding intelligence that goes its own way, a way often quite different from that of the examination syllabus. Watts's teachers hoped that he would win a history scholarship at Trinity College, Oxford. His chances of doing so were, one might think, excellent, and without such a scholarship there was no chance of the Wattses' being able to afford to send their son to a university.

But Watts did an odd thing. Instead of simply sitting the examinations like anyone else and doing the best he could with them, he took it into his head to answer the questions in the manner of Nietzsche, a whim so quixotic that it lost him his scholarship. Various explanations come to mind. Was it pure arrogance, a feeling that he should be allowed to do anything and get away with it? Was it a kind of contempt for Oxford and its examinations? Was it a fear of failing so great that he felt a need to provide himself with a perfect excuse? To have tried openly and honestly and then failed might have felt like an intolerable humiliation. Or was it that he needed to escape from the pressure of his parents' high expectations? His own, later explanation of his action and failure was that he was bored by school and by the idea of Oxford, and was much more interested in his own program of reading, thinking, and experience than anything the university was likely to provide.

It is easy to accept his suggestion that nothing was lost by his missing Oxford, that on the contrary he gained by getting a more unusual education. Certainly his mind was naturally scholarly, and he combined this quality with an originality of thought shown by few academics. Yet it is difficult also not to suspect a hurdle he was afraid to jump, dreading competition from others possibly more clever than himself, a possible blow to his self-esteem. The gesture of failing the scholarship, apart from being a bitter disappointment to Laurence and Emily, started him off on a career as an outsider, one he was often later to regret. He had stepped off the path prescribed for Englishmen entering the professions — prep school, public school, university — and was never able to find it again. It could have been a courageous act, or an act of protest against the elitism of the Brahmins, but it looked a lot more like pique or loss of nerve.

By the time he sat the scholarship examination, of course, he was thoroughly impatient with the whole system — the Anglicanism, the "boiled beef" culture, and in particular the absence of girls. He longed to get to know girls, but was shy about it when opportunity offered.

By the autumn of 1932 he had become head boy of his house, the Grange, and no longer had to live in a cubicle in a dormitory. His own room was Elizabethan, with fine windows and ceiling moldings, which lent dignity and prestige to its temporary owner. More important, it also gave him privacy. In the winter he could light a fire in the grate and sit up late studying, and here he began to learn about meditation. At first he sat and puzzled about what it was that the Oriental masters of meditation described, his mind picturing all the theories he had read about snapping round his heels like little dogs. He writes of his first successful attempt at meditation, "Suddenly I shouted at all of them to go away. I annihilated and bawled out every theory and concept of what should be my properly spiritual state of mind, or of what should be meant by ME. And instantly my weight vanished. I owned nothing. All hang-ups disappeared. I walked on air."[30]

# Three

# Christmas Zen

## 1932-1938

CHRISTMAS HUMPHREYS was a man with the kind of panache that had already appealed to Alan Watts in other models. Initially he enjoyed the security and confidence of a wealthy patrician background, but this confidence was badly shaken when his brother was killed during the First World War. It was then that he began to seek something that offered him more than the conventional and unquestioned Anglicanism of his class. This search gradually led him to Buddhism. As an undergraduate at Cambridge he had read Helena Petrovna Blavatsky's works, and in company with Henry Dicks, later a distinguished psychiatrist, he had taken up Theosophy. He was called to the bar and eventually became a well-known judge. In the twenties he became seriously interested in Buddhism, and he started what was known as the Buddhist Lodge in London.

At a time when many Britons showed a kind of imperialist contempt for religions other than Christianity, it was unusual for a man of Humphreys's social and professional distinction to show a deep and abiding interest in Eastern religion — this interest revealed his originality, his openmindedness, his almost unshakable self-confidence, and, maybe, his wish to be singular. As the Buddhist Lodge began to grow, his fellow British Buddhists recognized that he was larger than life, a born performer with just a touch of ham, a kindly and generous man who did much to further the knowledge of Buddhism in England. "One cannot fairly characterize Mr. Humphreys as a great spiritual original," a fellow Buddhist wrote after his death in 1983, "one who attained deep insight or realization, nor as a guru or spiritual teacher in the strictest sense. Rather he was a great proselytizer, popularizer and energizer — a great catalyst, in fact. He got ideas — Buddhist ideas — circulating; he got groups going; he got things happening. And he was able to do this because he was endowed with a unique combination of talents and advantages — most of them of an unusually high order."[1]

Having corresponded with Toby, as Christmas was known to his friends, while at school, Alan Watts started attending Buddhist Lodge meetings during the holidays, which took place in the flat of Toby and his wife Aileen (she was known as Puck) in Pimlico. Emily and Laurence, with their habitual loyalty to Alan and his enthusiasms, accompanied him on his voyage outside the Christian faith, Emily as an occasional visitor, Laurence eventually as a practicing Buddhist who later became treasurer of the Lodge. Humphreys introduced a very English, and curiously Protestant, note into the proceedings — Emily, who had reason to know, complained that he ran the Lodge like an old-fashioned Sunday School.

The young Watts, however, found in the silence, the conversation, the ideas, the obvious admiration for him of Toby and Puck, who had no children of their own, exactly the spiritual home he was looking for. For his part, Humphreys felt some special quality in Watts.

"The boy didn't just talk *about* Zen," Humphreys used to say later, to fellow Buddhists, "he *talked* Zen."

Watts began to go more and more to the Humphreyses' flat — it was

> a hideaway with a bright fire, Persian rugs, incense, golden Buddhas, and a library of magical books which promised me the most arcane secrets of the universe. . . . Toby and Puck gave me an education which no money could possibly buy, and the depth of my gratitude to them is immeasurable. Even though I now [that is, in 1973] remonstrate against some of Toby's interpretations of Buddhism, I shall love him always as the man who really set my imagination going and put me on my whole way of life.[2]

To begin with, Watts was probably as fascinated by Theosophy as by Buddhism. He was avid for "arcane secrets." All his life he was someone who loved to "know," either the kind of secrets that gave him technical mastery, or the deeper kinds of knowledge that offered intellectual grasp or control — there always seemed something boyish about this, as of the little boy convinced that the adults were conniving at keeping some essential secret from him.

One of the appeals of Buddhism for Watts was that it seemed to offer some release from the guilts of Christianity with its deep-dyed sense of sin, and from the lonely responsibilities of Protestantism. The Buddhist belief in karma, which suggested neither praise nor blame, merely a recognition of the energy bubbling through the universe, was much more congenial. Buddhist *bodhi*, or wisdom, seemed to Watts more loving in practice than Christian *agape*, or love.

Humphreys resisted Watts's attempts to turn him into a guru, but for some years Watts's life centered on the flat in Pimlico, and many of his friends, ideas, and aspirations were filtered to him through it. In some ways Humphreys was a natural successor as a role model to Francis Croshaw — the easy wealth, the aesthetic taste, the unconventionality, the interest in the exotic were all there. His arrival in Watts's life at this time was fortunate; Croshaw had just suffered a tragic death by falling from an upstairs window in his home in circumstances that might have indicated suicide.

Like Croshaw, Humphreys loved travel and the arts. The Diaghilev ballet was in London, and Toby and Puck introduced Watts to the sweeping staircases, velvet curtains, and glittering chandeliers of Covent Garden. Toby dressed splendidly for the occasion in a cape and top hat; he carried white gloves and an ivory-handled cane. Watts, used to his parents' more sober tastes at home and the austerity of school life, was captivated by it all.

Through the Humphreys and the ballet Watts got to know many Russian émigrés and acquired a love of Russian music. He was also introduced by Humphreys to a *budokwai*, a school of judo and *kendo* (fencing), as well as a Japanese form of exercise, *juno-kata*, rather like what many people know now in its Chinese form as tai chi. He never became a great exponent of any of these arts, but said that they taught him "how to use my feet, how to dance, how to generate energy by following the line of least resistance."[3]

Humphreys's glowing admiration for the boy who talked Zen was in strong contrast to the feelings of many of Watts's own relatives, who could only see him as a boy who had thrown away on a whim his chance of attending a university. The Great Depression was not a promising time to emerge into the adult world without either the degrees of the professional man or the skills of the workman, and family councils were held about "what to do with Alan." Laurence, with the help of Uncle Harry, had recently got himself a job as a fundraiser in an organization called the

Metropolitan Hospital–Sunday Fund. By pulling strings he managed to get the seventeen-year-old Watts a job there too, and the two of them traveled up each morning from Chislehurst to the Mansion House, the official residence of the lord mayor of London, where the fund had its offices. The job never seemed to engage very much of Watts's attention, but it left him free to pursue his own interests in the evenings and at weekends. In fact, finding himself at last turned loose in London, free of the restrictive world of school, felt glorious to him.

The London of the early 1930s was quite an exciting milieu. The worlds both of the arts and of psychology were hugely enriched by the many distinguished refugees from Hitler's Germany, and politics and religion were widely discussed with enthusiasm. A number of these currents crossed in the Humphreyses' drawing room, and Watts, so alert, so alive, so enthusiastically intelligent about all that life had to offer him, moved enraptured from one enthralling conversation to another. Part of the charm of this new world was that, unlike the world of school, it included women, and Watts was anxious to get to know women. So far he had not overcome a lingering sense of shyness, but he felt he only needed a bit more practice and the help of a willing female accomplice to explore the mysteries of sex with him. Meanwhile he practiced his charm on his cousin Joy, who remembers him affectionately from this period of their lives. To her he seemed a confident, highly articulate youth, one who was kind and thoughtful to his younger and shyer cousin, talking to her at length, doing his best to make her laugh, telling her funny stories, and drawing her pictures.

The main problem facing Watts at this time was that he still lived at home. Like many a young man, he dreamed of a flat of his own where his evenings and any potential romances would

not be cut short by his need to catch the late train home. Not
surprisingly, he also longed to get away from Emily. His relationship with her had come to be one of courteous emotional distance,
as it would be for the rest of their lives. His friendship with his
father, on the other hand, bloomed and flourished:

> He went for long walks with me on weekends through the hills of
> Kent, during which we discussed all the basic problems of life,
> admired haystacks, views of the Weald, and ancient churches and
> mansions. We drank beer and ate excellent bread and cheese — the
> tart and solid Cheddar, and sometimes the blue Cheshire — at vil-
> lage pubs. Almost invariably he accompanied me to sessions at the
> Buddhist Lodge. . . . He is a quiet, serene man who never says any-
> thing unless it is really worth saying, and I cannot imagine a more
> companionable father.[4]

Laurence Watts might, one supposes, have expressed his disappointment that Alan had not lived up to his parents' hopes of a
university scholarship, but Watts says he fell readily in with his
son's plan to design his own "higher education." Maybe Alan had
convinced his father that "no literate, inquisitive, and imaginative
person needs to go to college unless in need of a union card, or
degree, as a certified lawyer, or teacher, or unless he requires access
to certain heavy and expensive equipment for scientific research
which he himself cannot afford."[5] Laurence had a way of thinking
almost everything about Alan perfect, at least until a later phase
of his life when he profoundly violated his father's moral code.
Still, on the long tramps through the Weald and over the lunches
of beer and bread and cheese, Watts's father was an important
source of companionship and support.

Quite quickly after leaving school Watts was able to get to know,
mainly through Humphreys's introductions, a circle of friends that

would have shocked his Evangelical relatives if they had known. One of these was a young man, Nigel Watkins, who ran an esoteric bookshop in Cecil Court in Charing Cross Road. The shop carried books on a most extraordinary range of subjects: "Oriental philosophy, magic, astrology, Masonry, meditation, Christian mysticism, alchemy, herbal medicine and every occult and far-out subject under the sun."[6] The shop was also a Mecca for an extraordinary range of customers: serious seekers of knowledge who could not satisfy their curiosity elsewhere in sober England, visiting Asians, people like Watts who wanted to learn "arcane secrets," and quite a few who were frankly curious about much that seemed to be left out of a conventional education. It thus became the haunt of a wonderful blend of gurus, priests, witches, psychotherapists, lamas, and mahatmas, and ordinary office workers who happened to have wandered in during the lunch hour.

Watts quickly became friends with Watkins, and especially appreciated the fact that Watkins was frank about which material in his shop he regarded as genuine and which as rubbish. He was well informed and equally frank about what various gurus in London had to offer. One day he introduced Watts to another customer also called Alan Watts, who, for a brief period, was an important influence on his young namesake. The elder Watts was living with a woman young Watts regarded as stunningly beautiful, and, emboldened by this fact perhaps, Watts asked all the questions about sex that he had never felt prepared to ask anyone at home or at school. The older Watts not only answered those questions sensitively and helpfully, but he also introduced him to the works of Freud and Adler and to the theory of psychoanalysis. Finally, he began to speak of a very special guru he consulted himself, Dmitrije Mitrinovic, from Yugoslavia, who, he told the young Watts, was probably "a high initiate into the mysteries of the universe."

Watts needed no more. This was just the kind of person he was looking for, and he wasted no time in getting to know Mitrinovic, who was exotic enough to live up to Watts's wildest hopes and expectations. Mitrinovic lived in Bloomsbury, on Gower Street, in those days a quiet, early Victorian street in a modest part of London where many writers had lived. Somehow Mitrinovic contrived to make his perfectly ordinary house seem like a secret and exotic Eastern sanctuary, to which it was an extraordinary privilege to be invited. The rooms were dark, heavily scented with incense, decorated with fine Oriental objets d'art and with rare editions of books, often with an Eastern flavor. He lived surrounded by friends who were more like disciples, and by women, all of whom seemed to the admiring Watts to be "adoring" of the masterful Mitrinovic. He often held court late at night — 11:00 P.M. was a favorite time for entertaining — which made it difficult for a young fellow who needed to get back to Mum and Dad in Chislehurst on a train that left before midnight. On one occasion when Watts threw discretion to the winds and stayed on, Mitrinovic sent him home at 3:00 A.M. in a chauffeur-driven limousine. He had what the young Watts most admired — style.

Part of his fascination was his appearance. He had a shaved head, high Slavonic cheekbones, black winglike eyebrows, and eyes that were large and hypnotic. For his rare daytime appearances he was meticulously dressed in a bowler hat, of the kind favored by Winston Churchill, a cutaway black morning coat, and striped trousers. He completed this outfit by carrying a walking stick with an amber handle. He paid all bills in the large, beautiful five-pound notes of the period, white, crisp, and designed to look like legal documents; he drank huge amounts of whiskey, without apparently becoming drunk; and he smoked outsize cigarettes.

Watts realized that he was fascinated by the man, but that he was also quite frightened of him — in Buddhist and Theosophical circles the word was out that he was a black magician. If he was, he never revealed the terrible secrets to Watts.

Mitrinovic obviously liked Watts, took him out with other friends to Hungarian, Russian, and Greek restaurants in Soho and home to long absorbing conversations. At home Mitrinovic put on loose robes and held court sitting on his bed. Watts remembers his discussing the principles of unity and differentiation in the universe — ideas important in Watts's later thinking — and how the two principles went together. In fact he was introducing Watts to what the Japanese call *ji-ji-mu-ge* — an understanding of the mutual interdependence of all things and events.

Although Watts, influenced by Humphreys's Theosophical ideas, went through a period of wondering whether Mitrinovic was one of the secret "Masters" in touch with the ancient knowledge, his relationship with him moved gradually onto a more ordinary level. One of Mitrinovic's ideas was to develop the thought of Alfred Adler on lines that would nowadays perhaps be called co-counseling. Mitrinovic, Watts, the other Alan Watts, a physicist, and a psychoanalyst, embarked upon a "no-holds-barred mutual psychoanalysis." For some months they met on a regular basis for some hours at a time during which period Watts remembered that they "resolutely destroyed and rebuilt each other's personalities."

Mitrinovic was remarkable for his times in that he seemed fully to grasp the kind of threat that Adolf Hitler posed and advocated stern opposition to him by Britain and France. He was a socialist of sorts, who believed in doing away with money and in making workers stockholders in industry. He followed Rudolph Steiner in his concept of the threefold state (with three assemblies, one political, one economic, one cultural) and in a federation of Europe. He invented a movement called the New Britain Movement, which planned to do away with money, and published a magazine out-lining his political ideas that Alan tried to sell for him at Piccadilly Circus.

In the years that followed, Watts was to show little interest in politics; rather, his two principal interests would later be psychology and religion, and both of these were foreshadowed by his youthful adventures in London. He became friends with the Jungian analyst Philip Metman and an even closer friend of the psychiatrist Eric Graham Howe. (It was typical of Watts that years later he clearly remembered what Howe had given him for lunch at their first meeting — a fine potato baked in its jacket and smothered with butter.) Perhaps what psychology seemed to offer was yet another form of arcane secrets, knowledge, or power. One day Howe introduced Watts to Frederic Spiegelberg, an Oriental philosopher who was to be important in Watts's life years later in California. Spiegelberg made an indelible impression on Watts: "He wore a hat with an exceedingly wide brim, spoke English with a delicate German accent which always suggests a sense of authority and high culture, and was propagating the theory that the highest form of religion was to transcend religion. He called it the religion of non-religion."[7]

The religion of nonreligion . . . It so happened that about the time he was considering Spiegelberg's ideas, Watts was being introduced by Humphreys to D. T. Suzuki, a tiny Japanese, with pebble glasses and a bow tie, who was to influence Watts and many other Westerners in an extraordinary way. Then in his late sixties, Suzuki had led an interesting and varied life. Born of samurai stock, he had nevertheless grown up in near poverty be-cause of the early death of his father. He had been a clever school-boy, working hard at other languages including English, and he

had been keenly interested in studies in Rinzai Zen. He studied
under Kosenroshi and then under Soyen Shaku. Soyen gave the
youth the *koan* Mu ("Nothingness" as a subject for meditation)
and Rick Fields, the author of *How the Swans Came to the Lake,*
movingly quotes his struggles with it:

> I was busy during those four years with various writings . . . but all
> the time the koan was worrying at the back of my mind. It was,
> without any doubt, my chief preoccupation and I remember sitting
> in a field leaning against a stack of rice and thinking that if I could
> not understand Mu, life had no meaning for me. Nishida Kitaro
> wrote somewhere in his diary that I often talked about committing
> suicide at this period, though I have no recollection of doing so
> myself. After finding out that I had nothing more to say about Mu
> I stopped going to sanzen with Soyen Shaku, except for the com-
> pulsory sanzen during a sesshin. And then all that usually happened
> was that the Roshi hit me. . . . Ordinarily there are so many choices
> one can make, or excuses one can make to oneself. To solve a koan
> one must be standing at an extremity, with no possibility or choice
> confronting one. There is just one thing which one must do.[8]

In the winter *sesshin* (a marathon of "sitting") Suzuki put all
his strength into solving the torturing *koan*, and realization happened. Walking back to his quarters in the moonlight the trees
looked transparent, and he knew himself to be transparent too. In
1897, at the age of twenty-seven, Suzuki went to live in the United
States, working in Illinois at a publishing house with religious and
Oriental interests. He began writing a book in English, *Outlines
of Mahayana Buddhism,* a book expressing his passionate belief
in the living quality of Buddhism. Later he would return to Japan
and marry an American women, Beatrice Lane, in 1911. Together
the two of them worked on an English-language journal, *The
Eastern Buddhist,* and in 1927 the British publisher Rider com-

bined some of these essays with new ones to bring out Suzuki's *Essays in Zen Buddhism*. It was this remarkable book that more than any other was to attract Westerners to Zen.

It was not an easy book to read. The mixture of learning and playfulness, not to mention the unconventional subject and the ideas surrounding it, left readers interested but baffled. Many people bought it — it soon went into second and third volumes of essays — but few seemed to know quite what to make of it. Japanese scholars at Western universities seemed to resent Suzuki's success and accused him simultaneously of "popularizing" Zen (they meant cheapening it) and of being impenetrably obscure. The American Oriental Society, famed for the austerity of its approach, gave the opinion in its journal that he was a dilettante, and others complained that he was not keen enough on "discipline."

Watts, however, following Christmas Humphreys, felt love, admiration, and reverence for Suzuki. One of the first times Watts ever saw him was during a particularly boring meeting at the Buddhist Lodge. Suzuki was playing with a kitten, and something about the old man's total absorption in the tiny creature gave Watts the feeling that he was "seeing into its Buddha-nature."

Something in Suzuki the man, as well as in his writings, told Watts that he had found the principal teacher for his private university, the master he had been looking for. Suzuki had none of the expensive, ostentatious habits, the easy cosmopolitan airs, or the cultural aims of Watts's other models, but his stillness and his smile touched something lonely and lost in Watts, offered a hint of a way out not merely from acting instead of being oneself, but also from the predicament of being isolated and human, from what Watts often thought of as a "bag of skin." Already interested in Zen, Watts was now fired with a passionate concern to absorb it. Like many writers before him, he found a way to give the utmost concentration to a new enthusiasm — he would write a book about it.

His working days were still devoted to raising money for the London hospitals, but with the self-discipline that was later to mark his use of time, he decided to devote a month to writing *The Spirit of Zen* in his spare time. Instead of spending his evenings eagerly dashing off from the office to fascinating meetings with his new friends, or his weekends haunting the Humphreyses, he went soberly home each night and wrote a thousand words or so, and within a month had fulfilled his aim — a book of around thirty-five thousand words. It is easy to sense the pleasure with which it was written, a particular sort of freshness and enthusiasm that is infinitely touching. He dedicated the book to his master Christmas Humphreys, but wrote a humble and moving preface to Suzuki, saying how much he owes to his writings, and urging the reader to attempt the *Essays*, presumably using *The Spirit of Zen* as a sort of guide.

The book is self-confessedly derivative, but it is an astonishing achievement for a writer of nineteen. Writing a preface to the second edition twenty years later, Watts wished that his knowledge of Chinese had been better when using translated texts, so that he could have been more critical, that he had had a more academic knowledge of Zen, and that, before he began the work, he had seen more clearly the ludicrousness of "explaining Zen." (If the purpose of Zen is to help people "go out of their minds" in order to stumble upon the nonrational truth, then explaining it is not likely to get them very far.)

Whatever failings Watts later perceived in the book, it had, and has, a very special quality, consisting partly of Watts's love for Suzuki and for Zen, and partly of the revelation of a new side of Watts — loving and undefended — which, as he grew older, would appear more rarely in public. There is also intelligence, simplicity, passionate enthusiasm, and the first evidence of a masterly gift for describing religious and philosophical thought lucidly and provocatively. There is nothing youthful in any crude or unskillful sense; it is balanced, thoughtful, and excellently written by a cultured mind.

For the first of many times in his life, Watts describes the isolation of the individual with his or her impossible cravings, and the Zen method of trying to shock or baffle a way out of this "defended castle." Here Watts follows the Buddha's insight into the unity of all living things, and his charge to replace hostility by divine compassion, *karuna*.

Watts sees Zen as a vigorous attempt to come into direct contact with the truth itself without allowing theories and symbols to stand between the knower and the known. The method, he says, is to "baffle, excite, puzzle and exhaust the intellect until it is realized that intellection is only thinking *about*." Similarly with the emotions, with which the aim is to "provoke, irritate and exhaust" so that it becomes clear that emotion is only "feeling *about*." All this so that a kind of leap can take place between secondhand conceptual contact and reality itself.

He moves on to look briefly at the history of Buddhism and the aspects of it that interest him most. The Buddha was once asked, "What is the Self?" and he refused for a long time to answer. Eventually he said that "man will find out only when he no longer identifies himself with his person, when he no longer resists the external world from within its fortifications, in fact, when he makes an end of his hostility and his plundering expeditions against life."[9] The alternative to this "philosophy of isolation," as the Buddha called it, was the sense of the unity of living things, and the need to replace hostility with *karuna*.

Watts examines the different views Mahayana and Hinayana Buddhism have on the question of the Self.

> What is found when man no longer resists life from behind the barrier of his person? Because the Buddha denied the existence of any "self-nature" in the person, the Hinayana takes this to mean that there is no Self at all. The Mahayana, on the other hand, considers that a true Self is found when the false one is renounced. When man neither identifies himself with his person nor uses it as a means of resisting life, he finds that the Self is more than his own being; it includes the whole universe. The Hinayana, realizing that no single thing as such is the Self, is content with that realization. . . . But the Mahayana couples this denial with an affirmation; while denying the existence of Self in any particular thing, it finds it in the total interrelatedness of all things. Thus Enlightenment is to deny the self in the castle, to realize that Self is not this person called "I" as distinct from that person called "You," but that it is both "I" and "You" and everything else included.[10]

Watts, in his search for nonseparatedness, was selecting the Mahayana path, and the particular form of Mahayana Buddhism known as Zen. Within that he concluded that "the true Self is not an idea but an experience," the experience which comes to pass when the "mind has voided every metaphysical premise, every idea with which it attempts to grasp the nature of the world." Although in our ignorance, we continually lose sight of this fact, the Self, the experience, is no less than "the Buddha nature." "An ordinary man is in truth a Buddha just as he is" — his difficulty is to be brought to know it.

In *The Spirit of Zen* Watts also recounts many of the famous Zen stories that show pupils, in laughter, pain, anger, grief, suddenly getting the point, achieving enlightenment in a sudden, astounding flash of intuition. By that flash of intuition, *satori*, the willed but painful separateness of egoism is overcome. Even *striving* after Buddhahood implies a fatal distinction between oneself and the Buddha-nature. "While the ego works at its own spiritual betterment it is already separated from the rest of life, isolated from other beings, and this is a lesser form of lunacy, for the lunatic is the most isolated person in the world."[11]

With hindsight we can see Watts preaching to himself the answer to his own painful loneliness and know that, as is the habit of preachers, he was never entirely to benefit from his own wisdom.

Curiously, in the book he treats Zen rather more like a work of art than a living discipline available to Westerners. He describes life in Zen monasteries with a rose-colored attitude that he would later renounce, but he does not seem to expect the reader to wish to try Zen techniques like *zazen*, and he does not trouble to give the outwardly simple details of how this is done. Zen, he says, is "for the few," as elitist a way of life, he implies, as a taste for Chinese and Japanese art is for the handful of people who have developed a "high culture." Later he would change this view, or rather, events would change it for him. But the book remains an important one for those interested in Watts; at the age of nineteen (twenty when the book was published by John Murray in 1935), he had managed to state, in a rudimentary way, most of the ideas that would interest and occupy him for the rest of his life.

He was to see much more of Suzuki. In 1936, "that year of true grace in my life," as Watts called it, the World Congress of Faiths met in London, sponsored by the Himalayan explorer, Sir Francis Younghusband. All kinds of distinguished scholars, philosophers, religious leaders, and writers were there, from many different kinds of backgrounds, but so far as Watts was concerned, Suzuki, with his simplicity, his spontaneity, his humor, stole the show.

> Suzuki's feeling for the basic reality of Zen was . . . elusive, and the moment you thought you had finally grasped his point he would slip from your grasp like wet soap . . . thereby showing that Zen is something like dancing or the movement of a ball on a mountain

stream. But neither is it mere chaos, just as the flow-patterns in flame and water are animated designs of great complexity, which the Chinese call *li*, the markings in jade or the grain in wood.[12]

Suzuki could be very critical of Zen as practiced in Japan, saying that it would be best if all the monasteries could be burned down. He practiced *zazen* only occasionally (it was one of the things his enemies had against him), but was known for being able to slip into *samadhi*, a sort of reverent concentration (or maybe it was sleep, no one quite knew which), at stressful moments. Like Jesus falling asleep during the storm on the sea of Galilee, Suzuki was good at dropping off during turbulent airplane flights, a child at home in the universe, unworried and serene. He seemed to live spontaneously, without calculation, and without rigid conceptual distinctions between himself and others, or between himself and objects or animals. He used the force of gravity, Watts mysteriously claims, "as a sailor uses the wind."

Suzuki gave a paper about Mahayana Buddhism, denying the Western cliché attitude that it was a rejection of life and an escape from it; on the contrary, said Suzuki, it meant total acceptance of all life's vicissitudes, it meant compassion for all sentient beings, and it meant becoming a master of *samsara* — the world of birth and death. Watts introduced the discussion of this notable paper, and thereafter he attended every lecture and seminar that Suzuki gave. The Zen "boom" in which distinguished psychoanalysts and therapists, artists, composers, and writers were to flock to Suzuki, Erich Fromm and Karen Horney among them, did not happen until the 1950s. Suzuki was not the easiest of teachers to follow, because his method was so strange. "Teaching," according to Rick Fields,

in addition to being a way of earning a living was a way of thinking out loud about whatever books or translations [Suzuki] happened to be working on, and it was not uncommon for him to lose students as he crisscrossed the blackboard with a bewildering maze of diagrams and notes in Japanese, Sanskrit, Chinese and Tibetan. Mary Farkas, a student who audited the class occasionally, remembers counting as many as a dozen people sleeping in their chairs one afternoon. Not that it bothered Suzuki. Once, John Cage tells, a low-flying plane drowned out Suzuki's voice in mid-sentence, but Suzuki simply continued speaking, without bothering to raise the level of his voice.[13]

The energy of young Watts was at its height. He was now reading and writing Mandarin Chinese quite well, he was still practicing martial arts at the *budokwai*, he had changed his handwriting to a beautiful italic, and trained himself in a thorough knowledge of graphics, layout, and lettering. He was reading widely not just in Buddhism, but in Vedanta, Taoism, and the Christian mystics; with Eric Graham Howe's advice he was also exploring the writings of Jung.

Would Watts have benefited more intellectually if he had attended a conventional university? Judging by contemporary biographies and autobiographies, relatively few undergraduates of the period read, wrote, or thought as studiously as Watts did. Oriental studies were fairly limited at English universities, and most students would not have had the chance to mingle as freely as Watts did with such an interesting variety of thinkers and talkers. All his life Watts had a knack for finding people who were original without being eccentric and of seeing quickly to the nub of their ideas before making them his own.

If his pursuit of knowledge and of interesting people came easily to him, his pursuit of "girls" did not. Watts had left school with the naive belief that women would be as eager as he was for sexual experiment, and all he needed to do was to find one who attracted him. To his surprise it took him a year or two to find any girls with whom he felt a sense of rapport, and even then, to his disappointment, they seemed unwilling to go beyond the preliminaries. He did not despise the pleasures of what was later to be known as "necking," but when weeks and months took him no further, he became exasperated. It was, as he inimitably put it, "all retch and no vomit." It was gradually borne in on him that girls were conditioned to withhold their sexual favors as a prize that went with marriage (their very real fears of pregnancy seem not to have occurred to him), and this made him feel that he was the victim of an infuriating game. If there could be no sexual freedom without marriage, and if, as he believed to be the case, there was no chance of his affording marriage until he was at least thirty, then the prospects for a lusty young man were deeply depressing.

Part of the torment was that he was not sure whether his failure with girls was due to lack of experience and technique. Infectiously self-confident in most other matters, he felt anxious and unsure about his sexuality. Looking back from the vantage point of nearly forty years later, he puzzled about his failure to consummate a relationship before the age of twenty-two (though this may not have been as uncommon among his contemporaries as he seems to assume). Perhaps in the end it came down to something quite simple: "They were scared, and I was afraid of rejection."[14]

He started his romantic life with a girlfriend named Betty, whose would-be liberated style was somewhat cramped by an overanxious mother. Finally, Betty alienated Watts by joining the Oxford Group, the religious organization later known as Moral Rearmament, which relied heavily on piety, guilt, and group confession. Anything less likely to appeal to the youthful Watts or less promising to the sexual adventurer in him would be hard to imagine. There was another girl called Greta who seemed constantly to promise ecstasies she was never ready to fulfill; in the end Watts got on rather better with her brother, with whom he went on camping expeditions. The most promising liaison was with a Danish au pair girl, Hilda, who would "kiss and hug like a mink," but deeper involvement was always interrupted by Watts's need to go and catch the 11:55 train. Perhaps he was more scared than he later remembered. In any case, the sexual mores of the time were against him. "Nice girls" were not expected to do much more than kiss before marriage, and in addition to warnings of pregnancy, they were told that "men wouldn't respect them" if they gave way to desire. Underlying all of this was a dimly understood belief that Christianity thought fornication was wrong, but also an atttiude toward sexuality that insisted that "ladies" didn't enjoy sex and that there was something beastly in men which regrettably did. It was not a healthy foundation for sexual experience, forcing many into marriage before they were ready for it, as the only "decent" way of satisfying their sexual desires. The young Watts, not surprisingly, was at war with this damaging and unrealistic approach to natural feelings, and there was pain and bewilderment at his initial inability to persuade well-brought-up young women to see the matter as he did. All this changed rather quickly, however, when Eleanor Everett came into his life.

The first time he saw her was at the Buddhist Lodge early in 1937. Her mother, Ruth Fuller Everett, had come to give a talk about her stay at a Zen monastery in Kyoto two years before. Mother and daughter, apparently devoted to one another, had an air of easy American wealth; money and the style that went with it had often fascinated Watts in the past, but this time it came in a new guise.

Ruth Everett, a rather formidable lady, knew more about Zen than Watts. Like many American society ladies she had, some

years previously, come under the influence of a man who, like
Aleister Crowley or Mitrinovic, could be described as a "rascal-
guru," one Pierre Bernard, who owned a sort of ashram in Nyack
on the Hudson River and taught tantric and hatha yoga. At Nyack
Ruth discovered the existence of Zen Buddhism and, with the sublime self-confidence that marked all her actions, simply took off
for Japan with the fifteen-year-old Eleanor and introduced herself
to Suzuki, who in turn introduced her to Nanshinken, the famous
*roshi* of the picturesque monastery Nanzenji. Ruth insisted on
being allowed to sit *zazen* at the monastery, thus making her and
Eleanor the first Western women ever to do so, but Nanshinken
seemed to prefer Eleanor's company and liked to sit out on his
veranda showing her pictures of sumo wrestlers he thought might
appeal to her as possible husbands.

Ruth, though she later became a serious student of Zen, was
perhaps initially seeking some solace for a wretched marriage. At
the age of eighteen she had married Warren Everett, a famous
Chicago attorney who represented well-known industrialists. It
became clear to her almost at once that Warren was less interested
in her as a woman than as a competent housekeeper and a decorative hostess. She had great intelligence and gradually acquired wide
aesthetic and religious knowledge as compensation for an empty
emotional life, but in the beginning she had been a timid girl with
a bullying husband, himself trying to compensate for having been
crippled as a child with polio. He was fearfully exacting about
how the house was run — Ruth remembered years later how the
biscuits served at the table had to have enough fat in them to stain
the napkin they stood on — and he took for granted that it was
her job to entertain innumerable business acquaintances whose
interests were entirely different from her own.

Gradually under these pressures a very powerful woman began
to emerge. Eleanor, as the only child of a strong-willed mother and

an irascible father, had a hard time simply being her own person. She had money to spend, beautiful clothes to wear, a background of extensive travel to exotic places that took Ruth's fancy, but she did not finish high school, probably because her mother wanted her as a traveling companion. In 1937, however, when Eleanor and her mother came to London, she decided that she wanted to study the piano, and she was working with a teacher named George Woodhouse, a man with a Zenlike approach to piano playing.

It is striking that Watts devoted as much space in his autobiography to Ruth as he did to Eleanor, and it is Ruth who comes across as the stronger and more interesting personality. Perhaps it was Ruth, with her knowledge, her formidable power, and her money who most deeply fascinated and attracted Watts, but the way to be close to Ruth was to be close to Eleanor.

He and Eleanor went to the opera and the ballet and to various piano concerts together, always with the most expensive seats, and she encouraged him to start playing the piano too — he got as far as a Scarlatti sonata. She also persuaded him to dance — a thing most inhibited Englishmen of his generation found almost unimaginable except in the most formal circumstances. Eleanor had picked up the hula on a trip to Hawaii and taught him the swing of the hips that makes true dancing possible.

Eleanor was not precisely pretty, but was a pleasing, slightly plump girl, with a vivacity that made her fun as a companion; she wore lovely clothes that Watts's cousins admired and envied, had money to spend and an air of sophistication. She was talented and appeared supremely self-confident. Always perceptive, Watts probably knew that beneath the culture, the fine clothes, the extreme high spirits, was a girl with little self-esteem who felt intimidated by her mother and unloved by her father. These feelings, however, would have touched on Watts's own weakness — his pleasure in playing a kind of Pygmalion role toward women, to mold them and give them confidence, no doubt in an attempt to relieve fears and neurotic tendencies of his own. Whatever the reasons, a romance had begun, one that caused interested speculation in the Watts/Buchan clan since Watts had committed himself to the point of describing Eleanor to them as "highly satisfactory."

He had other pleasures in 1937, in particular the publication of his new book, *The Legacy of Asia and Western Man.* The *Church Times* described it in a review as a "witty and perverse little book," but Watts himself in later years found it somewhat embarrassing. This may have been because it attempted to cover too much ground, but it is a lucid and interesting book, and it reveals much about the way Watts's mind worked in the period immediately following *The Spirit of Zen.*

In some ways it is a response to the rather shallow arguments against Buddhism that his first book provoked, the sort of criticism of which Watts had been happily and unselfconsciously aware when he began to write. In his second book he felt obliged to tackle questions of whether Buddhism is "impersonal," whether it "devalues" the individual, whether it lacks "love" and social concern.

Watts, however, took on a bigger task than defending Buddhism. He began to see every religion as having special gifts of its own to bring to mankind: Hinduism a very deep understanding of mysticism, Taoism a sense of oneness with the principles of life, Buddhism in all its forms, a developed method of freeing the mind from illusion. Inevitably Christianity, the traditional religion of most people he was writing for, had somehow to be rediscovered for his purposes. He approached it with a certain amount of distaste, still resentful of the guilt and shame that surrounded its moral teachings, still angry about heaven and hell used as carrots and sticks to control the simpleminded, and still dubious of the Christian Church's claim to ultimate truth.

Yet despite distaste for a religion that, it seemed to him, had gone collectively sour, Watts admitted to feeling a kind of pull toward it: "However much we may imagine ourselves to have cut adrift from the Church's symbols, they return to us under many forms in our dreams and phantasies, when the intellect sleeps and the mind has liberty to break from the rational order which it demands."[15]

Because Christianity had lost its life and vigor, Watts felt that modern Western man had lost himself in the "rational," in humanistic, scientific, and technocratic modes that derived from a purely rational attitude to life. "It is precisely to preserve us from a 'rational' civilization that a vital Christianity is necessary."[16] Having thrown Christianity away he began to feel it return like a boomerang.

In *The Legacy*, borrowing from Jung, Watts suggested that Christianity must learn to see itself much more in symbolic and mythical terms than in historical ones, so that, for example, the Passion and Resurrection of Christ become the pain of the individual torn between the contradiction of the opposites, and achievement of their eventual resolution, or the birth of the Divine Child becomes the birth of intuitive love in every person. Watts also believed that assimilating Asian wisdom — in particular the wisdom relating to the relativity of good and evil, and the recognition of the way mankind is torn by duality — gave a chance for escaping the alienation of duality.

The young Watts was applying himself to some of the central questions for Western man, doing his best to grasp the nature of the tragedy. As part of the new understanding he believed that psychotherapy was essential; within the triangle of Eastern religion, Western religion, and psychotherapy, a new beginning for human salvation, a new healing, was to be sought.

In his two books Watts had now outlined his lifelong preoccupations: the synthesis of Eastern and Western thought, in particular the synthesis of Buddhism and Christianity, and the links of both with healing, particularly in the form of psychotherapy. For the rest of his life he would think and struggle, read and argue, teach and discuss, make jokes and tell stories about precisely these questions.

Eleanor shared Watts's Buddhist preoccupations just as Ruth did. Able to sit in the full lotus position, she came with him to Buddhist meetings to sit in *zazen*, and the two of them faithfully practiced meditation together at home. Once when the two of them were walking home together from a meditation session he began to talk about how difficult he found it to concentrate on the present. "Why try to concentrate on it?" Eleanor asked. "What else *is* there to be aware of? Your memories are in the present, just as much as the trees over there. Your thoughts about the future are also in the present, and anyhow I just love to think about the future. The present is just a constant flow . . . and there's no way of getting out of it."[17] Watts found this comment of Eleanor's a minor revelation, one for which he remained grateful to her for the rest of his life. "You could have knocked me down with a feather," he said.

He was just as grateful to Eleanor for her eagerness to embark on sexual adventures. Perhaps it accorded with the more liberal sexual ideas of her new religion, perhaps the sense of wealth made the possible consequences seem less alarming, perhaps she sensed Ruth's rather obvious complicity. Ruth went back to America, leaving Eleanor to Watts's tender mercies, perfectly aware that the two were spending most of their spare time together. They took advantage of the opportunity, two virgins anxious to lose their virginity, two attractive young people who liked each other's company. They very quickly started to believe that they were in love.

Ruth's total cooperation is perhaps a little surprising. Known in Chicago as a social climber, she might have sought and found a better match for her daughter. She might have feared (perhaps with justification) an element of fortune hunting in Watts's courtship of her daughter, not in any crude sense, but in his simple expansive pleasure in the good things of life — good seats at the opera, good restaurants — otherwise not available to him. She probably found him physically attractive, as Eleanor did, and she may have felt that his good manners, his elegant Britishness, his cheery insouciance made up for a good deal he lacked in other ways. Certainly his lack of money, or a career, kept the young people under her control to some extent. It was not that she had any very high opinion of his abilities and potentialities, despite his two published books. When she left England for America her only comment about him to Eleanor was, "He's all right, but he'll never set the Thames on fire."

The two young people continued to try out all the sexual techniques of which Watts had read in books — Eleanor tended to prefer the more conventional methods — and instead of traveling home on the 11:55 train every night Watts often spent the night at Eleanor's apartment, something which cannot have had Emily's approval. "Living together" was still rather frowned on for any but the most bohemian. Perhaps this reason pushed the two of them, young and inexperienced as they were, towards the possibility of marriage.

Watts took Eleanor to tea with Emily and Laurence at Rowan

Cottage — they had by now moved back and had just celebrated their silver wedding anniversary. Eleanor found Rowan Cottage charming and talked, with her easy American manners, about her home in Chicago, her life in London. Emily, a little stiff as always, had put herself out to entertain "Alan's girl," and Laurence was openly delighted with her. It did not surprise him that his son should attract a girl so rich and stylish.

Social expectations swept them along; young people in love were supposed to get married, especially if they could afford to do so. Watts proposed to Eleanor, she accepted, feeling a wonderful sense of release from the tyranny of life with her parents, and the two of them were invited to spend Christmas 1937 with Eleanor's family in Chicago. They sailed for New York on the *Bremen* on December 17, but the day before, an engagement party was held at Rowan Cottage, with all Watts's uncles, aunts, and cousins there to meet the "very sophisticated American fiancée."

The journey to America was a delight to Watts. Although he sensed that the visit to Chicago was set up to be an inspection of him, he had no qualms of his success and dived into the delicious food on the liner with tremendous pleasure. New York was the next excitement — thrilling and beautiful — and then the two of them boarded the *Commodore Vanderbilt* train for the night ride to Chicago. The fields gleamed white with snow under the moon, many of the towns and villages were lit with colored lights for Christmas, and Watts went to sleep to the sound of the old steam whistle as the engine pounded through the night, through towns with magic names like Poughkeepsie, Schenectady, and Ashtabula. In the morning at the La Salle station, they were met by the Everetts' Philippine chauffeur, who tucked them under rugs into a sleek limousine, and Watts was on his way to meet the family for their holiday celebration, given for them on a royal scale.

Warren Everett, who, at the best of times, was a bad-tempered man with a bullying lawyer's manner, was by now an invalid badly afflicted by arteriosclerosis, which did not improve his character. To everyone's surprise, he and Watts took to one another on sight, Watts later thought because they enjoyed some similar vices — smoking cigars, telling ribald stories, and thumbing through girlie magazines. Despite his youth Watts was not frightened of Warren, and he showed a genuine interest in the older man's long and varied career. Although Watts found most of the other Everett relatives he met to be rather boring, he got on quite well with a number of Eleanor's friends. Then it was back to England again on the *Bremen*, to the fun of trying to dance the Viennese waltz on a rolling deck to the music of a Bavarian band.

Before taking him home to visit her parents Eleanor had changed Watts's style of dress, as she was changing so much else in his life. Always biased towards the formal, he had been in the habit of sporting a mustache, a black Homburg hat, a black formal coat with striped trousers, a silver-gray tie, chamois gloves, and a rolled umbrella. Eleanor got him out of this rather pompous and old-fashioned gear and into tweed jackets and colored ties.

Although a date had not yet been set for the wedding — indeed their parents might have discouraged setting one until Watts had a "proper job" — in February 1938 Eleanor became pregnant by Watts, and they immediately decided to get married in April. Eleanor was eighteen, Alan twenty-three. Looking back on it afterwards, Watts "could not understand" how it was that two Buddhists managed to get married in a Church of England ceremony, at Saint Philip's, Earls Court, one at which Eleanor promised to "love, cherish and obey." Perhaps the reason was simply that Ruth could have the big society wedding that she had set her heart on.

The bride, on Watts's insistence, entered the church to the

*Meistersinger* overture, and the couple left to a theme from the last movement of Beethoven's Ninth Symphony. During the taking of the vows the organist gently played a Tchaikovsky melody, which, years later, when it was turned into a popular song, Watts was amused to notice had the new title "Will This Be Moon Love, Nothing but Moon Love?" These musical details were about the only say the two of them had in the planning of their wedding.

Ruth had taken a maisonette (duplex) for them at Courtfield Gardens in London, a huge Edwardian mansion with vast rooms. Watts does not make it clear whether the house was already furnished, whether Ruth undertook the task for them, or whether he and Eleanor set about spending her very considerable allowance from her parents. But the place was curtained with yellow Chinese damask, carpeted in dark purple, and set about with pieces of Elizabethan and Jacobean furniture. "Almost palatial" was Watts's description of it.

They did not stay long to enjoy the splendor. Even the temporary respite of Munich made it clear for those who chose to see it that war with Germany was bound to come, and that if it did, Watts would be conscripted. He had not the slightest intention of becoming a soldier — the idea appalled him from every point of view — nor did he intend to endure the public obloquy and possible imprisonment inflicted on conscientious objectors. The only alternative was flight, and for the young Wattses flight to the United States was very easy, with moneyed relatives waiting to receive them. Perhaps sooner or later the United States would have lured Watts anyway. Ever since the enchanted journey to Chicago he had been excited by the challenge it offered — perhaps some of the wealth would rub off on him?

So with Eleanor in the last months of pregnancy, they set off for New York. Entering the continent via Montreal Watts was stopped by a U.S. immigration officer who noticed that he carried a stick.

"Whaddya carry a cane for? You sick?"

"Not at all," Watts replied. "It's just for swank."

Once in New York, the young couple was installed by Ruth in an apartment next to hers at the Park Crescent Hotel, at Eighty-seventh and Riverside, and here in November Eleanor gave birth to a daughter, Joan. The future, despite the war, looked personally promising.

*Four*

# The Towers of Manhattan
## 1938-1941

MANHATTAN SEEMED DANGEROUS, fast, foreign, almost unbearably exciting to the young Alan Watts, entirely different from the familiarity and coziness of 1930s London. He was fascinated by the sight of so many different races of people in the streets and by the enormous streamlined towers beneath which men were as tiny as ants. He loved going to drugstores and inventing amazing sundaes for himself (concoctions that made the later, gourmet Watts squirm at the recollection), such as "vanilla ice cream globbed with butterscotch, ringed with maraschino cherries, topped with whipped cream and chopped nuts."[1] He liked the huge steaks, the food in Jewish delicatessen shops, and the many kinds of exotic cooking. He was amused when he gave his name in stores and they spelled it *Watz*. He thought the New York girls beautiful and beautifully turned out, and never tired of watching the passing show in the streets.

Apart from the joys of exploring New York, it was good to be married, and married to Eleanor. The misery of being without a sexual partner and the humiliation of trying to persuade various unwilling girls to oblige him were things of the past. Marriage to Eleanor had also had the additional bonus of taking him away from the uncomfortable relationship with his mother and the burden of difficult relatives in general. As a young, attractive, moneyed couple, the Wattses found themselves part of an interesting social circle, constantly invited to parties, to weekends in country houses, and to dinner parties with friends. Their friends were musicians, painters, scientists, psychologists (the sort of people Watts was to know and enjoy for the rest of his life), who talked of Buddhism, mysticism, Jungian analysis, and much else. Watts was already a brilliant talker who knew a great deal about these subjects, and he enjoyed an instant popularity. If his rather courtly British manner and "Brahmin" accent seemed slightly affected to his new audience, they nonetheless exerted a perverse attraction of their own.

He was less successful as a father. It was not that he didn't like the baby, more that he was bored by all the daily labor that went with her, which interested him much less than his own ideas and pursuits. In this he was aided by the mores of the time, which did not have high expectations of paternal involvement, especially when, like the Watts couple, the parents could afford "help." Their social life was not seriously disrupted. Little Joan did, however, sleep in their bedroom, and Watts seemed to enjoy what he called her "burbling" and "bubbling" and the way she developed "a lilting language of her own that sounded like a mixture of Hopi, Japanese and Malayan."[2]

Ruth Everett was living next door to them, alone, since Warren Everett was now permanently confined to a nursing home with arteriosclerosis. Pursuing her interest in Zen, she found herself in 1938 a new master, Sokei-an-Sasaki. Funded by a rich Japanese businessman, Mr. Mia, Sokei-an had taken a couple of rooms on

West Seventy-third Street and founded the Buddhist Society of America in May 1931. "I had a house and one chair. And I had an altar and a pebble stone," said Sokei-an. "I just came in here and took off my hat and sat down in the chair and began to speak Buddhism. That is all."[3]

Sokei-an had led an adventurous and interesting life. He had begun by studying art and becoming a painter, carver, and sculptor in Tokyo, with a particular skill in carving dragons, but he had gone on to become a Zen student with the famous master Sokatsu Shaku. With Sokatsu and some of his students he had gone in 1906 to California, where they tried unsuccessfully to farm at Hayward near San Francisco. Sokatsu arranged a marriage for Sokei-an, and he had three children by his wife, Tomoko. Much of his life had been one of conflict, as he was torn between first his Zen studies and his work as an artist, and then between his duty to Tomoko and his children, and his longing to lead a lonely and independent life. Eventually he separated from his wife and returned to Japan where his old teacher was now living; there he gave himself up at last to his Zen studies. At the age of forty-eight he was authorized to teach by Sokatsu and told to return to the United States where his life's work would henceforth be. The first years in New York were painful, as he tried to eke out an existence without money or a permanent place to live. Then Mr. Mia took him up, and slowly he began to acquire students.

By 1938, when Ruth Everett met him, Sokei-an had about thirty students who met for *zazen* for about half an hour. They sat upright on chairs rather than crosslegged on the floor because Sokei-an was convinced that Westerners would not endure the crosslegged posture. His major teaching was not *zazen* — there was no *sesshin* at his *zendo* (room for meditation) either — only *sanzen*, the private interview in which *koans* were assigned and discussed.

Hearing of the remarkable Sokei-an from Ruth Everett, Watts decided to go along and see the master for himself. He found him in "a small temple in a walk-up . . . just one large room with a shrine that could be closed off with folding doors, and a small kitchen. Here Sokei-an lived in extreme simplicity with his Maltese cat, Chaka."[4]

Watts was very taken with both the simplicity and convenience of Sokei-an's way of life and asked the old man if he could become his student, to which Sokei-an agreed. The method of training was that the pupil was given a *koan* that, following the formal method devised by Hakuin, had to be answered in a specific way.

Beginning with enormous enthusiasm, Watts worked extremely hard at his *koans*, only to find that, bored and angry, he reached a point of nearly intolerable frustration and felt as though he were looking for a needle in a haystack. Ironically, in *The Spirit of Zen* he had described this sort of discouragement as an essential stage in the pupil's development, the suffering described as an iron ball in the throat that could neither be swallowed down nor spat out. It was indeed precisely the experience of being driven "out of one's mind" and thus onto another level of awareness altogether that the *koan* so uncomfortably existed to promote.

Perhaps Watts did not have enough trust in Sokei-an to undergo this ordeal at his hands, or perhaps he found the role of apprentice too humiliating to be bearable. Whatever the reason, after some eight or nine months of study Watts lost his temper in *sanzen*, shouting at his teacher that he was right.

"No, you're not right," Sokei-an replied. That was the end of formal Zen study.

Other pupils saw Sokei-an very differently. When he sat in the *roshi* chair to conduct *sanzen*, the small, rather insignificant-looking man inspired awe. He was formidably silent, and the silence created a vacuum in which the pupil was drawn out of his or her habitual self into a new awareness of the One. Ruth Everett, admittedly always deeply fascinated by Sokei-an, felt that, in his teaching guise, he was not so much a man as an "absolute principle."

Sokei-an liked to lecture, which he did hesitantly and with a strong Japanese accent. His astonished audience would see him change before their eyes, becoming the animals or the people or the forces of nature he was describing: a golden mountain or a lonely coyote, a princess or a geisha. According to one of his pupils, in Sokei-an's teaching "there was something of Kabuki, something of Noh's otherworldliness, something of a fairy story for children, something of archaic Japan. Yet all was as universal as the baby's first waah."[5]

Either Watts did not see this or his envy of the rival spellbinder was insupportable. It was not exactly that he had decided that Sokei-an had no more to teach him, rather that he resented the teacher/pupil role. He solved this problem through a kind of surreptitious observation of Sokei-an, a study of how a Zen master lived as he went about his daily life.

There was ample opportunity for him to do this, since Sokei-an was now spending a lot of time at Ruth Everett's apartment, eating with her and going on trips with her, and Watts and Eleanor were frequently invited along. "A photograph of the period shows . . . Alan and Eleanor, Sokei-an and Ruth, out for the evening on the boardwalk at Atlantic City — mother and daughter looking like sisters in their long evening gowns, Watts resembling a young, handsome David Niven in his tuxedo, and Sokei-an, also in evening clothes, but wearing glasses, and a large false nose and moustache, looking very much like a Japanese Groucho Marx."[6]

Watts's observation of Sokei-an at close quarters deepened rather than lessened his admiration. There was something true and somehow inexplicable about his calm, his laugh, his ribald, earthy humor (often rather shocking to American sensibilities; he liked to use farting as an example of a spontaneous Zen moment), his skill as a woodcarver, and his scholarship in the Buddhist classics. Watts noticed that he had none of the nervous embarrassment of other Japanese he had known, but "moved slowly and easily, with relaxed but complete attention to whatever was going on."[7]

Ruth Everett's organizing energy had begun to make a difference to Sokei-an's modest beginnings of a Buddhist society. She had persuaded him that, Western or not, his students must sit crosslegged on the floor, and she took on the editorship of the society's journal, *Cat's Yawn*. She and Sokei-an began working together on a translation of the *Sutra of Perfect Awakening*.

Formidable woman that Ruth was — her granddaughters point out that she was born on Halloween, under the sign of Scorpio, and that her Japanese name meant "dragon's wisdom" — Sokei-an clearly enjoyed her company a great deal.

Warren Everett died in 1940. Even before his death, Watts and Eleanor had noticed, unbelievingly at first, that Ruth and Sokei-an appeared to be falling in love. Watts had wanted to observe the conduct of a Zen master at first hand, but he had scarcely anticipated the experience that now came to him of watching one in "the first bloom of romance." Absolute principle and dragon, this unlikely pair seemed to match one another in power, perhaps both finding love for the first time in their lives, she "drawing out his bottomless knowledge of Buddhism and he breaking down her rigidities with ribald tales that made her blush and giggle."[8]

In November 1941 Ruth set up a sort of house-cum-temple for Sokei-an on East Sixty-fifth Street. Here she took her splendid library and Oriental works of art and set up the First Zen Institute of America. This was intended to be Sokei-an's future home. In

December, however, Japanese forces attacked Pearl Harbor, and almost at once the FBI began rounding up Japanese, American citizens or not. The Buddhist Society was regarded as an object of particular suspicion, and Ruth and Sokei-an were extensively questioned.

In July 1942 Sokei-an was taken to an internment camp in Wyoming. He had just had an operation for hemorrhoids at the time and, according to Watts, was "put in a hut from which he had to walk some fifty muddy yards to the nearest latrine." The major in charge of the camp liked Sokei-an and did his best to ease his living conditions, in return for which Sokei-an carved him a stick with a dragon climbing on it. Ruth hired a famous lawyer to work on his case, and eventually he was allowed to return home, his health seriously undermined. The couple married at last in 1944. In 1945 Sokei-an died, according to Watts with the parting words, "Sokei-an will never die," and to Rick Fields with the saying, "I have always taken Nature's orders, and I take them now."

Meanwhile, the marriage of Alan and Eleanor was running into difficulties. They were very close, too close Watts was later to think, so that the unhappiness of one could pull the other down into deep gloom. This might not have mattered so much but for the fact that Eleanor was becoming seriously depressed. Maybe it was the responsibility of having a child to care for when she was still very young herself, maybe it was, as Watts seemed to believe, the difficulty of living with him instead of a more conventional husband, maybe the sexual disagreements that were later to become central to their marriage were beginning to be apparent. Whatever the underlying reason, Eleanor was deeply sad. She put on a lot of weight, developed eczema and a tendency to put her jaw out, presumably from tension, tended to drink too much, and to worry, quite unnecessarily, over money. No doubt being the rich wife of an unemployed husband posed its own threats to the marriage; at one point, because she wanted to make Watts feel, as he put it, "more of a man," she handed over her considerable holdings in stock to him. They continued to live comfortably off the dividends, supplemented with occasional handouts from Ruth. Eleanor began to have treatment from a psychiatrist friend, Charlie Taylor.

Watts was deeply affected by Eleanor's distress. He entered into her symptoms and the possible cures with the kind of friendly sympathy he always showed to those around him; it was not easy to see what was troubling her. Eleanor "had everything," as people say — money, a nice apartment, an attractive husband who loved her, and a contented baby — yet she was showing signs of severe stress. Watts is oddly silent about the relationship between Eleanor and Ruth at this time.

Eleanor, who had been frightened and controlled by her mother all her life, can scarcely have wished to live next door to her in adult life, nor to have lived off her money, with all the possibilities for power that such an arrangement provides. But getting out of Ruth's pocket would have required Watts to take up a successful career, which he showed no sign of doing. In one sense, Watts was her ally against her mother, an attractive husband who was theo-retically on her side. But the trouble was that Watts was deeply fascinated by her mother, perhaps even to a degree in love with her. His previous models in life had been men, rich, clever, eccen-tric figures, whose knowledge and taste exceeded his own and from whom he could learn. But his mother-in-law was wealthier than Francis Croshaw, cleverer than Christmas Humphreys, better read in the Oriental classics than Watts. Her ideas, her conversation, her library, her style, her taste ("infallible" so far as Oriental objets d'art were concerned) all compelled him in spite of himself. Partly it seemed that wealth had always cast the sort of spell over him that it sometimes does upon the genteelly poor; partly perhaps, in the days of Ruth's unhappy marriage to Warren Everett, Watts sensed a deep sexual frustration that attracted him more than he knew. For all these reasons he could not be free of Ruth, and Eleanor, who despite gifts and talent of her own had never quite emerged from the shadow of her mother, felt more trapped than ever.

Although Watts could not see his way to taking a job, he had none of the characteristics of the layabout or ne'er-do-well. Much as he liked parties and relaxed evenings with friends, he had a natural self-discipline, liked to rise early and use every moment of the day. He spent his time reading seriously and deeply, working at his Zen studies, practicing photography, calligraphy, and painting — he worked in watercolor, ink, and tempera. He also painted icons and sometimes made erotic drawings to please his friends. Ruth suggested that he work for a Ph.D. and take up teaching, but just as he had once felt that he could do better than go to Oxford, now he felt that he could do better for himself than take up the patient molelike digging of the academic life. He was either too proud or too wise, too frightened or too self-confident, too lazy or too easily bored — perhaps a bit of all of these.

In fact, he had begun teaching, though not within the academic system. He lectured at the Jungian Analytical Psychology Club, talking about "acceptance," in the sense of contentment, and he conducted rather successful seminars in Oriental philosophy that were well attended. He turned his Jungian lecture into a book — *The Meaning of Happiness* — which Harper enthusiastically bought. It came out in May 1940 "just as Hitler moved into France and no-one wanted to read about happiness and mysticism," though it was warmly praised by the *New York Times*. As a result of the book's success, Harper began to use Watts as a manuscript reader, and he began to sell the odd article to magazines interested in Asian ideas and religion.

The subject of the book was a simple one. Of what did human happiness consist? The religion and psychology of both West and East maintained that it was about union or harmony between the individual and the principle of life itself — God, the Self, the unconscious, the inner universe. The individual, Watts thought, needed first to become aware of this, and then to recognize that he or she was, as it were, already *there*. Harmony was not, in his view, achieved by tremendous efforts, but by perceiving the real state of affairs:

> At this very moment we have that union and harmony in spite of ourselves; we create spiritual problems simply through not being aware of it, and that lack of understanding causes, and in turn is caused by, the delusion of self-sufficiency. As Christianity would say, the Grace of God is always being freely offered; the problem is to get man to accept it and give up the conceit that he can save himself by the power of his ego, which is like trying to pick himself up by his own belt.[9]

This idea that we are already *there* was to be central to all Watts's thinking thereafter. It had practical consequences for his daily life, in particular that he was unable to follow "systems," as he had been unable to accept the teaching of Sokei-an. Similarly, he was fascinated by depth psychology, but unable to undertake the discipline of psychoanalysis.

The purpose of all disciplines for the mind, it seemed to him, whether religious or psychological, was enlightenment, mystical experience, "transforming consciousness so as to see clearly that the separate and alienated ego is an illusion distracting us from knowing that there is no self other than the eternal ground of being."[10]

What he had against the systems, however, was that they subtly encouraged the disciples to postpone enlightenment to some future in which they were "good enough." A system, it seemed to this supremely confident young man, might be

> an elaborate and subtle ego-trip in which people inflate their egos by trying to destroy them, stressing the superhuman difficulty of the task. It can so easily be mere postponement of realization to the tomorrow which never comes, with the mock humility of, "I'm not ready yet. I don't deserve it." . . . But what if this is just self-punishment and spiritual masochism — lying, as it were, on a bed of nails to assure oneself of "authentic" existence? Mortification of the ego is an attempt to get rid of what doesn't exist, or — which comes to the same thing — of the feeling that it exists. . . . My point was, and has continued to be, that the Big Realization for which all these systems strive is not a future attainment but a present fact, that this now-moment is eternity, and that one must see it now or never.[11]

This idea followed very naturally from the Zen leap, the "direct path up the mountainside," which he had written about in *The Spirit of Zen*. He was older now, however, and his students and contemporaries in the United States were harder on him than the Buddhist Lodge had been on the twenty-year-old boy. At his age, they wondered, what did he know of wisdom, of suffering, of mystical experience? Where was his apprenticeship to a guru, his initiation, his gradual growth into God-consciousness? Wisdom demanded that the disciple work away faithfully until crisis point or breakdown was reached, and in that crisis grasp the truth;

the Buddha himself had followed the pattern. Yet here was young Alan Watts claiming that you could get there without the agony, that you could fly in by airplane, as it were, instead of making the long, painful journey by foot and camel. Who did he think he was?

Close to the question of whether or not discipleship was necessary was another conundrum about religion which Watts set out in an article for the *Columbia Review of Religion*.[12] His thinking about whether one attained mystical experience through a supreme effort of will, or whether the effort was precisely what prevented one from having the experience, reminded him of the ancient Christian dispute between Pelagius and Saint Augustine. Pelagius held that man's salvation must come by his own efforts, and Saint Augustine that it could only come by way of divine gift or "grace." Prompted by Suzuki, Watts had long ago noticed that Mahayana Buddhism struggled with a very similar conflict. There were those, such as the Zen meditators, who pinned their hopes of liberation on *jiriki* (self-power, the effect of one's own dutiful efforts towards enlightenment), and those, like the Jodo Shinshu sect (Pure Land Buddhists), who believed that liberation can only come by *tariki* (other power), the power of Amidha or Amitabha, a transcendental form of the Buddha revered in Southeast Asia. As Watts toiled at these ideas for his *Review* article it began to occur to him that Zen, Jodo Shinshu, and Christianity might all three be approaching the same goal (enlightenment) by different routes. With growing excitement he began to see Christianity as part of the common experience of the human race, instead of a religion he found embarrassingly and uncomfortably unique. If Christians could be persuaded to give up their rigid, defensive stance, their "imperialistic claims to be the one true and perfect revelation," then there might be a chance to rediscover Christianity's mystical depths and, for many Westerners who had never seriously considered it, to discover it for the first time. He also thought that it might be possible for a growing number of people to get into the habit of "passing over" from one religion to another in search of whatever sustenance they needed.

It is impossible to divorce these intellectual struggles of Watts from his emotional conflicts. Throughout his life Watts seemed to need to reconcile his childhood religion with his adopted religion. He had taken in Christianity with his mother's milk, but had digested it uneasily, as Emily had before him. He had longed to find it better than it was, even, perhaps, as he had longed to find Emily tenderer and prettier than she was.

To accept spiritual guidance from a teacher was to put himself back in a state of dependence, and there was in him a mixture of longing and fear, of self-destructive willfulness and calculated self-interest, which made it too difficult to accept help, even from a Sokei-an. He had to be independent and self-sufficient because any kind of dependence brought back the guilt and shame of dependence upon Emily. It seemed to be what mothers, even when disguised as Zen monks, exacted as the price of such nourishment.

It was of course true that many adults made themselves ridiculously dependent upon priests, *roshi*, gurus, and other kinds of teachers, and it was equally true that sometimes in their dependence they believed nonsense that no intelligent person should believe and submitted to all sorts of practices and disciplines that at best were harmless and at worst actually got in the way of real understanding and insight. Often they had little or nothing to do with the inner leap of Zen, or liberation in any of its Western or Eastern forms.

That is not to say, however, that there were no masters from whom Watts could benefit. Indeed, as a young man he clearly longed to find a teacher he could depend upon, and he turned, with varying degrees of success, to Toby Humphreys, Ruth Fuller Sasaki, Sokei-an Sasaki, and possibly D. T. Suzuki, as later in life he would try to trust a psychoanalyst. But in the end his nerve always failed, and he had to detach himself as he had from Sokei-an. To refuse so much wisdom and loving care, however skillfully he rationalized it, reduced him to an isolation, which, for all his marvellous openness, produced a particular kind of rigidity, the rigidity that comes from self-sufficiency, from always "knowing better." It was a lonely path to have chosen.

It was all the lonelier since Eleanor's neurotic problems were growing worse. The jolly girl who had once taught him to dance the hula had turned into a sad woman who felt too miserable to cope with life at all. One day, wandering into Saint Patrick's Cathedral when she felt tired on a shopping expedition, Eleanor had a vision of Christ. It filled her with deep disquiet, and she began a round of visits to priests and others who might tell her what it meant. No one seemed able to do this in a way that she found helpful.

Given the closeness of Watts and Eleanor at that time, it is perhaps not very surprising that Eleanor somehow anticipated his revived interest in Christianity. From the time of his *Review* article onwards, Watts had been taken up with the idea of a work of resuscitation. What had repeatedly shocked him was the sense that few Christians really knew or cared about the "innerness" of their religion. Most knew much about the basic teachings and practices of Christianity, but had no conception of the mystical content that Watts felt gave the religion vitality and meaning. He wanted both to revive the lost mystical tradition of Christianity and to integrate Christianity among the great religions of the world. For Watts it had a place, but not, as Westerners often believed, the sole place.

This was an exciting if ambitious plan for which it is possible to feel some sympathy — an attempt at healing the great divide of East and West, as well as, maybe, the great divide within Alan Watts. It was one of many ways in which he was ahead of his time, anticipating ideas that would not truly come into their own for another twenty years.

This was not enough for him, however. He at once moved on from this position in his thinking to wonder whether, if he was to be listened to in his criticisms of Christianity, he should find a stronger strategic position from which to do it. As he put it, he began to think that the best thing would be to "fit myself into the Western design of life by taking the role of a Christian minister."[13]

However generously Watts's motives are interpreted, it is diffi-cult not to feel a twinge of cynicism about this scheme. A young man who has been a Buddhist for the past ten years of his life suddenly decides to become a Christian priest, not from any sudden conviction that Christianity is the "way of liberation," but because, to put it bluntly, it provides a convenient way of earning a living. Unemployed, tired of living off his wife and his wife's relatives, knowing that he knows a great deal about religion, and that he is a natural speaker, singer, and theologian (much more skillful at all these things than the average parish priest), he adds all of these considerations together and decides that switching religions may be the answer.

Watts did not, in fact, make any pretence of conversion, but such was the enthusiasm of the Christian clergy who encouraged him, or such was the unconscious arrogance in the church that all "right-thinking" people are Christian at heart, that he encountered no difficulties when he proposed to take up paid employment in a religion no longer his own. Such criticism as there was came not from Christians, but from his friends and students.

> Our personal friends . . . were astonished. They knew Eleanor as an earthy girl with a rich belly-laugh, and me as a fathomless source of bawdy limericks with a propensity for outlandish dancing and the kind of chanting which, today, brings calls to the police, the citizens supposing that the Apaches — in full war paint — are in their midst. The . . . possibility of such persons being also a minister and a minister's wife was beyond belief. Were we about to repent our sins and become godly, righteous and sober?[14]

Eugene Exman, the religious editor at Harper, apparently thinking that it was faith rather than a paid job that was the issue, urged him to become a Quaker. Watts's students, not unreasonably, had mixed feelings.

> I had discussed Buddhism as a key to the inner meaning of Christianity in seminars, and many of them, especially those with Jungian inclinations, had no difficulty in seeing Christian symbols as archetypes of the collective unconscious which is common to mankind as a whole. Others felt instinctively uncomfortable with Christianity for, although they could grasp the rationale of my explanations, they could not stand the atmosphere of church and churchy people.[15]

Ruth took the line of "how nice that you dear children have at least found a belief that really means something for you."[16] It was a subtle insult, implying that Buddhism had not really meant very much to Watts, and it is difficult to see how she could regard the change with much admiration.

The most quizzical response came from Robert Hume, Indologist and translator of the Upanishads, who taught at Union Theological Seminary; alone of Watts's friends he questioned the integrity of what was going on. Watts reports his attitude rather scornfully: "How *very* interesting, how really remarkable that I

— Alan Watts — should be contemplating this momentous STEP. He would be fascinated to know in just what ways I had come to feel that Buddhism was insufficient."[17]

Watts's daughter Joan suggests another reason for Alan's "conversion." In 1941 he was in danger of being drafted, and having escaped the war in England he did not propose to have it catch up with him in the United States. As a minister he would be safe from the draft, although it is not a reason he mentions in his autobiography.

With their new plan in mind Watts and Eleanor began shopping around the Episcopal churches in New York. The low churches, which offered simple morning prayer, clearly would not do for such a ritualist as Watts, but on Palm Sunday they discovered Saint Mary the Virgin on West Forty-sixth Street. After attending the blessing of the palms and solemn high mass, all carried out in Gregorian chant, they realized that they had found their new home. They returned for Tenebrae on Maundy Thursday. First there was a prolonged chanting of psalms, interspersed with bits of Palestrina. "One by one they extinguished the candles on a stand before the altar and gradually the church went into darkness. . . . There was undoubtedly magic in that church."[18]

Watts introduced himself to Fr. Grieg Taber, the rector of Saint Mary's, and told him about his wish to become a priest. It is not recorded that Father Taber had any doubts on the subject. Was this because Watts was so plausible, because he really seemed to have the makings of a priest, or because Father Taber was not accustomed to men approaching the idea with quite so much cool calculation as Watts did?

Pages of slightly uneasy explanation and justification are given in the autobiography. Watts had not *abandoned* Buddhism and Taoism, in fact he had always thought the Gospels inferior to the

*Tao te Ching*. But perhaps it did not matter all that much if he was not very interested in Jesus. What mattered when celebrating mass was conveying the *mystery*, the mystery that all religions celebrated. He could really do a great service to people by suggesting that "Christianity might be understood as a form of that mystical and perennial philosophy which has appeared in almost all times and places."[19] As a priest he would be "sincere but not serious."

The excuses and explanations multiply, but never do they seem to justify such a significant change. What seems to be lacking is any sense of passion, or, as the Christians say, vocation. Becoming a priest for Watts was, in the main, a way of making a career out of religion. An incidental inconvenience was that it also implied some degree of disloyalty to the Buddhist beliefs he had practiced and advocated for years. There is a deep and disturbing sense of his refusal to face the implications of what he did, and underlying that, an unattractive self-seeking. Becoming a priest would solve some urgent problems in his life. His final word on the subject is a chillingly practical comment on his defection from Buddhism and his sudden espousal of a religion he had affected to despise: "It was simply that the Anglican Communion seemed to be the most appropriate context for doing what was in me to do, in Western Society."[20]

Father Taber sent Watts to see Dean Fosbrooke at the General Theological Seminary, and Fosbrooke pointed out his lack of a degree. What a young man like him needed was some academic background, more particularly in history. One way to get into the priesthood without a college degree was to find a bishop who was favorably impressed, and then, with his sponsorship and approval, it was occasionally possible to make a short cut in the academic training. Wallace Conkling, the bishop of Chicago, seemed a likely sponsor, since he was just the sort of Anglo-Catholic Watts aspired to become. And the Everetts, though far from keen churchgoers, were a well-known family in Evanston, with many of the right connections necessary in just this sort of situation.

All went as planned. The bishop took to Watts, and Watts, rather unexpectedly, took to the bishop, deciding he was a *bhakti* mystic (one who achieved enlightenment through devotion) and a man of high culture. Watts was at once sent off to talk to Bishop McElwain, the dean of Seabury-Western Theological Seminary in Evanston, who felt that the degree might possibly be overlooked and that Watts might be enrolled as a special student, if he could show that he had read reasonably widely in religion and history. The reading list that Watts then prepared astounded the old man, accustomed as he was to less scholarly students. The bishop prescribed a two-year course for Watts, with courses in New Testament Greek, the Old Testament, and theology.

The young couple cheerfully packed up their possessions in New York, pausing only for Watts to paint a mural of the tree of life in the white space on the wall left by taking down a Japanese screen. They moved to Clinton Place in Evanston, next door to a flautist in the Chicago Symphony Orchestra, who introduced Watts to the delights of poker, usually played with other members of the orchestra. The new milieu was suburban, and, determined to live like his neighbors, Watts bought insurance, went to football games, and attended church socials and dances, though with a playful spirit that indicated a certain lack of conviction. The chameleon had entered a new phase.

Five

# Colored Christian

## 1941-1947

AFTER THE MYSTERY AND NUMINOUSNESS of Saint Mary
the Virgin, the churches of Chicago struck the Wattses as rather
arid. The seminary chapel at Seabury-Western did not appeal to
Alan Watts much either: "a colorless alley lined with oak choir
stalls where the black-gowned seminarists sat in somber rows to
chant the psalms of Matins and Evensong."[1]

Nor were his Evanston neighbors all that much to his taste.
The main preoccupation of most of them was making money,
which Watts thought might be rather fun to do — a clever game,
like bridge — only people seemed to have to pretend not to
enjoy it.

It must most definitely be classified as *work*; as that which you *have*
to do as a duty to your family and community, and which therefore
affords many businessmen the best possible excuse for staying away
from home and from their wives. The Nemesis of this attitude is
that it flows over into the so-called leisure or non-work areas of
life in such a way that playing with children, giving attention to
one's wife, exercising on the golf course, and purchasing certain

luxuries also become duties. Survival itself becomes a duty and even
a drag, for the pretense of not enjoying the games gets under the
skin and tightens the muscles which repress joyous and sensuous
emotion.[2]

Watts clearly was still struggling with his own Protestant roots,
using his resentment of them to make observations about the
link between work and play.

For him the barrier between work and play did not exist. At
Seabury-Western Watts threw himself into reading with a tremendous intellectual appetite. He had been afraid at first that he
would have difficulty in keeping up, since unlike most of his
fellow students he had not been to college, but his old Brahmin
training and his habits of scholarship stood him in good stead.
He quickly discovered that his rusty Greek was the best in the
class, and that he could manage all the required reading by working one night a week, which left the rest of his study periods free
for the reading that interested him. By his second year he was so
far ahead that his teachers excused him from classwork and taught
him on a tutorial basis. So it came about that for two years Watts
gave himself up to serious theological reading, day after day, the
study of a man who cared intensely about theological ideas and
had a boundless curiosity about what others had made of those
ideas. He read Harnack's *History of Dogma*, Clement and Origen,
the Gnostics, Athanasius, Irenaeus. There was one period when
he threw himself into reading Saint Thomas Aquinas and his
modern exponents, Maritain and Gilson. There was a Russian
phase when he read Vladimir Soloviev, Berdyaev, the hesychasts.
He intensely scrutinized the classics of Christian mysticism —
every well-known mystic from Pseudo-Dionysius to Leon Bloy,
together with Evelyn Underhill, Friedrich von Hügel, and Dom
John Chapman.

Somewhere in all this Watts became fascinated by the "un-knowing" tradition of Christian mysticism, as in *The Cloud of Unknowing*: "silence of the mind and being simply at the disposal of God without holding any image or concept of God."[3] It was here, Watts felt, that Christianity and Mahayana Buddhism came close to touching hands.

A chance encounter during this period was with Aldous Huxley. On an Easter visit to Ruth in New York in 1943 Watts was intro-duced to Huxley, and they both made tentative overtures in what was to be a long, though not close, friendship. Watts found Huxley kind and sensitive, as well as mordantly witty and intellectual. It was a pleasure for Watts to hear again the forgotten cadences of English beautifully phrased and spoken by an English voice. Huxley told him about the group of Englishmen — Gerald Heard, Christopher Isherwood, Felix Greene, and himself, all living on the West Coast — that was studying Vedantist ideas. Heard and Huxley in particular were working towards some sort of synthesis of Christianity and Oriental mysticism, but in Huxley's excellent exposition of it at least, it came across as too "spiritual," too ascetic. Huxley seemed to Watts a Manichaean who hated the body. Watts's own thoughts along these lines were that Christian-ity's "Word made flesh" must be about a transcendence of the dualism of mind and matter rather than a denial of the flesh, and it seemed to him that this expressed much the same idea as Pure Land Buddhism.

> This very earth is the Pure Land,
> And this very body the Body of Buddha.[4]

At home at Clinton Place Watts and Eleanor had done what they could to make a rented house feel homey. When they arrived it was all painted institutional buff, expensively antiqued on the moldings. They painted it, moldings and all, in pale green. They were living in a style unimaginable for most students and enjoyed the services of a maid.

Eleanor's depression had not notably improved, however. She found it difficult to cope with the demands of a small child, and sometimes turned violently on Joan. She was aware of the popularity her husband found wherever he went, and although she was capable of holding her own socially, she felt left out and envious. All these problems were aggravated by the fact that, soon after they arrived at Evanston, she found herself pregnant once more. She did not want another child yet, but consoled herself with the thought that it might be a son, which she did want. In August 1942, however, she gave birth to a daughter, Ann (often, as a young child, to be called Winkie). Eleanor was disappointed and inclined to blame Watts for her plight. Ann had come into a painful inheritance — a mother who did not want children and who would have preferred a boy, and a father who, both sisters were later to feel, really preferred Joan. From quite early on, unable to cope with all the tensions of her family life, Eleanor was physically cruel to Ann.

Watts's response to Eleanor's growing misery and to the distress of the children was to withdraw still further into his academic work. No doubt he had once thought he could save Eleanor from her various problems, including her mother; now he began to feel her as a drag on his life, and her mother, who had interested him so much, was far away in New York. Eleanor fought with him or had long bouts of crying; she was less and less interested in the sexual side of the marriage. She rebuked Watts continually for not giving enough of his time to the children, and Joan remembers the frequency of rows at Clinton Place.

Watts did not spend much time with his children (either in this marriage or his subsequent one), but this made the time that he did spend with them especially treasured and memorable. On one wonderful weekend, Joan remembers, he set himself to paint the inside of the barn with monsters and demons until he had transformed it into a place of magic. When Watts played with his children he played as if he was a child himself, totally absorbed. He wasn't there a lot, but the time he gave was, says Joan, "quality time."

A few years later Ann found herself sick in the hospital with scarlet fever. Using his position as a minister to get to see her, Watts sat down and produced on the spot a magical chain of cut-out paper dolls. He had the sorcerer's gift of producing something out of nothing, a gift that his children loved and remembered. Writing about his children years later Watts had his own sort of guilt about neglecting them, and his own excuse.

> By all the standards of this society I have been a terrible father, with a few disastrous attempts to be a "good" one, for the simple reason that I have no patience with the abstract notion of "the child," which our culture imposes on small people; with the toys and games they are supposed to enjoy, with the books they are supposed to read, with the mannerisms they're supposed to assume, and with the schools in which they become lowest-common-denominator images of each other. I am completely at ease with the infant who still enjoys nonsense and plays spontaneously at un-programmed games, and then again with the adolescent who is calling the brainwashing into question. But the Disneyland "world of childhood" is an itsy-bitsy, cutie-pied, plastic hoax; a world populated by frustrated brats trying to make out why they are not treated as human beings. . . . If my children have found me distant and aloof, this is the explanation.[5]

Perhaps Watts's children did not so much find him distant and aloof in any emotional sense, as simply *not there*, in the most ordinary physical sense, to which Disney and his artefacts were irrelevant. They needed their father to counter Eleanor's sadness and to control her anger against them, and he was too busy becoming an Episcopalian.

It was not easy for someone who was still basically a Buddhist to pass as a man of Christian conviction. The need for an element of concealment was there, since Watts was exasperated at being constantly in the company of those whose emotions were "colored Christian." He detested the atmosphere of guilt, repentance, and confession, and hated the idea of God as *He. She* might have corrected the balance a bit, he felt, but really if he was to speak of God at all (and he found it difficult to take that idea seriously), he would have preferred to use the word *It* or *That.*

His Christian teachers for their part accused Watts of pantheism and wondered if his inability to relate to God as a person might indicate an inability to relate to persons in general. This was a fairly offensive observation, but no doubt they sensed that something was not quite right about Watts's sense of vocation and that he was holding back feelings and thoughts from those who were supposed to be friends and future colleagues.

Watts describes this period of his life in mock-innocent, "Where did I go wrong?" tones: "I chose priesthood because it was the only formal role of Western society into which, at that time, I could even begin to fit. . . . But it was an ill-fitting suit of clothes, not only for a shaman but also for a bohemian — that is, one who loves color and exuberance, keeps irregular hours, would rather be free than rich, dislikes working for a boss, and has his own code of sexual morals."[6] To which the Christians might have replied, if they had understood his rather dubious motives, that no one was compelling him to be a priest.

However, on Ascension Day 1944 Watts was ordained an

Episcopal priest in the Church of the Atonement, Evanston (he managed to get the date wrong in his autobiography); he had put on the ill-fitting suit of clothes and was condemned to wear them for another six years.

He could not imagine himself as a parish priest and hoped that Bishop Conkling might let him be a sort of priest-at-large in Chicago, maybe running a retreat house with a strong emphasis on contemplative prayer. Much later, by the 1960s and 1970s, Christians were to develop a renewed interest in contemplative prayer, but Watts was ahead of this development. The best the church could do for him was to make him chaplain at Northwestern University.

Watts threw himself into the job with a will. It provided a home for his family at Canterbury House on Sheridan Road in Evanston. Canterbury House was designed to be both the chaplain's home and a sort of student center, and it contained within it Saint Thomas's Chapel. Eleanor, who had skill and taste, set to work to give the house a welcoming beauty and style.

Watts meanwhile worked out a program to attract students both to services and to the intensive course of education and discussion in which he wanted to involve them. In one of the pamphlets he had printed for students, he pointed out that at the most, a high school graduate had had 360 hours of religious instruction in school as compared with 1,800 hours of English or mathematics. That meant that a grown-up girl or boy had about reached the third grade where religious teaching was concerned. One of his hopes was to encourage intellectual curiosity about religion.

The Church is here on campus to provide what college education neglects — a mature understanding of those doctrines and the real answer of Christian philosophy to the central problems of life, in ignorance of which no-one can call himself educated. . . .

What am I for? What causes me to exist? Is it a mechanical process or a living intelligence? What is God, the ultimate life and reality? Can I have actual knowledge of God, and if so how? These most fascinating of all questions are in the mind of every member of this university, for even the most hard-boiled agnostic has *some* interest in religion.

Through lack of time and resources the religious teaching given in the average Sunday School (or even sermon) is so elementary and superficial as to be actually misleading to a grown mind. Thus the popular impression of Christian doctrine is a wild caricature of the reality. No wonder people don't believe it![7]

The pamphlet that offered this release from religious ignorance advertised a series of lectures at 7:30 on Sunday evenings, many of them given by Watts himself, on such subjects as "Religion and Science," "Christianity and Psychoanalysis," "Popular Religious Art" (with slides for illustration), and "The Painting of Eternity" (also with slides). It also offered individual instruction with the chaplain for any member of the university who cared to ask for it. Individual instruction would cover the following subjects: the aim of religion; the doctrine of God; the doctrine of man; the Incarnation; the Church and sacraments; prayer and the spiritual life; Christian ethics; Christian worship.

In addition to this educational program Watts also offered personal counseling to those who wanted it, and he made it clear that he and Canterbury House were always available:

Canterbury House is *not* a "social center." It has no "organizations," no "committees," no "programs." It is supported by the Episcopal Diocese of Chicago to serve the spiritual life of Northwestern University, to give proofs of God's existence, his supreme importance and our utter dependence upon him, and of the impossibility of rational life and thought without him; to combat the silly and pernicious views of agnosticism, humanism and pseudo-scientific materialism so fashionable among modern educators; and to afford you the opportunity to bring your own faith in God and his Church to maturity and conviction.

Although it is not an organized social center, Canterbury House is "Open House," especially on Sunday afternoons from 4 to 6. People are always coming in to talk and pass the time of day; the Chaplain thoroughly enjoys it; you cannot waste his time![8]

This was an enthusiastic and generous approach to a job for which Watts was paid a tiny salary. It was difficult for Eleanor and the children to carry on their family life with such busy coming and going of students, but Eleanor was determined to play the part of "the minister's wife" to the best of her ability. Watts soon became a well-known figure on campus, bicycling from one place to another (bicycling was rare enough at that time to be regarded as eccentric), dressed from head to toe in clerical black. He was bearded too, which was unusual, and it was rumored that he fasted and went in for other ascetic practices.

Fired by the intensive reading of the past few years, Watts had begun a new book entitled *Behold the Spirit: A Study in the Necessity of Mystical Religion*, for which his seminary was to award him a master's degree. In the course of his switch to formal Christianity, which the book represents, he enormously increased his theological knowledge. The intensive course of reading that preceded his ordination introduced him to the Fathers, to the *Summa Theologica*, to the riches of medieval Christianity, and to the Counter Reformation saints, all of which subjects were previously unknown to him. He began to realize that there was more to his native religion than Protestant ethics, guilt, and sentimental devotions to Jesus. Fired by this discovery he recovered the clarity and energy of style evident in his early books about Zen.

Like all Watts's books *Behold the Spirit* asks how liberation, or enlightenment, is to be achieved. The book begins from the assumption that "Church religion is spiritually dead," as evidenced by its organizational busyness, inadequate teaching, excessive moralism, doctrinal obscurantism, lack of conviction, absence of reality, and disunity. What the Church did not succeed in doing was in relating "man to the root and ground of reality and life. . . . At times man *knows* his need of religion; at others he only *feels* it as an unexplained void in the heart."[9]

The problem seemed to be as great among those who went to church and followed Christian spiritual disciplines as among those who had abandoned or never known such practices.

> Christian faith and practice have lost force because the enormous majority of Christians . . . do not know what they mean. Let it be said at once that such knowledge is not a matter of mere learning, of philosophical and theological acumen. Indeed, the theologian has often just as little grasp of the meaning of his religion as anyone else. He knows ideas; he knows the relations between these ideas; he knows the historical events — the story of Christ — upon which these ideas are based. He knows the doctrines of the Trinity, the Incarnation, the Virgin Birth, and the Atonement and can describe them with accuracy. But because he does not know, or even apprehend, what they mean, having no consciousness of union with God, his description of them — while correct as far as it goes — is uninformative and lacking in significance.[10]

The main trouble with church religion, Watts says, is that people are taught to carry out spiritual exercises on a sort of imitative basis. Because the saints said their prayers, received the sacraments, and performed the conventional Christian gestures, others suppose that the way to become saints is to copy them, and if no inner transformation takes place, they are enjoined to practice "holy patience" forever if necessary. But this approach does not take account of the terrible vacuum at the heart of such piety. Imitation does not feed spiritual hunger. "They want God himself, by whatever name he may be called; they want to be filled with his creative life and power; they want some conscious experience of being at one with Reality itself, so that their otherwise meaningless and ephemeral lives may acquire an eternal significance."[11]

Watts suggests that such wistful seekers are ignorant of a vital secret:

> They do not know that the Church has in its possession, under lock and key (or maybe the sheer weight of persons sitting on the lid), the purest gold of mystical religion. Still less do they know that creed and sacrament are only fully intelligible in terms of mystical life. And they do not know these things because the stewards and teachers of the Church do not, for the most part, know them either. For while holding officially that eternal life consists in the knowledge of God — and in nothing else — churches of every kind are concerned with almost everything but the knowledge of God.[12]

For Watts it came down to this:

> Knowledge of God, the realization of one's union with God, in a word, mysticism, is *necessary*. It is not simply the flower of religion; it is the very seed, lying in the flower as its fulfilment and preceding the root as its origin. . . . It is the *sine qua non* — the *must* — the first and great commandment. "Thou shalt love the Lord thy God with all thy heart, and with all thy soul, and with all thy mind." On this hangs all the Law. On this all rules and techniques depend, and apart from it mean nothing.[13]

To suggest that people *must* know God is to say something at once too difficult and too simple to be grasped. Mysticism is not so much a doing as an undoing, a removing of the barriers, a taking down of the defenses, a creating of space, a getting out of the way. Mysticism is "an action in the passive."

The time had come, Watts suggested, to recover the deep mystical sense Christianity had previously known, but with a new emphasis. Medieval Christians had felt at one with God and with religious symbolism in a primitive, childlike way. The Renaissance and the growth of humanism could be seen as a kind of rebellious adolescence, necessary as a movement towards maturity, but not maturity itself. This was followed by a tremendous awareness of human power in action, in science and technology. But this enormous upsurge of energy and action was followed not just by weariness, but by the spiritual maturity of age.

Following Oswald Spengler Watts suggests that Western culture was on the verge of a "Second Religiousness" that in some ways would be quite different. It would be "an interior, spiritual and mystical understanding of the old, traditional body of wisdom. . . . What the child understood as an external, objective, and symbolic fact, the mature mind will see also as an interior, subjective, and mystical truth. What the child received on another's authority, the adult will know as his own inner experience."[14]

Watts goes on to consider what a twentieth-century mysticism could be like. In the past Christian mysticism had had a kind of "unholy alliance" with Manichaeism, denying the fleshliness proclaimed in the Incarnation, "the Word made flesh," by despising the body — supposing it, its senses, and in particular its sexual fulfillment, to be inimical to the life of the spirit. A true understanding of the Incarnation involves a recognition of the redemption of body as well as spirit, that "the eternal life of God is given to man here and now in the flesh of each moment's experience."

Release from our own isolating egoism comes partly from recognizing the hunger for God, partly from a sort of relaxation. Egoism itself is "like trying to swim without relying on the water, endeavoring to keep afloat by tugging at your own legs; your whole body becomes tense, and you sink like a stone. Swimming requires a certain relaxation, a certain giving of yourself to the water, and similarly spiritual life demands a relaxation of the soul to God."[15]

Union is often thought of as a tremendous attainment, needing huge struggles. But there is a whole other method, as in Zen *satori*, which suggests that what knowing God is about is not effort and attainment, but realization: "The soul striving to attain the divine state by its own efforts falls into total despair, and suddenly there dawns upon it with a great illuminative shock the realization that the divine state simply IS, here and now, and does not have to be attained."[16]

Yet there was, Watts suggested, some perverse determination in us that it had to be difficult, some self-regarding romantic picture of our own heroic labors: "We flatter ourselves in premeditating the long, long journey we are going to take in order to find him, the giddy heights of spiritual progress we are going to scale." The tragedy is that we thus miss the obvious:

> God is not niggardly in his self-revelation; he creates us to know him, and short of actual compulsion does everything possible to present himself to our consciousness. In saying that God gives us union with himself here and now, we are saying also that here and now he exposes himself right before our eyes. In this very moment we are looking straight at God, and he is so clear that for us complex human beings he is peculiarly hard to see. To know him we have to simplify ourselves.[17]

Watts makes the very interesting suggestion that the mystical consciousness of God (as opposed to the more direct, beatific vision) may be very like the sort of awareness we have of ourselves:

> For while we cannot perceive our own egos directly, we know that we exist. We do not know what we are, but we know ourselves as existing, and this knowledge is present as an undertone in all other

knowledge. Similarly, the mystical knowledge of God is a knowledge of God in the act of his presence and union with us, but is not immediate vision and apprehension of the divine essence.[18]

The amazing joy of this sort of apprehension, partial as it is, is that we know ourselves to be part of a "living mystery, which imparts life, power and joy." The price of knowing this mystery is the cutting off of the "possessive will."

Always practical about spirituality, Watts goes on to consider what this view of God means. He is not against formal religion. For some it is a necessary way to discover ultimately that God cannot be possessed. For others it is a precious way of tracing out the symbolic and analogic patterns of God in order to move on to "the Reality beyond symbols." For others again, formal religion has such repugnant associations that it is almost impossible for them to espouse it.

Watts envisages a new flexibility in Christian worship, with a formal liturgy at one end of the scale for those who want it, and wordless contemplation at the other for those who want that. Sermonizing, moralizing (especially where the dubious lever of guilt is employed), and excessive theological speculation, seem to Watts totally fruitless. What the whole religious endeavor is about is in finding God in the most hundrum moments — this, he believes, rather than by "devotions" to Jesus, is the way to discover "the mind of Christ." He would like to see the Church give informal teaching on "digging potatoes, washing dishes and working in an office." There must, he thinks, be a Christian way of washing your hands.

This is an interesting view of Christianity, obviously much influenced by Zen. In his perception of people's hunger for mystical experience Watts anticipated much that was to come within the next thirty years — the search for mystical experience outside the

Church and the renewed interest in contemplative prayer within it. In other ways, too, he was prophetic. He saw that the time was coming when the "male God" would seem incongruous, and that the elevation of the Virgin Mary, though important, did not touch the real need. He saw the need for Christians to undo their Manichaean heritage and finally accept the messy body, able to feel at one with God even when, or especially when, in *flagrante delicto*.

When *Behold the Spirit* came out in 1947 the reviewers were rapturous. An Episcopal reviewer, Canon Iddings Bell, said that the book would "prove to be one of the half dozen most significant books on religion published in the twentieth century," which was high praise indeed. Another Catholic author noted with interest that the book recognized "contributions from Oriental religion which simply are not present in contemporary Western religion. More than this it shows how the traditional Western doctrine of the Incarnation and the Atonement can be reconciled with and combined with the intuitive religion of the Orient, such as that of Zen Buddhism. These are exceedingly important and outstanding achievements."[19]

Meanwhile Watts was setting to work to transform the liturgical experience of students. On Sundays at 11:00 A.M. he conducted a service at the Chapel of Saint John the Divine on Haven Street, which, though it stuck basically to the Book of Common Prayer, managed to achieve colorful and dramatic effects unknown to the Episcopal students before. He introduced incense, the slow, casually formal processions that he had learned about from Hewlett Johnson, short arresting sermons, Gregorian chant and Renaissance polyphony, sung by a specially trained ensemble from the music school. Worshippers came into a church fragrant with smoke, brilliant with vestments and candles, in which the prayers were spoken in Watts's beautiful resonant English and the ritual was performed like the gestures of a play. Something of the mystery that Watts had learned from Friar Taber was there too and something of his own feeling for language and use of intelligence and humor. The students began to flock to Saint John's in large numbers, even though lively liturgy and strong preaching was on offer in the neighborhood of the campus. Watts was one of the latest fashions.

He was also hardworking. In the Anglo-Catholic style he celebrated Mass every morning except Mondays at 7:15 A.M. in Saint Thomas's Chapel, and most of the rest of his waking hours were spent either conducting services, taking seminars, or entertaining students in his own home.

His growing popularity was looked upon a little sourly and suspiciously by colleagues and others. The dean of the seminary wondered aloud what sort of preparation Watts's example would provide for the work his theological students would be taking up in very ordinary parishes where the "bells and smells" of Saint John's would not be appreciated. The mother of one of the seminarians quoted in Watts's biography expressed this point of view more succinctly: "The religion you are giving these people is not the religion of Saint Luke's and Saint Mark's here in town, and from what I can see it isn't the religion of the Episcopal Church anywhere."[20] Perhaps she sensed an element almost of leg-pulling in the sheer elaboration of ceremonies; she had, at least, an inkling that Watts was up to something. He had also managed to upset the scientists on the faculty of Northwestern by attacking their antireligious attitudes.

The students, not surprisingly, took a more adventurous view of his activities. His imaginative liturgies appealed to many of them. They dubbed Richard Adams, a student with whom Alan planned the liturgies, "the Sorcerer's apprentice," a joking recognition of the shaman quality they noted in Watts. They appreciated the individual attention Watts was prepared to give to people in intellectual or emotional difficulties, and they enjoyed the social life of Canterbury House, a mixture of fun and endless discussion, as life with Watts was apt to be. Watts and Eleanor kept open house, and the house, Watts remembered, "was the scene of an almost perpetual bull session, involving students, seminarists and members of the University faculty." On Sunday afternoons there were tea parties, which lingered on into the cocktail hour "and became decidedly merrier than anything ordinarily foreseen in the prospect of tea at the vicarage."[21] On Sunday evenings, when Watts had completed his seminar, people gathered round the piano and sang rather racier material than the hymns at Uncle Harry's. Later there was dancing.

Perhaps because the members of the group at Canterbury House did have such a good time together they appeared as a bit cliquish to those outside, though Watts was welcoming to anyone wishing to join the fun. He was not very interested in being a good colleague to his fellow clergy, or perhaps was simply not very interested in them at all. One former student remembers trying to get him to a surprise birthday party for a curate in another parish and getting a frosty response.

As time went on the parties got wilder, as members of the group around Canterbury House came to trust one another more. Forgetting the proprieties expected of him, or simply sick of them, Watts would play with as much relish as any of his students. Joan remembers him in competitions with students to see who could pee the highest, and making "bombs" with them of matchheads in milk bottles, which they exploded in the back garden. Watts himself remembers one of his students demolishing a streetlight with an air rifle from inside a car, and though he did not actually encourage the student to do it, Watts was driving the car at the time. On another night the same student and he attached a wire and a wad of sanitary napkins soaked in gasoline to a helium balloon, lit it, and let it blow away over Lake Michigan. Chicago's inhabitants, seeing a flame floating in the night sky, excitedly reported sightings of flying saucers to the police.

While Watts had been training to be an Episcopal priest and preparing to write his book about the failures of Christianity, the war in Europe and in the Far East had had little impact on his life. Perhaps the only effect on him was that his parents had been prevented from visiting him in his new country. In 1946 they were able at last to visit Evanston. Apart from the pleasure of seeing their much-loved only child again, they were glad to see Alan apparently so settled with wife and children, making a success in a career that Emily in particular admired. Did they, one wonders, have any inkling when they played with the children, or talked to Eleanor, or saw Alan in the pulpit, that all was not sound? A photograph taken during the visit shows the older couple looking pleased and happy, Watts looking evasive, Eleanor looking unhappy and embarrassed, and Ann looking sad and vulnerable. The older Wattses' visit was much appreciated by the two little girls, who responded to their gentleness and loving interest.

The next year Joy Buchan and Aunt Gertrude set off from England on the exciting trip by boat and train to visit their relatives. Joy went on alone to Evanston from Minneapolis where they had been visiting Uncle Willy. She was met at the Chicago station by Watts, and the only change she discovered in him was his beard. She found the children sweet and attentive and Watts very pleased to see her. He showed her his drawings and paintings, calligraphy and photographs, and gave her a copy of *Behold the Spirit.* The life of a clerical household went on around her: choir practices, in which she took part, discussion groups, people dropping in, visits to the church where Watts preached and celebrated Communion. Like any visitor from Britain in that austere postwar period she was fascinated by the variety of food and wrote at length of delicious meals consumed either in the Watts household or at restaurants. Her companion on some of these jaunts to restaurants was a young mathematics student, Dorothy De Witt ("Doddy"), who was often a babysitter for Joan and Ann. Sometimes too there was a musical evening at Canterbury House, with Eleanor and Ann, Doddy, and a young musician called Carlton Gamer playing for them, or all of them listening to records together.

Joy's diary paints a very favorable picture of the chaplain's household, a portrait of a man faithful in his pious duties, attentive as husband and father, generous and thoughtful as a host, busy and devoted about the occupations of suburban Evanston. Eleanor perhaps emerges as a little distant, performing the duties of a hostess; Joy was, in any case, Alan's cousin, not hers. Emily and Laurence must have loved hearing all the details of the visit when Joy got home again to Bromley. Beneath the conventional happy family facade, however, all was not well. A heavy drama was about to be played out, and in her diary Joy unwittingly had introduced the main characters.

# Six

# Correspondence
## 1947-1950

"MY DEAR BISHOP CONKLING," Eleanor Watts wrote in a cliffhanger of a letter dated June 29, 1950. "I have never taken any steps to acquaint you with this matter as I have hoped it would prove unnecessary for me to uphold my status at the cost of another's reputation whom I cannot bring myself to judge. But Father Taber insists that the time has come when my silence can no longer protect the Church, and that I must set before you the complete facts of the case that you may be able to act in full knowledge of the truth."

Eleanor was writing not from Canterbury House at Evanston, but from her mother's house in New York, where she had fled with her children to the psychiatric care of Charlie Taylor and the spiritual care of Father Taber.

"During the first two years of my marriage I became aware that Alan's preoccupation with sexual matters was extreme," Eleanor went on, "but as his 'demands' on me were not frequent I considered it highly probable that my lack of understanding of such things was coloring my view. His 'demands,' however, were of a type that made intimate relations most uncomfortable to me and

I also discovered that he was a frequent masturbator, although I did not draw any inference from this knowledge at that time."[1]

The bishop may not have known of Eleanor's depression, frigidity, and invalidism, but he must have wondered at this point in the letter whether Watts's "demands" were unreasonable, or whether he was dealing with a prudish woman who was repulsed by her husband's normal expectations.

Most bishops then, and perhaps now, were accustomed to a situation in which clergy gave so much of their time to caring for their parishioners that they often had very little energy left over for their wives and families. Clergy wives, he would know, were often seething with rage that they received very little of their husbands' love and attention. Yet it was difficult for them to get sympathy if they complained, since their husbands were dedicated to God, and God was an impossible rival, worse than another woman. Watts had certainly worked unceasingly since he arrived in Evanston, and Eleanor had watched him become an important figure on campus, with students flocking to services and later into her home to carry on conversations with him. Once vivacious and attracting attention herself, Eleanor was depressed by her present contrasting role as housewife and mother, and took out some of her temper on the children, particularly on Ann.

Eleanor did not tell the bishop of the boredom and frustration of being the chaplain's wife, however. On the contrary she describes how she had dutifully cherished Alan's vocation to the priesthood in the hope that the discipline and ideals of the church would make him steady and responsible. But, she complains,

So far, i.e., before his ordination, I had had the entire responsibility for the home upon my shoulders both financially and socially, as well as the upbringing of our daughter. Alan lived in his own particular "ivory tower" and the practical world seemed to have no reality for him. To my surprise and concern the change to a lovely home, another child, and a new career did nothing to help this state of mind, in fact he retreated further than ever from his family and his responsibilities as the head of the family. Our intimate relations became more infrequent, another matter of concern which I put down to "consideration" on his part.[2]

Eleanor's tone, if somewhat self-righteous, nevertheless suggests what a miserable married life they had been pursuing.

"In May, 1944," Eleanor goes on, "we moved into Canterbury House. Here again I was left with the full responsibility for the home and the rearing of the children. Our intimate relations were few but as his attitude towards me in this sphere was increasingly distasteful to me, and as I was not well, this state of affairs, although unhappy, seemed all that could be expected."

The strains between the Wattses, still unnoticeable when Joy Buchan visited, began to be apparent even to casual visitors. Jean McDermid, Alan's cousin from Minneapolis, was out motoring one day with her new husband Malcolm, whom Watts had never met, and they stopped in to pay a call on the Wattses. Watts answered the door, but was not his old jolly self, nor did he seem pleased to see them. He showed them into his study and made polite conversation for a bit. Lunch time came, but the half-expected invitation did not come with it. All of a sudden the door shot open, Eleanor marched furiously in, placed a tray with one plate on it in front of Watts and went out without speaking to them. Watts uneasily ate his pork chop. Shocked by this scene, the McDermids went angrily away, swearing that they would never call on the Wattses again.

Eleanor went on:

In the early summer of 1946 Alan came to me with the story that one of his students was desirous of having relations with him and asked my advice as to how to handle it. He had visited her in her

*Overleaf:* Alan Watts performing the
Zen tea ceremony (*Pirkle Jones*)

Emily Buchan Watts

Laurence Wilson Watts

*Opposite page, top:* Laurence and
Emily Watts at Rowan Cottage,
Watts's boyhood home, in Chisle-
hurst, Kent

*Opposite page, bottom:* Watts's own
drawing of the unheated bathroom at
Rowan Cottage, part of the dreaded
upstairs world

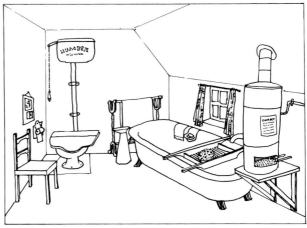

Alan at five months with Emily, 1915

Alan at age six, 1921

As a young scholar at King's School,
Canterbury, 1929

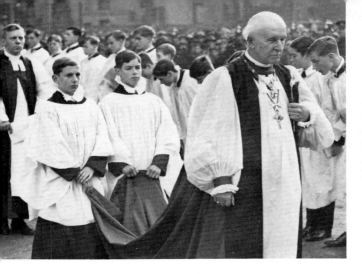

Always partial to ritual, Watts (*center*) carries the train of the newly ordained Archbishop Lang, 1928.

Emily and Laurence make a visit to the United States, 1946. *From left:* Alan, his first wife, Eleanor, their daughters, Ann and Joan, Laurence, and Emily

*Above:* Watts lunches with Christmas Humphreys (*left*) and D. T. Suzuki (*right*) at the Rembrandt Hotel in London, 1958. (*Buddhist Society*)

*Left:* As Dean of the American Academy of Asian Studies, 1955 (*courtesy of KPFA*)

*Right:* Watts practicing calligraphy, 1958 (*Ken Kay*)

Watts lecturing on Zen, 1958

Giving a seminar on the *Vallejo,*
Sausalito, 1966 (*courtesy of Alan
Watts Educational Programs*)

Watts in later years

*Alan joins us in thanking
you for your farewell message.
Listen and rejoice, as his
laughter circles the universe.*

Jano's reply, with Watts's own
calligraphy, to those who mourned
Watts's death in 1973

rooms on several occasions and had indulged in "necking parties" with her. This announcement came as a complete surprise. I tried my best to point out to him the incongruity of such a relationship for one in his position and how it endangered both his vows as a priest and as a husband. After much argument and discussion we *seemed* to come to an agreement as to principles.[3]

Watts's misery in his marriage and his guilt about his sexual longings had become too much for him. Later he was to say that he thought that he and Eleanor had clung together so hard in the beginning that "mutual strangulation" had taken place. This made each of them the other's "chattel," and with hindsight he thought this a hopeless kind of relationship: "You must so trust your partners as to allow full freedom to be the being that he or she is."[4] There seemed to be no freedom between him and Eleanor, and each was exasperated at the other, Watts seeing a frigid invalid, too depressed to care for her children, and Eleanor a man whose sexual desires frightened and disgusted her. She makes it clear to the bishop just what the euphemism, "uncomfortable," which she had used in her letter, meant to her:

Alan at last confided to me the whole story of his sexual difficulties. I can only repeat his story to you to the best of my ability.

He had been sent to boarding school at the age of seven and there had been introduced to certain sexual practices by older boys and even a master. In his Preparatory school [she means King's School, Canterbury] this early start was nourished further. Apparently sex in all its forms was a constant topic of interest and experimentation and added to that was the type of discipline administered there [flagellation] which set the pattern for Alan's sex life. He told me that he had practiced masturbation more than once daily from his schooldays to the present and that as the phantasy life which accompanied this practice grew more compelling he spent hours in drawing pornographic pictures and reading pornographic literature to excite his interest. He also inflicted various tortures upon himself in order to achieve orgasm. [It is interesting in this connection to recall his suggestion to his headmaster that beating be abolished at the school.]

At the time that he married he had hopes that a normal sexual relationship would prove to be a settling influence but he found to his dismay that it became increasingly difficult for him to complete such a normal relationship without some extraordinary stimulus.

Over the years of his marriage pornographic interests and phantasy, while more attractive to him than the normal marriage relationship, lost some of their power to stimulate him and he began to seek stimulation from women outside his marriage.[5]

It is not difficult to imagine how shocked the prudish young Eleanor must have been as her husband tried to tell her what he needed from her. Without experience, maturity, or even enough love for him to try to imagine his feelings, she was left feeling "uncomfortable" and with the conviction that her husband was incurably "abnormal."

"On hearing this story," she tells Conkling, "I was horrified but, at the same time, sympathetic. I could not see wherein he was to *blame* and after much discussion I agreed to do my best as a wife to try to help him overcome his difficulties. I urged him to see a psychiatrist which he refused to do."

It is easy to imagine the couple talking far into the night, Watts, having begun to speak freely of his sexual distress, almost unable to stop talking, Eleanor too taken up with her own generosity to take in fully what he was trying to tell her. At one point he openly invited her to beat him, but she indignantly refused. He began to consider finding a woman who might respond to his needs, but the image most people had of the clergy made such requests difficult.

They struggled on with their insoluble sexual problem until

March 1947 when Eleanor became ill and took to her bed for a few days. Dorothy De Witt, the "Doddy" of Joy Buchan's diary, came to run the house. She was a very intelligent graduate student in mathematics who had become a close friend of both Watts and his wife and a regular babysitter for them, although Joan and Ann heartily disliked her.

> In June Alan told me that since that date [that is, her illness] he had been having relations with this young woman. I was stunned. As we had already been through the moral aspects of such affairs the previous year, I was at a loss to know how to handle this. We had already discussed the question of marriage and priesthood and he was not at all ignorant as to how I feel about such things. He admitted as much.

By this stage Watts had had enough of being humbled and told he was in the wrong. His painful confession had brought him no nearer a solution. He went over to the attack.

> [He] began seriously to question *my* state of mind and I discovered that he considered monogamous marriage to be quite out of date and unable to fulfill the "natural needs of the male." He then attacked me for my lack of understanding of "male nature" as well as what he chose to call my frigidity and prudishness. He assured me that he had never had any intention of remaining "true" to me and that my "ideals" were merely the produce of my own psychotic mind and that I was merely taking refuge in ancient codes to "excuse" my inability to adapt to modern ways. He was not the slightest bit repentant and absolutely refused to discuss his affairs with an older priest as he said that such a priest "could not be honest as he would have vested interests" to consider.

Watts by now felt certain that Eleanor could not help him, that the only way he could cope with his sexual needs was to look outside his marriage, a fairly desperate situation for someone whose job demanded monogamy and sexual circumspection. He began to nag Eleanor ceaselessly to change her "ideals" and Eleanor, in despair, consulted a priest herself, a Father Duncan. Father Duncan asked Watts to visit him, but Watts refused, and Duncan's recommendation to Eleanor was that she leave him. Explaining to Bishop Conkling why she did not do that, Eleanor remarked, piously, that

> I believed in his religious teaching and felt bound to save that at any cost. I was sure his priesthood would suffer if I left him and besides I considered myself a married woman and did not wish to run away from what I considered to be my responsibility to Alan. I realize now that I was quite wrong to attempt to protect him in this way. It was not honest, but the summer I had lived through with the pressure from Alan had so confused me that I thought perhaps he *was* right and that my "Ideals" might be as foolish and unreal as he considered them to be.

In fact during 1947 Eleanor had become friends with a music student, Carlton Gamer, ten years younger than herself. They had arranged that he would give her a weekly piano lesson in return for a Sunday dinner at the Wattses' house. Gradually Eleanor and Carlton discovered many tastes in common, she confided her unhappy marital situation to him, and before long the two of them had fallen in love. Eleanor reported this new development to Watts, obviously expecting him to behave like an outraged husband, only to discover that he seemed rather to like the idea. He even read her a little lecture about getting it right. "He hoped I would not make life miserable for Carlton by my frigidity and prudery and that as long as I gave up any idea of divorce, he could see no hindrance to an affair for us. . . . To my horror I discovered that he still expected me to fulfil my 'wifely obligations' to him, the fact that I was loved by another man being very stimulating to him."[6]

At Watts's suggestion both Carlton and Dorothy moved into Canterbury House; Joan was moved out of her bedroom to make this possible. It was a bizarre arrangement for any household, but particularly so for a clerical family in the 1940s. Joan still remembers trying to puzzle out why their home life seemed so different from other people's. Eleanor undoubtedly had a greater enthusiasm for this arrangement than appears in her disingenuous letter to Bishop Conkling in which she suggests that she only put up with it for the sake of helping Watts keep his job. In fact she and Watts went on a long motoring holiday to California with Carlton during the summer of 1948, and soon after that she became pregnant by Carlton. Watts cannot have been as content with the arrangement as Eleanor makes him appear. He knew that campus gossip, or Eleanor's growing bitterness, could destroy him. Although he did achieve sexual fulfillment, it was at the price of nagging worry and an impossible domestic arrangement.

In June 1948 Eleanor flew to New York to consult Ruth, who suggested that she pay another visit to the psychiatrist, Charles Taylor, who had helped her in the past. Taylor, Eleanor claimed, urged her to leave Alan and to remove the children from his influence.

She returned home with a challenge. Either Watts must receive psychiatric treatment, or she would leave him. Well aware that refusal meant that he would lose his job, since he was required to appear happily married, Watts did visit a psychiatrist, but soon showed that he had no intention of changing. He refused once again to accept the help of a fellow priest.

Michael, Eleanor's son by Carlton, was born in June 1949, an event both the Wattses' daughters remember with pain. Always ambivalent in her feelings about her daughters, particularly Ann, Eleanor suddenly switched all attention away from the two little girls and concentrated it on the longed-for son, perhaps in part to teach her husband that she no longer cared for him at all. Joan and Ann, already suffering in a difficult and bewildering situation, felt this loss of affection very acutely. Joan went away to boarding school at Versailles, Kentucky, while Ann continued unhappily with her mother.

Finally, in July 1949, Eleanor set off once again for New York to consult Ruth, Ruth's lawyer, and Dr. Taylor. All three of them recommended a divorce, and in September Eleanor finally left Watts, taking the three children with her to settle in New York with Ruth. She was in a dilemma. She wished to be free to marry Carlton and wanted the sort of divorce that proved the matrimonial fault to be Alan's, yet the birth of a child by another man made her seem other than the innocent victim she pretended to be. She could only vindicate her own actions by exaggerating the oddness of Watts's behavior. Father Taber, who, only a few years before, had encouraged Watts to become a priest, now thought that an annulment was the answer, so early in 1950 Eleanor went off to Reno and secured her annulment on the grounds that at the time of her marriage her husband had concealed from her that he was a "sexual pervert." (Alan's version of this in his autobiography was that the Nevada annulment was obtained on the grounds that he believed in "free love.") Anxious to absolve herself in Bishop Conkling's eyes Eleanor wrote,

> As far as I myself am concerned I can only say that throughout this affair I have acted in the only way I saw possible, wrong as that has been. I have constantly had the good of the Church in my mind although I have made dreadful mistakes in endeavoring to accomplish that good, nor have I understood in what that good consisted. However, I have made my peace with the Church and perhaps my honesty with my advisors here has been an important

factor in the mercy and consideration they have shown me, and the faith they have that I am ready for a "Christian marriage."[7]

Bishop Conkling had every faith in Father Taber's assessment of the situation. He was deeply touched at the thought of all that this wealthy penitent had endured and sent a sympathetic reply. Unfortunately, Carl Wesley Gamer, Carlton's father, saw it all very differently, and he in his turn wrote to the bishop. The Gamers had slowly become aware that their son did not wish to come home for vacations, that he preferred to spend his summers in Evanston, and in 1948 he announced that he was to go on a car trip through the western states with the Wattses, with all expenses paid by them. Only gradually did his parents discover that Carlton was living in a ménage à quatre, and at last they learned with horror that he had had a child with a married woman, ten years older than himself and the wife of a minister. Not unreasonably Carl Gamer felt that the Wattses had exploited his son while he was under 21, that Eleanor had seduced him, and her husband had connived at the fact. He considered bringing charges against Watts, especially after hearing from Carlton that in view of Eleanor's annulment there would now be no objection to a marriage, either civil or ecclesiastical. Father Taber had even pointed out the relevant canon to the couple that would allow them a church marriage.

Sickened by this piece of casuistry and determined to impede an unpromising marriage, Gamer senior attacked the church for its apparent complacency in Eleanor's conduct and suggested that even under the lenient law of Nevada, Eleanor could not have obtained an annulment if the full facts had been known to the court. In a letter to Bishop Conkling he writes, "Her annulment was a case of 'clear fraud' perpetrated upon a court. In addition to that, Eleanor by her affaire with Carlton, appears to have violated the criminal statutes of both Illinois and New York State and furthermore a federal statute which carries with it confinement in the penitentiary."[8]

Bishop Conkling was able to sidestep the issue of Eleanor's remarriage since it came under the jurisdiction of the bishop of New York, but Watts, on the other hand, was his concern.

As the situation worsened between him and Eleanor during 1949, Watts knew that it was only a matter of time before his private life was public knowledge. He had worked well and enthusiastically at his chaplain's job, and he dreaded the thought of the gossip and rumor, knowing it would destroy his career and uncover his private wounds. The humiliation of being the object of sexual gossip, the shock and disappointment of his parents, the surprise of friends and relatives who had believed the two of them to be happily married, the loss of his children, the bitter return to unemployment all made the future look hopeless. He continued alone at Canterbury House knowing that sooner or later the blow would fall.

Even before he received Eleanor's letter, Bishop Conkling had begun to hear rumors that the Wattses' marriage was breaking up, and he wrote to Watts in May of 1950 to ask for information. Was it true that Eleanor was divorcing him? He asked Watts to come to see him.

Watts, just back from a trip to Kentucky, to see Joan at boarding school, wrote that he hoped divorce would be avoidable. When he went to see the bishop, Watts managed to suggest that he and Eleanor were having a temporary separation, and that the marriage would continue.

By the end of June, when Eleanor wrote her long letter to Bishop Conkling, she had already secured her Reno annulment. Her letter blackened Watts successfully in the bishop's eyes, and he was touched by the picture of the suffering woman — until a few weeks later when he heard the Gamers' side of the story.

Regardless of who was to blame for what, it was plain enough to Watts that it was all up so far as his career in the church was concerned. His pride was badly hurt, and rather than waiting for processes of dismissal or even working out his resignation, he left Canterbury House for Thornecrest Farmhouse in Millbrook, New York, where a friend lent him a house. He took Dorothy with him. All the hard work and enthusiasm he had put into his work as chaplain was destroyed.

He was in no mood for penitence. Furious over what had happened, he wrote the bishop a long letter full of abrasive criticism of the church and its hypocrisy. He said that he had now decided to abandon not only the priesthood, but also the communion of the Episcopal church: "Part of the reason is that, having in mind both the proper care of my two girls and my own essential needs, I am quite sure that I must marry again."[9]

His original attraction to the priesthood, he says, had really been one of nostalgia, part of the common tendency to yearn for the securities of the past. Gradually, he had come to feel that the ancient forms of ritual, beautiful and profound as they were, no longer spoke effectively to modern men and women. His own ministry had enjoyed a kind of success because he had tried some original approaches, some of them borrowed from other spiritual traditions. Yet he was full of doubt about Christianity. "Somehow or other the language, the forms, of the Church are ceasing to be either relevant or communicative. Forms lose their power, perhaps because all material things die, or because the Spirit within them is breaking them as a bird breaks from its shell."

Spiritual life, he thought, now depended upon ceasing to cling to any form of security. "Forms are not contrary to the Spirit," he lectures his bishop, "but it is their nature to perish. I wish I could take this step without hurting the Church. For the Church is people — people whom I have learned to love. Yet for that very love, I cannot be a party to their hurting themselves and others by seeking security from forms which, if understood aright, are crying, 'Do not cling to us!' "

It is difficult to take these high-minded reasons for leaving the church at their face value when Watts had shown no signs of wishing to leave until his position became impossible — he had taken the church's money and preached its accepted wisdom fairly uncritically. Whatever truth in his observations, it seems too striking a coincidence that the church's value in general seemed to decline in Watts's eyes just at the moment that it rejected him.

The church's mistake, he said, was to insist that it was the "best of all ways to God." "Obviously one who has found a great truth is eager to share it with others. But to insist — often in ignorance of other revelations — that one's own is supreme argues a certain inferiority complex characteristic of all imperialisms." This claim to supremacy, anxiety for certainty, and wish to proselytize, seemed to him a tragic form of "self-strangulation."

In the letter he also returned to the idea that there was something strange and absurd about treating a clergyman as a "moral exemplar." It was "an aspect of that unfortunate moral self-consciousness which has so long afflicted our civilization."

It was no good telling people they ought to love and then blaming them if they couldn't do it, he added with feeling. "The moralism which condemns a man for not loving is simply adding strength to that sense of fear and insecurity which prevents him from loving. You may help him to love neither by condemning nor consoling, but by encouraging him to understand and accept the fear and insecurity which he feels." Instead of this healing acceptance he felt that Christian attitudes to sex had aggravated people's fear, had taught many to "foster a simulated love which is fear in disguise." This approach made the church's dealings with marriage clumsy and inept, more concerned with protecting a social institution than helping people to love.

He is not, he says, an antinomian.

> What I see is what life has shown me: that in fear I cling to myself, and that such clinging is quite futile. I have found that trying to stop this self-strangulation through discipline, belief in God, prayer, resort to authority and all the rest, is likewise futile. For trying not to be selfish, trying to realize an ideal, is simply the original selfishness in another form. I can understand worship as an act of thanksgiving for God's love, but the formularies of the Church make it all too plain that it is likewise to be understood as a means of spiritual self-advancement.
>
> The more clearly I see the futility of trying to raise myself by my own spiritual boot-straps (of which asking the grace to be raised is but an indirect form), the less choice I have in the matter: I cannot go on doing it. At a yet deeper level — the more I am aware of the futility of clinging to self. I have no choice but to stop clinging. And I find that in this choiceless bondage one is miraculously free. . . .
>
> I have no thought of trying to persuade anyone to "follow my example" and leave the Church likewise. You cannot act rightly by imitating the actions of another, for this is to act without understanding, and where there is no understanding the vicious circle continues. I have no wish to lead a movement away from the Church, or any such nonsense. If any leave, as I do, I trust they will do so on their own account, not from choice, not because they feel they "should," but only if, as in my own case, understanding makes it clear that, for them, there is no other alternative.

Watts continues by saying that he has no intention of joining any other religious body. He expects to devote his working time to writing and talking "because I love this work more than any other, and believe I have something to say which is worth saying."[10]

It was a startling letter for Bishop Conkling to receive. He must have felt rather as a judge might if he were to receive a moral lecture from a prisoner on whom he was about to pass sentence. Here was Watts, having committed adultery and encouraged his wife to commit adultery, causing a public scandal to the church, and running away from his job without asking leave, telling his bishop in no uncertain terms that the whole thing was the church's fault. Whether or not one agrees with his strictures, some of Watts's statements are movingly self-revelatory. If nothing else, he deserves top marks for cheek. With an amusing effrontery that Coyote might have affected, he appeared to saunter away from the encounter with the air of one who thinks he is the victor. Bishop Conkling was left to fret and fume, writing strong expressions in the margin of Watts's letter: "What conceit!!" "This is *not* true," "What does he mean by love?" "rationalizing for his own desire," and "a perverted man's perverted sight!" Surprisingly, in the end he wrote Watts a rather courteous letter.

My dear Alan,

Though your letter grieves me yet it is not a surprise. I do not believe there is any need for comment on your position. When an individual moves as far as you have from the group, words have little avail. Sometimes the individual proves to be a leader and to have a genius for truth; more often he shows himself in a much less complimentary position. . . . I am grateful for all you tried to do for good in your ministry and I commend you to the justice and mercy of God.

Sincerely yours, Wallace E. Conkling, The Bishop of Chicago.

Chicago, Illinois, July 5, 1950.[11]

Watts had robbed Bishop Conkling of any chance to dismiss him. He had already written his letter of resignation to the appropriate committee and had married Dorothy De Witt, an action that automatically secured excommunication, since in the eyes of the Church he was still married.

*Seven*

# A Priest Inhibited

## 1950-1951

WATTS AND HIS NEW WIFE moved to a temporary home, Thornecrest Farmhouse, in Millbrook, New York, in July 1950, "one of those archaic rural structures whose rooms are severe closetless boxes with small window-frames decaying from much painting."[1] It was bitterly cold that winter, and they found themselves spending much of their time in the kitchen to keep warm. Watts spent a lot of his day writing — letters to his friends and to others explaining or justifying the turn his life had taken, and a new book, to be called, appropriately enough, *The Wisdom of Insecurity.*

His financial situation seemed, at first, rather desperate. From being a rising young priest-theologian who had written a very good book about Christianity and was enormously in demand as a lecturer, he had suddenly become a pariah within the Christian community. He had lost his job and his income and the riches that accompanied life with Eleanor — after their annulment he had felt bound to return the stock she had made over to him. His studies and his natural inclination only fitted him for one thing: "to wonder . . . at the nature of the universe," as he put it. The difficulty was to see how to make a living at it. Very fortunately the writer Joseph Campbell intervened for Watts and got him a grant from the Bollingen Foundation, an institution founded on Lake Zurich by a wealthy patient of C. G. Jung, which was prepared to finance research in myth, psychology, Oriental philosophy, and many other subjects that interested Watts. The theme of his new book qualified for enough money to keep the Watts household for six months.

The new situation might have been easier if Watts had been deeply in love with Dorothy, but love was not one of his main reasons for marrying her. In the first place, what he felt for her was more of a sexual infatuation than a deep love. In the words of Joan and Ann, she "had a hold over him," perhaps because, unlike Eleanor, she was not too high-minded or inhibited to understand that part of his sexual drive was strongly sadomasochistic. He viewed their relationship with a mixture of fear and relief. Spared as he had been by Eleanor's money and by the care of his parents from any real need to come to terms with the more humdrum details of life, he also felt dependent on Dorothy's sheer practicality to help him through this difficult phase. Each of them, it seemed to him later, had hopes of "making over" the other into the person each *really* wanted to be married to. Finally, and most important, he believed that marriage gave him the opportunity to offer a home to Joan and Ann, whom he deeply loved. It is ironic that, even before his marriage, both of them loathed Dorothy, so much so that Joan, aged ten, solemnly and wisely warned him against it. Ann, in fact, had difficulty for years in believing that Watts had actually married "that woman," as she thought of her.

Dorothy, for her part, found herself in a most painful position. Whether or not she believed that Watts loved her, the glamorous young priest who had been so much admired at Northwestern and who had seemed an enviable lover, was suddenly a disgraced man without job or income. During the holidays she was saddled with Joan, who detested her. (Ann had gone to New York to live with Eleanor and her grandmother.) She had had to give up her own graduate work in mathematics and was stuck in a bleak farmhouse with an unhappy man uncertain of the future.

Even in adversity, however, Watts was good at enjoying whatever was to be enjoyed. During evenings and weekends he set himself to learn cooking, a skill he would be proud of all his life. He and Dorothy began to cook ambitious meals together to such an extent that they were able to serve an elegant Christmas feast of *pâté de veau en croûte* and turkey with chestnut stuffing to such house guests as the Campbells, their benefactors, Ananda Coomaraswamy's widow Luisa, and the composer John Cage.

Not a bitter man by nature, Watts was, however, angry about what he felt as his public disgrace, endlessly going over it all in his mind, explaining and justifying it all to others. Even when he came to write about it in his autobiography, over twenty years later, the details still rankled. He published the circular letter he had sent to his friends, itself a working over of the long exculpatory and critical letter he had sent to Bishop Conkling. The responses were various. The one he found most unforgettable, because of its tone of moral superiority, was from Canon Iddings Bell, the reviewer who had thought *Behold the Spirit* one of the half dozen most significant books of the century.

Canon Bell wrote reproachfully:

It is not easy, not possible, to undo spiritual commitments. You are a priest forever — and a priest inhibited. You think you can wipe our your ordination, restore that which was before your ordination, start all over. You can't. Life is not like that. What has been, still is.

I remain your friend, but I see no good in our seeing one another,

nor in correspondence, at least for as long as you are able to persuade yourself that you are content. If ever this becomes no longer
possible, call on me and count on an understanding response.[2]

Penitence was a price Watts had no intention of paying. He
replied, saying that he knew perfectly well that he was always a
priest, but "I have no thought whatever of going back to a former
state, or making a fresh start." There is an insecurity, he suggests,
to be welcomed by those who will not use religion as a guarantee
of safety: "One may embrace this kind of insecurity as a gesture
of adolescent bravado. One may also embrace it, because, having
seen the futility of other courses, there is nothing else to do. As a
result I feel my priesthood to be uninhibited rather than, as form-
erly, inhibited."[3]

Other clerical friends were shocked at his suggestion that
Christianity might have anything to learn from other religions.
"There are many religions. There is but one gospel," wrote one of
them. "Religions are man's search for God; the gospel is God's
search for men." To which Watts replied that he believed Christ
was not the only incarnation of God: "The identical theme of
God's search for man is the essence of the Hindu doctrine of the
Avatars, and the Buddhist Bodhisattvas. For me they are all in-
carnations of 'the only begotten Son'."[4]

Another correspondent, Theodore Green, wrote warmly of
Watts's new position, a letter without judgment or criticism,
which Watts quoted in his autobiography.

As a layman in the church I have been in doubt again and again
as to whether my proper course should be to remain in the church,
and, in all humility, try to fight its multiple failures and abuses, or
whether I should leave it and join the vast army of the unchurched.
Rightly or wrongly I still feel that I should take the first course and
that is what I am doing, although with great misgivings at times.

Meanwhile, you have a tremendous contribution to make as a scholar and teacher from your new vantage point.[5]

Depressed as he was, and disillusioned both about himself and the world that had rejected him so resoundingly, Watts began to think more about God and about the God-filled person "wholly free from fear and attachment." Such a person was to be envied, he thought.

> We, too, would like to be one of those, but as we start to meditate and look into ourselves we find mostly a quaking and palpitating mess of anxiety which lusts and loathes, needs love and attention, and lives in terror of death putting an end to its misery. So we despise that mess, and put "how the true mystic feels" in its place, not realizing that this ambition is simply one of the lusts of the quaking mess, and that this, in turn, is a natural form of the universe like rain and frost, slugs and snails.[6]

The blessing that came to him in his distress was the realization that his own "quaking mess," as he called it, was natural, even a part of the divine. What he needed to do was live it, not fight against it. Eleanor's departure had released him forever from the need to pretend to be something he wasn't, a "respectable" person as defined by the mores of his time. "I am a mystic in spite of myself," he wrote, "remaining as much of an irreducible rascal as I am, as a standing example of God's continuing compassion for sinners or, if you will, of Buddha-nature in a dog, or light shining in darkness. Come to think of it, in what else could it shine?"[7]

It was this new insight that Watts explored movingly in his new book, which was dedicated to Dorothy, his partner in insecurity. Swinging sharply away from Christianity he suggests that it is not dogma but wonder that is the window on life. Writing out of his own uncertainty he says that "salvation and sanity consist in the most radical recognition that we have no way of saving ourselves."[8] Instead of the pitiful human tricks to avoid insecurity by clinging to one idol or another, and in particular to the idols buried in the heart of religion, the answer is to embrace insecurity by living each moment intensely as it happens.

In a desperate attempt to avoid the moments of pain and to know only pleasure, the Western mind had fallen into a tragic duality in which body and mind were dangerously split. Body, with its fine instinctual wisdom, had become the enemy of "will," the device with which we fondly imagine insecurity can be defeated. The body became both feared and despised, "Brother Ass," as Saint Francis dubbed it and as many Christian saints had experienced it. But to lose touch with the body, said Watts, is to lose touch with our real feelings and emotions, and to sink into an "insatiable hunger" for possessions, food, drink, sexuality without tenderness, and crude sensation of all kinds. The answer is to rediscover the rhythms and wisdom of the body, to help it to live naturally and spontaneously. Aiming at security "means to isolate and fortify the 'I,' but it is just the feeling of being an isolated I which makes me feel lonely and afraid."[9]

Watts was beginning to speak in the voice that would become famous in the sixties, a voice that would speak for the loneliness and alienation of many. The loss of his clerical career was pushing Watts back to a rediscovery of his old Buddhist beliefs.

*Eight*

# The Wisdom of Insecurity
## 1951 -1960

IN FEBRUARY 1951 Alan Watts and Dorothy drove westward, away from the harsh winter of the East, heading for Los Angeles and eventually San Francisco. On the earlier visit, with Eleanor and Carlton, Watts had been captivated by California. Now it delighted him all over again as he came upon the Mojave desert, the palm trees and dates of Indio, the misty San Bernardino range, finally Los Angeles itself. There Aldous Huxley and Christopher Isherwood had set up a meeting for him with Isherwood's guru Swami Prabhavananda and his Vedantist followers. Predictably Watts disagreed with the swami's emphasis on asceticism, sexual continence, and will power, and he mischievously let it drop that he thought orgasm was analogous, if not in some sense identical with, *samadhi*, or mystical experience. The swami's response was equally predictable; he was dismayed at the idea that enlightenment might come without effort and discipline.

In early March the Wattses passed through the country between Los Angeles and San Francisco, where Watts was overwhelmed by the beauty of the Santa Lucia range of mountains. At Big Sur he stopped to call on Henry Miller (who was away), but he fell in love with Partington Ridge, with its waterfalls, aromatic herbs and hay — "sage, wild thyme, sorrel, Indian Paintbrush, and acres of dangerous fire-prone golden grass three to four feet high, amidst which one can sometimes discover rattlesnake grass with its light, fragile, and airy heads designed like the rattlesnake's tail, or like those Japanese fish ornaments."[1]

From there they continued on to San Francisco itself, where an old London acquaintance, Frederic Spiegelberg, had had the idea of setting up what he called the American Academy of Asian Studies and had invited Watts to join him. The plan, as understood by the backers, was that the academy should be an information service at graduate level, an independent school granting master's and doctor's degrees, that would meet the new American interest in all things Asian. Its offerings would include Asian languages, art, histories, politics, and religion taught at a more practical level than the more formal Oriental departments at existing universities. Businessmen, government officials, teachers, and interested travelers would, it was thought, benefit from such courses, and initially funds came from such business, which set the academy up in the financial district of San Francisco.

At heart, however, both Spiegelberg and Watts had a more ambitious plan, nothing less, in Watts's words, than "the practical transformation of human consciousness."[2]

With the latter rather than the former plan secretly in mind they built up the staff of the new academy. Prof. Haridas Chaudhuri came from the University of Calcutta. Sir C. P. Ramaswamy Aiyar, previously dewan of the state of Travancore, was another recruit, "a princely man, close to seventy, who somehow reminded one of the elephant god Ganesha."[3] Judith Tyberg, who came to teach Sanskrit and yoga, a Japanese lama, Tokwan Tada, the Polish/English writer Rom Landau, who taught Islamic studies, and a Thai scholar who was also a princess — Poon Pismai Diskul — made up the rest of the staff.

Watts, for whom six months previously life had looked so grim, had found himself a paying job that couldn't have been more congenial to him in a climate and part of the world that he found a joy to live in. He, Dorothy, Joan (during her school vacations), and Ann moved briefly to Palo Alto, and then to a house on Woodside Drive off Skyline Boulevard. When the children first saw it they loved it; it was a log cabin surrounded by woods where they could play at tracking and camping, a magical place where their imaginations could run free.

In other ways the children's lives were not so happy. The two of them, ten and six years old, while visiting Ruth's house in New York, had been summoned separately to the library of the brownstone and asked to choose which parent they wanted to live with. The pain was acute. Joan described it this way:

> It was like being asked to choose between the devil and the deep blue sea. We loved our father; he had been most caring towards us during the difficult times at Evanston. If ever our parents were going anywhere, Eleanor was always the one who didn't let us come; basically she didn't want us around. Whereas Alan always said, "Sure, come along." Even though we couldn't stand Dorothy we still had this tremendous feeling of our father loving us, and I am sure that colored our choice — we both chose to live with him. We moved in with him and Dorothy, and Dorothy proceeded to live up to our worst fears. She was terrible.

Dorothy was a good housekeeper, with stern Pennsylvania Dutch standards of cleanliness and order, no sense of humor, and no feeling for, or real experience of, the way small children saw the world. Both Ann and Joan were already very unhappy at their parents' divorce, and Ann had spent some wretched months with

Eleanor and Michael at Ruth's house. Eleanor continued to ignore her in favor of Michael and to find her naughtiness intolerable.

Although both Ann and Joan chose to live with their father, they were bitterly resentful of Dorothy. They pitted their youthful strength against her, seeing her as their cruel stepmother, defying her when they dared, avoiding her, doing all that they knew to disrupt the household and damage the relationship between her and their father. During this time, Dorothy was pregnant and when the pregnancy ended in a miscarriage, she blamed the children, who felt all the more angry and wretched for being made to feel guilty. When Dorothy gave birth to a daughter, Tia, the situation felt to Ann and Joan like a repetition of Michael's birth.

Joan hated to go off to boarding school and leave her little sister alone with Dorothy. And just as though she were living out the Cinderella story, Ann bore the burden of Dorothy's misery and despair. In a sort of dumb insolence Ann found a phonograph record of the Cinderella story and played it over and over again in Dorothy's hearing, a ploy that enraged her stepmother.

There were escapes from the nightmare for Ann, partly into the blessed world of school, partly, as she began to read, into the fantasy world of books. She had some children's books with beautiful illustrations given her by Ruth and by her parents, and alone in her room, or late at night in bed, she would pore over them for hours. One of the new hardships of her life, though, was that as she grew older, Dorothy expected her to do a large share of the household chores. At the age of eight she was forced to do all her own personal laundry, to wash up alone after dinner parties given by Dorothy and Alan, to make all the beds before going to school, so firmly and perfectly that you could "bounce a fifty-cent piece off them," and to iron shirts to an almost professional standard. She had become, in her own words, "a little workhorse."

There were wells in the desert, however. Sometimes Watts, who knew how to set up a treat, would take her alone with him to a restaurant, usually where the cooking was exotic, and feeling very grown-up and proud to be out with him, she would loyally develop tastes for strange kinds of food. When she was ill her father could be very kind to her, bringing her hot toddies, reading to her, playing with her. As a result she longed to be ill and tried to bring it about by standing out in the rain without a coat. Sometimes he would take her with him to the academy where she wandered about happily, talking to faculty and students while Watts lectured or went to meetings. Maybe people at the academy perceived something about her unchildlike sadness and her need for love. In particular, Watts's secretary Lois became a friend and used to take her out on expeditions, treating her, to her delight, as if she were grown up. She received the love and attention eagerly, drawing from it an element of sanity that seemed missing from her family life.

At home Ann's relationship with Dorothy continued to deteriorate. One day there was a row between Watts and Dorothy after which Dorothy herself began to cry. This offended Ann's childish sense of logic, and she at once marched into Watts's study and demanded how it was that Dorothy was allowed to cry if she was not permitted to do so. It was really a way to tell her father about the pain of her present life and to get a response from him, but Watts just shrugged his shoulders and said, "Oh, that's just women, I guess!" Ann went back to her room bitterly let down and felt that at that moment she gave up any expectation of real help and understanding from her father: "I just thought, it's not gonna happen. He just isn't going to be a father." Child as she was, she dimly perceived that there was something unreal in Watts's attitude to women, that he was sometimes afraid of them, allowing them to behave tyrannically towards him, and that he would not stand up either for himself or for his children.

Joan too was having problems with her father at the time. She remembers waiting at school with other girls to be fetched for a half-term vacation. One by one the others disappeared with relatives, until it gradually became obvious that no one was coming to fetch her. Out of kindness a teacher offered to take her home for the holiday.

Watts had distanced himself both from Dorothy and from his responsibilities as a father. For most of his waking hours he was busy at the academy or with friends.

The academy was attracting students. It was a simple building of classrooms and offices, with a library largely stocked with books from Watts's huge collection. Many of the pupils who came were artists or poets, and once a week Spiegelberg held a colloquium in which there was intense discussion about the contributions of East and West, the nature of the self, methods of meditation, and other such ideas that had interested Watts for years. Watts pushed the idea, which some of his Asian colleagues already believed, that "the egocentric predicament was not a moral fault to be corrected by willpower, but a conceptual hallucination requiring some basic alterations of common sense." Chaudhuri said that the illusion of the isolated, separate ego could only be overcome by yoga and meditation. Watts replied that to try to unseat the ego by summoning up its own strength and resources to help you to do it was like trying to lift yourself off the ground; it couldn't be done. Methods of meditation, he said, only worked if they showed the ego and its will to be unreal. Fellow members of the faculty affectionately accused him of laziness.

The school was turning out to be a wonderful meeting ground

for unusual and interesting people. A group of artists, including Jean Varda and the surrealist Gordon Onslow-Ford, attended the academy, and so later on did Michael Murphy and Richard Price, the founders of Esalen. The poet Gary Snyder was among the pupils. Snyder was later described by Watts as "a wiry sage with high cheek-bones, twinkling eyes, and a thin beard, and the recipe for his character requires a mixture of Oregon woodsman, seaman, Amerindian shaman, Oriental scholar, San Francisco hippie, and swinging monk, who takes tough discipline with a light heart. He seems to be gently keen about almost everything, and needs no affectation to make himself interesting."[4] He had read the prospectus of the academy in a journal of Asian studies and thought it seemed worth looking at. He had studied anthropology and linguistics in Indiana and had decided to attend the University of California for graduate studies in classical Chinese and contemporary Japanese. He went to hear Watts lecture, got talking to another man in the audience, Claud Dahlenberg, who later joined the San Francisco Zen Center, and as a result got taken along to the academy and began to attend Watts's lectures.

From the beginning Watts and Snyder got on very well. Because there were still few students, Watts had plenty of time to talk and to enjoy informal meetings. He was, at this stage, Snyder remembers, "very straight, very British, short hair, necktie." On Friday nights the two of them started going to a study group at the Berkeley British Church; one night Watts drove Snyder home from a meeting and they finished a bottle of wine together and talked deeply about Buddhism. The friendship really took off, however, when Snyder sent Watts a letter on some points of discussion between them and wrote it in italic calligraphy. Calligraphy, one of Watts's great enthusiasms, became another shared pleasure between them like their interest in classical Chinese. Details of translation and interpretation became a running topic between them, and at Watts's invitation, Snyder gave readings of his Chinese translations at the academy. His relationship with Watts at this time, he remembers, was comfortable, respectful on his part, the relationship of a pupil with a good teacher.

Another of Watts's students at this time was Lock McCorkle, later to be a key man in est. McCorkle, like a number of other students at the academy, was a pacifist; he was fighting a jail sentence for resisting the draft, and Watts gave evidence in his defense in court.

Watts was excited by the originality and intellectual vitality of his students. One of them, Leo Johnson,

> had been haunting the University of California in Berkeley as a voracious reader and auditor of courses without the slightest interest in credits, examinations or degrees. . . . He was . . . simply interested in knowledge. His material ambitions were minimal; he lived in extreme simplicity; such money as he had went mostly for books, which he gave away; he had a ribald, bawdy, belly-laugh attitude to life which came out at unexpected moments, and was so informed with intellectual expertise that it was a real risk to expose him to scholarly company. . . . Leo impressed upon me the important idea that the ego was neither a spiritual, psychological, or biological reality but a social institution of the same order as the monogamous family, the calendar, the clock, the metric system, and the agreement to drive on the right or left of the road. He pointed out that at such times such social institutions became obsolete . . . and that the "Christian ego" was now plainly inappropriate to the ecological situation into which we were moving.[5]

Another student, Pierre Grimes, had been "nurtured on Plato," but in working with Watts

> he had graduated to Nagarjuna and began very practical experiments with that great Mahayanist's philosophy. He saw that Na-

garjuna's method was a dialectical process that went far beyond sophistry and intellectual acrobatics, and could be used as a very powerful instrument for what I had in mind — namely, the dissolution of erroneous concepts felt as precepts. Pierre devised an encounter group on the metaphysical level. That is to say, he worked out a situation in which the participants would probe for each other's basic assumptions, or axioms, about life, and then demonstrate that they were no more than assumptions; not truths, but arbitrary game-rules. This dialectic was as traumatic for a logical positivist as for a Hegelian, for as basic assumptions crumbled, members of the group would begin to show intense anxiety. He would then probe for still deeper assumptions underlying the anxiety until he could bring the group to a state of consciousness in which they could happily relax, and abandon the frustrating and futile project of trying to make a false hypothesis called "I," on the one hand, get mastery over another false hypothesis called "experience" or "the world," on the other. The process seemed extraordinarily therapeutic both for Pierre himself and for those who worked with him. I had feared that he would become a scornful, prickly intellectual, but he turned out to be a man of singular compassion and humor, as well as of good sense in the practical matters of life.[6]

The academy was an arena in which people asked the hardest questions about living; it was a long way from the "information service" it had once purported to be. But its success in touching spiritual and philosophical depths did not help it financially. In the autumn of 1952 the "angel" who had maintained it thus far ran out of funds and could no longer pay the salaries. Frederic Spiegelberg resigned as director and went to teach at Stanford. But Watts, "having nothing else to do, decided that the Academy was an adventure too interesting to be abandoned, and slipped by default into the position of its administrator." The academy moved from the financial district to a rambling old mansion on Broadway in Pacific Heights. For another four years Watts managed to keep this offbeat and exciting project alive. He invited many interesting people to lecture, among them D. T. Suzuki, G. P. Malalaskera, Buddhist scholar and diplomat, Bhikku Pannananda from Thailand, the Zen master Asahina Sogen, the Thera Dharmawara from Cambodia, and his ex-mother-in-law, Ruth Fuller Sasaki, "who entranced the whole student body with her formal and definitive lecture on the use of koan in Zen meditation." It was as a result of Ruth's visit, and Watts's introduction of Gary Snyder to her, that Snyder was later given a scholarship grant to take him to Japan.

San Francisco was, in many ways, an ideal setting for the academy. Faculty and students visited, on the warmest terms, with the Chinese Buddhist community of San Francisco. Japanese Buddhists in the city also became deeply involved with the academy. Hodo Tobase, a Zen master at the Soto Zen temple on Bush Street, taught calligraphy at the academy, his assistant priest gave Watts lessons on Zen texts, and another Zen master, Shunryu Suzuki, saw the possibilities of developing "Western Zen" on the West Coast and went on to found San Francisco Zen Center. On one occasion Watts took a whole party of students on a "joy ride" to visit Krishnamurti at Ojai, camping at night on a beach at Carpinteria, with fires of driftwood.

In 1952 Laurence and Emily visited Alan and Dorothy and were distressed at the relationship between Dorothy and Ann, and were even more distressed at Ann's state of physical and psychological health. Ann, at ten years old, was afflicted with gastric ulcers. In a recent episode, Dorothy had given away all of Ann's books as a punishment for reading in bed at night. Gently, Laurence and Emily suggested a way out — that Ann might come to live with them in England — and so Ann returned with them to Rowan

Cottage. This was the beginning of a much happier time for Ann. Emily, who had so longed for a daughter, poured love and care on the little girl, who felt as if she was allowed to be a child for the first time in her life. She stayed with her grandparents for the next eight years, going to school at Farrington's, behind the garden at Rowan Cottage.

In 1953 Watts, Dorothy, Joan, and Tia moved to Mill Valley in Marin County. There was a big garden — a former garden nursery — with a big lawn, four great pine trees, twenty-seven fruit trees, a stream, cats and chickens, nice neighbors, a Volkswagen bus in which to transport the children, and a big library.

Dorothy, according to Watts, had very much wanted the suburban life, and it may be that he relished its comforts more than he later cared to remember. In any case the move to new surroundings was a distraction from the real difficulties of the marriage, from Dorothy's resentment that Watts was away for most waking hours and for some of the sleeping ones too. He was at the academy, or he was out with friends, or he was broadcasting on the Berkeley radio station KPFA or appearing on the educational television station KQED. In addition, Dorothy was suspicious, with good cause, that he was unfaithful to her with other women. She had reason to be bitter, not least because she was expecting another child, Mark, and she enjoyed very little of her husband's care and attention.

In 1954 the Japanese artist and printmaker Sabro Hasegawa visited the academy, and Watts was so delighted by his personality and his skills as a lecturer and teacher that he immediately invited him to join the staff. Not only was he a fine teacher of *sumi-e* (spontaneous ink painting derived from Zen practice), but he also became a kind of informal therapist for the faculty.

He was, among other things, a tea master, and when Watts and Lois were becoming intolerably harassed by administrative problems he would wander into their office and suggest that they take time out for tea. Then in Hasegawa's room, "where the enshrined image of the Buddha was a piece of driftwood that had originally been the lathe-turned leg of a very ordinary wooden chair," the three of them would sit on the floor, and "with easy conversation, watch him spoon powdered green tea into a primitive Korean rice-bowl, cover it with boiling water from a bamboo ladle, and then whisk it into a potion which has been called 'the froth of the liquid jade'."[7] Lois used to say that one tea with Hasegawa was worth fifteen visits to a psychiatrist.

The friendship between Watts and Hasegawa went deep. When, a few years later, Hasegawa died of cancer, Watts unofficially became guardian to his daughter Sumire, acting as confidant and adviser. Because of the calm and wisdom of Hasegawa, Watts also took to wearing a kimono and found it much more comfortable than formal Western clothing.

The influence of the academy had brought Watts full circle back to his early passion for Zen. In 1956 he wrote *The Way of Zen* (published the next year), perhaps his most famous book, and dedicated it to "Tia, Mark and Richard who will understand it all the better for not being able to read it." (Richard was the Watts's newborn baby.) It covered some of the same ground as *The Spirit of Zen*, written twenty years before, but it had the benefit of all the Chinese studies he had worked at since.

In his preface he says firmly that he does not want to get himself labeled as a "Zenist or even as a Buddhist, for this seems to me to be like trying to wrap up and label the sky."[8] It is more that he wants Western readers to take pleasure in Zen, to enjoy its art and its literature, and to borrow any ideas that might be of service to them in leading their own lives. He longs to see Westerners give the same respect to the "peripheral mind" as they do to conscious intelligence, and part of that process is to go back to the Taoist beliefs, which preceded Zen Buddhism, with their clear certainty that "the natural man is to be trusted."

The freedom that lies in Zen is the discovery that we deny our own freedom by determinedly manufacturing our own ego, with all its attendant problems, from moment to moment. "Man is involved in karma when he interferes with the world in such a way that he is compelled to go on interfering, when the solution of a problem creates still more problems to be solved, when the control of one thing creates the need to control several others." The remedy is an "insight and awakening" that suggests an alternative, a way to get off the roundabout. "Sitting" meditation is not a spiritual exercise, it is simply "the proper way to sit," a method without ulterior motive, an action performed, like all Zen actions — like eating, or walking, or shitting, or yawning — for its own sake. As always with Watts, the thing that matters most is getting rid of the subjective distinction between "me" and "my experience," the painful dualistic split: "The individual, on the one hand, and the world, on the other, are simply the abstract limits or terms of a concrete reality which is 'between' them, as the coin is 'between' the surface of its two sides."[9]

By 1956 Watts realized that he could not make the academy work financially and that he was becoming bored with academic and administrative life. Dorothy was perpetually angry with him, with good reason, and with some idea of making a fresh start with her he decided to take up the free-lance life. Although she supported him in his resolve to work independently, he felt that she was putting pressure on him "to suburbanize myself, to live a more ordinary life, to mow the lawn, play baseball with the children, and abandon my far-out bohemian friends." The return to the job wilderness was not without pain. There was again the sense of failure, "voices from the past echoing in my skull: Alan, why can't you be like everyone else? Why are you so weird? Why don't you come down to earth and face reality?"[10] But all the same, in the spring of 1957 he resigned from the academy (which tottered on for a year or two before collapsing) and thenceforward would earn his living as a writer and as a peripatetic teacher, lecturer, broadcaster, philosopher, and entertainer. Meanwhile, Dorothy had given birth to another child, Richard.

The longing to write that had helped precipitate Watts's resignation from the academy soon found expression in a new book — *Nature, Man and Woman*. It discussed the duality of mind and body that Christian spirituality had so often unconsciously encouraged. In the Western tradition woman was often depicted as "Eve," the temptress leading men away from God into sin; by projection she had become synonymous with "the flesh" or "the body," and sexuality itself was seen as a regrettable lapse into weakness for those who had not the strength and determination to be celibate.

Watts believed that a new approach to sexuality could transform it. Neither man nor woman had to be seen as a lonely abstract entity wandering like an orphan through the world. Rather, each should be considered part of the very fabric or expression of the world, so love-making becomes one part of nature recognizing another part, while also recognizing that other part as itself.

One problem, he said, was that we are afraid to let go of the "chronic cramp of consciousness," the narrowed, serial thinking, the memory-stored stream of impressions that give us a sense of "ego," which gives us the feeling that we are, as it were, the driver of the machine. But the same ego inflicts upon us an awkward loneliness, a self-consciousness, a separateness that inhibits joy. We need, Watts thinks, to recognize that the ego is no more than a convenient fiction, to learn an awareness that is diffuse and comprehensive rather than sharp and selective, and to discover that there is no longer the "duality of subject and object, experiencer and experience. There would simply be a continuous, self-moving stream of experiencing, without the sense either of an active subject who controls it or of a passive subject who suffers it. The thinker would be seen to be no more than the series of thoughts, and the feeler no more than the feelings."[11]

Such an outlook makes possible a spontaneity of feeling, where the "organism is no longer split into the natural animal and the controlling ego. The whole being is one with its own spontaneity and feels free to let go with utmost abandon. Pain, which we have been taught to avoid, and pleasure, which we have learned to seek, become indistinguishable in orgiastic response. Shame, on the other hand, is part of the frightened opposition of the conscious will, the ego, to that which it cannot control."[12]

After writing at length of the release of feeling and of ecstasy, Watts goes on to look at the relation between man and woman.

For Watts the union of two lovers is the overcoming of *maya*, the illusion of duality and separateness. Without fear, shame, or desperate need for gratification, the two gain a glimpse of a real, rather than an ideal, vision of how things are. Their vision, not just of each other, but of the world, can be transformed: "Sexual contact irradiates every aspect of the encounter, spreading its warmth into work and conversation outside the bounds of actual 'love-making'." Within love-making duality may be overcome: "At a particular but unpredetermined moment they may take off their clothes as if the hands of each belonged to the other. The gesture is neither awkward nor bold; it is the simultaneous expression of a unit beneath the masks of social roles and proprieties. . . . There is not the slightest compulsion to assume a pretended character."[13]

In the spring of 1958 Watts was invited to Zurich to give lectures at the C. G. Jung Institute. It was his first visit to Europe since he had left England as a young man twenty years before. Photographs show him still slim and youthful looking at forty-three, with a short haircut.

En route he went back to Chislehurst. He enjoyed visiting the cottage with the enormous garden he had loved as a little boy, and Chislehurst itself was still the same small country town surrounded by woods, ponds, and common land. There were still the same advertisements printed on sheets of metal at Chislehurst station — for Stephens' ink and Palethorpe's sausages — the old high street contained the same sweet shop, the chemist's shop still run by the same owners, and he could still walk across the green and round by the ancient church for a drink with his father at the Tiger's Head. Even the vegetables grown by his parents had the same delicious taste that he remembered from the past — twenty years of heavy smoking had not completely spoiled his taste buds.

Despite the delights he had mixed feelings about being back in England. He had always enjoyed the company of Laurence, now retired from business. But Emily, despite her love and care for him, still filled him with ambivalence, the more distressing since most of his relatives considered her very lovable and could not understand the emotions she aroused in him. He could only reflect that he had always felt that she hated her own body, felt cold to him, and had seemed physically unattractive for as far back as he could remember; he felt a fear in her presence and a sense of the impossibility of living up to her expectations.

England itself, after so long an absence, also felt like a chilly mother. It was peaceful, but weary, obsessed with its imperial past. He spoke in Cambridge at the invitation of the Departments of Theology, Anthropology and Oriental Studies and found them a dull and unimaginative audience. He felt hurt that none of his books seemed to be read much in his native country.

He went to London and lunched with Christmas Humphreys and D. T. Suzuki, both of them his boyhood mentors at the Buddhist Society, and he had his photograph taken with the pair of them, looking, beside the patrician High Court judge and the twinkling little Japanese, a rather ambiguous figure not quite at his ease, neither solidly British anymore, nor unequivocally American.

Zurich, somewhat to his surprise, turned out to be much more fun. Watts talked about the Hindu doctrine of *maya*, suggesting that the illusion of duality arose not from the evidence of the senses but from our mistaken concepts. The mystic, or enlightened person, lived in the same natural world as everyone else but saw it differently. He had got past the riddle of duality and regarded himself not as separate from the rest of the world but as part of it.

Watts enjoyed the audience, composed partly of the young studying to be psychotherapists and partly the company of "elderly, refined, and extremely well-educated ladies of formidable appearance who set the tone of the Institute."[14] He felt, however, that he rather blotted his copybook by going about Zurich with a young woman, called Sonya, a former patient who had been abandoned by the Jungians as hopelessly psychotic.

The high spot of his visit was the trip out to Jung's lakeside home at Küsnacht. The old man began with one of his favorite gambits, assuring Watts that he himself was not a Jungian, and then the two of them got down to a subject of mutual interest — Oriental philosophy. They discussed the concept of the unconscious, Watts suggesting its similarity to the Mahayana Buddhist term *alaya-vijnana*, the "store consciousness," which, like Jung's "collective unconscious," was the origin of archetypal forms or images. Watts also remembered how Suzuki had sometimes translated the Japanese term *mushin* (*no mind*) as *the unconscious*, meaning by it a sort of aware unselfconsciousness.

They went on to talk of the effects computers might have on human psychology and finished by discussing a pair of swans they could see on the lake.

"Isn't it true," Watts asked, "that swans are monogamous?" Jung said that yes they were, but the odd thing about their first mating was that they invariably began by picking a fight, which was resolved when they worked out the method of mating.[15]

Watts found Jung open, eager, without conceit, full of humor and intellectual curiosity.

When Watts returned to the United States *Nature, Man and Woman* had just come out, and it was enthusiastically reviewed. There was, however, a sad irony in his publishing a book about sexual intimacy and the union of lovers. He and Dorothy were by now barely on speaking terms; the experiences that had begun to release him from his old sexual fears had mostly been with other women. He had discovered that many desirable women found him attractive and lovable and that he could be a successful lover, neither awkward nor frightened, nor ashamed. Only at home did he feel captive and wretched, emotions that he chose to blame more and more on the suburban atmosphere of Mill Valley, where he had taken on the expenses of luxurious family life. Bitter that he was not free to do as he wished, he complained that life at home was like something out of *Sunset* magazine: "picture windows of the ranch-type house, the outdoor barbecue, the children playing ball on the lawn, the do-it-yourself projects of tiling the bathroom and putting up shelves, and the station-wagoning of loads of sun-browned and quarrelsome papooses and brats to picnics on the beaches or marshmallow roasts in state parks."[16]

In 1959 Gary Snyder returned from Kyoto and borrowed a log cabin from a friend in Homestead Valley, in walking distance of Watts's home. At once the two men resumed the friendship begun at the academy. Snyder took out one of the walls of his cabin, put in an altar stone, and made a small *zendo*. Watts, with other friends, came over two or three nights a week to sit *zazen*. From December 1 to 8 they sat *rohatsu sesshin* (a winter marathon of *zazen*) together.

On New Year's Eve, Snyder was invited to a party at Mill Valley given by Watts and Dorothy. Snyder liked Dorothy — he thought her intelligent, clear, and cool; she ran the household on orderly and immaculate lines and seemed a good mother. He observed, however, that she and Alan did not behave like a couple. Watts was out most evenings at parties alone and seemed detached from home and family. It struck him that Watts was still very much part of the affluent bourgeois life, often formally dressed, refusing marijuana when it was passed to him at parties. "He had not yet," Snyder decided, "shifted gears into counterculture."

Watts was, in fact, in the agonizing dilemma of those who know that their marriage is a disaster, but who have not quite summoned the courage and strength needed for separation and divorce. Watts now had four children by Dorothy — Tia, Mark, Richard, and Lila — in addition to Joan and Ann. He knew that his income was and would remain uncertain, that Dorothy would, naturally enough, expect substantial financial guarantees in the event of a divorce, and that would mean that, however hard he worked, he would be a poor man. As painful as any of these worries was the sense of being once again a failure. "He was one," Snyder remarks mildly, "who sowed problems wherever he went."

Watts wrote about the problem later, in self-justifying terms:

> It is well known that — for men especially — the forties are a "dangerous" decade, because if they have been well brought up, it takes them this long to realize that one sometimes owes it to other people to be selfish. . . . Dutiful love is invariably, if secretly, resented by both partners to the arrangement, and children raised in so false an atmosphere are done no service. . . . Permanence may fairly be expected of marriages contracted and families raised under the ancient system of parental arrangements for then the partners are not required to feel romantic love for each other. But modern marriage involves the impossible anomaly, the contradiction in terms of basing a legal and social contract on the essentially mystical and spontaneous act of falling in love. The partners to such folly are sometimes lucky, and that is the best that can be said for it. They may sometimes become wise in the ways of the human heart by suffering each other, but such wisdom may also be learned in a concentration camp.[17]

Watts was spending nearly all of his time away from home and was drinking heavily, vodka mostly. In *The Wisdom of Insecurity* he had written poignantly of the plight of the alcoholic:

> In very many cases he knows quite clearly that he is destroying himself, that for him, liquor is poison, that he actually hates being drunk, and even dislikes the taste of liquor. And yet he drinks. For, dislike it as he may, the experience of not being drunk is worse. It gives him the "horrors" for he stands face to face with the unveiled, basic insecurity of the world. Herein lies the crux of the matter. To stand face to face with insecurity is still not to understand it. To understand it, you must not face it but *be it*.[18]

The "horror" had moved closer to Watts since he had written those words, nearly ten years before.

Ironically he was increasingly in demand as a broadcaster, seminar speaker, and lecturer, gaining a reputation all over the country as someone who could tell people how to live. He tried to insist that he was a "philosophical entertainer," "in show biz," "a genuine fake," and an "irreducible rascal," perhaps to help him endure the sense of hypocrisy that his fame gave him, but most of his listeners were no more than mildly puzzled by such statements, perhaps thinking them a sign of a rare sort of humility.

Watts was doing a lot of teaching in New York. In the late fifties Charlotte Selver was giving remarkable seminars there on bodily awareness, using techniques to teach people to notice their own bodies and to be more acutely aware of the world around them, and she and Watts began to teach together in a particularly lively series of seminars. One student at these seminars in 1960, a woman of around Watts's own age, was Mary Jane Yates — Jano, as she liked to be called — and gradually she and Watts started to see a lot of one another. Together they drank and dined in Greenwich Village, exploring the small shops that then housed a number of craftsmen selling their wares. Before long Watts began to fall in love with her.

Jano hailed originally from Wyoming. She had been the first woman reporter on the *Kansas City Star* and had worked for some years in New York as Mobil's chief public relations officer. She was interested in many things that interested Watts, particularly in Taoism and Zen. He was, he says, fascinated by

> her voice, her gestures, the humor of her eyes, her knowledge of painting, of music, of colors and textures, her skill in the art of the loveletter and her general embodiment of something I had been looking for all down my ages to be my chief travelling companion.

. . . My first idea was to whisk her off to a lonely shack by the Pacific, where we could sit on foggy nights by a log fire and talk over a bottle of red wine.[19]

So Watts left his family. The saddest feature of this desertion was that Dorothy was once again pregnant; in one of those painful episodes of attempted reconciliation or seduction that sometimes come right at the end of an unhappy marriage, she had again conceived. So Watts was leaving the comfortable suburban house, a pregnant wife, and four children. "At the age of forty-five I broke out of . . . this wall-to-wall trap, even though it was a hard shock to myself and all concerned. But I did it with a will and thus discovered who were my real friends."[20]

Among those who experienced the "hard shock" were Watts's parents in England. Brought up in a very different age, they had been shocked enough when Alan and Eleanor parted. They found the circumstances of this second failure deeply distressing; Laurence, usually a rather overadmiring father, wrote a sympathetic letter to Dorothy when she gave birth to her youngest child, Diane, after Watts had left, saying that he regarded Alan as a failure as a husband and father.

Watts's justification for his "breaking out" was that he felt himself stifled emotionally: "I had been slipping into the emotional constipation peculiarly characteristic of genteel academia — the mock modesty, the studied objectivity, the cautious opinion, and the horror of enthusiasm."[21]

Not only with Jano but also with one or two close friends Watts began to enjoy an emotional warmth of which he had not believed himself capable. Two of these friends were Roger Somers and Elsa Gidlow. Somers was a jazz musician and an architect-carpenter of great brilliance and originality, who had come to the Bay Area from a puritanical Midwest background and had gradually discovered himself as a joyful pagan. "He is an incarnation of the Greek god Pan," Watts wrote of him enthusiastically, "if you can imagine Pan based on a bull instead of a goat. . . . For his physique is formidable, his grizzly hair sticks out like short horns, and his energy is endless. He plays the saxophone, the oboe and all kinds of drums. He dances — free form — like a maniac, and his shrieks of delight can be heard all over the hill."[22] Elsa Gidlow was a gifted landscape gardener and a poet who made no secret of the fact that she loved women more than men.

In the late 1950s, Elsa, Roger, and Roger's wife found a beautiful and secluded site in a eucalyptus grove on Mount Tamalpais, and they planned to build houses and landscaped gardens there for themselves and for a few friends. They called it Druid Heights and had already invited Watts and his family to join them there. Only Dorothy's disapproval and dislike of Elsa had prevented this from happening.

Now, with his new sense of freedom, Watts found himself frequently visiting them. Perhaps because Elsa offered no sexual challenge, Watts enjoyed her as a comforting and sympathetic elder sister, or maybe as a sort of white witch, practicing her good magic. He liked watching her choosing herbs from her garden or talking to her cats. Roger encouraged a kind of freedom and unselfconsciousness Watts had never known before. In Somers's beautiful Japanese-style room, with its Buddhist household shrine and its gold and redwood walls, the two men played drums, or practiced a sort of freedom singing, or chanted, or danced. Watts remembers it as the discovering of a *yoga*, a joining with the energy of the universe, and as such, a sort of religious exercise.

In New York, too, in the Greenwich Village loft of jazz musician Charlie Brooks (soon to be the husband of Charlotte Selver) Watts found himself breaking free of his old inhibitions. "So it

was," he says simply, "that I found a new self." It was as if he had
learned something quite new about being close to people. "I found
myself among people who were not embarrassed to express their
feelings, who were not ashamed to show warmth, exuberance and
earthy *joie de vivre*. . . . I found too that these friends had always
considered me a little distant and difficult to know, and had chari-
tably put it down to British reserve."[23]

Elsa made it possible for Watts to realize his fantasy of an idyll
with Jano. She owned a lonely cottage on another part of Mount
Tamalpais, which she lent to them. In the cottage and in the
garden that Elsa had made they rediscovered a childhood world
lost by adult busyness and responsibility. They looked together at

> the convolution of a leaf, the light in a drop of water, the shadows
> of a glass in the sun, patterns of smoke, grain in wood, mottle in
> polished stone . . . we slowed down time. We watched the sun
> blazing from a glass of white wine and watered the garden at sun-
> set, when the slanting light turns flowers and leaves into bloodstone
> and jade. We studied the forms of shells and ferns, crystals and
> teazels, water-flow, galaxies, radiolaria, and each other's eyes, and
> looked down through those jewels to the god and the goddess that
> may be seen within even when the doubting expression on the face
> is saying "What, *me?*" We danced to Bach and Vivaldi and listened
> to Ravi Shankar taking hold of the primordial sound of the uni-
> verse and rippling it with his fingers into all the shapes, patterns
> and rhythms of nature.[24]

Going down to the sea and hunting for sand dollars at Stinson
Beach, wandering the lonelier paths of Mount Tamalpais, looking
and talking and making love in Elsa's cottage, they were slowly
discovering each other and themselves.

# Nine

# Counterculture

## 1960-1968

CALIFORNIA. San Francisco. 1960. Something new could be felt in the air. Later, journalists and social commentators found words for it. *Utopianism, radical divergence, revolution, religious revival, San Francisco Renaissance, counterculture* — each caught a bit of the action, without successfully describing the whole.

Looking back, a decade later, Alan Watts perceived that "something was on the way, in religion, in music, in ethics and sexuality, in our attitudes to nature, and in our whole style of life. We took courage and we began to swing."[1]

The roots of the counterculture were Eastern religion — particularly Buddhism — jazz, poetry, the "alternative reality" of psychedelic drugs, and perhaps behind that the transcendental tradition. A major preoccupation was the relation of the individual self to his or her surroundings; how was the lonely and alienated self to find release? Gestalt therapy, owing a great deal to Buddhist insights, and other kinds of therapy, such as the encounter group, vied with various religious disciplines to offer an answer.

The swift movement towards counterculture coincided with the

radical change in Watts's private life when he left Dorothy. Watts
had a new sense of hope, as did many in the counterculture, that
these social changes would bring a new freedom. The first step
toward this freedom was going with Jano to live on an old ferry-
boat called the *Vallejo* ("a dilapidated old hulk") moored at
gate 5 in Sausalito in 1961. Nothing could have plunged Watts
so successfully into a new bohemian world. The boat was owned
by a painter, Gordon Onslow-Ford, who had already let half of it
to another painter, Jean Varda, one of the most colorful characters
of the waterfront. Instead of becoming exasperated by Varda or
envying the ease of his social contacts, particularly with women,
Watts in fact admired and enjoyed him immensely, using him, as
he had used other admired friends, as a model of the sort of person
he would like to be himself. Varda seemed to him to be "a marvellous amalgamation of exuberation, sensuality, culture, and
literacy, salted with that essential recognition of one's own rascality
which is the perfect preservation against stuffiness and lack of
humanity."[2]

One of the things Watts admired about Varda was that he was
poor and preferred it that way — he said it led to less bother with
the tax people. (Struggling to pay alimony on a free-lance income
Watts needed the example of someone who seemed to meet poverty with a light heart.) With Varda, or Yanko, as he was always
known (the Greek word for uncle), there was always wine, good
food, and marvellous company. Yanko held court in his big peacock chair "at the end of a long table scratched and stained with
the memories of innumerable banquets of minced lamb in vine-
leaves, stuffed peppers, and fish cooked in herbs and wine."[3]

Varda had arrived in California from Greece in 1940 and
settled first at Big Sur. A painter by training, he was already less
interested in painting than in mosaics, collages, and sculpture made
out of whatever material came to hand — pipes, bottles, cans. His

favorite subjects were women and "The Celestial City," visions of which ran through all his work.

He lived with enormous joie de vivre, a joy that attracted all kinds of visitors to the *Vallejo*. "In the fifties," said the *Pacific Sun*, "Varda was sporting strawberry-colored pants and driving through Sausalito in a purple car. He would sometimes wear mismatched socks. 'Why limit yourself?' he would say in his high-pitched Greek-accented voice. And people loved him. He was always surrounded by young, desirable women. All who knew him swear he was a romantic, not a lecher. Each person who entered his life felt beautiful, wanted, special."[4] Varda's pleasure in living was derived from his gift for living in the moment.

On Sundays there were wonderful sailing trips on board the *Perfidia*, Yanko's lateen-sailed dhow, which often had a crew of women and was "supplied with loaves and cold chicken and gallons of wine."[5] The boat had no engine and was often in danger of running aground because of the insobriety of the crew, but it survived, maybe because of the great eye on the prow, put there, Greek fashion, to avert the "evil eye." There were parties on neighboring beaches or aboard the *Vallejo* itself.

On weekdays both Watts and Varda rose and began work early. "As I sat at my typewriter," wrote Watts,

> I would hear him hammering and rustling about in the studio. A little after eight I would often light a cigar and wander over for coffee with him. . . . Even at this hour there would be others at the table — his current mistresses, or young men helping him with boat construction; and as the day wore on a stream of visitors would be in and out — diplomats, professors, ballerinas, fishermen, pirates and models — for hour after hour of multilingual badinage. By lunchtime there were jugs of wine, jack cheese, and sourdough bread on the table, and towards evening Yanko would get together lamb or fish with olive and peppers, vine leaves and lemons, egg-

plant and onions . . . mixing salad in an immense wooden bowl. . . .
All the while he would regale us with anecdotes, real and imaginary,
and outrageous commentaries on art, women, nautical adventures.[6]

What Yanko so effortlessly lived, Watts had spent years trying
to understand, to explain, in books, articles, and talks on radio
station KQED. His quarrel with Christianity was that it did not
believe that "the natural man is to be trusted." Its emphasis on the
will, together with the continual need to watch oneself and to curb
the lusts of the flesh, seemed to him to heighten the human predicament, the "hard knot" of the mind seeking to know the mind,
or the self seeking to control the self. Continually watching oneself
made one lonely and also encouraged a kind of hallucination —
that the self was real. "When that tense knot vanishes there is no
more sense of a hard core of selfhood standing over against the
rest of the world."[7]

Watts had explored this idea at length in *Nature, Man and
Woman* (1958), suggesting that the split between mind and body
that Christianity inherited from Greek dualism, had affected all
subsequent attitudes toward women, since fears about the wayward
flesh or body were often projected upon women. With both tenderness and realism Watts was trying to explore new ways in which
men and women might relate to one another.

Many of these ideas about Zen Buddhism and about sensuality
had been explored before Watts by the group known as the beats,
or the beat generation. The poets of North Beach, San Francisco,
had often gathered in the early 1950s to drink and read poetry. In
the spring of 1955, many of them met at the Six Gallery — Gary
Snyder, Kenneth Rexroth, Philip Whalen, Michael McLure, Law-
rence Ferlinghetti, and others — and there Allen Ginsberg read
his poem *Howl*, a devastating attack on contemporary society delivered by a man with the temperament of an Old Testament
prophet. Jack Kerouac sat on the side of the tiny platform, drink-

ing wine, and "giving out little wows and yesses of approval and even whole sentences of comment with nobody's invitation but in the general gaiety nobody's disapproval either."[8]

There was a lot of interest in Zen Buddhism among the beats, the most enthusiastic exponent being Gary Snyder, already a close friend of Watts.

Jack Kerouac, who had written the influential book *On the Road*, a beat generation odyssey that had sent many young people traveling around the country on freight trains, fell under Snyder's spell and wrote a new book about their friendship and about Buddhism titled *The Dharma Bums* (1958). The two main characters in the novel, Ray Smith and Japhy Ryder, take part in wild, wonderful, drunken parties round bonfires, in which many of the guests take off their clothes for the pleasure of walking around naked. They believe that to live in poverty, religious belief, and joyful sexuality is the way to overcome the consumer society.

*The Dharma Bums* and *On the Road*, along with Watts's writing, gave the young a new ideal, as well as the ideas and words of a religion that seemed more exotic and exciting than their native Christianity.

Watts observed Kerouac's brand of Zen with a certain amount of doubt and suspicion, feeling that it mistook sloppy, undisciplined art, selfishness of all kinds, and idleness for spontaneity. Watts was, however, careful to exempt Snyder from his strictures.

Kerouac, for his part, obliquely mocked Watts, whom he knew from parties and poetry readings as well as in print. Watts appears in *The Dharma Bums* as Arthur Whane. He arrives at a party at which most of the guests have chosen to be naked.

> Whane stands there in the firelight, smartly dressed in suit and necktie, having a perfectly serious discussion about world affairs with two naked men.
>
> "Well, what is Buddhism?" someone asks him. "Is it fantastic

imagination, magic of the lightning flash, is it plays, dreams, not even plays, dreams?"

"No, to me Buddhism is getting to know as many people as possible." And there he was going round the party real affable shaking hands with everybody and chatting, a regular cocktail party.[9]

The vision that Watts, Snyder, and Kerouac shared was the renunciation of the values of bourgeois and suburban life. In 1962 Herbert Marcuse was to claim in the preface to *Eros and Civilization* that there is a kind of revolution that breaks out not in hopeless poverty, but at the very heart of affluence. Freed from acute anxiety about survival, human beings begin to ask more of life, and in particular they ask about meaning, in work, in relationships, in society, and in religion. It was to the search for this kind of meaning that the contemporary historian Theodore Roszak applied the term *counterculture* in 1968, a word that was widely taken up and used.

In 1960, when Watts and his contemporaries "began to swing," Kennedy had just been elected president and there was a feeling of hope and newness in the air, of the possibility of new moves toward peace and racial integration, an intoxicating sense that things could be different. Kennedy championed civil rights, had talks with Martin Luther King about racial problems, seemed to show a new initiative toward the Soviet Union, enjoyed and encouraged the arts. Idealism with style offered a way forward.

On the college campuses this idealism took the form of a radical activism that seemed more colorful and less grim than the old-style Marxism; students rather than the working classes were to be the new agents of change. Folk music, hitherto associated with rural settings and traditional themes of love and death, began to be adopted by urban idealists who gradually adapted it to express other passionately held sentiments about brotherly love, peace, and racial equality.

One of the most profound differences between the college generation of the sixties and their parents' generation had to do with sexuality. The earlier generation, lacking effective contraceptives and still firmly in the grip of a Christian ethic that believed "fornication" to be a sin, had officially held to the ideal of sexuality expressed only within monogamous marriage. The young, however, took their models from such books as *The Dharma Bums*, in which, for example, Japhy Ryder and a friend, sharing the delectable girl they call Princess in what she calls *yabyum*, roll delightedly on the floor in sexual ecstasy. They were repudiating the America that Japhy Ryder remembered from when he was a "kid," the America of the Protestant work ethic, of nervous liquor laws, of censorious attitudes toward sensual experience, and of devotion to the ideal of the family.

Watts was speaking — about sexuality, about sensuality, about religion, about psychedelics, about food, about clothing, about how to live — on campuses all over the United States, and weekly on the radio. In 1961 he spoke at Columbia, Harvard, the Yale Medical School, Cornell, Chicago, and at other schools, and gave seminars on the *Vallejo* and elsewhere. He was the sort of speaker who used his voice as consciously as a pianist uses his fingers. Sandy Jacobs, who was later to record Watts extensively on tape, remembers the way he captured an audience and how effortless it seemed.

He didn't *prepare*. He had a fine library, of course, and he did extensive research for his books, but for his lectures? No way. He would just wander into an auditorium someplace — some college town. He'd walk up on the stage, and he'd say, "Let's see, today we were going to discuss, say, Ramakrishna." Right away, some totally brilliant opening would suggest itself to him, he'd gather up the audience with some incredible beginning which would draw people in. There'd be this long, rambling middle, which would keep people's interest — jokes, laughs. He had a mental watch which said, "Hey! It's fifty minutes," and he'd draw it all in, and come up with this cliffhanger, a conclusion, but it was a pregnant moment where everybody would say, "God, that's fantastic!"

In 1962 Watts received a two-year travel and study fellowship from Harvard University's Department of Social Relations, and he began a series of visits to Harvard. Here he began to see quite a lot of Timothy Leary, whom he already knew slightly. Leary had turned his house into a sort of commune, in which all kinds of people gathered in the kitchen for meals and conversation. Watts, always fastidious in his personal habits, said later that he could not understand how anyone who had had his or her consciousness raised by psychedelic drugs could tolerate the squalor of the Leary household — the unswept floors and the unmade beds. Messiness apart, though, he liked Leary; later he was surprised when Leary proved to have a genius for getting into trouble that even exceeded his own.

Leary too remembered the evenings in his kitchen when

the wizard held court, drinking heavily, spinning out tales of fabled consciousness expanders of the past. [Watts talked of Madame Blavatsky, Annie Besant, Krishnamurti, and Gurdjieff.] . . . He gave us a model of the gentleman-philosopher who belonged to no bureaucracy or academic institution. He had published more influential books than any Orientalist of our time. Although he could teach rings round any tenured professor, he had avoided faculty status, remaining a wandering independent sage, supporting himself with the immediate fruits of his plentiful brain. . . . Watts taught us to divide mystics into two groups — the lugubrious and the witty.[10]

Watts was to participate in Leary's life at intervals thereafter, once coming to a pagan festival Leary held to celebrate the vernal equinox at Millbrook. There was a huge bonfire, and the congregation sat in a candlelit circle while Watts consulted the *I Ching*. Watts, Leary says, probably admiringly, "whose orientation was past and Eastern rather than scientific and Western, used the *I Ching* as an elegant mumbo-jumbo tea ceremony, which raised the esthetic level of our gathering and made us feel part of an ancient tradition."[11]

Leary and Watts were each, in different ways, to affect people's use and understanding of drugs, but ahead of either of them in exploring this territory was Aldous Huxley. In 1953, at the invitation of a psychologist conducting research, Huxley took mescalin, a natural drug that, like the synthetic drug lysergic acid, has chemical similarities to human adrenalin.

"One bright May morning," wrote Huxley in *The Doors of Perception*, "I swallowed four-tenths of a gram of mescalin dissolved in half a glass of water and sat down to wait for results." Within an hour Huxley, a man who on his own admission had a poor visual imagination, was looking at something utterly extraordinary. A flower vase on the table containing a rose, a carnation, and an iris, which had interested him briefly at breakfast, became the focus of his attention: "I was not looking now at an unusual flower arrangement. I was seeing what Adam had seen on the morning of his creation — the miracle, moment by moment, of naked existence.

'Is it agreeable?' somebody asked. . . .

'Neither agreeable nor disagreeable' I answered. 'It just *is*.'"

The "Is-ness" (*Istigkeit*) of which Meister Eckhart had spoken — the Being of Plato — suddenly Huxley saw it in the flowers. "A transience that was yet eternal life, a perpetual perishing that was at the same time pure Being, a bundle of minute, unique particulars in which, by some unspeakable and yet self-evident paradox, was to be seen the divine source of all existence."[12]

All the hints and painful attempts at explanation that Huxley had read in the mystical literature suddenly made sense. This was what the beatific vision was like, or *Sat Chit Ananda* (Being–Awareness–Bliss). And when the Zen novice asked his master what the dharma-body of the Buddha was like (dharma is the doctrine or method by which freedom is attained), he got the baffling answer "The hedge at the bottom of the garden." This was what the master saw.

It began to seem to Huxley that the function of the human senses and nervous system was to filter out the extraordinary wealth of information constantly available to it in order to enable the individual to deal with simpler necessities. But potentially, and in our earliest baby awareness of the world, each of us is, has been, Mind at Large, aware of everything, remembering everything. Mystics, schizophrenics, and those under the influence of such drugs as mescalin, see life without the filter. Painters, Huxley thought, see that life in part.

He emerged from this profound experience feeling that he had seen into the deeps of contemplation and could at least imagine the deeps of madness. He felt that contemplation demanded that something be added to it (as the saints and bodhisattvas believed), some effort of active compassion that could release others from suffering. In Eckhart's phrase they should be ready to "come down from the seventh heaven in order to bring a cup of water to a sick brother."

Partly because of Huxley's experiment and his vivid description of it, a wider group of people became interested in hallucinogens, such as mescalin, lysergic acid, psilocybin, and peyote. Anthropologists who had long known about the tradition of taking cactus buds (peyote) and "the mushroom" (psilocybin) in Mexico and in some countries of South America among the Indian populations were interested in the effect of drugs that had previously been used primarily as part of religious rituals. Psychologists were interested in the drugs for any light they might throw on the subject of perception and for revelations they might produce about schizophrenia. Religious people were interested in the information they might offer about mystical experience. Painters and musicians were after new perceptions of light, color, form, and sound.

In 1958 Watts, who, unlike the beats, had always been wary of drugs, was invited to take part in an experiment by Keith Ditman, the psychiatrist in charge of LSD (lysergic acid diethylamide) research in the Department of Neuropsychiatry at the University of California, Los Angeles. One of the things that encouraged him to do so was the way he thought that the mescalin experience had made the ascetic Aldous Huxley warmer, more human. So he went along to Ditman's office and took one hundred micrograms of LSD. Perception was changed in a fascinating way: time was slowed down, plants and grass and a church across the road were all great marvels, and a book of *sumi-e* paintings was a revelation; yet he was faintly disappointed. It seemed to him that he had had a wonderful aesthetic experience, but one that did not approach the mystical unity that Huxley had described. Later he was to believe that the clinical/laboratory atmosphere of a formal test in a hospital had itself imposed certain limitations on his response, though it is also true that the dose is a small one.

He let a year go by and then tried a series of five experiments with the drug, varying the dosage from seventy-five to one hundred micrograms. These trips were extraordinarily rewarding. Perhaps the most remarkable effect had to do with time, what Watts called "a profound relaxation combined with an abandonment of purposes and goals. . . . I have felt, in other words, endowed with all the time in the world, free to look about me as

if I were living in eternity without a single problem to be solved."
Within this freedom was another astonishing freedom: "I was no
longer a detached observer, a little man inside my own head, *having*
sensations. I *was* the sensations. . . . It is like, not watching, but
being, a coiling arabesque of smoke patterns in the air, or of ink
dropped in water."[13] An irresistible feeling of beauty and wonder,
absent from his first experiment with the drug, took over.

Watts writes of one experiment conducted late at night at his
house in Millbrook:

> Some five or six hours from its start the doctor had to go home, and
> I was left alone in the garden. For me, this stage of the experiment
> is always the most rewarding in terms of insight, after some of the
> more unusual and bizarre sensory effects have worn off. The garden
> was a lawn surrounded by shrubs and high trees — pine and euca-
> lyptus — and floodlit from the house which enclosed it on one side.
> As I stood on the lawn I noticed that the rough patches where the
> grass was thin or mottled with weeds no longer seemed to be blem-
> ishes. Scattered at random as they were, they appeared to constitute
> an ordered design, giving the whole area the texture of velvet
> damask, the rough patches being the parts where the pile of the
> velvet is cut. In sheer delight I began to dance on this enchanted
> carpet, and through the thin soles of my moccasins I could feel the
> ground becoming alive under my feet, connecting me with the earth
> and the trees and the sky in such a way that I seemed to become one
> body with my whole surroundings.
>
> Looking up, I saw that the stars were colored with the same reds,
> greens and blues that one sees in iridescent glass, and passing across
> them was the single light of a jet plane taking forever to streak over
> the sky. At the same time, the trees, shrubs, and flowers seemed to
> be living jewelry, inwardly luminous like intricate structures of
> jade, alabaster, or coral, and yet breathing and flowering with the
> same life that was in me. Every plant became a kind of musical
> utterance, a play of variations on a theme repeated from the main
> branches, through the stalks and twigs, to the leaves, the veins in
> the leaves, and to the fine capillary network between the veins. Each

new bursting of growth from a center repeated or amplified the basic design with increasing complexity and delight, finally exulting in a flower.[14]

The beauty of the experience reminded Watts insistently of something, and he realized that the garden had the kind of exotic beauty of the pictures in the *Arabian Nights*, of scenes in Persian miniatures or in Chinese and Japanese paintings. Those artists too had seen the world like this. Was that because they too were drugged and seeing therefore a strangely heightened and beautified version of the world, or was it that the effect of LSD was "to remove certain habitual and normal inhibitions of the mind and senses, enabling us to see things as they would appear to us if we were not so chronically repressed?"[15] What the Oriental artists saw in their health and wisdom, Watts is saying, he could see with the help of LSD.

Inevitably Watts wondered about the possibilities of a drug so potent. Writing in 1960 he says that "the record of catastrophes from the use of LSD is extremely low, and there is no evidence at all that it is either habit-forming or physically deleterious. . . . I find that I have no inclination to use LSD in the same way as tobacco or wines and liquors. On the contrary, the experience is always so fruitful that I feel I must digest it for some months before entering into it again."[16] It was a drug, he goes on to say, to be approached with the care and dedication with which one might approach a sacrament.

He continued to experiment with it throughout the next couple of years and achieved, in an experience with his friends at Druid Heights, a piercing sense of how very lonely he had felt all his life, "a bag of skin," chronically and hopelessly cut off from all other "bags of skin" — "the quaking vortex of defended defensiveness which is my conventional self." Sitting up on the ridgepole of the barn with Roger and his friends, laughing helplessly with them at the sight of a broken car standing in Elsa's garden, sitting round a table on the terrace, sharing homemade bread and wine, he had the most extraordinary intimation of peace, of having "returned to the home behind home."[17]

This sense of being loved and cared for, of a place of deep trust, made it possible for him to know what he called the "helpless crying of the baby." The confident talker and performer and entertainer suddenly knew himself as an infinitely needy and sensitive self, "a blithering, terrified idiot, who managed temporarily to put on an act of being self-possessed. I began to see my whole life as an act of duplicity — the confused, helpless, hungry and hideously sensitive little embryo at the root of me having learned, step by step, to comply, placate, bully, wheedle, flatter, bluff and cheat my way into being taken for a person of competence and reliability."[18]

It was both a wonderful and an agonizing discovery, one that raised even more interesting questions as to what this amazing drug could achieve. Writing *The Joyous Cosmology* in 1962 Watts had come to see drugs like LSD and mescalin as a kind of medicine for sick modern men that would give them the experience of being "temporarily integrated." Like medicine, transforming drugs were not, in his view, a way of life. You took them if you needed them, you deepened the experience "by the various ways of meditation in which drugs are no longer necessary or useful."

In 1961 LSD was only just beginning to become available outside the medical world. Watts shared Huxley's feeling that it might be shared by minds already developed by aesthetic, philosophical, and religious ideas and practices. Unlike Huxley he guessed at the danger of a widespread availability of LSD, fearing that it would produce the chemical equivalent of bathtub gin. One of the reasons for writing *The Joyous Cosmology*, Watts claimed, was to inform people about the drug while there was still time, to encourage them to approach it with a kind of reverence, rather than with a desire simply for "kicks."

In this he was entirely opposed by Timothy Leary. Leary came relatively late to LSD, not actually trying it until 1962. But for several years before that he and Richard Alpert (a psychologist, who later became Ram Dass) had experimented extensively with psilocybin and had tried unsuccessfully to persuade the psychology faculty at Harvard to set up a series of systematic drug experiments there. So instead Leary and Alpert worked with university staff members and volunteer students and their families. There were a lot of volunteers.

Partly because of a series of experiments involving use of psilocybin by prisoners in the Massachusetts prison system, in which he found that he could make prisoners less depressed and hostile and more responsible and cooperative, Leary began to feel that psychedelic drugs might have something to offer everyone, and he developed a kind of evangelical zeal to share his discoveries. He gave out mushroom pills freely, particularly to writers; Robert Lowell, William Burroughs, Gregory Corso, Jack Kerouac, Arthur Koestler, and Allen Ginsberg all "took the mushroom" with Leary.

He was following a tradition that the British philosopher Gerald Heard and the psychologist Oscar Janiger had begun in the 1950s of deliberately initiating people into LSD, believing that it was God's way of giving the twentieth century the gift of consciousness and saving it from Armageddon. "When you made contact, it was like two people looking at each other across the room, and with a sort of nod of the head that acknowledged that you 'too!' "[19] wrote Leary. Janiger had turned on a number of Hollywood film stars and directors, Cary Grant, Jack Nicholson, and Stanley Kubrick among them. He had also run tests with people from many walks of life, a number of whom had felt illuminated and changed by the LSD experience, and he had had some encouraging results working with depressed patients.

The rumors of the effects of psychedelic drugs began to cause a kind of excitement that boded ill for the sort of controlled initiation Huxley or Watts or Janiger favored. At Harvard Leary was continually being approached by students who wanted to try LSD. When he obeyed college rules and refused to oblige them, they got supplies in Boston or New York. The chemistry students synthesized their own. Leary described it this way: "In this the third year of our research the Yard was seething with drug consciousness." Dozens of Harvard students had visions. Some dropped out and went to the East. "Not necessarily a bad development from our point of view," Leary wrote with his usual insouciance, "but understandably upsetting to parents, who did not send their kids to Harvard to become Buddhas." Worse still, "dozens of bright youths phoned home to announce that they'd found God and discovered the secret of the universe."[20]

In California, LSD, not yet illegal, was being widely distributed, much of it synthesized by an entrepreneur named Stanley Owsley. Leary's *Psychedelic Review* disseminated information about methods of taking it. Braver or wilder souls, like Ken Kesey, author of *One Flew over the Cuckoo's Nest*, held rock-and-roll dances in which the place of honor in the middle of the floor was given to a baby's bathtub full of punch spiked with lysergic acid.

The words *hipster* and *hippie* were coming into the language and were applied to the new "far-out" crowd by the beats. By the end of 1965, in the words of a harassed police captain, "the word is out that San Francisco is the place for the far-out crowd," and within San Francisco the old student neighborhood of Haight-Ashbury had become the most far-out, both because of its cheapness and because of the attractiveness of its Edwardian houses. As if to fit in with the landscape many of the hippies started wearing Edwardian and Victorian clothes — they were cheap and good to look at during LSD trips or when stoned on marijuana.

Golden Gate Park became a sort of extension of the neighborhood, together with a handful of favorite stores and coffee houses that stayed open all night. A professor opened an experimental college in the Haight in which students could decide what they wanted to study, outline a course, get a faculty sponsor, and hire a teacher. There was a preponderance of people wanting to study art, psychology, and occult religion.

Street theatre became a common sight, and it mostly reflected antiwar or antiracist sentiments. The new rock-and-roll, which, to begin with, was not interested in much besides "love," was gradually adopting antiestablishment ideas. Already by 1965 many folkies were turning to the electric guitar and were singing songs, like Dylan's "Subterranean Homesick Blues," that caught the new mood. The hippies listened to the new bands, like the Jefferson Airplane, the Grateful Dead, and the Byrds, and to new singers, like Janis Joplin and Jimi Hendrix. They admired the Beatles, but began by thinking them a bit "cozy." The bands played against and within light shows in which their audience danced in the light of strobes, ultraviolet light, and overhead projectors. Charles Perry describes a message displayed by projector at one light show that went: "Anybody who knows he is God go up onstage!"

The Haight was beginning to get into the drug market. By the early sixties marijuana (once enjoyed mostly by Latins and working-class blacks) had become popular on campuses, and by 1963 people were smuggling it from Mexico. Most of the selling was done by hippies who found it a way of making a living. Ounces ("lids") sold for eight to ten dollars, a kilogram at around sixty dollars. The hippies broke up the kilos and sold smaller amounts at a good profit.

LSD was still legal (until October 1966), and the extraordinary perceptions and fantasies, images and colors associated with it began to influence pop art, clothes, and songs. The Beatles' new album *Revolver* gave broad hints that the Beatles themselves were "turning on," while a new paper, the *Oracle*, with an amazing use of colored inks, exploded in a vast rainbow that included all hippie preoccupations in one great Whitmanesque blaze of light and camaraderie. American Indians, Shiva, Kali, the Buddha, tarot, astrology, Saint Francis, Zen, and tantra all rubbed shoulders in one edition, one that sold fifty thousand copies on the streets. When the *Oracle* printed the *Heart Sutra*, it devoted a double spread to the Zen Center version, complete with Chinese characters.

There was, briefly, a touching kind of innocence about the hippie movement. In the early days of Haight-Ashbury there was a café on Eighth Street where people threw their spare change into a tray so that those who could not afford the price of a cup of coffee or a meal could eat. There was a movement of people called "the Diggers," who handed out free meals to all who came, an action based on the ideology that food belonged to the people. Young people from all over the United States regarded San Francisco and the Haight as a mecca to be reached at all costs, and many of them received a free meal and a free bed before either returning to home and school or joining the growing population around the Panhandle, the handle-shaped extension of Golden Gate Park.

During the years 1960 to 1965, Alan Watts visited Japan two or three times a year, escorting tourists to Kyoto. He was helped with the practical chores of tour guiding by Gary Snyder, who had extensive knowledge of the country; installed in his monastery, Snyder sorted out accommodation and currency problems for Watts and gave him a welcome bolt-hole from the responsibilities of looking after his charges. Snyder was by this time advanced enough in Zen studies to be able to discuss some of the things Watts was curious about, such as what actually went on in the silence of a Zen monastery, for example, and how the system was structured. Snyder introduced Watts to his *roshi* and to some of the head priests, and arranged for him to attend lectures at the monastery, as well as some of the ceremonies, which Watts enjoyed tremendously.

"I got to like him more and more, even though I realized he was getting naughtier and naughtier," says Snyder. "Which was all right because I was naughty too. So we enjoyed each other's company."

Watts's spoken Japanese was poor — "only enough to direct taxis and order food in restaurants, helped out with Chinese characters on a scratch-pad" — but he felt very at home in Japan, particularly in Kyoto. He visited temples and gardens, filled with wonder and joy, and was fascinated by all the rituals of tea, and by the shops with materials for "ink-and-brush meditation," a pastime he had long enjoyed. One day he and Jano

took a day off for meditation at Nanzenji, not in the temple itself, but on the forested hillside behind it, where we sat on the steps of some ancient nobleman's tomb, supplying ourselves with the kit for ceremonial tea and a thermos bottle of hot saké. Zen meditation is a trickily simple affair, for it consists only in watching everything that is happening, including your own thoughts and your breathing, without comment. After a while, thinking, or talking to yourself, drops away and you find that there is no "yourself" other than everything which is going on, both inside and outside the skin. Your consciousness, your breathing, and your feelings are all the same process as the wind, the trees growing, the insects buzzing, the water flowing, and the distant prattle of the city. . . . The trick, which cannot be forced — is to be in this state of consciousness all the time, even when you are filling out tax forms or being angry.[21]

In the grounds of one of the ruined temples, Jano and Watts, by now married, served each other LSD, each pouring the liquid into the other's tiny cup, as the Japanese serve sake.

Watts's repeated visits to Kyoto brought an old acquaintance back into his life, Ruth Sasaki, by now the abbess in the Rinzai sect of Zen. He and Ruth at this stage in their lives had a sort of amused respect for one another.

Watts's writing and speaking about Zen at public lectures and seminars, on tape and television, in books, and above all on public radio, gave him a strong influence on the hippie culture. He talked of what interested him — mystical experience, drugs, food, clothes, lifestyle, poverty and wealth, pacifism — and he did it brilliantly. Theodore Roszak remembers the fascination these broadcasts held for all sorts of people, and the way conversation with friends the next morning often turned on "what Alan Watts said last night." He was struck by Watts's deep scholarship and by the courage of his efforts to translate the insights of Zen and Taoism into the language of Western science and psychology.

He has approached his task with an impish willingness to be catchy and cute, and to play at philosophy as if it were an enjoyable game. It is a style easily mistaken for flippancy, and it has exposed him to a deal of rather arrogant criticism: on the one hand from elitist Zen devotees who have found him too discursive for their mystic tastes (I recall one such telling me smugly, "Watts has never experienced satori"), and on the other hand from professional philosophers who have been inclined to ridicule him for his popularizing bent as being, in the words of one academic, "The Norman Vincent Peale of Zen."[22]

Roszak believed that, on the contrary, Watts's intellectual grasp and achievement was real and solid; he was more interested in sharing his ideas with the world at large than in reserving them for a small academic circle.

The charisma of Watts began to make him a revered figure in the whole Bay Area. People who wanted to be his disciples or to have their problems straightened out by him turned up unannounced at the *Vallejo* or insisted on telephoning him at all hours of the day and night. There was a woman who came and knelt at his feet on one occasion when he was dining out at a San Francisco restaurant. As a man who seemed to have answers, to know something others didn't, he drew the lost, the worried, the depressed, and the seeking like a magnet. Watts's cheerful talks often began from the proposition that his listener was in a sort of trap:

> You feel the world outside your body is an awful trap, full of . . . people, who are sometimes nice to you but mostly aren't. They're all out for themselves like you are and therefore there's one hell of a conflict going on. The rest of it, aside from people, is absolutely dumb — animals, plants, vegetables and rocks. Finally, behind the whole thing there are blazing centers of radioactivity called stars, and out there there's no air, there's no place for a person to live. . . . We have come to feel ourselves as centers of very, very tender, sensitive, vulnerable consciousness, confronted with a world that doesn't give a damn about us. And therefore, we have to pick a fight with this external world and beat it into submission to our wills. We talk about the conquest of nature; we conquer everything. We talk about the conquest of mountains, the conquest of space, the conquest of cancer, etc., etc. We're at war. And it's because we feel ourselves to be lonely ego principles, trapped in, somebody inextricably bound up with a world that doesn't go our way unless somehow we can manage to force it to do so.[23]

This way of looking at ourselves, Watts said, this view of the world about us over against our own ego, is hallucinatory, a completely false conception of ourselves as (a favorite expression of his) "an ego inside a bag of skin."

A truer way of looking at things, according to Watts, is to see our own body, along with animal and plant life and everything else, as part of a natural environment in which we are all intimately connected, human beings depending on air that is within a certain range of temperatures, and on the nutrition that natural life provides. People "go with" their environment, exactly as a bee goes with a flower — neither bee nor flower could exist without the other.

Watts regarded the ego, the need to think of ourselves obsessively as "I" and to build elaborate images about that persona, as an illusion — "an illusion married to a futility." The trouble is, in his view, you can't get rid of such a powerful illusion just by trying; conscious effort, even effort aimed at losing the ego, only reinforces the condition. So what is the answer?

> You find that you can't really control your thoughts, your feelings, your emotions, all the processes going on inside you and outside you that are happening — there's nothing you can do about it. So then, what follows? Well, there's only one thing that follows: You watch what's going on. You see, feel, this whole thing happening and then suddenly you find, to your amazement, that you can perfectly well get up, walk over to a table, pick up a glass of milk and drink it. . . . You can still act, you can still move, you can still go on in a rational way, but you've suddenly discovered that you're not what you thought you were. You're not this ego, pushing and shoving things inside a bag of skin. You feel yourself now in a new way as the whole world, which includes your body and everything that you experience, going along. It's intelligent. Trust it.[24]

This way of looking at the ego, compounded with the insights gained from taking LSD, chimed perfectly with the spirit of the counterculture. The passion for transformation, for inner change, that was a central feature of the movement, had found a quasi-religious leader in Alan Watts. Describing himself as a "philosophical entertainer" and a "genuine fake," he had clearly and well thought out things to say about many of the traditional constituents of religion — about God, about the self, and about the self's relationship to God and to fellow creatures.

At the time some theologians were discussing the idea of the "death of God." It was not, Watts suggested, God who was dying, but a particular way of thinking and talking about him that had died "by becoming implausible." Watts suggested a return to the God of the Theologia Mystica of Saint Dionysius, a God not limited by our concepts, or our pitiful need for security. "The highest image of God is the unseen behind the eyes — the blank space, the unknown, the intangible and the invisible. That is God! We have no image of that. We do not know what that is, but we have to trust it. There's no alternative. . . . That trust in a God whom one cannot conceive in any way is a far higher form of faith than fervent clinging to a God of whom you have a definite conception."[25]

Watts put some of his thinking about God into a new book, *The Two Hands of God* (1963). It was a book about overcoming the Western obsession with duality, the duality that separated the ego so painfully from its environment; it explored the themes of light and dark, life and death, good and evil, as well as Oriental imagery — the Cosmic Dance, the Primordial Pair, and legends of dismemberment and resurrection.

Next came *Beyond Theology* (subtitled *The Art of God-manship*; 1964), a cheerfully naughty but carefully argued book that approaches Christianity with determined irreverence.

Perhaps I can best indicate the spirit and approach of this book by asking you to imagine that you are attending a solemn service in a great cathedral, complete with candles, incense, chanting monks, and priests in vestments of white, scarlet and shimmering gold. Suddenly someone pulls you by the sleeve and says, "Psst! Come out back. I've got something to show you." You follow him out by the west door, and then go around the building . . . into the sacristy or vestry. This is the ecclesiastical equivalent of the green room in the theater, and you are about to enter by what, in a worldly setting, would be called the stage door. However, just outside you notice a couple of clerics — in their vestments — lighting up cigarettes.[26]

Watts then transposed this scene to heaven and himself to the role of a kind of jester or fool at court, unmasking the solemnity that surrounds the idea of God, debunking the crushing reverence that makes it impossible to reason about some of the more baffling statements of Christianity. Watts returns to some favorite targets.

How can an all-powerful God permit the Devil, or evil, to be at work in the world, unless he has somehow planted him there to heighten the drama? Watts imagines God playing hide-and-seek with himself in the world, then forgetting that it is a game and losing himself (in the person of his creatures) in scenes in which the drama gets altogether out of hand.

Why are Christians sometimes declaring themselves to be gods and sometimes insisting that they are terribly sinful? Why can they not see that asceticism and eroticism are two sides of the same coin? Their unwillingness to see this, Watts suggests, exacts a terrible price in prudery, misery, and warped lives: "The game is just too far-out."[27]

Two years later, in a book called *The Book: On the Taboo Against Knowing Who You Are,* Watts went back to his favorite themes of ego and non-ego, of living in the moment, of spontaneity, of ecstasy and the importance of living fully in the body, to repeat his favorite message — You are It. He was now moving into Vedanta with Hindu concepts to make his points, but the points were much the same.

Since his early experiments with LSD, his shared life with Varda and Jano, his friendships at Druid Heights and elsewhere, and his involvement with the counterculture as articulator and charismatic leader, Watts had changed a good deal. According to Gary Snyder, by about 1967, the summer of love as it was called, Watts had become a full-scale flower child, as committed to the colorful, the experimental, the provisional, and the original as any campus dropout or high school runaway. His shyness, primness, and correctness, eased by the warmth of the sixties climate, gave way to confidence, pleasure in acclaim, flowing hair, and a wonderful range of garments, including a sort of chasuble made from hairy material which kept him warm in cooler weather, a Philippine sarong ("the most comfortable garment ever invented"), and the Japanese *yucata* in which he liked to work. (He was particularly opposed to trousers for men, regarding them as "castrative.")

Waves of counterculture, often carrying Watts's messages with them, were washing around most of the Western world. Experimentation with psychedelics was widespread, not infrequently producing the sequence Timothy Leary had advised — "Turn On, Tune In, Drop Out" — and thousands of young people did just that, abandoning study or regular employment, giving themselves up to drugs or meditation, living as beggars. Others, not prepared to go to such extremes, nevertheless found their habits and outlook changed. When he came to look back on this period some years later Watts still felt astonished at what had happened.

I could not have believed — even in 1960 — that, say, Richard Hittleman, who studied with me at the Academy, would be conducting a national television program on yoga, that numerous colleges would be giving courses on meditation and Oriental philosophy for undergraduates, that this country would be supporting thriving Zen monasteries and Hindu ashrams, that the *I Ching* would be selling in hundreds of thousands, and that — wonder of wonders — sections of the Episcopal Church would be consulting me about contemplative retreats and the use of mantras in liturgy.

It was not only the young who were affected. "One by one," says Watts of his middle-aged friends, "I watched this change coming over my friends as if they had been initiated into a mystery and were suddenly 'in the know' about something not expressly defined."[28]

A strongly pacifist mood was growing; horror as the details of the Vietnam War became better known, resentment at the draft, and the newfound wonder at the natural world, all made war seem deeply repulsive and produced the slogan "Make love not war." "Flower power" gradually hardened into a more overt kind. Theodore Roszak describes "the troubles" at Berkeley in 1966:

> A group of undergraduates stages a sit-in against naval recruiters at the Student Union. They are soon joined by a contingent of nonstudents whom the administrators then martyr by selective arrest. . . . Finally, the teaching assistants call a strike in support of the menaced demonstration. When at last the agitation comes to its ambiguous conclusion, a rally of thousands gathers outside Sproul Hall, the central administration building, to sing the Beatles' "Yellow Submarine" — which happens to be the current hit on all the local high-school campuses.[29]

In October 1966, it became a misdemeanor to possess LSD or DMT in the state of California and a felony to sell them. They were widely available, however, and the ban on them only increased the interest in the drugs and their effects. In Berkeley a hillside that high school students had been in the habit of painting with the name of their school and their class year now bore the legend in huge letters, LSD. The initials were also spelled out in a song,

"Lucy in the Sky with Diamonds," in the Beatles' new album *Sgt. Pepper's Lonely Hearts Club Band* (1967).

Life in the Haight had taken on a psychedelic quality in itself, as Charles Perry says, "like a running Beaux Arts Ball. . . . People brought things to share, such as food or Day-Glo paints with which to decorate each other's bodies or paint designs on the floor [the dance halls all had ultraviolet lights to make Day-Glo fluoresce more brilliantly]. Or little toys: soap-bubble blowers, bells, convex mirrors, . . . sparklers, yo-yos or pens that glowed in the dark."[30] Stores flourished that had caught the new mood, with names like Wild Colors, the Psychedelic Shop, Far Fetched Foods, the I/Thou Coffee Shop.

In January 1967 the counterculture staged what was to be its biggest show, the "Be-In," or "Human Be-In." It was held in the polo field in the Park Stadium of San Francisco, and the day, January 14, was decided through consultation with an astrologer. "Jerry Rubin told reporters the Be-In would show that hippies and radicals were one, their common aim being to drop out of 'games and institutions that oppress and dehumanize' such as napalm, the Pentagon, Governor Reagan and the rat race, and to create communities where 'new values and new human relations can grow.' "[31]

The *Berkeley Barb* said about the Be-In, "The spiritual revolution will be manifest and proven. In unity we shall shower the country with waves of ecstasy and purification. Fear will be washed away; ignorance will be exposed to sunlight; profits and empire will lie drying on desert beaches; violence will be submerged and transmuted to rhythm and dancing."[32]

On the morning of January 14, Snyder, Ginsberg, Watts, and others performed *pradakshina*, a Hindu rite of circumambulation

at the polo field. It was a fine day, and from early in the morning
people began walking from all over the city toward the meadow.
Tens of thousands were there, some with banners, some in robes
and exotic clothing, others in denims. "The proper ecstatic note
in dress was usually provided by a bright shirt or scarf, or a string
or two of beads or buttons with drug or peace messages. But many
people brought fruit, flowers, incense, cymbals and tambourines,
. . . bells, mirrors, feathers or bits of fur, the kind of thing people
had long carried on Haight Street to blow the mind of a passing
tripper."[33]

Speakers, rock bands, and Shunryu Suzuki-roshi of the San Francisco Zen Temple meditating on the platform and holding up a
flower passed the afternoon. According to Charles Perry, some
people hoped a flying saucer "with good news" might come down.
In the event what came down was a parachutist said to be Owsley.
At sunset Gary Snyder blew on a conch shell, Allen Ginsberg led
a chant, and the crowd drifted away, some of them to build fires,
chant, and pray on Ocean Beach. An unexpected spin-off from the
Be-In was the comment of Police Chief Thomas Cahill.

"You're sort of the love generation, aren't you?" he asked a
delighted group from the Haight, a title which was instantly
claimed.

For all the love, ecstasy, religious devotion, and peaceful aims
of the love generation, there were signs that the wave had reached
its crest and was beginning to crash. One of the major problems
was in the Haight itself. So well publicized was it that it became
a mecca for teenagers from all over the country, some who came
for a weekend, some who had the idea of dropping out of school
and staying permanently. Along with this crusade of the innocents
came the drug pushers and a world of criminality.

As early as 1967 Nicholas Von Hoffman noted in the *Wash-*

*ington Post* how the flower child world of Haight-Ashbury had disintegrated into a nightmare of murderous criminality, as the drug entrepreneurs, interested not in expanded consciousness but in money, fought for territory. Unintentionally, Von Hoffman said, the hippies had come to constitute "the biggest crime story since prohibition."

The money tray no longer waited in the café on Eighth Street. Too many people had come to Haight-Ashbury looking for an easy buck. A doctor who ran a "radical clinic" for hippies spoke about the downfall of the neighborhood like this:

> I think the mass media were primarily responsible for the destruction of HA; they had for three, four years a quite interesting social experiment and with some health problems, but in general we were all doing a good job and then all of a sudden hippies became publicity material, the word had spread throughout the United States, and every disturbed kid, runaway teenager, ambulatory schizophrenic, drug addict, knew about HA and they knew that if they came to HA or at least they thought, there would be love and peace and people sharing, which is exactly what happened about three or four years ago, but you can't share items that are necessary for three hundred people with three hundred thousand, you know, and the community just became destroyed as a result of this mass influx, also the media publicized the hippies so much that it aroused the anger of the dominant culture and it was declared a Communist conspiracy or un-American and it's amazing the hostility that mystical, non-violent, long-haired youth can evoke in the conservative element in the United States.[34]

There *was* a growing anger against the "love generation." Clergy began to preach sermons against it, and police opposition hardened. Leary was deported, first from Mexico because of pressure by the CIA, then from Dominica. Some of the hostility was richly deserved. There were groups like that around Andy Warhol in New York, indifferent to vision and spiritual experience, but unashamedly into "booze, speed, downers, . . . drugs that provide escape, that turn off, toughen, and callous the nerve endings."[35]

Leary's original hope (never fully shared by Watts), that if people could experience the sense of meaning, unity, and wonder given by LSD, then social problems would be solved, began to look very naive. Mental hospitals bore pathetic witness of practical "jokes" played on unsuspecting victims who had drunk a soft drink or a cup of coffee containing the drug, and were full of people who could not "come down" after one or more trips.

The more idealistic among the young had begun to think in terms of moving into the country, of growing their own food, of starting their own farms, and a number moved out into Marin County, California, and beyond.

Others, influenced initially by Watts and Snyder, moved on from drugs to Zen. Snyder quoted D. T. Suzuki as saying that people who came to the *zendo* from LSD experiences showed an ability to get into good *zazen* very rapidly. Snyder told the English Benedictine monk Dom Aelred Graham in 1967 that "LSD has been a real social catalyst and amounts to a genuine historical unpredictable. It's changing the lives of all sorts of people. It's remarkable and effective and it works in terms of forms, devotions, personal deities, appearances of bodhisattvas, Buddhas and gods to your eyes. It doesn't work in terms of non-forms, emptiness. ("This isn't form is the same as emptiness," one Zen teacher who tried it reported, "this is emptiness is the same as form.")

"In several American cities," Snyder also observed, "traditional meditation halls of both Rinzai and Soto are flourishing. Many of the newcomers turned to traditional meditation after an initial acid experience. The two types of experience seem to inform each other."[36] (D. T. Suzuki later appeared to go back on the qualified respect he had shown for the LSD experience and announced that the meditation experience was quite distinct from Zen.)

Many who had used LSD as an opening to the inner world were attracted to formal meditation. By the fall of 1966, according to Rick Fields, "close to a hundred and fifty people were sitting zazen and attending lectures at the San Francisco Zen Center; fifty or sixty sat at least once a day, and eighty people, twice as many as the previous year, had attended the seven day sesshin. . . . As Zen Center itself grew, it naturally spawned a number of satellite centers run by senior students . . . in Berkeley, Mill Valley and Los Altos."[37]

San Francisco Zen Center raised a large sum of money to buy land at Tassajara Hot Springs in the Los Padres National Forest, and the Tassajara Zen Mountain Center was founded. More than a thousand people contributed money.

"It is for us in America," wrote Watts, "to realize that the goal of action is contemplation. Otherwise we are caught up in mock progress, which is just going on toward going on, what Buddhists call samsara — the squirrel cage of birth and death. That people are getting together to acquire this property for meditation is one of the most hopeful signs of our times."[38]

So the counterculture had moved by way of color, free sex, civil rights, rock music, brotherly love, LSD and other psychedelics, and innovative lifestyles toward — at least for some people — a serious interest in meditation. A few years later Watts was to say that people who had experimented with psychedelic chemicals might find that they had left them behind, "like the raft which you use to cross a river, and have found growing interest and even pleasure in the simplest practice of zazen, which we perform like idiots, without any special purpose."[39]

# Ten

# The Home Behind Home

## 1969-1973

In 1969 WATTS AND JANO moved to Druid Heights. The *Vallejo* had become so well known from films and photographs that Watts had begun to be pestered by disciples on the Sausalito waterfront, and he badly needed a place where he could not easily be found. He continued to use the boat for seminars and meetings of the Society for Comparative Philosophy, the organization he and Jano had founded in 1961 to promote ways of understanding drawn from many religions and cultures. But henceforward home was on Mount Tamalpais.

Ever since his sequence of LSD experiences Watts had seen Druid Heights as "home" and "the home behind home." Now he and Jano lived in their circular house, built by Roger Somers, high up over a valley with a view of great beauty. It was a kitchen, sitting room, and bedroom all in one. The bed disappeared out of sight during the day, so that Watts did not have to retire to a separate bedroom in the way that he hated, and there was a sun deck for outdoor living.

The house "is hidden in a grove of high eucalyptus trees," wrote Watts, "and overlooks a long valley whose far side is covered with a dense forest of bay, oak, and madrone so even in height that from a distance it looks like brush. No human dwelling is in view, and the principal inhabitant of the forest is a wild she-goat who has been there for at least nine years. Every now and then she comes out and dances upon the crown of an immense rock which rises far out of the forest."[1]

In 1968 Watts lost his earliest home: Rowan Cottage. In 1961 Emily died, and Watts, somewhat to the shock of his relatives, did not return to England for the funeral. Now Laurence had grown too frail to live on his own and had moved to an old people's home called Merevale. (It was pronounced Merryvale, but Laurence, with contempt, took pleasure in calling it Mere Vale.) Watts had gone to England to help him with the sad task of going through his possessions and getting rid of them — the legacies of many years of happy marriage.

Watts sadly put Rowan Cottage up for sale, having offered it to Joy Buchan, who declined the offer. One day as he was clearing the house he came upon "the Housetop," the enormous bureau that in his childhood had seemed to contain an arcane secret; he found himself going through its contents almost feverishly. "There were lots of interesting treasures and trinkets — but in all such quests and searches, as also in my pull to the West, it keeps coming back to me that the secret is in the seeker."[2] He was looking, he thought, for a jewel. Just as he had often searched Persian miniatures with a magnifying glass, losing himself in their tiny mystical worlds, he thought that the concentration on a tiny perfect whole — a dewdrop, a jewel, a snowflake, a flower — was an image of the universal of which we ourselves are a part. Looking for the jewel in the Housetop was his search for the universal and eternal, for the energy that had formed him, but from which he had so often felt cut off.

His years of fame had not in a sense helped him to find the

jewel. Film taken of Watts in 1969 shows him looking seedy, ill, and older than his fifty-four years; friends were concerned about his obvious fatigue and about his heavy drinking.

Gary Snyder, who had just returned to California from one of his periods of study in Japan, this time with his wife Masa and his son, Kai, began to notice that drinking had become a serious problem for Watts. Watts had arranged to rent Gary and Masa a house at Druid Heights, so the two men saw a good deal of one another. In Kyoto, Snyder had noticed that Watts drank more than was necessary, but now he had moved into a phase of heavier drinking.

> I told him as best as I could to get off it, but by this time he was stuck with an enormous alimony payment, and he was having to take far more gigs than anybody in their right mind would want to do just earning money, and he was also spending more money than he had to. He lived very well, and he was also supporting lots of people, including a full-time secretary. So he had to keep working, and as you keep working, you know, you got to play these roles, and you also keep drinking 'cause there's always these parties and so forth, so that doesn't help you slow it down. So he just wore himself out. It was out of his control, that was my feeling. The dynamics of his life had gotten beyond his control, and he didn't know what to do about it.
>
> The amazing thing was that he kept such expansiveness, such good humor, you know, with that great big laugh. . . . He never showed a waver or a wobble in his self-esteem, in his confidence. He never let a little crack open that "I'm having trouble." But he was putting away a bottle of vodka a day — I saw those bottles under the sink.

Roger Somers believed that the "tragic flaw" in Watts was that he suffered a deep neurotic shyness when it came to small groups, as for example at the sort of cocktail party that was usually given before or after one of his lectures:

He would sweat blood before these events and was quite uncomfortable in them. Then one day he discovered that if he had two, maybe three martinis, he was not only comfortable, but the life of the party. He could not have gone on with his lecture tours and the cocktail parties that went with them with any ease at all without that lubrication. . . . He could talk to people one to one, or a hundred to one, but cocktail party banter had him trembling and perspiring.

Paula McGuire, his editor at Pantheon Books, remembers Watts's telling her in 1968 that he was suffering from an enlarged liver, and that his doctor had warned him that he must give up drinking. For some months he did so, to the relief of his family and friends. Elsa Gidlow remembers the disappointment of sitting beside him at a Druid Heights lunch party and noticing that he was drinking again.

"Oh *Alan!*" she said, as he reached for the brandy.

"If I don't drink, I don't feel sexy," he growled in reply.

Perhaps the drinking came from a deep sense of loneliness that he had so often written about, a loneliness that increased with the cocktail parties and the fame. Considering Watts's lifelong interest in psychotherapy it seems odd that some wise and clever therapist could not help him; the trouble was that though Watts seemed to think psychoanalysis a good idea for other people, he could no more undertake and sustain it himself than he had been able to sustain *sanzen* with Sokei-an. He recounted how, at his one attempt, he felt that the analyst had turned the tables and was asking him for help. Jano, he claimed, had had the same experience, and she had cheekily suggested that she and her analyst adjourn to the nearest bar where he could buy her a drink and talk about *his* problems. The comment is scathing, superior, and is meant to suggest that Watts and Jano knew so much about themselves that no analyst could help them — a somewhat unlikely state of affairs. It also might be a defense against painful revelations. If there was a choice between maintaining the precarious self-control of the "know-it-all" adult and the humble discipline of trying to rediscover the lost child in himself, Watts was not prepared to make it.

Another kind of therapy comes to many people through love affairs or marriage. Perhaps Watts never quite despaired of this sort of healing, although his attempts at loving had often brought down storms of accusation on his head. By the time he married Jano he knew that he was incapable of monogamy. What he offered her instead was public loyalty and private devotion that was unswerving.

Life with Watts was hard for Jano, though. An intelligent woman, well-fitted to be his intellectual companion, she soon found when she traveled with him or sat in on his seminars that people sat spellbound at the feet of her guru-husband and had little interest in her ideas, even when they were just as good as his. She was too blunt, too honest, too little in awe of Watts, too human, not to be exasperated by this. As time went on she got into the habit of arguing with him or contradicting him in public. Sandy Jacobs, who first recorded Watts on tape, remembered how often on recordings you could hear the guru laying down the law as the awestruck pupils lapped up his pronouncements. Then Jano's voice chipped in with "No, Alan, you've got it wrong. . . ." Watts seemed to accept this correction meekly, as if he felt he needed it.

If she undermined him at his seminars, he had subtle ways of undermining her elsewhere. Joan and Ann, who were fond of her, noticed how when Jano started to cook a meal, Watts would gradually take over from her, leaving her with nothing to do. Even in small areas of life, he "knew better," needed to be in control.

Early in the marriage he was already having affairs, usually with very bright, attractive, younger women he met on his travels.

He used to say to friends, though not to Jano, that he "could not bear to sleep alone." So he would pick up a pretty girl on a university campus and take her to bed with him. There were many women who were happy to accommodate him; he was reputed to be an accomplished lover, and fame was a predictable aphrodisiac. He was a fine lover so long as he did not feel there was any attempt to hold him or trap him into marriage, and there were deeper, more lasting relationships with women friends with whom he could relax. He made it clear that there was no question of his ever leaving Jano.

Roger Somers thought that Watts might have made a better job of marriage if he had married women with whom he did not feel the need to play the Pygmalion role.

> He would have felt insecure if he'd been with some really heavy, finger-popping, laughing, gay woman, yet that was the kind of woman he sought in extracurricular ways. He saw them freely, was quite effective with them, and loved them, but to *live* with one of those — here was the crack in the vase: his unwillingness to accept joy. Instead his self-importance was demonstrated by their inability to cope — he would take over from them — and of course, they would end up morbidly dependent upon him. This was not like the man who was talking to us about Zen. That's not Zen — that's Zen backwards.

Watts refused to acknowledge any of this when Roger brought it up in conversation. "He would be a little awkward about it, and it was not easy as a rule for me to make him feel awkward."

Jano, as well as Watts, was drinking a good deal — the strains of their life together, as well as the mutual example of heavy drinking, exacerbated the problem for both of them.

Paula McGuire remembers an evening when she and the writer Joseph Campbell were to dine out with the Wattses in New York. Instead of accompanying them Jano was sent home in a taxi, suffering, according to Watts, from hypoglycemia. "We just thought she was drunk," says McGuire. Whether or not she was drunk on that occasion, Jano did suffer from a blood sugar problem that affected her health and was not helped by her heavy drinking.

Quite apart from his marriage, Watts was living under considerable tension. There was Dorothy's alimony and the cost of maintaining her five children and paying their medical expenses, in addition to the living expenses of Jano and himself (and Jano, on occasion, was given to wild bursts of spending). The life of a free-lance writer is a notoriously anxious one, even for those with a modest number of dependents; for Watts to meet his financial commitments meant a life of almost unceasing industry: writing, lecturing, broadcasting, appearing on television, traveling to speak on university campuses, or going abroad to take part in other talks and television appearances. The periods of idleness, which for Watts permitted inner development and change, became fewer and fewer. Though his writing was always professional, competent, and often brilliant in its perception and exposition, Watts began to repeat himself and covered his lack of energy with a self-assurance that some found very irritating. From clothes, to food, to lifestyle, to sex — Watts knew best how it should be managed.

Many people, however, were fascinated by the "know-it-all" touch, perhaps interpreting it as an authentic bit of British arrogance, perhaps merely liking to be told what to do by someone who had interesting and original ideas. They allowed Watts to tell them to sleep on mattresses on the floor of the living room, to wear loose Oriental clothes, to cook with fresh, natural ingredients, to dance, to chant, to make love freely and joyfully, and to despise chairs and plastics, both of which he disliked. What he wanted, he told his readers, was that they should "come to their senses." The advice was good, and many people were probably the better for following it.

Watts did try to insist that he was a fake, a rascal, and, primarily, an entertainer, but that only added to his fame and his following. The tragic underside of this fame could be seen in the furious and bitter letters from Dorothy complaining that he did not send enough money (though he was faithful in keeping up his commitment), in an unhappy Jano who only stopped drinking when he went away on his travels, and in his own desperate dependence on vodka.

Fame did at least put Watts in touch with a kind of international brotherhood of people interested in the same sets of ideas. He knew scientists and priests, Buddhist monks and artists, psychotherapists and craftsmen, academics and doctors. It seemed to him that the ideas of people from disparate disciplines were converging in important areas. By listening to theologians, religious thinkers from East and West, anthropologists, psychiatrists, psychotherapists of many schools, and neurologists, Watts might begin to try to join together ideas derived from different experiences of the human body, mind, and spirit. He knew, or corresponded with, Thomas Merton; Dom Aelred Graham; Shunryu Suzuki and his successor at San Francisco Zen Center, Richard Baker-roshi; Lama Govinda; Lama Chogyam Trungpa; anthropologist Gregory Bateson; scientist John Lilly, the Zurich Jungians; a group of Stanford neurologists working on the human brain; R. D. Laing, Fritz Perls, and Abraham Maslow; and the Esalen people.

Snyder observed that Watts moved from Zen to social and psychological concerns, then to visionary concerns, and finally, late in the sixties, to an interest in Taoism. Snyder saw Watts as part of a group of visionaries helping to give birth to a new consciousness. Much of the time, Snyder felt, Watts was right on top of what was going on, understanding it, and helping it on its way. And by about 1967 Watts had turned into a full-scale flower child.

Once or twice Snyder challenged Watts about the sort of popular books he was writing, wondering if they were worthy of the ideas he was trying to expound.

> I was beginning to question what seemed to me the easiness of his books — but his argument was that these ideas needed a skillful and popular exponent. As I got a chance to browse in his library, I was very impressed and convinced that perhaps he knew what he was doing; obviously this was no lightweight thinker. . . . He had really done his homework, and that deepened my respect for the kind of work he was trying to do.

Christians and Christianity still interested Watts a good deal. When Dom Aelred Graham, the author of *Zen Catholicism* and a Benedictine monk from Ampleforth Abbey in England, wanted to visit Kyoto to hold lengthy conversations with the *roshis* and monks at the Zen temples there, Watts seemed a natural adviser and guide. The conversations were later published in book form.

Considering that Watts was not an official participant in the conversations, he recurs surprisingly often in the text. One of the Zen exponents, Prof. Maseo Abe, commented a little severely on Watts:

> *M.A.*: I think he's a very clever man, clever interpreter of Zen, but I don't know how much he has practised Zen meditation.
> *Graham*: Not much, I don't think; but one can't be sure.
> *M.A.*: Maybe not.[3]

Watts had given Dom Aelred two fans, on one of which he had drawn the calligraphic characters for "Form is emptiness" and on the other the circle representing *sunyata, ku,* roughly translated as "emptiness." They became a focal point in several of the interviews. The Rev. Kobori Sohaku at his subtemple at Daitoku-ji Monastery was scarcely more enthusiastic than Professor Abe, once the Japanese interpreter had explained the origin of the fans. He dealt with the situation by using the Zen trick of disclaiming all understanding.

> *K.S.*: I hope you will explain the meaning. I don't know!
> *Graham*: I have come all the way to Japan to find out.
> *K.S.*: I don't know the meaning. It is taken from scripture, a very famous saying. He is quite good at calligraphy, Mr. Watts. The fan is too little for you — you need a much bigger one.[4]

Dom Aelred also interviewed Gary Snyder about his beat background, and about how Snyder would compare the insight given by LSD and similar drugs to the insight acquired through sitting in *zazen*. Snyder saw the grave dangers of such drugs, but also believed that the insights they gave were real. Watts came into this conversation too, in a joking way.

> *Graham*: Alan's going to found a new religion in San Francisco, I understand.
> *G.S.*: Which Alan?
> *Graham*: Alan Watts.
> *G.S.*: Is he going to start a new religion?
> *Graham*: Called Hum. On September fifteenth in San Francisco.
> *H.T.* [Harold Talbot]: He's not founding it; he's drawing attention to it.
> *G.S.*: That's nice.[5]

Dom Aelred was, in fact, having a wonderful time in Watts's company, accompanying him to parties of hippies and on all sorts of interesting trips in Japan. On one occasion they took LSD together. "I think there was a touch of genius about him," Dom

Aelred says, "and that he did much good for lots of people, especially perhaps in California. Like the rest of us, of course, he had
his weaknesses. He could lift the elbow regularly and frequently,
but he was generous and kind, and I never heard him speak
harshly of anyone."

Watts's private expeditions in Kyoto were a source of great pleasure. His favorite haunt was Tera-machi Street where, in the tiny
shops, he could buy implements for the tea ceremony, wonderful
tea, ancient pottery, rosaries, books, incense that smelled of aloes-
wood (the essential smell of Buddhism, according to Dr. Suzuki),
writing brushes, paper, and fine ink. One of his finds was a small
stick of vermilion ink covered with gold leaf. He said that to use
it he rubbed it on a windowsill, early in the morning, using a drop
of dew for water.[6]

On that same trip Gary Snyder remembers Watts's pleasure in
a big party at Kyoto, which was full of congenial guests: Japanese
poets and artists, priests from the Jodo Shin sect in California who
were particularly fond of jazz, and Hindu visitors. The party
seemed to catch the worldwide, cosmopolitan nature of the
counterculture.

Then, as so often, Watts's extraordinary capacity to enjoy himself came to the fore. It was his gift for play that his friends enjoyed most.

Roger Somers, who had noticed a similar quality in some of the
great black jazz musicians he had met, felt that Watts had the
greatest quality of play of anyone he had ever known. Living close
to Watts allowed him to know and appreciate the small details of
Watts's life and habits that most people did not know about. He
remembered how, when the two of them sat together out-of-doors,
butterflies would come and settle all over Watts, while scarcely

one would settle on him. He remembered Watts's taste for shooting arrows straight up into the air above his own head. (Jano once saw one of the arrows come down to land, quivering, between his feet.) He remembered Watts's awkwardness in handyman tasks around Druid Heights; the Brahmin education had spoiled him for those sorts of skills.

Jano's niece, Kathleen, herself now part of the boat community of Sausalito and an artist and craftswoman, remembers the extraordinary way Watts played with her and her brother when she was still a child. Once in New York he took them to the zoo and bought helium balloons for all three of them. While the children happily clutched theirs, Watts deliberately released the string of his and watched it float up into the sky — an act that made a deep impression on the children.

In 1964 Watts met the Jungian analyst June Singer at a cocktail party. June Singer had recently become a widow after a long marriage and was suffering from depression. At the party, given in Watts's honor, a sense of sympathy and recognition passed between them. She had just moved into a new apartment, and the next morning, a beautiful sunny day, she was sitting staring at a row of paint pots and thinking that she should begin work on repainting when she decided on an impulse to call Watts at his hotel and find out how he was getting along. He was delighted to hear her voice and suggested that they spend the afternoon on the beach, a meeting that was the beginning of a long and happy, though intermittent, love affair.

Watts would stay with her whenever he found himself in Chicago, and little by little she came out of her depression. Shaped by an "uptight" Jewish background and a rather correct Jewish marriage, she was surprised and delighted by Watts's attitude to life and to sex. His extraordinary energy, his readiness to dance or to sing or to make love, his pleasure in all the sensual joys of life deepened her own capacity for happiness. She was amazed at Watts's ability to unwind; after a grueling evening as a speaker in which he had been giving out for hours, he would curl up like a cat, utterly relaxed.

She knew also that Watts's pleasure in the relationship came partly from the absence of demands, and she did not make them upon him. From the beginning she was aware of his intense devotion to Jano. He seemed to her responsible but not guilty in his attitude to his marriage.

She found the public aspect of Watts difficult, the act of what she called "I am Alan Watts" when they went to a restaurant together. After a year or two their friendship temporarily foundered. She was working hard at her doctoral dissertation and told Watts to keep away since she did not want to be distracted. Hurt by what he felt as rejection Watts did not come back, and it was only after they met by chance on an airplane runway that their relationship continued.

Watts helped her with her writing and suggested the title for her book *Boundaries of the Soul.* Throughout much of their time together Dr. Singer was working on an idea that she later expressed in her book *Androgyny*; her theory was that human beings were developing in the direction of psychological androgyny, and that the more advanced people among us, in evolutionary terms, already showed marked characteristics of both masculine and feminine in their make-up. Watts seemed to her the perfect androgyne, active in his masculine aspect, receptive in his feminine. Besides this, she felt he had a gift of seeing the spark in people, in knowing where life and growth lay.

But like many of his friends she was saddened to see how heavily he was drinking. On one occasion she visited him in the hospital, where he was suffering from delirium tremens, and she realized that he knew how destructive the habit had become.

"That's how I am," he said to her sadly. "I can't change."

By 1970 his other friends were growing more concerned about his obvious fatigue and the effects of his drinking. Robert Shapiro, who thought he was being "eaten alive" by his many dependents, discussed the problem with him. The strain of making enough money to keep everybody and of living out his extraordinary role in the counterculture was slowly killing him. The solution, Shapiro said, was for him to get out of it all for a bit. It was absurd that a man of his interests had never been to China. What he should do was to go away to China for a year, giving no address, and leaving Robert to handle the claims and complaints of his relatives. It was a gesture of friendship and seemed to offer real hope for Watts to get his health and his energy back. He set off on the first leg of his journey, but then Robert received a telephone call. The guilt was too great; he could not abandon Jano, even temporarily.

Despite failing health Watts continued to lead the bohemian life, going to parties, staying up late, drinking and smoking heavily. Yet even for a bohemian and a drinker, he was very disciplined, rising early to write, coping well with business and with his vast correspondence, never missing an airplane or a deadline. His publishers always received meticulously typed manuscripts on time.

He never admitted in public to making very serious attempts at meditation, implying that the closest he came to *zazen* was going for a walk. Gary Snyder, however, believed that he sat in *zazen* more and more often in the last years of his life — they talked a lot about *zazen* together and Gary noticed the well-worn meditation cushion in front of the altar in Watts's house.

In a growing number of incidents the public facade almost cracked. Joan and her husband Tim remember going to collect Watts when he was due to give a public lecture — as his drinking had grown worse he had given up driving — and finding him heavily drunk. They drove a few blocks, and Watts insisted that they stop at a liquor store, where he bought a bottle of vodka. He put it on the back seat, and they drove off with Watts sitting between them in the front, but soon he had to turn round and take a swig out of the bottle. Joan was amused at the sight of the famous Alan Watts with his bottom in the air drinking neat vodka; she was also fully aware of the tragic implications. When they arrived at the lecture hall Watts walked onto the podium and gave his usual admirable lecture. (This was a miracle frequently repeated.) Only those who knew him very well could have guessed that he was very drunk indeed. Questions from the floor were more difficult. Watts seemed not to be able to make sense of what he was being asked, or to be answering some other question altogether. Occasionally he appeared to have gone to sleep between the asking of the question and his answering of it. Such was the awe in which he was held in the Bay Area, or such was people's readiness to attribute any eccentricity to some rare piece of Zen insight, that groups continued to ask him to speak; he gave good value. He no longer thought in terms of giving up drinking. He knew now that he was riding a tiger and that it was too late to get down.

It was ironic that his reputation, which had declined slightly at one point in the sixties when he did not involve himself with civil rights or with the peace movement, seemed to be rising again as his own grasp on life was failing. Apocryphal legends about him abounded, many of them absurd, though he did seem to have unusual perceptions and intuitions. For instance, Joan remembers talking to a woman who had gone to Watts for counseling. He interrupted her in midsentence and told her to stand up. He placed a steadying hand on her shoulder and at that moment there was quite a severe earthquake shock. Watts had been aware of the coming shock waves several minutes before she was.

Watts's relations with his older children were good. Joan and Ann and eventually Mark and Ricky, his two sons by Dorothy, were all fond of him and saw a good deal of him; the daughters of his marriage to Dorothy, on the other hand, never overcame the distance set up by his desertion in 1960 and were perhaps strongly influenced by Dorothy's bitterness toward him. On occasions when he tried to visit the family there were verbal attacks on him, and he used to take Joan or Ann with him to try to forestall these outbursts.

He gave each of his children a particular legacy. At the age of eighteen or so he would offer them LSD and care for them most lovingly through the trip, a remarkable memory for each of them. (Others, such as the friend Ruth Costello, who first took acid with Watts also remember how careful and helpful he was.)

Mark, who was parted from his father at the age of thirteen when Watts left Mill Valley, got to know him again in New York just before his eighteenth birthday. It was a happy reunion; they had a great time together. Watts arranged for him to take a photography course in the East Village, and Mark remembers with pleasure a visit by Watts to New York when Watts took him to visit friends at the Chelsea Hotel. Up in the penthouse suite of the hotel they played a wicked game on the passersby with a tiny laser beam device that they shone down upon the baffled people below.

"There was this wino," Mark remembers, "who was convinced he had seen Jesus."

Later on, at Druid Heights, Watts would take his vodka and
Mark would take a joint, and they would go and sit up on the hills
together and talk about things. Mark, like the others, was troubled
by his drinking: "I'd say to him, 'Dad, don't you want to live?'
and he would say, 'Yes, but it's not worth holding onto.'"

In 1971 was Laurence Watts's ninetieth birthday, and Watts and
Jano returned to Chislehurst to hold a celebration for the old man.
They gave a big family party at the pub by Saint Nicholas's
Church, the Tiger's Head, and after dinner Watts sang the Pete
Seeger song "Little Boxes" as part of the entertainment. His
cousins formed the impression that both Alan and Jano were a
little strange, that they were "on" something. Believing the wild
rumors of life in California the cousins assumed it must be drugs
rather than alcohol.

Watts also made such a long after-dinner speech to wind up the
evening that the waiters, wanting to clear up and go off duty, were
visibly impatient. Visible, that is, to everyone except Watts who
went on talking.

"If Confucius here would just stop talking we could go home,"
one of the waiters was heard to remark. When Watts eventually
realized their irritation he was surprised and concerned. He had
not meant to be arrogant; he was just absorbed in the pleasure of
talking to his friends and relatives.

On that same trip Watts and Laurence motored up to Cambridge, at the invitation of Bishop John Robinson, to conduct a
"liturgy of contemplation" at Trinity. The chapel was packed with
undergraduates. Watts had sent his usual meticulous instructions
to Bishop Robinson before the service, and the occasion had a moving and simple drama about it. A chair had been set in the middle
of the altar steps with a candle alight on a chair beside it. Many

who came to the service sat on cushions on the floor in front of
the speaker with a half circle of chairs behind them. Watts came
in wearing a cassock, sat down, and talked about contemplation:
"Man discovers himself as inseparable from the cosmos in both
its positive and negative aspects, its appearances and disappear-
ances."[7] Then he intoned the first line of "Veni Creator," the ancient hymn that invokes the action of the Holy Spirit, while the
lights dimmed overhead. He conducted a meditation, with long
periods of silence. Then they sang the Nunc Dimittis and a litany,
after which Watts gave a benediction and the choir sang a long
Gregorian amen. Watts could still orchestrate a moving and beautiful service.

This liturgical experiment was not an isolated occasion. Licensed
by Bishop James Pike in San Francisco, Watts had held similar
services in Grace Cathedral, which were enthusiastically attended.
News of his involvement with the church caused rumors that he
was thinking of asking to have Anglican orders restored to him,
but rumors were all they were. Far from returning to the church,
he still managed to offend Episcopal high-church sensibilities on
occasion.

On one such occasion, entertained by senior clergy in New York,
he had been drawn into discussion of the Anglican Holy Communion service as compared with the Catholic Mass. The complacency of his companions over the rather sober rite used at the time
pushed him into his now famous outrageousness.

"Holy Communion?" he was heard to remark. "Why, it's like
fucking a plastic woman!" In the silence that followed the only
sound to be heard was the bishop's wife biting nervously and
noisily into an apple.

More seriously, he had written about "the problem" of the
churches. "What are we going to do with an enormous amount

of valuable real estate known, not quite correctly, as the Church —
whether it be Catholic, Episcopalian, Presbyterian, Lutheran,
Methodist, Congregational, or Unitarian?"[8] Strip them of pews,
was his suggestion, leaving only a few chairs for the sick and
elderly, and putting carpets and cushions down for the rest. Abandon the "interminable chatter" of sermons and petitions, and substitute instead a liturgy that helped the worshippers into mystical
contemplation and silence — by way of chanting, singing, dancing,
meditative rituals, and dramatic enactments of the Mass.

For Christmas 1971 Laurence made a tape wishing Alan and his
grandchildren well and reciting the Kipling poems that he loved.
Watts played it during Christmas dinner at Joan's house in Bolinas,
and then one by one Watts's grandchildren, Joan's husband,
Tim, Elsa Gidlow, Jano, and finally Watts himself, sent their
good wishes to "Granddaddy." On the tape Watts described the
turkey lunch, complete with *pâté en croûte* made by him, and
Joan's daughter Elizabeth described how Joan had just given her
a doll that had once belonged to her, together with a four-poster
bed and a doll's wardrobe made by Laurence and a quilt and an
embroidered stool made by Emily. Jano described how, as soon as
Christmas was over, she and Alan were to go off on vacation to
Mexico "away from mails, the telephone, and family." In fact,
they went on this rare vacation before Watts finished the tape.
Completing the recording in May Watts described how, in the
first few months of 1972, he had given lectures all over New
Mexico and in Boulder, Colorado, and how he had spoken in
Vancouver and on Cortes Island and then in Chicago. He had, he
added laughingly, been obliged to pay a tax bill of ten thousand
dollars in April, so he had had no choice but to work hard.

   And work hard he did, for despite the alcoholism, his energy
for his projects had not diminished. He had gone to Esalen to

work with Army officers on the drug problem in the U.S. Army. The formal meetings had not yielded much, since the officers would talk in "memorandese," but the informal conversations had made him feel more hopeful and had given him insight about official attitudes. In addition, he, Mark, and Sandy Jacobs were making a series of half-hour video cassettes in preparation for the growing video market. Up at Druid Heights Elsa Gidlow and Roger Somers were considering selling land to the government on a one-hundred-year lease and building a Japanese-style library for Watts's books.

Another significant publication was in the works, Watts's autobiography. In 1970 Paula McGuire had suggested to Alan that he might like to write an autobiography, which he did, and in 1972 Pantheon published *In My Own Way*. Mrs. McGuire remembers her disappointment when the manuscript came in. Though an interesting book in many ways and one that was bound to sell, there was something too coy, too knowing about it, an infuriating air of effortless ease. It was honest as far as it went, but it hardly went far enough, in her opinion. "I sensed he had not really written about his mother at all," she says. There was something thin and unsatisfying about it, a lot of name dropping, perhaps to make up for the other omissions of the book, and it had the air of having been dictated rather carelessly. The material was haphazard in its order; Watts repeatedly returned to discussing his childhood and his schooldays long after he had passed on to later stages of his life.

It is easy to guess at some of the difficulties that Watts had as he approached this task. The book was a guaranteed seller in advance, and he needed the money, but a truthful autobiography would have imposed impossible conditions upon him.

He could not write easily of his feelings about his mother without causing great distress to his father (though within strict limits he made a brave attempt). In fact, other interesting omissions may have occurred, in part, from Watts's attempt to spare his father's feelings. There is no account of his parents' removal from Rowan Cottage when economic hardship overwhelmed them, nor does he mention the pain of Laurence's unemployment. Not only did Laurence write the foreword, but he also read the book in draft, suggesting many omissions.

Watts also could not write truthfully of the sexual difficulties that had gradually destroyed his marriage to Eleanor and had lost him his job in the Episcopal priesthood without alienating most of his admirers. He could not write of his present marital difficulties; in fact, he gives Jano a slightly patronizing pat on the head whenever he mentions her, as if, like a sulky child, she will become difficult if not publicly noticed. He is, however, generous to both his other wives in the book, probably because it was not in his nature to be bitter. Eleanor was deeply touched by the book when she read it and felt largely reconciled to Watts because of the way he described their marriage.

In the early seventies Watts paid a couple of visits to the Sierra Nevada, where Gary and Masa Snyder had built Kitkitdizze, a Japanese-style house and a *zendo* deep in the woods. Watts admired the house; lying on his back on the floor and looking up into the pitched ceiling he said that it was "a very noble view." Gary remembers their shooting arrows together and sitting outside peeling apples, preparing to dry them. They had "lots of sake and gossip" and talked, among other things, about whether LSD was a good idea or not.

Their feeling by this time was that "letting it loose in the society" had done harm. The first people to experiment with peyote, LSD, and similar drugs had been artists, poets, psychologists, and students of religion, and most of them had handled it well, finding it an interesting and creative experience. Consequently, no one was prepared to see that when LSD became more widely used in society the results would be bizarre indeed, with people who were not in any way ready for the experience becoming monomaniacs and self-appointed messiahs. It was just too potent for those who were psychologically, aesthetically, or spiritually unprepared for it.

Watts's own religious interest was now centered on Taoism. In a journal he wrote during 1971–72, *Cloud-hidden, Whereabouts Unknown*, he describes his feelings on watching the mountain stream after the rains on Mount Tamalpais:

> When I stand by the stream and watch it, I am relatively still, and the flowing water makes a path across my memory so that I realize its transience in comparison with my stability. This is, of course, an illusion in the sense that I, too, am in flow and likewise have no final destination — for can anyone imagine finality as a form of life? My death will be the disappearance of a particular pattern in the water.[9]

The human problem, as Watts sees it, is the attempt to gain control of the "streaming," a habitual tension that sets up a chronic frustration, the belief that force or effort or will can solve our difficulties.

In contrast to this Western approach to "how things are" is the Chinese concept of the Tao, the course of nature, that which flows of its own accord, says Watts: "You can get the feel of it by breathing without doing anything to help your breath along. Let the breath out, and then let it come back by itself, when it feels like it." Once the breather has "let go" of the breath and allowed it to go its own way, it becomes slower and stronger. "This happens because you are now 'with' the breath and no longer 'outside it' as controller." In the same way, thoughts, feelings, and all experiences may be allowed to follow their own course, watched detachedly by the one who has them. "If you find yourself asking who is watching and why, take it as simply another wiggle of the stream."[10]

Our fear, says Watts, is that if we don't control everything, events will run wild — our suspicion of what is natural and spontaneous is deep. Letting go is an experiment few are prepared to make. Letting go works in the paradoxical sense that creative and constructive action comes from a knowledge that

> every willful effort to improve the world or oneself is futile, and so long as one can be beguiled by any political or spiritual scheme for molding things nearer to the heart's desire one will be frustrated, angry or depressed — that is, unless the first step in any such scheme is to see that nothing can be done. This is not because you are a victim of fate, but because there is no "you" to be fated, no observing self apart from the stream.[11]

Once the illusion of the separate self is dissipated, then, he says, it is like restoring balance in dancing or in judo; once the "you" knows itself as part of the stream, then the true energy or power works through it.

Watts began a book developing these ideas: *Tao: The Watercourse Way*, continuing with his image of the stream. He had been teaching, both at Esalen and at Sausalito, with the tai chi master Al Chung-liang Huang. A friendship quickly grew between them as they worked over Chinese texts together, trying out various translations, trying to decipher all the possible meanings.

In their last teaching session together at Esalen Al Chung-liang Huang remembered a joyful afternoon session in which their pupils ended up dancing and rolling down the grassy slopes:

> Alan and I started to walk back to the lodge, feeling exuberant, arms around each other, hands sliding along one another's spine. Alan turned to me and started to speak, ready to impress me with

his usual eloquence about our successful week together. I noticed
a sudden breakthrough in his expression; a look of lightness and
glow appeared all around him. Alan had discovered a different way
to tell me of his feelings: "Yah . . . Ha . . . Ho . . . Ha! Ho . . . . . . ."
We gibbered and danced all the way up the hill.[12]

Watts finished five chapters of the new book, one on the Chinese
use of ideograms and the difference such a language makes to the
understanding of those who use it. By contrast the linear language
of the West has resulted in an emphasis on progress and thus on
control, as opposed to the cyclic Chinese view of time and history.

The next chapter described the two poles of cosmic energy, the
yang and the yin, otherwise thought of as the light and the dark,
the firm and the yielding, the strong and the weak, the rising and
the falling, the masculine and the feminine — the complemen-
tarity that is the key to harmonious existence.

In the third chapter he repeats the image of the stream, the
watercourse way from which you cannot really deviate even if you
wish; you can only fight against it like a swimmer exhausting
himself by trying to swim against the tide. Next, Watts discusses
*wu-wei*, the famous principle of nonaction, the refusal of counter-
feit action, meddling, forcing, working against the grain of things.

Finally, he writes about *Te* — virtue — a way of contemplation,
of "being aware of life without thinking about it," the expression
of the Tao in actual living.

When these five chapters were completed Watts told Al Chung-
liang Huang with glee, "I have now satisfied myself and my readers
in scholarship and intellect. The rest of this book will be all fun
and surprises!"[13]

Before he could get on with the fun and surprises, however, he
had another exhausting lecture tour to Europe planned. He wrote
to Laurence on September 5, 1973:

Dear Daddy,

I have made arrangements for Jano and I to arrive in London on the morning of September 25th and to stay at the Charing Cross Hotel until about October 4th, when we have to go to the Continent — Frankfurt, Heidelberg, Amsterdam and Geneva.

In the meantime, I have opened a London bank account. This is at Barclays, 27 Regent Street, SW1 and the number is 20–71–64 20048305. I can't imagine that they have more than 20 million clients, but that is it!

During the visit to England I shall need to take two days out to go to Cambridge and York — to see Joseph Needham and John Robinson, and to confer with the Benedictine fathers at Ampleforth. I have a date with Toby [Christmas Humphreys] on the 29th.

Otherwise, take it that we shall come down to Chislehurst on the afternoon of the 25th and have dinner together at the Tiger, and make up our plans from there on. Will you let Joy know that we are coming. We would also very much like to see Leslie and Peggy.

I am more than halfway through my next book — a rather scholarly though simply written study of Taoism.

Much love from us both,
    As ever, Alan.

The eve of the trip, however, found both Watts and Jano in poor shape for such a demanding undertaking. Early in September Jano's twenty-one-year-old niece Kathleen came over from Europe for a holiday at Druid Heights. The plan was for her to spend a few weeks with Watts and Jano and then accompany them back to Europe when they went on the trip. When she arrived, full of excitement and enthusiasm, she found Jano far too ill as a result of drinking to go anywhere at all, and Watts in only marginally better shape. Having admired this unusual couple from afar for most of her youth she felt very shocked and let down.

"Uncle Alan, *why*?" she asked him, as his children had so often done.

"When I drink I don't feel so alone," he told her.

Kathleen offered to stay behind and look after Jano while Watts was away in Europe; in his absence, as on other occasions, Jano stopped drinking.

Watts's trip to Europe included a trip to the Benedictine Abbey at Ampleforth at the invitation of Dom Aelred Graham and the then abbot, Basil Hume (now cardinal). The previous year Watts had been to a conference held by the Benedictine monastery of Mount Savior, in New York,

> to which the good fathers invited a whole gaggle of gurus for a five-day contemplative retreat. It was a marvellous and most encouraging experience. For . . . we found that any real opposition between the I–Thou [devotional or bhakti] attitude and the All-is-One attitude could be transcended in a silence of the mind in which we all stopped verbalizing. It was fascinating to take part with Hindu swamis and Trappist monks in 4:30 A.M. sessions for Zen meditation where we all seemed to get into a state of consciousness in which there was nothing left to argue about — as well as to attend sessions for the Hesychast Jesus prayer conducted by an Archimandrite whose theological views were extremely conservative. It all ended up with everyone dancing on the green to the guitar music of a Hassidic rabbi! Lex orandi lex credendi.[14]

The visit to England included taking part in a television program about drugs called "The Timeless Moment." Other participants ranged from a simple-minded acidhead at one end of the scale to a disapproving clergyman at the other. Watts took a moderate line on taking drugs: "I don't exactly advocate it. I say it's a very useful adjunct to human knowledge to have these drugs, just as microscopes and telescopes are, but they have to be used with greatest care because all investigation into these realms is dangerous." But he thought the changed perception that found the world so amazingly beautiful, the sudden understanding about how foolishly we rush and worry in the world, and the sense of unity between the individual and the universe was valuable. "It teaches you — it teaches you to feel, not merely just to know intellectually, but to feel in your bones that you are one with the whole natural environment, and therefore you respect it as you respect your own body."[15]

After England there were to be trips to Germany, Holland, and Switzerland, and more public appearances. First there were occasions for family meetings, however. There was a visit to his cousins Leslie and Peggy in Kingston Vale. Peggy remembered waiting an hour and a half to pick up Watts and Laurence at the Putney tube station. Then Watts arrived, happily oblivious of any offense caused.

On another evening he met them for dinner at Simpson's in the Strand, a very traditional and sober restaurant. He was wearing a turtleneck shirt and sandals, and the doorman politely declined to let him in.

"You don't like my wear?" asked Watts in amusement. He went back to the Charing Cross Hotel to change and reappeared, still wearing his sandals, but in a necktie and jacket.

"Are you happy now I look like all the other undertakers?" he asked.

His relatives found him warm, loving, fun to be with, generous. He dominated the conversation, but was well worth listening to. He seemed to them, however, always "in a world of his own."

In October Watts returned from his visit to Europe exhausted and lay on the couch "jet-lagged." A friend brought him a red balloon to play with, and as he watched it float away from him he said, "This is just like my spirit leaving my body." He had spoken of death a good deal in the previous year or so, telling Baker-roshi on a long motor ride just what kind of funeral he would like to have. When someone made a joke about the telephones at Druid Heights being tapped, he said that after his death he would watch the situation, and if the phones were tapped he would come in a lightning flash and knock out the underground cable. He had made his will, and he had told Sandy Jacobs and his son Mark, who had both worked on his tapes and videocassettes, that now he would be able to communicate "without carrying this body around."

Gradually Watts had been overtaken by the sense that living was a burden. His strength was clearly declining, yet the financial demands on him grew no less. As for his marriage, far from re-energizing and comforting one another, he and Jano seemed to aggravate each other's problems; something in the chemistry of life between them was decidedly destructive to Jano.

On the morning of November 16 Jano tried to wake Watts but found him "strangely unmoveable." With deep shock she realized he was dead. When the doctor came he certified that Watts had died of heart failure. In Joan's words he had "checked out." He was fifty-eight.

There were strange stories surrounding Watts's death: that the great gong on the terrace of Druid Heights sounded when there was no one there to strike it. That on December 21 of that year, the winter solstice, a lightning flash knocked out the underground cable at the top of the lane that led to Druid Heights, and that this must be Watts fulfilling his promise.

Jano believed, and said as much in a letter to Laurence Watts, that Watts had been experimenting with breathing techniques to reach *samadhi*, had somehow left his body, and had been unable to get back into it again.

. . .

As the news of Watts's death was announced, messages poured
into Druid Heights, and Jano and the Druid Heights community
sent out a letter of reply with a circle drawn on it in Watts's
calligraphy and stamped with his Chinese seal. "Alan joins us,"
it read, "in thanking you for your farewell message. Listen, and
rejoice, as his laughter circles the universe."

In her letter to Laurence, Jano wrote of her grief and of his.

> Besides the "this isn't so" feeling I get often when coming out of
> sleep, and it's often dreadful, there are all those "reality" tasks,
> thank heavens. Things that must be done, and things that I get
> excited about in planning projects for my own life, and to keep
> Alan's life-after-death name alive. Both with objectives in mind —
> financial and idealistic. Alan left me everything — all loose ends
> to tie up, if possible: the chance to make my own way: the decisions
> related to the "health, education and welfare" of his children and
> other heirs. Wow!

Jano went on to speak of the rites of Alan's death and her disappointment that her mother, who had loved Alan, was too ill to
attend. She felt she now understood better her mother's grief at
the death of Jano's father.

> Excuse me, a few tears. It happens several times a day, and I re-
> cover. And it's so odd that from the time of Alan's death until after
> midnight on the Winter Solstice, when I spent the night before his
> altar and ashes in the library, I had not shed one tear. I was no-
> where. Then I had a dialogue with him, a long one, and he said,
> in short, "Do it, baby, while it lasts. Have a ball; I toss it to you."
> And I really cried — endlessly that night.
>
> Oh Daddy, there is so much I want to discuss with you, not
> practical details, which can be handled by correspondence, but
> about why, maybe, and how, maybe, this fantastic event, Alan's
> death, occurred. And I just can't say this or that was the reason,
> although I suspect that he knew he would not last too long, with

all that mental and psychic strength carried by a not-so-strong body. And he refused to care for his physical being, anything said by me or Joan or anyone being considered an interference to his own responsibility.

She writes of the various hints there had been that he expected to die before long.

Anyway, Daddy, with all that seems to have been lost so early with Alan's death, I sometimes wonder. His very last lecture was a string of pearls — of all the best things he had said many, many times, word for word: his unfinished book on Taoism isn't really unfinished: it's perfect. It only needs a summation as to how such a philosophy can be applied today, and he had prepared several persons to do that. [Al Chung-liang Huang actually did it.] All is being considered. Alan did fantastic things in his lifetime. With his resting, all he said may become, oh dear, gospel. Maybe. Alan's statement, one that sticks with me: The secret of life is knowing when to stop. That's like opening a fortune cookie, only more profound.[16]

There was a requiem mass in February at Druid Heights, the scattering of ashes there in front of Watts's library, and the interment of ashes beneath the stone stupa on the hillside behind the Zen Center's Green Gulch Farm. It was the one-hundredth day in the Buddhist calendar. Full honor was given to Watts as an "ancestor" by the abbot of the San Francisco Zen Center.

At the Crossing Over ceremony Zentatsu Baker-roshi — carrying the monk's staff Alan Watts had once given Suzuki-roshi at Tassajara — gave Watts a Buddhist name, Yu Zen Myo Ko — Profound Mountain, Subtle Light — to which he added the title Dai Yu Jo Mon — Great Founder, Opener of the Great Zen Samadhi Gate — a title, he said, "given very rarely, once a generation or a century."

Gary Snyder wrote:

He blazed out the new path for all of us and came back and made
it clear. Explored the side canyons and deer trails, and investigated
cliffs and thickets. Many guides would have us travel single file,
like mules in a pack train, and never leave the trail. *Alan* taught
us to move forward like the breeze, tasting the berries, greeting the
blue jays, learning and loving the whole terrain.[17]

In the last year of Watts's life, his daughter Joan had told him of
her unfulfilled wish to conceive another child.

"After I'm dead," Watts told her, "I'm coming back as your
child. Next time round I'm going to be a beautiful red-haired
woman." He had written in *Cloud-hidden, Whereabouts Unknown*
of the "completely rational" belief in reincarnation that he held.
He thought that the energy that had made him in the first place
was bound to do it again in some other form. "After I die I will
again awake as a baby."

Joan was not sure how lighthearted he was being in his promise
to return as her child, but not long after his death she did conceive
and eventually gave birth to a very pretty red-haired daughter,
Laura, whose character sometimes reminded Joan of her father.
Once, when Laura was a tiny girl, she and Joan visited a friend's
house, and Laura went to the cupboard where the liquor was kept,
pushed a number of bottles out of the way, reached in, and removed a bottle of vodka from the back of the cupboard. Joan
laughs as she tells this story, neither quite believing nor disbeliev-
ing her father's promise.

# Notes

All quotations for which references are not given are taken from conversations I have had with Alan Watts's relatives and friends. The context makes it clear who these are.

## 1. THE PARADISE GARDEN, 1915–1920

1. Emily Watts to William Buchan, December 25, 1912.
2. Alan Watts, *In My Own Way: An Autobiography* (New York: Random House, Pantheon Books, 1972), p. 22.
3. Ibid., p. 15.
4. Ibid.
5. Emily Watts to William Buchan, March 17, 1918.
6. Laurence Wilson Watts, foreword to Watts, *In My Own Way*, p. vi.
7. Watts, *In My Own Way*, p. 13.
8. Ibid., p. 35.
9. Ibid., pp. 30–31.
10. Ibid., p. 8.
11. Ibid., p. 9.

12. Ibid., p. 38:

> Il y avait un jeune homme de Dijon
> Qui n'aimait pas la religion.
> > Il dit, "O ma foi,
> > Comme drôle sont ces trois:
> Le Père, et le Fils, et le Pigeon."

Which Watts translated as:

> There was a young fellow of Dijon,
> Who took a dislike to religion.
> > He said, "Oh my God,
> > These three are so odd —
> The Father, the Son, and the Pigeon."

In ruder vein is a limerick Watts taught to Gary Snyder:

> There once was a Bishop of Buckingham,
> Who took out his thumbs and was sucking 'em,
> > At the sight of the stunts
> > Of the cunts in the punts
> And the tricks of the pricks who were fucking 'em.

## 2. THE EDUCATION OF A BRAHMIN, 1920–1932

1. Alan Watts, "Clothes — On and Off," *Does It Matter? Essays on Man's Relation to Materiality* (New York: Random House, Pantheon Books, 1970), p. 57.
2. Watts, *In My Own Way: An Autobiography* (New York: Random House, Pantheon Books, 1972), p. 89.
3. Ibid., p. 89.
4. Ibid., p. 93.
5. Ibid., p. 44.
6. Ibid., p. 14.
7. Ibid., p. 69.
8. Ibid., p. 68.
9. Ibid., p. 69.
10. Ibid., p. 66.
11. Ibid., p. 26.

12. Patrick Leigh Fermor, *A Time of Gifts* (London: John Murray, 1977), p. 15.
13. Watts, *In My Own Way*, p. 98.
14. Ibid., p. 54.
15. Leigh Fermor, *A Time of Gifts*, p. 17.
16. Watts, *In My Own Way*, p. 91.
17. Ibid., p. 99.
18. Leigh Fermor to the author, December 18, 1983.
19. Watts, *In My Own Way*, pp. 103–4.
20. Ibid., p. 61.
21. Leigh Fermor to the author, December 18, 1983.
22. Watts, *In My Own Way*, p. 57.
23. Ibid., p. 71.
24. Laurence Watts to William Buchan, May 25, 1929.
25. Watts, *In My Own Way*, p. 76.
26. Ibid.
27. Watts to Gertrude Buchan, c. 1931.
28. Ibid.
29. Watts, *In My Own Way*, p. 83.
30. Ibid., p. 86.

## 3. CHRISTMAS ZEN, 1932–1938

1. Editorial, *The Middle Way: Journal of the Buddhist Society* (August 1983). Memorial issue on Christmas Humphreys.
2. Alan Watts, *In My Own Way: An Autobiography* (New York: Random House, Pantheon Books, 1972), p. 77.
3. Ibid., p. 113.
4. Ibid., p. 106.
5. Ibid.
6. Ibid., p. 107.
7. Ibid., p. 116.
8. Rick Fields, *How the Swans Came to the Lake: A Narrative History of Buddhism in America* (Boulder, Colo.: Shambhala, 1981), p. 137.

9. Watts, *The Spirit of Zen: A Way of Life, Work, and Art in the Far East* (New York: Grove Press, 1958), p. 26.

10. Ibid., pp. 27–28.

11. Ibid., p. 75.

12. Watts, *In My Own Way*, p. 121.

13. Fields, *How the Swans Came to the Lake*, p. 189.

14. Watts, *In My Own Way*, p. 127.

15. Watts, *The Legacy of Asia and Western Man: A Study of the Middle Way* (London: John Murray, 1937), p. 61.

16. Ibid., p. 43.

17. Watts, *In My Own Way*, p. 132.

## 4. THE TOWERS OF MANHATTAN, 1938–1941

1. Alan Watts, *In My Own Way: An Autobiography* (New York: Random House, Pantheon Books, 1972), p. 160.

2. Ibid., p. 161.

3. Quoted in Rick Fields, *How the Swans Came to the Lake: A Narrative History of Buddhism in America* (Boulder, Colo.: Shambhala, 1981), pp. 180–81.

4. Watts, *In My Own Way*, p. 142.

5. Quoted in Fields, *How the Swans Came to the Lake*, p. 189.

6. Fields, ibid., p. 190.

7. Watts, *In My Own Way*, p. 145.

8. Ibid., p. 145.

9. Watts, *The Meaning of Happiness* (New York: Harper & Row, 1940), xxii.

10. Ibid., p. 65.

11. Watts, *In My Own Way*, p. 149.

12. Watts, "The Problem of Faith and Works in Buddhism," *Columbia Review of Religion* (May 1941).

13. Watts, *In My Own Way*, p. 157.

14. Ibid.

15. Ibid., p. 159.

16. Ibid., p. 158.

17. Ibid.

18. Ibid., p. 161.
19. Ibid., p. 156.
20. Ibid., p. 163.

## 5. COLORED CHRISTIAN, 1941–1947

1. Alan Watts, *In My Own Way: An Autobiography* (New York: Random House, Pantheon Books, 1972), p. 178.
2. Ibid., p. 176.
3. Ibid., p. 180.
4. Ibid., p. 183.
5. Ibid., p. 141.
6. Ibid., p. 186.
7. Watts, pamphlets describing the work at Canterbury House.
8. Ibid.
9. Watts, *Behold the Spirit: A Study in the Necessity of Mystical Religion* (New York: Random House, Pantheon Books, 1947), pp. 4–5.
10. Ibid., p. 13.
11. Ibid., p. 15.
12. Ibid.
13. Ibid., p. 16.
14. Ibid., p. 29.
15. Ibid., p. 70.
16. Ibid., p. 110.
17. Ibid., p. 155.
18. Ibid., p. 180.
19. F. S. C. Northrop, *Church Times*, November 2, 1947.
20. Watts, *In My Own Way*, p. 189.
21. Ibid.

## 6. CORRESPONDENCE, 1947–1950

1. Eleanor Watts to Bishop Wallace Conkling, June 29, 1950.
2. Ibid.
3. Ibid.

4. Alan Watts, *In My Own Way: An Autobiography* (New York: Random House, Pantheon Books, 1972), p. 203.

5. Eleanor Watts to Bishop Conkling, June 29, 1950.

6. Ibid.

7. Ibid.

8. Carl Wesley Gamer to Bishop Conkling, July 20, 1950.

9. Alan Watts to Bishop Conkling, June 29, 1950.

10. Ibid.

11. Bishop Conkling to Alan Watts, July 5, 1950.

## 7. A PRIEST INHIBITED, 1950–1951

1. Alan Watts, *In My Own Way: An Autobiography* (New York: Random House, Pantheon Books, 1972), p. 226.

2. Ibid., p. 213.

3. Ibid.

4. Ibid., p. 215.

5. Ibid., p. 217.

6. Ibid., p. 223.

7. Ibid.

8. Watts, *The Wisdom of Insecurity: A Message for an Age of Anxiety* (New York: Random House, Pantheon Books, 1951), p. 9.

9. Ibid., p. 52.

## 8. THE WISDOM OF INSECURITY, 1951–1960

1. Alan Watts, *In My Own Way: An Autobiography* (New York: Random House, Pantheon Books, 1972), p. 244.

2. Ibid., p. 247.

3. Ibid., p. 246.

4. Ibid., p. 378.

5. Ibid., p. 251.

6. Ibid.

7. Ibid., p. 270.

8. Watts, *The Way of Zen* (New York: Random House, Pantheon Books, 1957), p. 14.

9. Ibid., p. 141.

10. Watts, *In My Own Way*, p. 276.

11. Watts, *Nature, Man and Woman* (New York: Random House, Pantheon Books, 1958), p. 70.

12. Ibid., p. 112.

13. Ibid., p. 199.

14. Watts, *In My Own Way*, p. 336.

15. Ibid., p. 339.

16. Ibid., p. 245.

17. Ibid., p. 304.

18. Watts, *The Wisdom of Insecurity: A Message for an Age of Anxiety* (New York: Random House, Pantheon Books, 1951), pp. 79–80.

19. Watts, *In My Own Way*, p. 306.

20. Ibid., p. 305.

21. Ibid.

22. Ibid.

23. Ibid.

24. Ibid., p. 307.

## 9. COUNTERCULTURE, 1960–1968

1. Alan Watts, *In My Own Way: An Autobiography* (New York: Random House, Pantheon Books, 1972), p. 311.

2. Watts, speech at Varda's memorial service, January 1971.

3. Ibid.

4. *Pacific Sun*, January 1–7, 1982.

5. Watts, *In My Own Way*, p. 319 .

6. Ibid.

7. Watts, *Nature, Man and Woman* (New York: Random House, Pantheon Books, 1958), p. 70.

8. Rick Fields, *How the Swans Came to the Lake: A Narrative History of Buddhism in America* (Boulder, Colo.: Shambhala, 1981), p. 212.

9. Jack Kerouac, *The Dharma Bums* (New York: Viking Press, 1958), p. 104.

10. Timothy Leary, *Flashbacks: An Autobiography* (Los Angeles: J. P. Tarcher, 1983), p. 149.

11. Ibid., p. 195.

12. Aldous Huxley, *The Doors of Perception* (New York: Harper & Row, 1954), pp. 12–17.

13. Watts, "The New Alchemy," *"This Is It" and Other Essays on Zen and Spiritual Existence* (New York: Random House, Pantheon Books, 1960), p. 140.

14. Ibid., p. 143.

15. Ibid., p. 152.

16. Ibid., pp. 152–53.

17. Watts, *The Joyous Cosmology* (New York: Random House, Pantheon Books, 1972), p. 73.

18. Ibid., p. 43.

19. Leary, *Flashbacks*, p. 132.

20. Ibid., pp. 158–59.

21. Watts, *In My Own Way*, p. 367.

22. Theodore Roszak, *The Making of a Counter Culture* (Garden City, N.Y.: Doubleday, Anchor Books, 1969), p. 132.

23. Watts, *The Essence of Alan Watts* (Berkeley: Celestial Arts, 1974), p. 4.

24. Ibid., p. 23.

25. Watts, *The Two Hands of God* (New York: George Braziller, 1963), p. 168.

26. Watts, *Beyond Theology: The Art of Godmanship* (New York: Random House, Pantheon Books, 1964), preface.

27. Ibid.

28. Watts, *In My Own Way*, pp. 310–11.

29. Roszak, *The Making of a Counter Culture*, p. 30.

30. Charles Perry, *The Haight-Ashbury: A History* (New York: Random House, 1984), p. 55.

31. Ibid., p. 122.

32. *The Berkeley Barb*, January 13, 1967

33. Perry, *The Haight-Ashbury*, p. 125.
34. "Dateline," BBC TV, March 27, 1968.
35. Aelred Graham, "LSD and All That," *Conversations: Christian and Buddhist* (London: Collins, 1969), pp. 53–87. Conversation between Gary Snyder and Dom Aelred Graham, September 6, 1967.
36. Ibid.
37. Fields, *How the Swans Came to the Lake*, p. 256.
38. Watts, *Zen in America: An Unconditioned Response to a Conditioned World* (Zen Center brochure).
39. Watts, ibid.

## 10. THE HOME BEHIND HOME, 1969–1973

1. Alan Watts, *Cloud-hidden, Whereabouts Unknown: A Mountain Journal* (New York: Random House, Pantheon Books, 1973), p. 13.
2. Watts, *In My Own Way: An Autobiography* (New York: Random House, Pantheon Books, 1972), p. 31.
3. Dom Aelred Graham, "Zazen and Related Topics," *Conversations: Christian and Buddhist* (London: Collins, 1969), p. 9.
4. Ibid., p. 8.
5. "LSD and All That," ibid., p. 82.
6. Watts, *Cloud-hidden*, p. 29.
7. Ibid., p. 184.
8. Ibid., p. 153.
9. Watts, *Cloud-hidden*, p. 17.
10. Ibid., p. 19.
11. Ibid., p. 20.
12. Al Chung-liang Huang, foreword to Watts, *Tao: The Watercourse Way* (New York: Random House, Pantheon Books, 1975), p. ix.
13. Ibid.
14. Watts to Bishop John Robinson, January 29, 1973.

15. "The Timeless Moment," BBC TV, August 10, 1973.
16. Mary Jane Watts to Laurence Watts, February 16, 1974.
17. Rick Fields, *How the Swans Came to the Lake: A Narrative History of Buddhism in America* (Boulder, Colo.: Shambhala, 1981), p. 360.

# Books by Alan Watts

*The Spirit of Zen; A Way of Life, Work, and Art in the Far East.*
London: John Murray, 1935.

*The Legacy of Asia and Western Man: A Study of the Middle Way.*
London: John Murray, 1937.

*The Meaning of Happiness: A Quest for Freedom of the Spirit in Modern Psychology and the Wisdom of the East.* New York: Harper & Row, 1940.

*The Theologia Mystica of Saint Dionysius.* Worcester, Mass.: Holy Cross Press, 1944.

*Behold the Spirit: A Study in the Necessity of Mystical Religion.* New York: Random House, Pantheon Books, 1947.

*Easter — Its Story and Meaning.* New York: Henry Schuman, Inc., 1950.

*The Supreme Identity.* New York: Random House, Pantheon Books, 1950.

*The Wisdom of Insecurity: A Message for an Age of Anxiety.* New York: Random House, Pantheon Books, 1951.

*The Way of Zen.* New York: Random House, Pantheon Books, 1957.

*Nature, Man and Woman.* New York: Random House, Pantheon Books, 1958.

*"This Is It" and Other Essays on Zen and Spiritual Experience.* New York: Random House, Pantheon Books, 1960.

*Psychotherapy East and West.* New York: Random House, Pantheon Books, 1961.

*The Joyous Cosmology.* New York: Random House, Pantheon Books, 1962.

*Beyond Theology: The Art of Godmanship.* New York: Random House, Pantheon Books, 1964.

*The Book: On the Taboo Against Knowing Who You Are.* New York: Random House, Pantheon Books, 1966.

*Myth and Ritual in Christianity.* Boston, Mass.: Beacon Press, 1968.

*The Two Hands of God: The Myths of Polarity.* New York: Macmillan, Collier Books, 1963.

*Does It Matter? Essays on Man's Relation to Materiality.* New York: Random House, Pantheon Books, 1970.

*In My Own Way: An Autobiography.* New York: Random House, Pantheon Books, 1972.

*Cloud-hidden, Whereabouts Unknown: A Mountain Journal.* New York: Random House, Pantheon Books, 1973.

*The Essence of Alan Watts.* Berkeley: Celestial Arts, 1974.

*Tao: The Watercourse Way.* With the collaboration of Al Chung-liang Huang. New York: Random House, Pantheon Books, 1975.

# Index

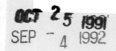